Praise for the novels of Sheila Roberts

"The beginning entry in this hopeful series will win over readers looking for a comforting escape."
—*Library Journal* on *Welcome to Moonlight Harbor*

"[A] delightful story of family, friendship and new beginnings. The vividly drawn coastal Washington setting comes alive."
—*RT Book Reviews* on *Welcome to Moonlight Harbor*

"The plot takes several unexpected twists and turns on its way to a delightful ending.... Can't wait to see what life has in store for Jenna in Moonlight Harbor."
—*FreshFiction.com* on *Welcome to Moonlight Harbor*

"*Welcome to Moonlight Harbor* will be sure to capture your attention as well as your heart."
—*HarlequinJunkie.com*

"Sheila Roberts makes me laugh...and come away inspired, hopeful and happy."
—Debbie Macomber, #1 *New York Times* bestselling author

"A lovely blend of romance and women's fiction, this insightful holiday treat hits all the right notes."
—*Library Journal* on *Christmas in Icicle Falls*

SHEILA ROBERTS

winter at the beach

mira

mira

ISBN-13: 978-0-7783-6995-0

Recycling programs
for this product may
not exist in your area.

Winter at the Beach

For Cheron and Christi

Dear Friend,

Thank you so much for spending some of your valuable time with the gang at Moonlight Harbor. If you've ever made plans only to have them go sideways I'm sure you can identify with the adventures of Jenna Jones and her family and friends.

I've planned some big events in my time and let me tell you, it's stressful. I still remember the day my hairdresser informed me that she'd discovered a bald spot at the back of my head. Thankfully, the hair grew back but... Yikes. Just. Yikes! And power outages? Oh, yes, we've gone through that. My kids always thought it was a big adventure. "We get to have a fire in the wood stove and tell stories," my son would say. And then stumble around in the dark and huddle around that stove to stay warm and go crazy because... "I CAN'T USE MY COMPUTER!"

Ah, but it's these little challenges that bring us closer together. And in retrospect we can always find something to reminisce or laugh about. I hope you'll find a few things to laugh at in this tale and come away with a smile on your face, maybe even a little encouraged. If you do, then I've done my job.

I got creative with the calendar in this story, jumping ahead to a year that worked for my purposes. I'm sure you'll forgive me though, right? Because after all, this is fiction.

I hope your winter is warm and cozy and that the storms in your life are few and short. Thank you for loving books and supporting writers. Without readers, what would we do?

Sheila

winter at
the beach

Chapter One

Life at the beach was good. It was even better when you ran a motel and had people staying in it.

Lately life at the beach hadn't been quite so good for Jenna Jones, manager of the Driftwood Inn in the beach town of Moonlight Harbor, Washington. Her great-aunt, Edie Patterson, the current owner, had offered Jenna both a home with her and a job after her divorce. Jenna had been grateful for the new start and Aunt Edie had been grateful for the help as the place had fallen into disrepair after the death of her husband, Ralph. Jenna would eventually inherit the motel, which offered her financial security.

It had been a win-win deal, and Jenna had whipped the place into shape, decorating on a shoestring, giving the rooms a different theme, depending on what color bargain carpet and what kind of thrift store décor she'd been able to find. The Driftwood Inn was now, if she did say so herself, a charming beach retreat. But she needed more heads in beds.

After Labor Day, when summer fun ended and families got busy with school and football season, reservations became scarce. Now, in October, well, if you were looking for a cute vintage motel to stay in, the Driftwood Inn had plenty of vacancies.

This was a problem because Jenna had mouths to feed, people depending on her, including her ex-husband, struggling artist Damien Petit (who wasn't struggling nearly as much as he deserved to be, thanks to the transitional spousal support Jenna paid him every month). More important, she was responsible for her daughter, Sabrina, and her great-aunt.

When she wasn't in the office with her friend and right-hand woman, Courtney Moore, or helping their lone maid, Coral, clean rooms, Jenna was working the kinks out of sore muscles. It was a good thing she'd been a massage therapist B.M. (Before Motel). It would give her something to fall back on while money was tight. And it sure was. The next summer's tourist season seemed a long way off.

But today was Monday, the beginning of a new week, and this week looked promising. She had clients booked for massages Wednesday, Thursday and Friday, and the Driftwood Inn had guests arriving on Friday afternoon.

Which meant they had a reservation for one room in a motel with twenty. That left seventeen to fill as two were permanently taken. And of those two they were only getting money for one.

Pete Long, the useless old coot who pretended to be a handyman, paid nothing and did as little as possible to earn his keep. The other room was occupied by Seth Waters, who had proven to be a lot more handy.

Unlike cranky old Pete, Seth paid for his room in addition to helping out, and Jenna was glad to have him around. Gorgeous, with muscles growing muscles. Smart and a hard worker, he was also a good listener.

And a great kisser.

But not so good at commitment. Jenna supposed it was understandable considering his past. A rash but noble decision had landed him in prison and he was easing back into his life with leery caution.

Which was just as well, Jenna kept telling herself. After her disastrous marriage to the artist who'd made an art out of cheating, she didn't need to rush into love. Although if ever there was a man who made a woman think about rushing, it was Seth.

Or Brody Green, successful Realtor and the other man in her life.

As a friend. A friend who'd like to be friends with benefits.

And she could easily imagine the benefits Brody could offer. Yes, she'd kissed him, too, thanks to too much to drink at dinner, followed by a sunset on the beach with Mr. Suave.

Both divorced, both with kids, they had things in common, and Brody was fun to hang out with, but she needed to focus on managing the motel. Which was a heck of a lot easier to manage than her love life.

Except it currently had seventeen rooms that needed filling.

Things were bound to pick up, Jenna assured herself as she walked across the parking lot from Aunt Edie's house, where she and her daughter, Sabrina, also lived, to the motel office.

There was plenty to do on a Monday. Catch up on paperwork, post some new pictures on Instagram, add a new Aunt Edie culinary creation to the Facebook page. Blog about the great weather they were having down at the beach. *It's still sunny. Come one, come all.*

She'd just gotten into the office when Coral pulled up in her dad's truck. Coral was only working part-time. Very part-time. More like barely any time since they didn't have any reservations. She was a sweet girl, nineteen and trying to earn money for college. Jenna wished she could give Coral more hours, but it looked like they were stuck limping along until summer.

"Hi," she greeted the girl. "This is a surprise. I didn't expect you in today."

"I know." Coral bit her lip.

Uh-oh. "What's up?" As if Jenna couldn't guess.

"I'm giving my two weeks' notice. I'm sorry," she added, looking as if she'd just confessed to shoplifting. "It's just that, well, I need to be making more money."

Didn't they all? "I understand," Jenna said. "I wish we had more work for you."

"Me, too."

"I'll be happy to give you a good reference."

"Oh, you don't have to. I already have a job."

"You do? Where?"

Coral's cheeks turned red as a stoplight. "The Oyster Inn."

Which was booked solid pretty much all year long. Jenna nodded and forced a smile, told herself not to be jealous of Patricia Whiteside's success. The woman had been in business in Moonlight Harbor forever, and she'd worked hard. She'd gone slightly more upscale with her establishment and it had paid off. The Oyster Inn was as charming as its owner. It boasted a small restaurant and a boutique shop, in addition to great views, and catered to visitors who wanted to enjoy a stay in someplace more high-end.

"Well, good. I'm glad," she said. For Coral anyway. For herself, not so much.

"I wouldn't have left, really. But…"

"I know," Jenna said. "I get it. No worries, okay?"

Coral bit down on her lip again, nodded and then bolted out of the office.

Jenna watched her go and sighed. Oh, well. The glass was still half full, right? Now she didn't have to pay someone to clean the rooms. She could probably get by without anyone until spring, and that would save money.

Darn it all, she didn't *want* to save money. She wanted to make money.

The phone rang. Someone wanting to make a reservation! She picked it up and sang a cheerful, "You've reached the Driftwood Inn where it's beach time all the time." (Her own clever slogan!) "This is Jenna. How may I help you?"

"We have a reservation for this weekend," said a female voice. "Smithers?"

Maybe they wanted to reserve another room. Extend their stay. Ms. Smithers could be calling for any number of reasons. *Please don't let it be…*

"I need to cancel."

Jenna's right eye began to twitch. "Cancel?"

"Yes. Something's come up, and we're not going to be able to make it."

It was all Jenna could do not to say, "Are you sure?"

"You haven't dinged our credit card yet, have you?"

"Oh, no. That's only to hold the room."

"And we're giving you more than twenty-four hours' notice."

"Yes, you are." *Good for you.*

"Thanks."

"I'm sorry it didn't work out. I hope you'll be able to come another time," Jenna added, but by then she was talking to dead air.

She scowled and left the office to take a walk on the beach, her favorite go-to place when she needed to cogitate. She only had to share it with the seagulls this morning. At eight thirty on a cloudy fall day, no one else was out. There was a serious nip in the air. Hardly surprising, considering the time of year.

October, and the scene remained the same. Water, sand and wind. The one difference was the color of the sky. Not that Jenna minded. She loved the beach, loved the constancy of the waves, loved hearing the sound through her open bedroom window of the steady lap of the tide coming in at night. It was all so comforting, so relaxing...

So stressful when no one was calling to reserve a room.

If only Moonlight Harbor had more deciduous trees. Business owners could lure people to town with the promise of seeing the changing colors like Icicle Falls over in the Cascades did every fall. But there was a preponderance of evergreens, both in Moonlight Harbor and on the state highway leading to it. And moss. A lot of moss hanging from trees. Sadly, it didn't change colors. Darn it all. Where were those changing colors when you needed them?

She sighed and turned back to the office. Time for

another Groupon offer. And time to tell Aunt Edie to start getting creative with stretching the grocery budget.

Jenna wasn't the only one frustrated with the tourism slump after the busy summer season. A lack of visitors appeared to be a common lament among the various business owners in town, and was a hot topic with the group of girlfriends who gathered at Aunt Edie's house for their regular Friday night get-together.

"We did well this summer," said Cindy Redmond, who, with her husband, Bruce, owned Cindy's Candies. "But it's going to be a long winter."

"We do get some people in to storm watch over the winter," Patricia Whiteside reminded her.

"Some, but not enough," Cindy said. "There's really not much to lure people down here until March when they come for the razor clam festival. That always brings them in."

"Maybe we need something in between," Jenna said thoughtfully.

"Yeah, the Bring Your Money and Keep Us Going Festival," cracked Nora Singleton, who owned Good Times Ice Cream Parlor and the funplex.

"There's got to be *something*," Courtney said. She'd been selling her women's clothing creations at the little boutique in the Oyster Inn's lobby and also had a website, but she wasn't making enough to live on yet. Helping Jenna at the reception desk evenings and weekends not only kept her supplied with fabric, it also kept her supplied with groceries. Another mouth for Jenna to feed.

"We'll just do what we've always done," Aunt Edie

said. "Hang on until summer. Summer will be here before we know it."

Dear, sweet Aunt Edie. Always optimistic.

Always clueless. If they hung on any tighter they'd break their fingers. Courtney was right. There had to be something else they could do.

"Anyway, it's nice to take advantage of the lull," said Patricia. "Travel, go see family and friends." Which she did every November. Patricia had a sister in Arizona.

Patricia also had a healthy bank account and plenty of staff to cover for her. But what about the business owners who weren't in such good shape financially?

"We'll have to hunker down and stretch the money," Jenna's friend Tyrella Lamb said to her later as the party was breaking up. Tyrella owned Beach Lumber and Hardware. She, at least, could be sure of customers all year long. "Or come up with a brilliant idea," she added.

A brilliant idea. No problem.

Jenna waved goodbye to the last of their guests and returned to the living room to find Aunt Edie seated in her favorite seashell chair, twisting the agate ring on her finger. That ring was her aunt's worry stone.

"We'll be fine," she told Jenna. Then added, "Won't we?"

"Of course, we will," Jenna replied. After everything they'd gone through to bring the motel back to life, no way was she letting it go out of business simply for lack of a few winter visitors.

She gave her aunt a hug and patted the covered cage where Jolly Roger, the parrot, was asleep for the night. Then she went upstairs to say good-night to her daughter, who'd been camped out on her bed, texting with her friend Marigold about the new "older man" in her life. Tristan Van Cliburn was a nerd. A very cute nerd, tall and skinny with glasses decorating a face waiting to fill out, along with the rest of him. He was a senior, and Sabrina was only a freshman, a big age difference when you were in high school.

But as Sabrina had taken to saying, "Love knows no age limits." Where the heck had she heard that?

They'd met when he'd answered an ad Jenna had put in the *Beach Times* Help Wanted section for a website designer. Sabrina had wandered into the motel office right after Jenna had hired him, and both their hormone centers had lit up like the Fourth of July. Before you could say *young love*, he was eating lunch with Sabrina and her two new friends, Jennifer and Hudson, every day at school, walking her home, trying to sneak in solitary walks on the beach.

Even though he seemed like a nice enough kid, Jenna didn't want her daughter jumping into a relationship with him. Or anyone, for that matter, and becoming sexually active at such a young age. They'd had a mother-daughter talk (okay, more of a mother lecture) but Jenna wasn't sure it had been very effective. It was so much easier to be a mother when your kids were little and you could keep them safely corralled in the backyard.

Boys, driving, the dangers of drug and alcohol abuse—so many land mines lay ahead. Ugh. How had she gotten here? How had she wound up with a teenage daughter? Oh, yeah. She'd turned forty.

On which one should she blame the gray hair she'd found hiding among the blond highlights the other day—the kid or the big 4-0?

"Don't pull it," her mom had advised during their last phone chat. "You pull one and two more come to its funeral." Melody Jones, the expert on gray hair. She'd been dyeing her hair since she was thirty.

The advice came too late. Jenna had pulled the thing. She'd heard that gray hair and wisdom went together, but she wasn't ready to be that wise yet.

"What are you and Tristan scheming now?" she asked as she kissed the top of Sabrina's head.

"Can I go to the Christmas ball with him?"

"Yes, when you're a senior. If he isn't engaged to some college brainiac, he can come back from MIT and take you."

"That's so not funny," Sabrina said, her sunny smile dipping behind a cloud of teen irritation.

"No frowny face," Jenna teased. "Santa's watching." This had been one of Jenna's favorite behavioral modification tactics, starting when Sabrina was four, and she'd used it plenty over the years, working it from November clear up to December 24.

"Lame, Mom," said Sabrina, who'd quit believing in Santa when she was nine. "Anyway, it's only October. You're way too early."

"I like to get an early start." Obviously, so did Tristan.

"Mom."

Every mother knew that tone of voice, half disgust and half pleading. "Maybe. Let me think about it."

Sabrina beamed at her. "That would be the best Christmas present ever."

"We'll have a great Christmas, no matter what," Jenna said, determined not to make any promises until

she'd had more time to consider. She gave her daughter
another kiss, then headed for her own room.

Christmas. It was her favorite holiday. The joy, the
lights, the parties, the hopeful message of peace on
earth, goodwill toward men. She loved the candlelight
church services, the cookies, the decorations and holiday songs, the gathering of family. Granted, her own
little family had been fractured, but she still had her
daughter and her mom and sister, and Aunt Edie, and
she was looking forward to enjoying their first Christmas together in their new home at the beach. Her mom
and Celeste, who both lived north of Seattle, would
come down, and it would be one long party. The beach
was always special, but even more so during the holidays.

Christmas at the beach. Hmm. Now, there was a
thought. Where could she go with it?

Someplace good, she realized as she crawled into
bed. A holiday festival was bound to lure people to
town. Who didn't like fairs and festivals, especially
holiday ones? She could see it now—the storefronts all
lit up with multicolored lights, trees in the restaurants
decorated with glittery shells and little lighthouses and
mermaids, amusement rides and cotton candy and hot
chocolate down at the pier, a live Nativity scene in front
of one of the churches. And a Christmas parade with
Santa bringing up the rear for a grand finale.

You had to include Santa. In fact, the jolly old guy
was such a draw, maybe they could include his name
in the festival. Sandy Claus? No, that was too close to
Sandy Claws, the pet goodies shop. Santa in the Sand?
That sounded like he'd gotten his sleigh stuck. Santa at

Sea. Sea, seaside… Seaside with Santa! Oh, that had a nice ring to it. *Come to Moonlight Harbor and experience the Seaside with Santa Festival. Waves of fun!*

Wow, was she brilliant.

Damien had always looked down his snobby artist nose at her various craft projects. She supposed she'd brought that on herself since when they first met she was the little crafter going to massage therapy school and he was the darling of the University of Washington's art department. But after a while it got old hearing, "You're just not creative, Jenna. Not everybody is, you know."

Right. Not everybody was as brilliant and special as him.

But guess what, Damien. Your former wife is more creative than you ever realized. And she's not mooching off her ex and sitting around making collages out of take-out containers. She's coming up with something to help a whole town.

Jenna smiled and snuggled under the covers, letting the sound of the surf lull her to sleep. Tomorrow at the Moonlight Harbor Chamber of Commerce meeting she was going to propose her brilliant plan. *Look out, Icicle Falls. You've got competition.*

Chapter Two

Jenna woke up every bit as excited about her holiday festival idea as she'd been when she went to sleep. "So, what do you two think?" she asked after she'd shared it with Aunt Edie and Sabrina at breakfast.

"Call the cops!" Jolly Roger suggested, bobbing and weaving on his kitchen perch, happy to be cage free.

"I think a festival sounds delightful," Aunt Edie gushed.

"If we have rides it'll be cool," Sabrina said. "And elephant ears and corn dogs."

"I love the idea of a parade," Aunt Edie continued. "Like our Flag Day parade only with Santa. Who would we get to play Santa?"

"I'm sure any number of men would be happy to volunteer," Jenna said.

At that moment Pete wandered in, following his nose right to where the bacon sat, fresh out of the oven on a foil-lined cookie sheet. Still unshaven, dressed in dirty, old jeans, a coffee-stained T-shirt and a rumpled windbreaker, he looked like he should have been squatting on a street corner holding a sign that said Anything Helps.

"Volunteer for what?" he asked, getting himself some bacon.

"For being Santa Claus in our holiday parade," Aunt Edie said.

Pete made a face. "Holiday parade. Since when do we have a holiday parade around here?"

"Since we realized we need to find a way to bring more people to town in the winter," Jenna replied. "We're thinking about a holiday festival."

Pete shook his head. "We don't need more people here in the winter. We have enough crowds in the summer. Edie, do we have any eggs?"

"I'll fry you one," Aunt Edie said, and got up, happy as always to wait on him.

"Hey, don't eat all the toast," he said as Jenna helped herself to a piece to go with her coffee.

"Don't worry, there's some left," she said.

"Just one piece!"

"We're tightening our belts," Jenna informed him. "Until we get more people staying down here, we need to cut back."

"An extra piece of toast isn't gonna break us." Pete snagged another slice of bread from the shrinking loaf on the counter and popped it in the toaster. Pete, the two-legged locust.

"You're welcome to contribute to the supplies," Jenna told him.

He scowled. "I'm on a limited income."

"So are we," she retorted.

"Well, now, what's on your agenda for the day, dear?" Aunt Edie asked her, obviously determined to distract Jenna from the irritation that was their so-called handyman.

"I hope you don't have a bunch of stuff for me to do," Pete said, taking a few more slices of bacon. "My back is killing me." Pete's bad back was becoming legendary.

"My back is killing me," Roger repeated. He'd heard that phrase often enough to have added it to his birdie vocabulary.

"I don't have anything for you today," Jenna told Pete.

"Good. 'Cause I need a day off."

He had more days off than he had on, especially with their lack of guests, but Jenna kept that observation to herself. There was no sense upsetting Aunt Edie by squabbling with him. He'd been a fixture at the Driftwood long before Jenna arrived, and her aunt was fond of him.

"Is this your chamber of commerce meeting day?" she asked Jenna.

"Yep. And I'm going to see what they all think about my idea."

"It's a dumb idea if you ask me," Pete muttered. As if anyone would?

"Well, *I* think it sounds like fun," said Sabrina, who'd been dawdling over her granola. The honking of the school bus outside galvanized her, and she jumped from the table and grabbed her backpack. She managed a quick kiss for her mom and aunt and then bolted out of the kitchen.

"She's gonna miss the bus," Pete predicted.

"They'll wait for her."

He retrieved his toast and buttered it. "When I was a kid you had to walk to school."

"Which is probably how you got your bad back," Jenna said sweetly, then took her coffee and left him to grumble and scarf down more bacon.

The school bus driver had, indeed, waited for Sabrina, and Jenna gave her a cheery wave as she walked across the parking lot to the motel office. She'd do a little research online and write up her idea, then print out copies for the chamber meeting. Hopefully there'd be more Sabrinas and Aunt Edies present than Petes.

"What have you got there?" Brody, who was president of the organization, greeted her when she arrived at the banquet room in Sandy's Restaurant for the lunch meeting with her handouts. As usual, he was looking like Mr. *GQ* in slacks and a blue twill shirt that showed off his broad shoulders and matched those baby blue eyes.

"An idea to bring more people to town. Can you add it to the agenda under new business?"

"Sure. We're always open to ideas."

She hoped they'd be open to hers. She thought it was a good one. Of course, she was the new kid in town, having only arrived a few months earlier. Maybe no one would take her seriously.

Lunch options consisted of either fish and chips or clam chowder in a bread bowl and a small tossed salad. Jenna was almost too excited to eat. Almost. But it was impossible to resist clam chowder. She ate the chowder and left the bread bowl. She already fought enough carb battles at home with Aunt Edie's baking binges, and a girl had to draw the line somewhere.

"I was never much of a seafood eater before Leroy and I moved here," confessed Tyrella, who was seated on one side of Jenna. "But I got hooked on fish and chips in a hurry."

"No pun intended," joked Nora Singleton, who was seated next to Tyrella. Brody had, as usual, claimed the seat on Jenna's other side.

Tyrella smiled. "Before we moved north, Leroy and I weren't big on seafood. With that man it was barbecue or fried chicken, macaroni salad and green beans or collard greens. Oh, and grits, of course. But after we came to Moonlight Harbor we sure changed our eating habits. Salmon, cod, fish and chips, sushi. Remember when my baby brother and his girlfriend came up to visit last year?" she asked Nora, who nodded. Tyrella shook her head. "I bought them salmon dinners right here in this restaurant. You'd have thought I'd tried to poison them."

"They did like my huckleberry ice cream, though," said Nora.

"You'd have to be from the moon not to like huckleberry ice cream," Jenna said.

Nora pointed a teasing finger at her. "I haven't seen you ordering any in months."

"If I ate everything you and Aunt Edie tried to feed me, I wouldn't need a car. I could just roll down the street."

"You worry too much about your weight." Tyrella told her. Tyrella was a curvy woman, and she never let concern over an extra pound keep her away from her mac and cheese. "But I get it. A lot of men like their women skinny, and you're still young." She cast a surreptitious look in Brody's direction. "You won't stay unattached forever."

Jenna was aware of Brody on her other side, eavesdropping, and her face suddenly felt hot. So did other parts of her.

"You're too young to go through life alone," added Nora.

"*I'm* too young to go through life alone," Tryella said and gave her dreadlocks a flip. "That darned Leroy, keeling over on me in the prime of my life." She sighed. "There'll never be another Leroy."

"You might meet someone else," Jenna said.

Tyrella rolled her eyes. "In case you haven't noticed, there aren't exactly a lot of middle-aged single black men down here at the beach."

"Online dating," Jenna said. "You could find someone and import him down here."

Tyrella didn't look thrilled with the idea of online dating.

"Just sayin'." Hey, if her friends could meddle in her love life, she could meddle in theirs.

"Speaking of dating," Brody said to Jenna, "what are you doing Saturday night? Want to catch a movie?"

"I might." But it wouldn't really be a date. Brody knew they were just friends. *With no benefits.*

"He's a nice guy," Tyrella whispered as Brody tapped a spoon on his water glass to get everyone's attention.

"We're just friends," Jenna whispered back.

"That's how Leroy and I started," Tyrella informed her. "Next thing I knew he was proposing. Get that boy whipped into shape first, though, cuz they don't change once they're married."

Was she kidding? Jenna had her hands full getting herself whipped into shape.

"I think we can begin now," Brody was saying. "Will our secretary read the minutes from our last meeting?"

Cindy Redmond pulled up the notes on her iPad and began to read. "We had an impressive influx for Labor Day weekend and our motels and B and Bs reported an uptick in guests. We had a lower turnout for beach cleanup the day after, and it was suggested by Rian that we get our local Boy and Girl Scout troops involved. It was also suggested that we hire a firm to do a study and show us how we can make Moonlight Harbor more attractive to tourists. Ellis West was going to get quotes for us."

"And did you, Ellis?" Brody asked.

"I did."

"Okay. We'll deal with that when we get to old business," Brody said.

Cindy finished her report, and the members voted to accept the minutes as read. Then their treasurer, Rian LaShell, reported on the current state of their budget, which hadn't changed much since her report the month before.

Then it was on to old business, with Ellis reporting what he'd found in the way of experts. He quoted a figure that dropped several jaws, including Susan Frank's.

Susan had worn one of the outfits from her shop, Beach Babes, to the meeting—beige slacks, which Jenna knew would have the same elastic waistline as all the slacks there. Her lemon yellow sweatshirt had a starfish embroidered on it. Beach Time is Happy Time it said. Susan, who was frowning as usual, obviously didn't subscribe to that philosophy.

"That's ridiculous," she said. "A waste of money. We already know what we need."

"And what would that be, Susan?" Nora goaded her.

"Better weather year-round," Susan snapped. "But that's not happening. This isn't California."

"The weather is what it is," Ellis said. "But people, especially people in the Pacific Northwest, don't let it dictate their lives. If they did, nobody would have a life. We need to find a way to let people know that the beach is a great place to be, no matter what the weather's doing. We need more attractions."

"Like an aquarium," said Kiki Strom, who owned the popular tourist shop Something Fishy. Kiki was still going strong at seventy. She wore her gray hair in spikes, sported glasses with bright red frames and wouldn't be caught dead in anything from Beach Babes. She had a reputation for thinking outside the box, and the crazy entrance to her store, which was shaped like a giant open shark's mouth, was proof of it. In fact, according to Kiki, there was no box. Period.

"We don't need to hire an expensive firm to tell us we need more attractions," Susan said.

"It wouldn't hurt to bring in an expert," Ellis argued.

"That's a lot more money than we have," Rian pointed out. "We'd have to convince the city to spend money."

"Good luck with that," Susan said with a sneer.

"It's worth a try," said Steve Hampton, who managed the Quality Inn.

Susan shook her head. "I move we table the whole thing."

"Well, I move we look into this more," Steve countered.

"We can only have one motion on the floor at a time," Brody said. "Susan, how long should we table it?"

"Forever," she said, and Brody frowned at her.

"That's not exactly tabling it," he said. "That's killing it."

"Okay, I move we kill it and put it out of its misery."

Brody kept his frown, but did his duty as the president and asked, "Do I have a second for Susan's motion?"

"I second it," Rian said firmly. "Let's be realistic, people."

"Okay, it's been moved and seconded that we bag bringing in an expert. All in favor say aye."

There was a chorus of ayes, some insistent, others reluctant.

"Against?" Brody asked, and Kiki and Ellis were the lone protesters.

The motion carried.

"There's a guy who specializes in helping towns and cities with struggling economies get on their feet," Ellis said. "I suggest—"

Susan interrupted him. "We're not struggling that much."

Rian cocked an eyebrow at her. "Oh, and you're getting rich over there at Beach Babes, are you?"

Susan didn't respond. Instead, she said to Ellis, "We just killed that idea."

"We killed the idea of hiring a firm. But this is another possible option. This guy offers webinars on how to build your city's economy. Those are more afford-able." Ellis quoted the price.

"Still too much," snapped Susan.

"Let's not take that totally off the table," Brody said. "It might be worth considering."

Discussion ensued, and finally Nora suggested, "Look, since we don't want to spend a lot and we know the city's on a tight budget, why don't we forget the expert and all do some research on our own? Maybe we can come up with ways to improve the town just by poking around online and seeing what other places have done."

Susan nodded in approval. "Now, there's a good idea."

"That *is* a good idea," Brody agreed. "Nora, you want to put together a committee to do that?"

Nora pulled a piece of paper from the yellow tablet in front of her. "I'll pass this around. Sign up if you're interested."

"Okay, that takes care of old business," Brody said. "Now, I think Jenna has some new business."

Oh, boy. She could hardly wait to see what Susan would have to say about this.

She cleared her throat. "Actually, I have a sugges-tion for a way to bring down more visitors during our slow time."

"We're all for that," said Patricia Whiteside.

Susan clamped her thin lips together and gave Jenna a look that dared her, the newbie, to come up with some-thing.

Jenna's nervous twitch put in an appearance. *Don't blink.* She blinked one last time and cleared her throat again. "Well, I was just thinking about other towns I've visited in the past and one that came to mind was Icicle Falls."

Susan rolled her eyes. "The cheesy German town."

"A lot of people find it charming," Jenna said. "It's awfully pretty, and they've done a great job of making themselves as authentic as possible. They always have something going to get people up there. In fact, I did some research online. They have festivals all year long, including a chocolate festival. Their tree-lighting ceremonies on the weekends in December bring in thousands of people."

"So, are you proposing we have a tree-lighting ceremony?" Susan mocked.

"No, but I *am* proposing we have a holiday festival."

"We just had a festival in August in case you forgot," Susan said snidely.

What was with this woman anyway? The town had done a good deed by putting on a festival to help Jenna raise money to restore the Driftwood after she experienced a financial setback. It had been such a success that the chamber had decided to make the Blue Moon Festival a tradition, with proceeds going to help other businesses in town in need of assistance. Jenna had benefited and other local businesses would as well, and Susan resented it? She was a crab in the pot. If she couldn't succeed, she didn't want anyone else to, either. And everyone knew her shop wasn't doing that well, especially now that Courtney was selling her own designs over at the Oyster Inn.

Well, pooh on her. Jenna handed papers to both Tyrella and Brody to start passing around the table.

"People love festivals. Remember how many came down for the Blue Moon one?"

"That was in the summer," Susan reminded her.

"I know. But people also love holiday festivals. We're looking for ways to get visitors down here in the winter. Why not put together a giant holiday party in Moonlight Harbor?"

Patricia Whiteside was reading Jenna's handout. "Seaside with Santa, that's cute. And I like all the suggestions you've made for activities. I really like the idea of making use of the pier."

"The weekend before Christmas?" Susan objected, frowning at her handout. "Who's going to want to come to something then? People will be getting ready to go see family, and they'll be finishing up their shopping."

"Why shouldn't they finish it here?" Jenna argued. "We have all kinds of cute shops. We have great places for them to stay while they shop and plenty of restaurants where they can eat. They may even want to stay here for the holidays. All we need is an event to lure them down. A festival could do it. And who doesn't like a parade? Look how many people turn out for the Macy's Thanksgiving Day parade."

"Look at the floats they have in that parade," Susan countered. "What sort of floats would we be able to put together down here?"

"Okay, maybe not the most impressive parade ever," Jenna admitted, "but I bet we could come up with something."

"I could get some of my employees to dress up as mermaids," said Kiki, "and stick 'em on a flatbed truck strung with fake seaweed." She grinned, clearly taken with her idea.

"We need more for our Moonlight Harbor Queen and her princesses to do," put in Nora. "They love riding in those old convertibles. You'll let us use your vintage Caddy, right, Ellis?"

"Well…" Ellis hesitated. "If it rains…"

"Which it probably will," said Susan. "Come on, people, be practical. You know what it's like down here in the winter, all wind and rain."

Patricia pooh-poohed that objection. "We've survived plenty of storms."

"Well, I think it's a bad idea," Susan said, scowling across the table at Jenna.

Maybe it was. Jenna's left eye began to twitch.

"I think it sounds great," said Elizabeth MacDowell. She and her twin sister, K.J., were new members of the chamber. They'd opened their arts and crafts store, Crafty Just Cuz, in September, and it was already one of Jenna's favorite places to hang out.

"We do need more business in the winter," said Cindy Redmond. "There's no getting around it. And doing something for the holidays could be fun. I say we give it a try," she added, and Jenna's eye stopped twitching.

"We'd have to get moving right away," Nora said, pulling another sheet of paper from her yellow tablet. "Who can help?"

"I can," said Ellis.

"Me, too," Brody said, smiling at Jenna. "Jenna, it's your idea. You'll have to chair the committee."

"Me?" she squeaked. Not that she couldn't take

charge. She was a firstborn, and Responsibility was her middle name. (Although her sister, Celeste, would probably argue that her middle name was Bossy.) She didn't have a problem with rolling up her sleeves and getting to work, but she also didn't want to offend old-timers like Susan Frank. "I'm sure someone else..." she began.

"Your idea, you have to do it," Susan goaded.

Jenna raised her chin. "I can do it." She'd survived rehabbing the Driftwood Inn. How much harder could it be to organize a festival?

In three months. Blink. Blink, blink, blink.

"Do I have a motion that we sponsor a Seaside with Santa Festival for the weekend before Christmas?" Brody asked.

"So moved," said Ellis. "I'm with you, kid," he told Jenna.

"I'll second," Nora said and reached across the back of Tyrella's chair to give Jenna's shoulder an encouraging pat.

"All in favor?" Brody asked.

"Aye," chorused almost everyone.

"Opposed?"

"Nay," Susan Frank said. "I'm telling you all, this is a bad idea. Make sure you put that in the minutes," she told Cindy.

"Motion carries," said Brody. He smiled down at Jenna. "Looks like we're going to be putting on a holiday bash."

"Holiday disaster," Susan grumbled from her side of the table.

What did Susan know? Blink, blink, blink.

Chapter Three

Jenna received plenty of encouragement and compliments on her idea after the chamber of commerce meeting broke up. Except from Susan, who vanished as soon as she'd paid for her lunch.

"Never mind her," Tyrella said as Jenna's new committee gathered for a quick chat. "Every great idea has its naysayers."

The committee consisted of Tyrella, Brody, Nora, Ellis and Kiki, all people Jenna liked and was sure she'd enjoy working with, not a naysayer in the bunch. After traveling the bumpy road of divorce and dealing with the stress of renovating the motel, she was determined to keep only positive people in her life. Everyone on her new committee was that kind of person. They were also practical and seasoned business owners, and she knew they'd be careful not to let her bite off more than she could chew. Except she might have already done that, so it would be more a case of keeping her from choking to death.

"When do you want to have our first meeting?" Brody asked her.

"The sooner the better," she said. The holiday clock was ticking. Loudly.

"I'm free tonight," said Kiki. Kiki was a busy woman. In addition to running her kitschy tourist store, she had her knitting group on Monday evenings, her church women's group on Wednesday nights, the seniors' bowling league on Thursdays, and her book club met once a month on Fridays. When she wasn't involved with those activities or at her shop, she volunteered at the food bank at least one day a week. Watching Kiki in action made Jenna tired.

"I'm always free," Tyrella said. Yeah, right. Tyrella was up to her eyeballs in church activities and just as busy as Kiki.

"How about the rest of you?" Jenna asked the others.

"I can make tonight," said Nora.

"Me, too," Ellis said.

"I'm there," said Brody.

"Why don't you all come over to my place?" Jenna suggested. Aunt Edie would love being in the thick of things.

"Is Edie baking?" Brody asked.

When it came to company there'd never be any belt-tightening. "What do you think?"

He grinned. "Let's go to Edie's."

"You tell her not to wear herself out," Kiki said.

"Too late. She was trying out a new brownie recipe today. You'll be saving my butt if you come over and help eat them." They'd already saved her butt in a major way last summer, with the festival they'd put on for her benefit. She loved these people, and she loved Moonlight Harbor.

"Let's make it dinner," said Ellis as they left the restaurant. "I'll bring over some popcorn shrimp from my place."

"You sure it won't get cold, coming all that way?" Kiki teased. The Seafood Shack was right next to the motel and Ellis only had to walk across the parking lot.

He pulled out a cigar to smoke. "I can manage it."

"I'll bring wine, then," said Brody.

"I'll bring ice cream to go with the brownies," Nora promised. As owner of the ice cream parlor, it was a given that Nora would always be responsible for contributing ice cream to any gathering.

"And I'll bring macaroni salad," Tyrella said, and that rounded out the meal.

Aunt Edie was thrilled, both to hear that Jenna's idea had gone over well and that they'd be having company. "I can serve my beach sandies. And I'd better bake some sugar cookies, too," she decided.

"That sounds great," Jenna said, and couldn't help a moment of evil glee at the thought of Pete not being able to pop into the kitchen and scrounge a free meal. He'd have to go somewhere and actually pay for his food, something he hated doing. She suspected he'd wind up at The Drunken Sailor, the town's popular pub.

He did manage to smell cookies baking, though, and made off with half a dozen.

Tristan wandered in after school with Sabrina. There went more cookies. But Jenna didn't begrudge the kids. Those carefree years disappeared in a hurry.

"I made a double batch," Aunt Edie told Jenna, "so

why don't you take a few over to Seth? I saw his truck pull in a while ago." Aunt Edie, the matchmaker.

Still, Jenna had no problem taking cookies to Seth. She and Seth were simpatico. If they'd met in another time, another place, they'd have been a couple.

So much debris had washed to the shores of their lives she wasn't sure they'd ever make it to coupledom. She was still working up the nerve to dip a toe into the uncertain waters of a serious relationship, and he wasn't ready to even get close.

She'd told herself it was a good thing that his mold-removal business was tapering off with the arrival of colder weather, and he was now working a couple of days a week at the hardware store. She couldn't see him every afternoon that way and feel both tempted and frustrated. Except that the days he was at the store seemed to be the days she needed to go in there for something. Just a coincidence.

Between him and Brody, Jenna spent a lot of time on temptation overload. If things didn't work out with her sister and her Mr. Perfect, she'd sic Celeste on them. Celeste was fun, bubbly and a little crazy.

Hmm. She'd probably be too much for Seth, who, for good reason, preferred calm waters. But Jenna could see Brody and Celeste together. When she wasn't seeing herself with him.… Good grief, she was a mess.

"You have time to figure things out," she reminded herself as she walked past the motel's empty rooms to the one second from the end where Seth had his headquarters. There was no need to hurry.

She had to knock more than once before he came to the door. Jeans, bare feet, a gorgeous bare chest sprinkled with dark hair and tousled, wet dark locks on his head were a big clue that he'd just gotten out of the shower.

"Hey, there," he said, and swung the door wide.

"Come into my parlor," said the spider to the fly.

Except Seth's room wasn't some lair set up to lure babes. It was spare, with only the usual motel furniture, his cooler, and piles of library books on the dresser and nightstands and the extra bed (twin—the Driftwood was built long before rooms were expected to have two queens or a king). No, there was no deliberate seduction setup here. Simply his presence that made it happen.

He motioned to the plate. "What did you bring me?"

"Cookies from Aunt Edie, of course."

He smiled as he took them. "All right. What's the special occasion this time?"

"A committee meeting."

An eyebrow lifted. "You got suckered into being on a committee today?"

"More like I got put in charge of a committee."

He settled on one of the beds and pulled the tin foil off the plate of cookies. "Yeah? Whose idea was that, the house-peddler's?"

Seth and Brody were probably never going to be buds. Too much rivalry. Seth might not have been ready for a serious relationship, but he also wasn't ready to share.

"No," she said, ignoring the jibe. "Mine." She smiled at the memory of her successful pitch.

"Okay, this should be good. Spill."

She sat down on the bed opposite him. "I came up with a brilliant idea, if I do say so myself."

"Yeah?" He held the plate toward her, and she shook her head. There was already enough temptation in this room without adding cookies. He shrugged and helped himself to one. "So, what is it?"

"We're going to have a festival," she announced.

"Another one?"

Her smile fell. "You sound like Susan Frank."

He held up a hand. "Sorry. I'm surprised is all. We just had one last summer. For a good cause," he quickly added.

Considering that it had been to help save the Driftwood Inn, yeah. "This is for a good cause, too. We need to bring more people to town in the winter."

He nodded. "I can see that. Hard to be a tourist town if you don't have tourists. But school's started and most people are done with their vacations."

"Exactly. Which is why we need to think of a reason for them to come to the beach."

"Sunsets and winter storms and good restaurants aren't enough?"

"Obviously not. You may have noticed that we lost our one booking for the weekend." Determined not to dwell on that, she returned to her news. "We're going to have a holiday festival, complete with a parade."

"A parade here in winter?"

"It can be done."

"Standing around outdoors in the cold and rain."

He sounded dubious. For an instant, she felt dubious, too. But, no, this *would* work. "Do you have any idea how many people stand around in the cold up in the mountains to watch Icicle Falls light up their giant tree?"

"So, you gonna import a giant tree?"

"No, but we're going to get the town all decorated."

He grunted. "I can see it now. Clamshells wearing Santa hats sitting by every cash register."

"Hmm, not bad."

"Tell me you've got more than that."

"Of course. We'll have all the businesses decorate. Customers can vote for their favorite. The restaurants can run holiday specials. The stores can have sales. Wc'll have the parade. Kiki's planning to make her employees wear mermaid tails."

"Topless? In the cold? Oh, yeah."

"Very funny," she said, frowning at him.

Unrepentant, he snickered and wolfed down a cookie.

"Anyway, it'll be a great way to get people here. They can come, do the last of their Christmas shopping, party a little. What do you think? Seriously?"

"Seriously? I think anything's worth a try. This is a cool town. More people should come here and check it out."

"I agree," she said.

"And more people should come and stay at the Driftwood."

"We *need* more people to come and stay at the Driftwood."

"So, if this will bring 'em in, go for it."

"Want to be on the committee?"

"No, thanks." He bit into another cookie. "Not my thing."

"You could join the chamber. You do own a business."

"And sit around and eat fish and chips and make

nice with people like that Beach Babes bitch? Oh, sure, sign me up."

"Most everyone's nice. You know that."

"I'm not a joiner. But hey, I'll help. I assume I'm going to get roped into something."

"Well, we do need some kind of float in the parade. And you know Pete won't be much use."

"No. Really?" Seth ate the rest of his cookie. "Sounds like you took on a mother of a job. I'm noticing a pattern here," he added with a smile.

Yes, she did seem to get in over her head on projects. First renovating the motel, now this. "I'm willing to if it'll help the town. And the Driftwood."

"I'm there for whatever you need."

"We need a Santa for the parade."

"I'm there for *almost* whatever you need," he amended.

Jenna left him and went to the office to do some bookkeeping. It was difficult to concentrate, though, because visions of the upcoming festival kept dancing through her mind, distracting her. She could already see the town bustling with holiday celebrants wandering from shop to shop, eating in the restaurants, spending money, making memories. She could see the floats and marching bands coming down Harbor Boulevard. This was going to be a success!

She finally shut down the computer and went back to the house, where she found Aunt Edie alone in the kitchen. No sign of Sabrina and Tristan, other than abandoned backpacks and a couple of plates with some cookie crumbs.

"Where are the kids?" she asked.

"They went upstairs to do homework," Aunt Edie said as she bent to take another batch of cookies out of the oven.

Jenna always made sure the pair stayed at the table to do homework where they could remain under the watchful eye of an adult. She realized now that she should've shared that rule with her aunt.

"Oh," Aunt Edie said when Jenna explained. "I'm sorry, dear. It didn't even occur to me that they'd be doing anything other than homework." Dear, sweet, trusting Aunt Edie.

Since homework could easily be done at the kitchen table, Jenna strongly suspected that her daughter and the boyfriend were working on something other than math.

She went upstairs, hoping she was wrong. Sabrina's door was shut. Not a good sign. *Let them be texting.* She heard a happy little moan that had nothing to do with solving an equation. *Not texting.*

Jenna granted them the courtesy of knocking. As she opened the door, Tristan scrambled off her daughter, his face lobster-red.

"Mom!" Sabrina scolded in outraged tones.

Stay calm. Don't yell.

But Jenna wanted to yell all kinds of things. *What are you doing? What were you thinking!*

But of course she knew what they were doing and thinking. It was the same thing she'd done and thought when she was young (but not as young as Sabrina!). It was the same thing she wanted to do again someday with the right man.

"You know the rule," she said to her daughter. "And there's a reason for it."

"I'm sorry, Ms. Jones," Tristan said, unable to look Jenna in the eye.

"Tristan, you're the older one. I expected better of you."

He hung his head, and Jenna almost felt sorry for him.

"There's a big age difference between you two," she reminded him. "In a few months you won't be a minor anymore. I'm trying to keep some guardrails in place so you don't run off the road. Do you understand?"

His face had gone from red to white, proof that he did, indeed, understand. He pressed his lips together and nodded.

"You're being mean. We weren't doing anything wrong," Sabrina cried.

Just warming up to trouble. "I think you'd better go home, Tristan. I need to have a talk with Sabrina," Jenna said.

He nodded and beat it.

"I'm sorry, Tristan," Sabrina called after him, almost sounding panicked.

"How about an *I'm sorry* for me?" Jenna asked, taking his place on her daughter's bed.

"We were just kissing."

"Lying on your bed with the door closed."

"Can't I have some privacy?" Sabrina demanded.

"Yes, but not when Tristan's over. You know the rule. No boys allowed upstairs."

Sabrina's only reply was to sit fuming, staring at the door through which her beloved had departed.

"Honey, things can get out of hand in a hurry," Jenna said gently. Especially when you were horizontal.

"We love each other," Sabrina said, her voice turning tearful.

Love. What a fire it built.

But that fire was also blinding, and it hurt like hell when it burned you.

"I don't want to see you get hurt, and you're going to have to trust me when I tell you that you're too young to go down this road," Jenna said. Crap. She was probably handling this all wrong.

"You don't understand," Sabrina accused, and threw herself face-first on to her pillow.

"I probably understand more than you think," Jenna said softly. "Even if I don't, I still need you to follow the rules. If I can't trust you two to behave responsibly here in our own house, how can I trust you enough to let you go to the Christmas ball?"

Sabrina sat back up, her eyes still glittering with tears, her expression hopeful. "You'll let me?"

"Do you think I should?"

Sabrina fell silent and dropped her gaze.

"I'm considering it. But I have to know I can trust you to be wise. You don't want to rush into anything and then be sorry later. You have all of high school in front of you. And you'll have more boyfriends in the future."

Wrong thing to say. "I love Tristan."

"I know you do. But you might fall out of love." *Your father did with me.*

"I won't," Sabrina insisted.

"Maybe you won't. But even if that turns out to be the case, you still have plenty of time. Sex is a big deal, Sabrina, and contrary to what anyone might tell you, it involves more than your body. You give yourself, you give your heart. You have to be sure." *Oh, what wise words. Better apply them to your own love life.*

"I *am* sure."

Jenna understood. She'd been there, done that. "If things don't work out, if he moves on, then he takes a part of you with him that you can't get back."

"He won't move on."

"Well, then, if he's going to stick around, he can afford to wait. And if he does turn out to be your one true love, he'll be a member of our family. You don't want to put him in a position where he's ashamed to look me in the eye."

Sabrina bit her lip and said nothing.

"So, can I trust you to honor the rules?"

It took a moment, but Sabrina finally heaved a sigh and nodded. "Okay."

"Good," Jenna said.

She kissed her daughter, then went in search of aspirin.

"I don't think I handled it very well," she said when she called her mother for a shot of encouragement.

"You did fine," Melody assured her. "Parenting has never been easy, but I think in today's culture it's harder than ever. You'll get through it, though. Meanwhile, you're smart not to ban them from seeing each other. You don't want to turn them into Romeo and Juliet."

"Oh, there's a charming thought," Jenna muttered. "Honestly, I'll be so glad when she's through high school."

Her mother chuckled. "If you think your worries will end then, you're sadly mistaken. Once a parent, always a parent. No matter how old your kids are, you always worry about them."

"Well, you don't need to worry about me," Jenna said.

"In twenty years, your daughter will be saying the same thing to you."

"I just want to get through the next four."

"You will. Now, go enjoy your committee meeting."

The holiday festival committee met in Aunt Edie's living room at 6:00 p.m., Jolly Roger supervising and begging for whiskey. Aunt Edie finally covered his cage and shut him up.

He hadn't been the only beggar in the house. Pete, on learning there'd be nothing coming from the kitchen for dinner, had grumbled just enough that Aunt Edie had actually made him a grilled cheese sandwich.

"Honestly, Aunt Edie," Jenna had protested after he'd wolfed it down and wandered off to The Drunken Sailor for a beer, "he's a grown man. He can fend for himself."

"I don't mind, really," said her aunt. "Pete was a big help to me before you came. I owe him a lot."

Pete was a big mooch before Jenna came, but she had to admit he'd probably been good for moral support. He and Aunt Edie had established their own boundaries long before she arrived, so why was she trying to move them?

Because he took advantage of her aunt's kindness and that bugged Jenna. They weren't married. Aunt Edie didn't owe him three meals a day. She certainly didn't need to cook for him every time he wanted something special. Of course, Jenna reminded herself, Aunt Edie didn't need to cook for her and Sabrina, either.

Jenna had said as much once, but her aunt had insisted she liked cooking for everyone.

"And I'm so grateful I have family with me now," she'd added. "You and Sabrina are truly making my golden years golden."

So there you had it. But Jenna would have prepared her own daughter's dinner if Sabrina hadn't been invited to her friend Hudson's house for pizza.

Thank God Sabrina had found friends. Jenna had begun to worry that her daughter would never settle in. But two new families had moved to town over the summer, both with girls Sabrina's age, and at the start of the school year the three outsiders had banded together. Hudson, Jennifer and Sabrina were all equally cute, so that took care of the competition factor. Most weekends the girls partied back and forth at each other's houses, did their nails, dyed their hair, played board games (often with Aunt Edie) and, of course, talked endlessly about boys. There would probably be much discussion on that ever-fascinating topic this night. Jenna supposed the whole Tristan thing would be discussed and she'd get the Mean Mother of the Year award, but she'd probably win that more than once over the next few years. Better to be a mean mother than an irresponsible one.

With Sabrina happily occupied, Jenna was free to plan the festival with her fellow committee members. "We should see if we can get a sponsor or two," she said as they began working their way through the evening's agenda. The chamber had voted to allot a small amount of money toward marketing, which would be enough to get them started, but Jenna knew they'd need more.

"I can talk to Sherwood over at the bank," Nora offered. "They often come through with money for city-wide events."

Nice to know they came through for something. They sure hadn't been there when Jenna needed a new roof for the motel. "Super," she said. She was happy to let Nora take care of that. She certainly had no desire to ask Sherwood Stern for anything.

Other possible sponsors were discussed, including the Porthole. "They might come up with five hundred," Brody said, and offered to talk to the owner. "And I think Beach Dreams Realty can manage to kick in another five."

"All right!" Jenna said, excited. "That's really generous of you. Thank you."

"A good tax deduction," Brody said, shrugging off her gratitude.

Ellis grinned at him. "Glad you offered, my man. That lets me off the hook."

"I'm sure we'll find plenty of other hooks to stick into you," Jenna told him.

They began listing what needed to be done and assigning it to committee members. Kiki volunteered to help with marketing and promised to have a website up for the event before the week was out.

"My grandson is a whiz with this stuff," she said.

"Oh, really? Does he live around here?" Jenna asked.

"As a matter of fact, he does. Goes to Moonlight Harbor High. He's a senior this year, and then he'll be off to college."

Senior, whiz with the internet… "What's your grandson's name?" Jenna asked.

"Tristan Van Cliburn. My daughter moved down

here three years ago after her divorce and is helping me with the business. She and Tristan live with me. Such a sweet boy."

Jenna managed a weak smile and poured herself another glass of Brody's wine.

"And he's smart as a whip," Kiki went on. "He built my website for me when he was only thirteen."

"He built mine, too," Jenna said, and decided to leave it at that.

"Well, then, you know how good he is," Kiki said proudly.

He *was* a good kid. He could hardly be blamed for wanting to do what every boy on the planet wanted to do with a girl he liked.

"We should probably have him manage our Facebook page, too," Tyrella said. "We'll need a like page for the festival."

Kiki nodded. "I'll get him right on it."

Excellent suggestion. Keep him busy.

The jobs continued to get divided up. Nora offered to take care of bringing in carnival rides and to be in charge of signing up vendors and artisans for booths on the pier. Tyrella said she'd contact the paper about an ad, get in touch with the *Seattle Times* and other media and also start involving the local businesses. Ellis was put in charge of money, and he and Brody teamed up to organize the parade, which would involve getting necessary permits, collecting fees from participants and setting out the parade route. Ellis also committed to being present on the big day to keep everything running smoothly.

"By the time we're all done, this will run like a well-oiled machine," Tyrella predicted as they dug into Aunt Edie's cookies and ice cream from Nora's.

"Machines break down," Ellis warned. "We may have a few bugs to work out this first year."

"Yes, but the good news is that people rarely see what's wrong behind the scenes," Nora said. "We might have a nervous breakdown or two, but our visitors will enjoy themselves."

"Let's hope so," Jenna said fervently.

"Anyway, it's not like we've never done a festival," Tyrella said. "We manage the razor clam one just fine, and don't forget what a success the Blue Moon was in August."

"Hey, I'm not trying to jinx us," Ellis said, holding up both hands. "But we need to be ready to roll with the punches."

Brody waved away his concern. "We'll be fine."

"You're certainly off to a good start," said Aunt Edie, who'd been nodding agreement and smiling throughout the entire meeting. "This is going to be a wonderful event."

"I hope so," Jenna said. One way or another she was determined to pull this off and prove Susan Frank wrong. And, even more important, fill up those vacancies at the Driftwood Inn.

The meeting broke up with almost everyone leaving for home. Brody lingered, and after Jenna had said goodbye to the others, he asked, "Am I imagining it or is something bothering you?"

"What makes you think that?" Jenna hedged.

"Maybe the fact that you looked like somebody was

offering you deep-fried slugs when Kiki mentioned her grandson."

"I didn't know he and my daughter's boyfriend were one and the same."

"So now you know he's a great kid."

He was, for the most part. It was those pesky hormones running on overdrive that were the problem.

"There it is again, the fried-slug face," Brody said. "Get your coat. Let's go to the Porthole for a drink-and-shrink session."

She hesitated. Should she really be telling her problems to the whole world?

"I'm a good listener," he promised.

So, ten minutes later, they were seated in a quiet corner of the Porthole, him with a beer, her having a cup of chamomile tea and once more fretting about how she'd handled the situation, worrying that she wasn't a good enough parent, that her daughter would wind up making poor choices.

"Don't be so hard on yourself. I think you handled the situation fine," he said. "Better than I would have. I'd probably have yanked the kid off her and punched his face in."

"Oh, you wouldn't," she scoffed.

"Oh, I would. It's a guy thing."

"I tried not to freak out. It's just that she's so young."

"I get that, and really, you handled it fine. But look at it this way. In medieval times she'd be married by now."

"We're not living in medieval times," Jenna said with a frown.

"True. But biology is biology, and feelings are the same now as they were back then. You're right to set rules, but if you want some unrequested advice from someone who's further down that road, remember that what she feels is real. They'll probably break up by the end of the year, so let her keep seeing him. And tell him I'll beat the shit out of him if he tries anything," Brody added with a grin, which made Jenna smile.

It did feel comforting to be able to talk over her worries with him. His son was in his first year of college and his daughter was a senior in high school, so in Jenna's mind he qualified as a parental stress survivor.

"I *have* decided to let her keep seeing him," Jenna said. "But seeing and dating are two different things. She can't date until she's fifteen and that's still a few months away. He can see her at our house and at school and parties, and that's it."

"That's fair," Brody said.

"Except she wants to go to the Christmas ball with him, and I don't know about that. Maybe if a group of them go together."

"Safety in numbers?"

"Something like that."

"Sounds like a reasonable compromise. If he wants her, he'll play by the rules. God knows I jumped through enough parental hoops when I was dating my high school sweetheart."

"What happened to her?"

Brody scowled. "I married her."

"Well, you were young. What did you know?" Jenna said in an effort to console him.

"Not much. And that's one of the advantages of getting older. You start to figure things out."

"I hope so," Jenna said, thinking of her own confused love life.

He picked up his glass and saluted her. "Here's to figuring things out."

She picked up her tea mug and echoed, "To figuring things out."

And to friends, she thought. She and Brody were definitely friends. Could she see them becoming more? Too soon to know, but it was certainly a possibility.

It appeared that Aunt Edie and Jenna and her committee weren't the only ones who were excited about the festival. Word spread quickly as the committee got busy, with various shop owners, hoteliers and restaurants happily signing on to decorate, offer specials and be in the parade.

Even Mayor Parker Thorne was excited when she came to Jenna for her Thursday-afternoon massage. "Of course, the city will be more than happy to print your posters and fliers," she promised.

"Thanks," said Jenna. All right! Getting the mayor on board was the commerce equivalent of getting a blessing from the pope. And the offer to take care of their printed materials would save them a nice chunk of change.

"I love the idea of a holiday parade," the mayor continued as Jenna worked out some tightness in her glutes. "You'll want a grand marshal, naturally."

Jenna hadn't thought beyond Santa, but she said, "Oh, yes."

"I'll be happy to do that for you." Stylish and pretty, Parker would, of course, make a perfect grand marshal.

She would also, of course, never miss an opportunity for a public appearance, but hey, that was politics. "And I told Ellis that my husband, Brewster, will play Santa. Brewster's a husky man. He'll do well at that. Oh, and I did remind Ellis he'll need to build a stage the floats can pass by."

Poor Ellis.

"I'll be happy to grant interviews to the area papers if needed."

That was fine by Jenna. The mayor could be counted on to say the right words, and she'd do a great job of promoting the festival.

"Whatever you need, the city is behind you one hundred percent."

That was good to know. Jenna had a committee of smart, talented people and the enthusiastic support of the mayor's office. Everything was coming together perfectly.

"School will be out by then," Celeste said when Jenna told her. She worked as a first-grade teacher in a school north of Seattle and spent as much time in Moonlight Harbor as she could. "I can come down early and help if you need me to."

"Want to be on our Driftwood Inn float?"

"Sure. I always wanted to be a princess."

"What do you mean? You've always *been* a princess," Jenna teased.

"One of the perks of being the baby of the family."

"Well, Princess Driftwood, you'd better plan to help us work on the float when you come down for Thanksgiving."

"I can do that. What's it going to be?"

"I don't know yet. Maybe we'll just pile a bunch of driftwood in the back of Seth's truck and you can sit on it."

"That sounds comfy. Maybe I don't want to be in the parade."

Jenna chortled. "Too late. But don't worry. We'll find a really cool costume for you. I know. You can be a giant fish."

"Gee, I can hardly wait."

Actually, so could Jenna. Seaside with Santa was going to be amazing.

Chapter Four

"I wish I could take the time off to come down," Jenna's mom said when Jenna called her on Friday to tell her about the growing enthusiasm for the festival.

"I wish you didn't have to work," Jenna said.

If only she could hurry up and get the Driftwood showing a profit. She could tell her mom to dump the job and come be part of the family business. Of course, knowing Mom, she'd insist on staying right where she was, checking groceries until she wound up with carpal tunnel. Still, if she was going to get it, she could get it working at the grocery store in Moonlight Harbor, too.

"I wish you'd move down here," Jenna said. "I could see if our grocery store is hiring."

"Oh, honey, that's sweet of you to want me. But I'm fine here. I only have a few more years before I retire."

"And then you can move down here with Aunt Edie and me."

"We'll see," Mel said, not committing to anything.

Widowed young, she had managed to make a good life for herself, but Jenna was convinced it would be better if they were together.

Of course, there'd be no Sabrina around by the time

her mother retired. Who knew where her daughter would end up or what she'd do with her life? All Jenna knew was that she wanted Sabrina to go out and see the world, do big things.

One thing she didn't want her to do was be in a hurry to get married. How did that old saying go? Marry in haste, repent at leisure.

Jenna had certainly done her share of repenting.

But she'd gotten a great kid out of the deal, and now she was someplace she really wanted to be, doing something useful. So what if she wasn't working toward becoming a famous artist like her ex? She was planning a festival, and that was pretty important, considering how many people would benefit. More people than would benefit from looking at sculptures made out of dumpster finds.

Okay, she told herself, *be generous. If Damien succeeds, you can be glad for him.* Mostly, though, she could be glad she was rid of him.

She ended the call with her mom and got ready for her first and best massage client, Frank the cop, who was currently working nights.

"Oh, man, I need this," he groaned as she started on his legs. "The job's a killer."

He made it sound like he pushed his muscles to the max chasing bad guys around Moonlight Harbor, but as there weren't currently any bad guys in residence, she knew his muscles couldn't hurt from racing into danger. And he wasn't exactly the fittest specimen on the police force, so she doubted he'd hurt himself working out at the community club gym. Frank's main reason for massage was to keep an eye on Jenna's love life. He never failed to ask about Brody, and she never failed to let him think they were an item. Maybe they were moving in that direction. She wasn't sure. But she *was* sure she and Frank weren't a match.

Once they'd gotten the usual banter out of the way, him talking about what a great catch he was and reminding her that money and good looks weren't everything, and her replying that she was entirely too superficial for him, they switched to the topic of the upcoming festival.

"Sounds like a good idea," he said. "Make sure you guys talk to the chief about putting extra cops on duty that day. You'll need 'em for crowd control."

She hoped so. She wanted a crowd.

She got Frank all fixed for the week, then worked on Patricia Whiteside.

"How's the poster design coming?" Patricia asked.

"I haven't quite hit on the right idea yet," Jenna confessed. She couldn't help remembering how Damien used to point out that he couldn't simply turn on creativity like a faucet when she nagged him to be more productive. Now, she had to admit, she got it. Inspiration was an elusive little bitch.

Not that Jenna hadn't been kicking around ideas. She'd known she needed to have Santa on the poster and she needed a nod to the beach, since Moonlight Harbor was a beach town. Santa riding on a whale? Santa under a beach umbrella? Santa sitting on a piece of driftwood? Nothing quite felt right.

Even if something did feel right she wasn't sure she'd be able to bring an idea to life on paper. As a child, she'd loved to draw, and she'd enjoyed her high school art classes, but marriage to Damien had sucked away much of her confidence in her artistic abilities.

"You'll come up with it," Patricia said.

She needed to do that soon. The festival clock was ticking, and those posters needed to get done and distributed.

Patricia left and Jenna took care of two more clients, then went over to the motel office to…do nothing. There were no new reservations, no guests to look after, no paperwork needing her attention. Okay, back to the house for lunch.

"Do we have any new reservations?" Aunt Edie asked when she came into the kitchen.

"We've had some inquiries," Jenna lied. She had a small nose, with room to grow a couple of inches, Pinocchio-style. She grabbed an apple and said, "You know, I think I'll just go work on the festival poster." Then she escaped before her aunt could question her further.

She settled at her desk in the spare bedroom, where she'd set up her massage table, and begged Ms. Inspiration to put in an appearance. What could she put on that poster? Santa in a fishing boat? Santa filling a stocking with…clams? Clams. Hmm.

Suddenly, just like that, she had it. It took her another couple of hours messing around, but she finally had something she liked, a drawing of a jolly Santa reclining on a giant clam shell, waving to festival-goers. A hint of sea in the background and she was good to go. Who said she didn't have any artistic abilities? Oh, yeah, her ex. Well, to heck with him.

She spent a little more time toying with her creation

and then scanned it and sent it to her committee members. She also printed off a copy to show Aunt Edie later.

She sat for a few minutes, staring at it. Pretty darned cute. Did poster design count as legitimate art? Surely it did. No matter. Jenna was pleased with what she'd created. She didn't need affirmation to feel good about herself.

Oh, who was she kidding? Of course, she did.

And it came in quickly from all her committee members.

This is positively brilliant, wrote Kiki.

So darling, declared Patricia. I knew you'd come up with something.

I love it, Tyrella enthused.

Ellis and Rian also gave it a thumbs-up, and Brody suggested they go out to dinner to celebrate.

Well, why not? She liked going out to dinner with Brody.

When Jenna finally surfaced, her daughter was home from school, enjoying Aunt Edie's freshly baked peanut butter cookies. Tristan was present, too, along with Sabrina's girlfriend Hudson. Tristan was having a hard time looking Jenna in the eye until she said hello to him and gave him a welcoming pat on the shoulder as she walked past. *You're welcome to come hang out, but behave yourself.* At the moment, all three kids were busy texting and posting cookie pictures on Instagram. So much better than kissing. *Text away, kids.*

"The poster's done," she announced, handing it to Aunt Edie.

"This is adorable," Aunt Edie gushed. "As soon as the posters are printed, we need to get one framed to hang in the living room. What do you think?" she asked, turning to show Sabrina and company.

"It's really cute, Mom," said Sabrina, and Jenna felt ridiculously pleased. She'd known she had something good, but to get the approval of her daughter, who had her daddy's artistic eye, was a big bonus.

"If you send it to me, I'll put it up on the Facebook page," Tristan said.

"Thanks," she said. Kiki was right. Her grandson was a good kid. He just needed to learn to control those hormone surges. To be fair, so did her daughter.

"Nobody's sent me anything to put up yet, and I've kinda been waiting for the poster graphic," Tristan continued.

"I'll get it off to you now. Thanks, Tristan. Having you do our Facebook page is a big help," she added, making him smile.

Aunt Edie invited Tristan and Hudson to stay for dinner, and there was talk of a game of Farkle after, which left Jenna free to go enjoy dinner out.

On her way to the Porthole, she stopped by Seth's room to drop off her design for the Driftwood Inn's float. It was simple, a miniature motel surrounded by driftwood. She'd wedge a chair in there for Celeste to sit on. Maybe Sabrina would want to be on it, too.

"Looks pretty straightforward," he said when she showed it to him. "You want some blue tinsel hanging from the bottom?"

"That would be great."

"Easy enough. Find me a chassis to build it over."

"A chassis?"

"You know, like from an old car?"

"A car," she repeated. Where was she going to find a car?

"Something has to drive the float," he pointed out.

Oh, yeah. Duh. But… "I don't have extra money to buy a car, even an old one." She could see her plan for a float floating away.

"Tell you what. I'll go over to Dino's tomorrow."

"Dino?"

"Lives outside town. Fixes cars, sells spare parts. He's got a couple of beaters sitting around. One of them might actually run."

Jenna had visions of their float stalling out halfway down the street. "Oh, boy," she said faintly.

"Don't worry. I worked on cars when I was in high school. Between the two of us, Dino and I can get something running for you."

"Do you think he'll want to donate to a good cause?"

"Probably. If not, he'll give us something dirt cheap."

"Until we get more people staying here, I can't even afford dirt."

"Don't worry," Seth told her. "I'm on it."

Then for sure she didn't need to worry. Seth Waters was hardworking and dependable. "Thanks!"

He took in her leggings and boots and once-stylish faux fur-trimmed jacket, her gold earrings and lipstick. "Going out?"

She blushed. Why did she always do that when the topic of her social life came up? Correction. She only blushed when her social life involved Brody.

But she didn't need to blush. If she wanted to have dinner with Brody, she darn well could. And she *did* want to have dinner with him. He was gorgeous, fun and good-hearted. Her mother had told her love hadn't given up on her, so why not give Cupid a chance to prove it? She was ready to go out with a man, and she didn't see Seth asking her.

Of course, he wouldn't, since he'd obviously decided he wasn't right for her.

Still, having him live on the premises was the equivalent of keeping chocolate bars hidden in the freezer. They were supposedly out of reach there, but you always knew where they were and you always wound up drifting to the freezer.

"With Brody?" Seth continued.

"Committee business." They would, of course, talk about the poster.

"Yeah, right," Seth said, and frowned.

Jealous but gutless. "I don't see you asking me out."

He gave her a lazy smile, and his eyelids dropped to half-mast. Whenever Jenna got caught with her eyes half closed in pictures, she looked drunk and idiotic. Seth Waters looked sexy.

"Don't want to tempt you," he said in his deep pirate voice.

Too late. He did. "What a feeble excuse."

"Don't want to tempt myself, either," he added. "Go on, gorge yourself on crab with the house-peddler. Try not to get too overheated."

"He *is* pretty hot," Jenna taunted.

"I meant from all the hot air he'll be blowing around."

"Admit it, you're jealous."

"You know I am. Now, get out of here before I turn into some sort of nineteenth-century rake and subject you to a fate worse than death."

Sex with Seth Waters. She'd die with a smile on her face. Ah, yes, the kids weren't the only ones with hormones on overload.

But in spite of the attraction, she didn't see anything happening with Seth. Maybe, in the end, nothing would happen with Brody, either. Who knew? One thing she did know for sure, if she took the plunge into the turbulent waters of true love, she wanted someone who was willing to stay in them with her and swim the distance.

Thinking about how hurt she'd been when her marriage crumbled, she couldn't help wondering if she'd ever find someone like that. Maybe she was meant to go through life alone.

You're not alone, she reminded herself. *You have Aunt Edie and Mom and Celeste and Sabrina.*

But Sabrina would be gone in four short years, either off to college somewhere or to learn a vocation. Aunt Edie and Mom would eventually leave Jenna, too, although not of their own volition. As for Celeste, she was too cute, and liked men way too much to settle into living forever single with her sister. No, someday it would be Jenna, all by herself.

Except she'd always have friends here at Moonlight Harbor. You were never alone when you lived in a tight-knit community like this one. She'd found the perfect place to land, the perfect safety net to fall into.

She bought a few things for Aunt Edie at the grocery store, and by the time she got to the restaurant, Brody was waiting for her in the lobby. "I could have come and picked you up, you know," he greeted her.

"I know, but I had an errand to run."

"I don't mind running errands."

He didn't mind much of anything. Nothing seemed to ruffle Brody Green. Patient and easy to be with, he was a nice change from her ex, who was high-strung and high-maintenance.

They didn't lack for conversation as they ate. Brody asked what kind of float the Driftwood was going to enter in the parade and heartily approved of her plan. "Give me a call if you need help."

"I think between Pete, Seth, Sabrina and me, we've got it covered."

The mention of Seth always made him frown, so she changed the subject. "How about Beach Dreams Realty? Are you going to have a float?"

"No, but we are going to do something."

"Oh? What?" she prompted.

"Two of my agents and I are going to be walking down the street as houses."

"As houses," she repeated.

"Yeah, we'll paint that spray insulation over some big cardboard packing boxes, the kind appliances come in, sculpt 'em and paint 'em, put roofs on 'em."

She chuckled. "You know what I just thought of?"

"I'm afraid to ask."

"Remember the old movie *To Kill a Mockingbird*?"

"Yeah. My high school English class read the book. I saved time and watched the movie."

She frowned at him. "Didn't that defeat the purpose of reading?"

He shrugged. "I got a B on my paper. Worked for me. So, where are you going with this?"

"Remember the scene in the movie when Scout's

walking home from the play wearing her ham costume?"

"What, you think I'm going to fall over in my house costume?"

She couldn't help grinning. "That could be amusing."

"Anyone ever tell you you're a sick little puppy?"

"Mmm, don't think so. By the way, didn't you always wonder why Atticus never came to watch the play and why he wasn't walking her home?"

He shrugged. "Maybe he already knew his kid was a ham."

"Ha, ha," Jenna said. "And maybe that was explained in the book."

"So, you never read it, either?"

"My English teacher didn't assign it," she said in her own defense. And most of her leisure reading had been—and still was—various suspense authors and romance writers such as Debbie Macomber and Susan Mallery.

"What classic did you have to read?" he asked.

"The Scarlet Letter."

"Which would never fly today," he scoffed. "Not exactly relevant anymore."

"It wasn't when we read it, but it also gave us a glimpse into another time. And isn't that what classics do?"

"Yeah, but I think it wouldn't hurt to add some current stuff, like John Grisham. Give kids a look into the legal world."

"It would certainly beat *Lord of the Flies*," Jenna said. "Just thinking about that book spoils my appetite."

"Hey, that was a cool book. So, what else did you read?"

"Shakespeare, of course. *Romeo and Juliet.*"

"Oh, yeah. Young love and death. Always a good read for kids."

"Sabrina's class is reading it and she loves it."

"Teenage girls love to read stuff they can cry over. My daughter did. Speaking of daughters and Romeo and Juliet, how are things with the boyfriend wannabe?"

"He's still with us. And they're remaining downstairs, where I can keep an eye on them."

"You sound like an overprotective dad," Brody teased. The minute the words were out of his mouth, he sobered. "Sorry, that was a dumb thing to say."

"Her dad isn't much use," Jenna said. That was putting it mildly.

"Have you told him about the boyfriend?"

Jenna shook her head. "He prefers to leave the parental heavy lifting to me."

"You might be surprised. He may be a loser as an ex, but deep down he's still a father."

"Too deep to drill," she said. Damien was happy shirking his duties.

"You've got it handled now anyway. But if you need a sounding board, you know I'm here." Brody reached out and placed a hand over hers, making those little fish tacos she'd been eating jump in her tummy.

Brody Green knew exactly what to say. And do. He had a way with women.

He'd had a way with half the women in Moonlight Harbor, from what Jenna could tell. Would he be content to settle down with just one?

She didn't ask and they returned to the subject of the festival. By the time they'd finished dessert, she was pumped and ready to go home and work some more, this time on luring people to stay at the Driftwood Inn for the festival.

She settled in at her computer and got busy. *Holiday Festival Stay at Charming Beach Inn*, she captioned her Groupon offer, and then made potential visitors a deal they couldn't refuse. Oh, yes, who wouldn't want to take advantage of that?

Finished with her promotion, she sat back in her desk chair and smiled. All right. Let 'em come.

Chapter Five

"Guess what I just found a Groupon for?"

Taylor Marsh wasn't sure she wanted to hear. It would be a bargain for some cool new restaurant opening up in Seattle or a great trip, and lately, hearing about her older sister's adventures was not bringing out the best in her. It wasn't that she didn't want Sarah to have a good life. It was that she didn't want to feel inferior because of it. And somehow, ever since Sarah and Chris Brown had gotten out of debt and managed to pile up some savings, it seemed that they'd become the experts on money management—always offering tips and unrequested advice to Taylor and Greg.

Taylor would be the first to admit their finances were currently a mess, but she hated having her nose rubbed in it—something her sister seemed to do in a million subtle and not-so-subtle ways. Taylor resented it, especially since it wasn't her fault they were in financial deep doo-doo. If Greg hadn't quit a great IT tech job to start his company, which was going nowhere—did the world really need another internet search engine?—if he hadn't drained their savings and pushed them into debt, they'd have been fine. Now it seemed they were up to their eyeballs in credit card debt and struggling to make their car payments. And he kept promising that any day this company was going to take off. It had been two years. How much longer did he need?

Of course, Sarah always had advice whenever Taylor made the mistake of complaining. "Lose the second car. You can't afford it."

"I need that car to show houses," Taylor would snap. "I can't exactly drive clients around in Greg's beater." Not that she'd made any money yet, but that was beside the point. She was still learning the business. The Seattle market was hot, and the money would come.

"That's the problem," Sarah the wise would say. "You have an excuse for everything you spend money on, and you don't need half of it. You don't need to get your nails done, you don't need to spend so much on clothes and you don't need to waste money on takeout and burgers."

"I don't always have time to cook," Taylor would retort, "and I need to look professional." Although she hadn't had her nails done in months.

"Not *that* professional."

Then the entire conversation would degenerate, with Taylor either shifting the blame onto Greg and his poor business skills or saying something rude to her bossy big sister that made her come across as a spoiled brat.

Taylor wasn't spoiling herself these days. She couldn't remember when she'd last bought herself any new clothes. And takeout? Well, okay, she'd done that a few times, but even hitting the fast-food drive-through had become nothing more than a memory in the last couple of months.

"So, don't you want to know what I found?" Sarah prompted, since Taylor was taking way too long to answer.

"A deal on cell phones?"

"We don't need new cell phones. And neither do you, by the way."

As if they'd planned on running out and getting new cell phones? Taylor let the comment slide. "Okay, then, a restaurant deal?"

"Even better. I just got us all a great holiday getaway."

Taylor blinked. "What?" Without even asking? Here they were struggling, and her sister wanted Taylor to come up with money for some crazy trip.

"To the beach."

"We always go to Mom's for Christmas," Taylor protested. What was her sister smoking?

"The trip isn't for Christmas. This is the weekend before. I got a bargain for a stay at a beach motel in Moonlight Harbor. It's a cute little town on the coast, only a couple hours' drive from us. They have a holiday festival going on that weekend."

Taylor loved festivals and fairs, and she loved the holidays. But almost every credit card she had was maxed out, so what was the point? "Sorry, we can't afford that."

"Sure, you can."

"You're always telling me I spend too much money," Taylor reminded her.

"I know. But this time you don't have to spend any because I'm paying. I booked rooms for both our families."

Just like that. Taylor was torn between gratitude and

irritation. It was a kind gesture, yes, but it would've been nice if her sister had asked first. What if they'd had plans?

Right. The only thing she and Greg did together lately was fight. But even that was preferable to a weekend of listening to Chris the know-it-all bragging about his financial wisdom and offering Greg advice at every turn, and having her sister watching with judgmental eyes every penny she spent. Of course, if Sarah was paying for the weekend, she'd feel she had the right to.

"We've got plans," Taylor said.

"Oh? Doing what?"

"Miranda has a party to go to." No lie. She did. A mother couldn't disrupt her daughter's social life, even when her daughter was only six.

The sound of footsteps and the high-pitched voice of an excited child told her that Greg was home from a day of scouring the planet for investors and had picked up Miranda from daycare. She needed to make this fast.

"I bet if you asked her, she'd rather go to the beach with Aunt Sarah and Uncle Chris and the cousins," Sarah said.

"Well, we promised, and we can't go back on a promise."

"Give it try," Sarah urged. "Tell them your family's demanding you spend time with them."

"I'll try," Taylor lied. "Greg's here. Gotta go." She ended the call and said a gushy hello to her daughter, who was excited to show her the drawing she'd made at school. Her greeting to her husband wasn't so gushy. The longer Greg kept dragging them down while he chased his go-nowhere dream, the less gushy she felt.

"You'll try what?" he asked after she'd only given him her cheek to kiss. After the big fight they'd had the night before he was lucky he to get even that.

"Nothing," she said.

"No, tell me."

"My sister wanted to rope us into something. I told her we weren't doing it."

"Oh." He nodded, acknowledgment that whatever Sarah wanted to rope them into was bound to be unpleasant.

Lately she'd been hounding them to go to a seminar sponsored by the same finance guru who'd inspired her and Chris to get out of debt. They'd both resisted, Taylor because she didn't want to give up any more of her lifestyle than she already had and Greg because he didn't want to give up his useless business. Which he *needed* to give up. It was his fault that her lifestyle was being affected. She'd cut back on everything she could think of. Even Christmas. All right, so what she'd ordered online had added up a bit, but all her purchases had been bargains, and she didn't want Miranda to suffer just because Daddy was being an idiot.

"What was she trying to rope us into this time?" Greg asked.

Taylor was very much aware of her daughter standing right there, all ears. Miranda would, of course, want to go to the beach. "Nothing. I'll tell you later."

He got the message and dropped the subject.

But he picked it up again later, after Miranda was in bed. Dinner had put Taylor in a better mood when he'd shared that it looked like he'd soon have a new investor on board, and they were side by side on the couch with glasses of wine and about to watch a movie. She was feeling mellow, so she told him about Sarah's big plan.

"Maybe we should go," he said. "A free getaway at the beach—Miranda would love it."

"You know it won't be free," Taylor said with a frown. "It'll be like getting a weekend in Hawaii where you spend the whole time listening to a sales pitch for a time share."

"But we wouldn't have to stick around and listen."

"We'll probably have adjoining rooms."

He shrugged. "Yeah, I guess. Bad idea. It would've been fun for Miranda, though."

Fun for Miranda. Those words stuck in Taylor's mind like a burr, poking her on a regular basis, making her feel downright uncomfortable. What right did she have to cheat Miranda out of a fun weekend? Who knew when they'd be able to afford a vacation?

Should she accept? She did love her sister. And when they weren't talking about money, they liked being together. They both enjoyed Hallmark movies and HGTV and, really, they'd always been there for each other. Taylor had been Sarah's personal chef for a week after her hysterectomy, and Sarah had taken Miranda for more than one overnight, back in the days when Taylor and Greg could afford to go someplace for the weekend. They hadn't been anywhere in ages. Besides the fact that they couldn't afford it, Taylor hadn't exactly had any desire for a romantic getaway with her husband, who up and quit his job without even discussing it with her.

She still didn't, but Miranda would have a good time with her cousins.

Oh, crap. How many lectures would Taylor have to endure for the sake of her daughter? She frowned. She would put a ban on all money talk, and if Sarah said anything, Taylor would shove a Christmas stocking in her mouth.

She finally called her sister. "Is your offer still good?"

"Of course," Sarah said, and Taylor could hear the smile in her voice.

"Okay. We'll go, on one condition. No money lectures." Her sister was paying for the weekend and she was setting ultimatums. Did that make her a jerk? Probably.

"Hey, I'm trying to do something nice here."

Yep. It definitely made her sound like a jerk. "I just don't want to be nagged all weekend."

"No nagging," Sarah promised. "It'll be fun."

It should be, but Taylor had her doubts. Crap. What had she gotten herself into?

"Holiday festival stay at charming beach motel," read Darrell Wilson as he sat with his laptop at the kitchen table in his home in Federal Way, Washington. Charming and holiday were key words when a man was planning a surprise anniversary getaway for his wife.

Kat loved the holidays. It was why she'd wanted a Christmas wedding.

And what a wedding they'd had. Two hundred guests, white and red roses and mistletoe everywhere, the bridesmaids in red gowns. His wife had looked stunning in a gown trimmed with white faux fur and all kinds of sparkles. She'd been a vision, and he'd been broke. He'd only been teaching math a couple of years and she'd been working at a daycare center by day and trying to become a published author by night. For their honeymoon, they'd gone to Icicle Falls, a little Bavarian-style town nestled in Washington's Cascades. It had snowed and the town had been lit up like a jewel box, and they'd been as happy as if they'd gone to Germany or Switzerland.

That was thirty years ago, and a great marriage had followed a happy honeymoon. Kat never did see any of her stories published, but she did get a job in a bookstore and decided she was happier surrounded by books and blogging about them than trying to write one. Their house was almost paid off, their kids were grown and their son had just married a girl they both liked. And, in spite of a few ups and downs and disagreements over the years, they were still each other's best friend. Their life together had been a good one.

Empty nesters, finally, with some money to spend, they'd planned to travel as much as possible before the grandkids started coming. In fact, before Kat's diagnosis he'd been thinking about finally getting them to Switzerland or taking one of those river cruises that stopped at all the European Christmas markets. But uterine cancer had hit them like an invading army, taking her hair, her energy and much of her joie de vivre. This would not be the year for international travel. She wouldn't be up to it.

Now he wished he'd done it for their twenty-fifth, when she was healthy. But next year, for sure.

There *would* be a next year. The cancer wouldn't come back. He refused to even entertain the possibility. He knew that sometimes she worried that it would, but he always steered her away from that particular conversation. She was still young, only fifty-one. She had lots of years left.

If only her doctors had caught the damned disease earlier. Then a simple hysterectomy would have taken care of the problem. They hadn't, though. So, after her operation they'd proceeded to the next ugly phase of treatment—chemo. After that, it would be radiation. His poor wife.

How he wished he could do more than just go to her treatments and doctors' appointments with her. Sometimes he felt so helpless. He felt especially helpless when she was wiped out by the treatments or suffering the painful side effects of the drug. He tried his best to keep everything going by hiring someone to clean the house once a week and by taking over in the kitchen. Since he sucked at cooking, his kitchen takeover consisted primarily of bringing home food from the grocery store deli and heating soup. Pretty pathetic, but his wife was a good cook and had enjoyed creating in the kitchen, so he'd never bothered to learn.

One thing he was not pathetic at, and that was planning anniversary surprises.

He had just snagged the Groupon offer when a voice behind him asked, "What are you doing?" making him jump.

Kat was supposed to be lying on the couch, watching a movie on TV. He quickly shut his laptop and turned to look at her. "Hey, why aren't you resting?"

"I came to see what you were up to."

"You missing me?" he teased.

"No, just making sure you're not spending money on DVDs and signed baseballs. It's getting too close to Christmas, and I don't want you messing up my plans."

"You already got me something?" Why should that surprise him? Kat shopped for Christmas all year long.

"Maybe. You're not spending money, are you?"

"Maybe."

She frowned. "On what?"

Ah, yes, his thrifty wife. They'd lived on a tight budget for so many years that thrift had become second nature to her.

"On a surprise. We do have an anniversary coming up, you know."

She smiled at that. "I sure do. And I have some plans of my own that I wanted to talk to you about."

Uh-oh. He probably should've checked with her before committing them to hitting the beach. It would only be a couple of days after her next chemo treatment, and she might not feel up to it.

"I saw this offer on Groupon."

He smiled. Great minds really did think alike. "For a holiday stay at a beach motel?"

Now she smiled. "You saw it, too?"

"Saw it and just bought it for our anniversary."

"Yes! Perfect." She plopped onto his lap and hugged him. He could still smell a hint of her perfume, and that soft little bottom in his lap made him think of other things besides anniversary trips. They hadn't had much sex since her operation, even though the doctor had cleared them for it. Somehow, she still seemed so fragile. He didn't feel right about it.

But he sure had no problem holding her. "You think

you'll be ready for it?" he asked, and kissed her cheek. "It'll be pretty soon after your treatment."

"It'll be relaxing, just what I need. And I'll have something fun to blog about. You're brilliant."

"No, I'm lucky. Lucky to have such a great wife."

She frowned and touched the pink cap on her head. "A bald wife."

The no-hair thing was a constant lament. How she hated not having her hair. It had been long and thick and wavy, the color of chestnuts. He used to love to run his fingers through it, used to love how it spread out on her pillow...

Of course, these days he never told her that. He reminded her (and himself) that hair grew back and told her he loved her no matter what, which he did. She'd shaved her head before chemo started, not wanting to deal with watching it fall out, and it had been a shock the first time he saw her bald. But she'd still had the same sweet smile. And she looked as attractive as ever in her scarves and fancy hats. And damn, what would he do if he lost her?

Oh, no. He refused to think about that. She'd be fine. They were going to make it clear to their fiftieth anniversary and beyond. And meanwhile, he'd give her the most special thirtieth he could.

"So, what do you think?" Lisa Whitaker asked her sister, Karen Owens. The two women had met for lunch and a shopping spree at the Tacoma Mall, which was a convenient halfway mark between Olympia and Seattle.

"It does sound good," Karen replied. "But you know, Doug..."

"Doug can suck it up for one weekend."

"He'll whine," Karen said, shaking her head.

"He whines about everything," Lisa said, dismissing both Doug and his whining with a flick of her hand. If you asked Lisa, her sister spoiled that man. She did everything for him short of cutting his meat at dinner. "You need to get away once in a while, have your own life. Chances are, you'll outlive him." Doug had high cholesterol and high blood pressure, plus he smoked—a triple threat. The reminder of her husband's bad health made Karen scowl, so Lisa quickly took a different tack. "And when was the last time we did something, just the two of us? We're past due for a girls' getaway."

Karen waffled. "I don't know..."

"Doug will survive without you for a weekend."

"It's so close to Christmas."

"We can finish our Christmas shopping at the festival. There's bound to be all kinds of craft and food items for sale." Honestly, when had her older sister become such a stick in the sand?

"True."

"And the pictures look really kind of nostalgic. We haven't been to Moonlight Harbor since we were kids. Remember how much fun we used to have there?"

"Hot dog roasts, flying kites, building sand castles." Karen pointed a finger at Lisa. "I did most of the work and you took most of the credit."

Lisa grinned. "That's how it works with little sisters."

"You've always been a pain in the neck,"

"We all have to be good at something. Now, are you going to do this with me or not?"

Karen heaved a long-suffering sigh, a sure sign that she was caving.

"I can come pick you up on the way," Lisa said, which she figured would clinch the deal. Karen was sixty going on eighty and she hated driving any distances, claimed it hurt her hip. The extra weight didn't help.

If you asked Lisa, her sister was turning into an old lady way before her time. When they were young and single they'd gone out dancing with their girlfriends until the wee hours of the morning every weekend. When they were raising their kids, they'd helped each other with huge home remodels and partied together with friends, staying up half the night playing crazy games like dark tag where they'd chase each other around a pitch-black living room, tripping over stools and chairs. In their forties, they'd taken up tennis and dragged their husbands to dance classes. Then Doug broke his foot and that was the end of the dancing, even after he was out of his cast. He began to put on weight and turned into a couch potato, and Karen had decided she preferred quilting and reading to dancing and smashing the tennis ball and joined him on the couch.

Lisa liked a steamy romance novel or a good murder mystery as much as the next woman, and she understood that quilting was a wonderful artistic outlet. But watching her sister become increasingly more sedentary was hard. It seemed these days that all Karen wanted to do was sit home and quilt or watch TV with Doug the slug. She needed to get out before she mummified in that two-bedroom downsized house of hers. They'd moved to an over-fifty active community, but these days she was about as active as a caterpillar in a cocoon. "Active is the key word. You're supposed to be doing stuff there," Lisa kept reminding her.

"We do," Karen would insist. "We go out for dinner every Friday."

It used to be dinner and dancing. Their waistlines were expanding, and their lives were shrinking. Doug could do what he wanted, but Lisa had no intention of letting him take her sister down with him. She was determined to find the butterfly Karen had once been before it was too late.

"So, how about it?" she pressed.

"I was trying to finish a quilt for Jillian for Christmas."

"You'll get it done." *It's all you do anymore.* And it wasn't as though Karen's daughter didn't have enough homemade quilts at this point. She yanked back the words before they could slip out of her mouth. "Think of the fun we'll have. Shopping, eating out. No cooking, someone to clean up after us." Heaven knew Karen did enough cleaning up after her husband, who'd become a throwback to the fifties, leaving her to wait on him hand and fat foot.

"It does sound like fun."

Lisa translated that as a *yes*, and pulled out her cell phone. "Good. I'm calling the Driftwood Inn right now."

"I'd better check with Doug first," said Karen.

"Give me a break," Lisa snapped and punched the number for the Driftwood Inn into her phone. "Since when do you have to ask permission to spend a weekend with your sister?"

"Since you got us lost finding the border in Canada."

"Anyone can get lost."

"From Vancouver? And with a GPS?"

Lisa frowned. "I know how to find Moonlight Harbor. Come on. This will be fun, I promise."

"Okay," Karen said with another sigh just as someone on the other end of the call said, "You've reached the Driftwood Inn where it's beach time all the time. This is Jenna. How can I help you?"

Beach time all the time. Oh, yeah, this was going to great. "I saw your Groupon offer and I want to reserve a room," Lisa told her. "Do you have any left?"

"For the weekend of Seaside with Santa?" confirmed the woman named Jenna.

"Yes. It sounds like fun."

"It will be. And we do have a couple of rooms left. I can give you one with a queen or one with two singles."

"Two singles," said Lisa.

"Singles," echoed Karen, horrified.

Lisa lowered her cell. "It's either that or a queen."

"We'll take the singles. I'm not sharing a bed with you. You're a bed hog."

"We'll take the singles," Lisa said to Jenna, then dug out her credit card and read off the necessary information. "My sister and I are going to do a girls' weekend," she said.

"She doesn't care," muttered Karen.

"This festival will be perfect for that," Driftwood Inn Jenna said. "We've got lots of vendors coming, and most of our shops and restaurants will be offering specials."

Oh, yes. This really was an inspired idea. "Now, admit it," Lisa said after she'd ended the call. "Aren't you glad we're doing this?"

"In theory, yes. But it seems like every time you and I take a trip together, something happens."

There was some truth in that. They'd gone to the tulip festival in LaConner, and Lisa'd had an allergic reaction. Who knew she was allergic to tulips? Then there'd been the three-day cruise when everyone on board had gotten sick. And yes, the weekend excursion to Canada when they'd gotten a little lost. But those experiences made for some pretty funny stories after the fact. Anyway, they'd had a couple of wonderful getaways, too.

"They haven't all been disasters," Lisa pointed out. "We survived your church's women's retreat and that trip to Portland with the girls."

"Let's hope we survive this," Karen said. But she sounded doubtful.

"We got another reservation today," Jenna informed Courtney when she showed up for her evening shift.

"That's great."

Courtney came around the reservation counter, ditched her purse and helped herself to one of the oatmeal cookies from the plate Aunt Edie had sent over for their guests—all three of them. One of them was a man on his way home from a business conference in Seattle who'd gotten tired of driving and wanted a place to crash for the night. The other two were an older couple who had just checked in and who didn't do gluten.

"Was this reservation, by any chance, another Groupon special?" Courtney asked.

"Yep."

"That turned out to be a smart move."

"It did. We've only got a couple of rooms left for the festival weekend."

"Hopefully, we'll get those booked tonight," said Courtney.

The bell over the office door jangled, and the female half of the older couple came in, wearing a frown.

"May I help you?" Jenna asked.

"Our room smells," the woman informed her.

The rooms had all been redone with new carpet. Jenna always made sure they were well cleaned and sprayed with room freshener.

"What does it smell like?" She'd cleaned the room herself that very morning.

"Like air freshener," the woman said, making a face. "I have a sensitive nose."

"Air freshener," Courtney repeated as if she was hearing wrong.

"I can't stand the smell of that stuff," the woman said.

"I'm sure we can find you a room that doesn't smell like air freshener," Jenna said pleasantly. She took a key for another room and suggested the woman accompany her. "Let's see how this one smells."

It had been shut up for a while and still held the faint odor of new carpet from the summer's renovation, but the woman sniffed the air and pronounced it acceptable and the switch was made.

"Air freshener? Seriously?" Courtney said when Jenna returned to the office with the other room key.

"It takes all kinds."

"I guess. And I can hardly wait to see what kinds you get from that Groupon special."

"I don't care how weird they are as long as their money's good," Jenna said. "I'll cry all the way to the bank."

And she meant it. Having the place completely booked for the festival weekend was all she wanted for Christmas.

Chapter Six

Jenna was working in the office the afternoon Seth's truck pulled into the motel parking lot, followed by a tow truck carrying the skeleton of a car. Half a skeleton, as it had no top. It looked like the big-daddy version of the go-carts Nora's sons rented out over at the funplex.

She put on her jacket and went outside to check out what had to be the beginnings of their float.

"Here it is," he greeted her, sweeping his arms toward it. "In all its glory."

"Nobody's gonna see this. All we care about is that it runs." He turned to the husky thirtysomething guy in the droopy jeans and dirty windbreaker, wearing a baseball cap, who'd emerged from the tow truck. "And it runs great. Right, Dino?"

"Yep," Dino said, and spat a stream of something gross onto the parking lot. He wiped off his scruffy beard with a hand grimy from car grease. "Dinner'll be great," he added, and grinned at Jenna, showing a set of teeth on their way to rotten.

"Dinner," she repeated weakly.

"What time do you want me to pick you up?"

"Um." What was going on here? Why was she having dinner with Dino? Jenna shot a frantic look in Seth's direction. He was busy examining the car's carcass.

Her hesitation made Dino frown. "Seth said you were up for going out."

"He did, did he?" She narrowed her eyes at Seth, but he missed it as he was still busy not looking at her.

"'Cause you're so grateful Dino came through for you with the chassis," he said.

This was the going price for a chassis, dinner with Dino? "Of course," she said.

"How's about seven? We can go to the casino. Tonight's all-you-can-eat crab night."

"Okay." She liked crab. Maybe she'd even like Dino. But that was a big maybe. "How about I meet you there? No sense you having to come all this way."

"I don't mind," he said with a shrug.

Jenna did. "It'll be easier for me to meet you there. Around seven? I, uh, have some errands to run first."

"Okay," he said. "Suit yourself."

He turned to his tow truck and began to unhook the carcass. Jenna tried to catch Seth's eye, but he was very busy helping Dino.

She stayed put and watched them. It was a nippy afternoon, but she wasn't cold. In fact, she was steaming.

The carcass slid to the ground in front of the two end units where Pete and Seth stayed. Then, his mission complete, Dino saluted Seth, told Jenna he'd see her later, climbed back into his tow truck, and rumbled off down the road.

"I'm gonna go over to the hardware store, pick up what we need," Seth said and bolted for his truck.

Jenna caught him by his jacket. "Not so fast. Why am I having dinner with Dino tonight?"

Seth shrugged. "All-you-can-eat crab. You love crab. And he's paying. Besides, Dino gave us this chassis for almost nothing."

"Almost nothing and me. You pimped me out."

"I didn't say you'd sleep with him."

"What, exactly, did you tell him?"

"Just that you were new in town and needed somebody to show you around. That you'd wanted to come with me to meet him but you, uh, couldn't get away."

"So I'd love to go to dinner with him?"

"Dinner out's a cheap price to pay."

"Then you go out with him."

"He's not into guys," Seth said with a grin.

Jenna pointed a finger at him. "You're enjoying this."

"Hey, you said you couldn't afford to pay anything."

"I can't."

"We got this for fifty bucks—and you for dinner."

She was going to kill Seth and feed him to the seagulls.

"Come on now, don't look at me like that," he said. "I'm trying to help you out here."

"I'd believe that if you didn't look like you're on the verge of an evil cackle."

"Guys don't cackle. Don't worry, Jenna. It's only dinner. I told him you don't put out on the first date."

"Gee, thanks," she said, and he chuckled and got in his truck and drove off.

Well, it was for a good cause. And underneath his rough exterior, Dino was probably a nice guy.

Or not. Dino was more cleaned up when Jenna saw him next. He'd exchanged his baggy jeans and dirty jacket for…baggy jeans and a sweatshirt. He'd lost the baseball cap, and his reddish hair was slicked back to show off the gauges in his ears.

She'd kept her own attire simple and as unsexy as possible, going easy on the makeup and wearing jeans and a loose sweater and boots. Unsexy apparently worked for Dino, and he looked her up and down like a thirsty man eyeing a tall glass of beer.

"You look nice," he told her.

"Thanks. So do you," she lied.

Dino grinned and puffed out his chest, which was almost as massive as his belly. "The food here's real good," he said. "I hope you're hungry."

He slipped a beefy arm around her and hauled her into the restaurant. Oh, boy. It was going to be a long night.

"We're doin' the all-you-can-eat crab," Dino informed their waitress, assuming Jenna was on board with that. Actually, she was.

She wasn't so on board with the beer he'd ordered, though, and switched that to Coke. "I have to drive," she said, and he shook his head and told her she should've let him pick her up. Captive in Dino's tow truck—when he'd had a bunch of beers. Oh, yes, she'd have loved that.

Dino wasn't shy and was perfectly happy to tell her all about his car restoration business and how good he was with his hands. This was accompanied with an eyebrow waggle that didn't do anything for Jenna's appetite. Neither did watching him inhale the pile of crab legs on his plate. Once they'd started eating, conversation stopped. Which was fine with Jenna. But after his second helping, Dino slowed down and decided it was time to chat again. Now the topic was TV shows. His favorites were *Breaking Bad* and *Luther.*

The fact that her favorite shows tended more toward romantic series like *Outlander* didn't leave them with much to talk about in that department.

"I like *Game of Thrones*, though," he said. "Lots of sex."

"Uh-huh," she said noncommittally.

"I like stuff with action," he went on. "You into monster truck drag racing?"

"Um. Not really."

Dino frowned. "Seth said you were."

Yep. She was going to feed Seth to the seagulls. "He must've misunderstood."

"I guess," Dino said, looking like a man who'd been given the old bait and switch.

Time for dessert. Dino was ready for ice cream. Jenna was ready to leave. She glanced at her watch. "You know, this had been great, but I really need to get going."

Dino's thick eyebrows dipped. "Without dessert?"

"I'm afraid so. It's been…" The eyebrows had lifted hopefully. *Okay, lie.*

No, don't. There was no sense in raising false hopes. "The crab was excellent." That she could truthfully say. "But I've got a lot to do back at the motel, and I have to get up early. Thanks for dinner, though." He was looking disappointed. He'd probably been hoping they'd connect and eventually move on to sex à la *Game of Thrones.* Having bruised his ego, she hurried to put on some salve. "And thanks for coming through for us for our float. Without your help and expertise, we would never have been able to have one."

She wasn't sure he was familiar with the word *expertise*, but he did know the meaning of *help*. He smiled. "Glad I had something that worked for you."

She wished she knew a woman who would appreciate Dino, who was probably a diamond in the rough. Alas for Dino, she didn't. She thanked him again for dinner, took care of the tip and scrammed.

The new base for their float was in the parking lot when she got back to the motel, but Seth's truck was missing. Obviously, he was avoiding her. Very wise.

But he couldn't hide forever. She was waiting for him the next day when he got home from treating several of the locals' houses for mold. "You are a skunk ball," she told him.

He didn't bother to feign ignorance. "Come on, admit it, you had a good time."

"Is that what you call it?"

"All you can eat Dungeness crab?"

"Enjoyed with Dino."

"He's an okay guy."

"Yes, he is, and I could tell from the minute we met that we were a match made in heaven."

"There you have it. Can I be best man?"

"You can be on my doo-doo list is what you can be."

He chuckled, unaffected by the threat. "So, I got what we need to make our platform, and rented what we need to build it. Is Pete around?"

Of course, Pete wasn't around. Pete had a nose for work, and once he caught the scent of it he vanished faster than Bambi in the face of a forest fire. "No. He's probably hiding out down at The Drunken Sailor." It was everybody's favorite pub, including Pete's.

"I'll go over there and see if I can pry him away from the garlic fries," Seth said. "Meanwhile, when you get a chance, go on down to the hardware store and buy the paint you want to use."

Picking out paint wouldn't be too hard since Jenna wanted to match the color she'd used for the motel. Of course, she did have to select the color for the base of the float. She supposed that would need to be some shade of turquoise to match the fringe for the bottom, something that would make people think of the sea. She could envision her little float sweeping along the parade route, people pointing to it with admiration.

They could use it again and again, bringing it out for the Flag Day parade and the Fourth of July.

They'd have to find a place to store the float. Seaside Storage had a couple of large garages for motor homes. She hoped they didn't charge too much. Otherwise, she'd have to ask Dino if he had some place on his property. Ugh. How many crab dinners would she have to commit to for that?

Well, never mind. One challenge at a time. She'd deal with where to store their mini Driftwood Inn once they had it put together.

It wasn't long before the float began to take shape. Unlike Jenna, Seth seemed to have a gift for actually getting work out of Pete, and from her post in the office, she watched them out there in the nippy fall air during the next few days, clambering over the evolving creation.

Pete was definitely going to deserve praise for this.

Which she was happy to give him, along with some cookies. Good behavior should always be rewarded. So should going the extra mile, which Seth was definitely doing. She gave him cookies, too, although she could think of other ways to show him her appreciation.

It's starting to take shape, Jenna texted her sister. We've got a cute bench for you right outside the office door. And we'll put Sabrina and Aunt Edie in front of one of the rooms on either side.

Celeste, the little ham, was now fine with the whole thing and was looking forward to being the resident mermaid. This didn't surprise Jenna at all, but Aunt Edie volunteering to ride on the float did. Aunt Edie said she was looking forward to it, and the possibility of standing in the cold didn't bother her in the least, although it worried Jenna. "I have a down coat and my knit cap. I'll be plenty toasty in them," Aunt Edie had told her. Even Sabrina was up for being on the float, especially after Jenna promised her a new outfit.

I still think you should be on it, too, Celeste texted back.

Too much to do behind the scenes.

And that was fine with Jenna. She much preferred to be on the sidelines, where she could watch the parade she'd envisioned coming to life. Her committee was insisting that, as the organizer of the festival, she be up on the viewing platform with the mayor.

The prospect didn't excite her, but she was enjoying the planning process, meeting with her committee, watching the festival come together as they checked things off their to-do list.

"The VFW's gonna have some old Jeeps in the parade

and the Rotary's entered a float," Brody reported when they met at Tyrella's. "We've got the high school marching band, and the royal court from Harbor Days. Ellis, you've got your other guys lined up with the cars, right?"

"Yes," Ellis said. "But if it rains, the convertible tops are gonna be up. I'd give my all for Seaside with Santa, but not the upholstery in my 1958 T-bird."

"It's not going to rain," Jenna said, convinced that if she said it often enough it would be true.

Kiki had the Facebook page up to show everyone. "We're getting a lot of hits," she reported as Tyrella poured more hot cider.

"Ellie Greenwald wants a booth for her Tupperware business," Tyrella said. "Johanna Wright confirmed that PAWS will have a booth, and Lisa Griebel and Kerry Schanberger are going to be selling their yoga DVDs. And Mary Harms just reserved a booth yesterday for her home décor business. That brings us up to thirty vendors."

"Good news," Jenna said. They had everything from roofers to wood carvers. "Between the vendors and the rides, and what the various shops and restaurants are offering, there should be plenty for people to do."

"And plenty of people to do it," said Nora. "I ran into Patricia at the bank the other day when I was picking up their sponsor check, and she said she's booked solid for the weekend. How are things looking over at the Driftwood?"

"We're almost at full capacity, too," Jenna said happily.

"I'm sure you and Edie are celebrating that," Nora said.

"You bet we are."

"Speaking of celebrating, don't forget the Halloween bash at my place," Brody said. "You got your costume?" he asked Jenna.

"Not yet. I've been too busy to think about Halloween costumes."

"Get busy," Nora told her. "We celebrate down here."

She was right. By the time Halloween arrived, all of Moonlight Harbor was dressed up and ready to party, with jack-o'-lanterns on house porches, garbage bag ghosts dangling from trees and skeletons hanging around in restaurant lobbies while scarecrows guarded cornstalks and pumpkins. Kids, both big and small, all over town had their costumes ready.

The Driftwood Inn was decorated with lit ceramic pumpkins in the office lobby. Aunt Edie had the house decorated as well, candles and pumpkins everywhere, and a vintage life-size plastic skeleton named Sylvester, who dangled in a corner by the window and creeped out Sabrina. Jenna had brought home a ceramic black cat she'd found on sale at Tyrella's hardware store and thought was adorable. But it had made Jolly Roger very nervous, so the cat had been transferred to the motel office to keep watch over the pumpkins.

Everyone in town got into costume and into party mode. Aunt Edie and Pete were going to The Drunken Sailor, Aunt Edie dressed as a pirate and Pete as her parrot, looking scary in neon-yellow jogging shorts, yellow tights that showed off his scrawny legs, a yellow leotard, big cloth wings and a beak.

"First prize is fifty dollars and a gift certificate for a free dinner. I hope we win," Aunt Edie said.

If they awarded a prize for the most fearless costume,

Pete had to win. Jenna was surprised that he was willing to go out in public looking like that.

She sent her aunt off with good wishes, then preapred to chauffeur Sabrina to a party at her friend Jennifer's house. Tristan had offered to pick Sabrina up, but Jenna was sticking to her guns; her daughter would not be dating until she was fifteen. Besides, she wasn't sure that turning the two of them loose alone in a dark car was a good idea, especially with her daughter looking more like eighteen than fourteen in her Wonder Woman costume.

"She's growing up so fast," she said to Seth when they ran into each other in the Driftwood Inn parking lot. "I'm not ready for it."

"No one ever is."

Jenna watched as her daughter came running toward her, coat parting to reveal long, slender legs. "She'll be grown before I know it."

"Make sure you've got a life. Then it won't be so hard," he advised.

She cocked her head at him. "How do you know all this stuff?"

He shrugged. "Beats me."

"No, seriously. That was profound."

"Yeah, that's me, profound," he said, clearly *not* taking her compliment seriously.

And sexy, she almost added. The only nod he'd given to Halloween was a pirate's patch over one eye. With his swarthy skin and dark hair, it was all he needed. Like Aunt Edie and Pete, he was on his way to The Drunken Sailor, where he'd most likely get swarmed by several man-hungry wenches wanting to play pool with him.

Jenna brushed away the moment of jealousy as she and Sabrina got in the car. She had no hold on Seth the pirate.

Brody, however, was a different matter.

"Are you, like, dating Brody?" Sabrina asked as they drove to her friend's house.

"Honey, this is just a chamber of commerce party."

"You know what I mean."

"We do things together," Jenna hedged. She wasn't sure that really counted as dating.

"Do you like him?"

What was *not* to like about Brody? "We're friends. Of course, I like him."

"I mean, as a boyfriend."

"Where are we going with this?"

"I just want to know. Daddy's got a girlfriend."

"Who you don't like. So, are you worried I'll hook up with someone you don't like, either?" Brody hadn't managed to rack up the teen approval points Seth had. If Sabrina disapproved of her getting serious with him, that would be a definite roadblock to taking things further.

Sabrina looked out the window and shrugged.

"Tell me what you're thinking." Maybe it wasn't as much about Brody as it was about her daughter simply not wanting another parent bringing a new person into the equation.

"I don't want you to be, like, miserable all your life."

Jenna had to smile. "Is there a *but* in here somewhere?"

"I guess Brody's okay. He's just kind of swog."

"Swog?"

"Uncool."

"Ah." Jenna nodded. "Well, who do we know my age who isn't swog?"

"Seth."

So her daughter had a favorite. "Seth and I are friends, too. I don't know if we'll ever be more than that. Anyway, I'm not in a hurry," Jenna said. "My number one priority is you."

Sabrina smiled. "Thanks, Mom. But if you want to be with somebody, it's okay with me. I hope you pick Seth. And if you want to have sex with him…"

Whoa there. "I don't think you have to concern yourself with who I have sex with."

"You do with me."

Oh, so was that the deal? Sabrina was hoping that if she gave her mom permission to go at it with someone, she could do it, too. "You're still underage," Jenna reminded her.

"And you're not getting any younger."

"Oh, ha ha, Miss Smart Mouth," Jenna said as they pulled up in front of Jennifer's house. "Get out of here and go have fun with your squad. And behave yourself," she couldn't help adding.

"I will, promise." Sabrina leaned over and hugged her. "And if you want to kiss Brody, it's okay. But I bet he won't want to kiss you. You stink."

She did, indeed, thanks to Aunt Edie's vintage witch costume that she'd insisted Jenna would look adorable in. The short skirt and fishnet stockings were sexy, and she liked her witch's hat and the cape appliqued with black cats and pumpkins. Sadly, she didn't smell as good as she looked. But Aunt Edie was pleased.

Brody had gone all out, dressing up as a devil for the

chamber of commerce party at his place. He was more than a little tempting in his shiny red cape.

"You look bewitching," he told her as they started a slow dance to "Witchy Woman."

"Even if I smell like I've been hovering over a cauldron full of mothballs all day?"

"I can't smell a thing," he said—obviously a lie. He drew her closer and whispered, "So, what can I tempt you to do with me tonight?" his breath tickling her ear.

Bubble, bubble, I'm in trouble. "Stop that, you devil," she replied, keeping the moment light.

Brody might not have been her daughter's favorite, but he was becoming increasingly more appealing to her. She could get serious with him.

If it wasn't for Seth… At some point she was going to have to quit standing at the fork in the road, hesitating over which way to go.

Not tonight, she decided. Tonight she was going to enjoy herself, right where she was.

After several dances, a lot of fattening goodies, and a ton of laughter, she was smiling when she left the party to go pick up her daughter. She wore the smile to bed that night.

She still had it on the following morning when Aunt Edie announced that she and Pete had won the costume contest.

"And how was your evening?" Aunt Edie asked. "Did you have fun?"

"I did, indeed." Life was great at the beach.

Until Jenna's phone started playing "Bad Boys," Damien's ringtone. There went the smile.

Chapter Seven

"Damien." *What an unpleasant surprise to hear from you.* Of course, mature adults who were taking the high road and trying not to be bitter about their exes's selfish and immature behavior did not utter those words. Although sometimes Jenna felt that maturity was overrated.

"How are things going down there?" he asked.

As if he cared? They'd hardly talked since Sabrina's summer visit fiasco.

"Sabrina's doing great in school. I'm sure she's texted you about all her adventures." Hopefully, not all of them.

"She has. Who's the boy?"

Now he was going to morph into a concerned father? Well, better late than never, she supposed. "He goes to her school."

"She says he's a senior. That's too old."

"They're not dating, Damien. They hang out at school, and he comes over here to see her. Is that why you called? If so, you don't need to worry. I'm keeping an eye on things." No way was she going to tell him what that eye had seen and why she was monitoring them so closely.

"Just like you did last summer?"

Her hand squeezed her cell phone tightly. "Do you really want to go there?"

"No, no. But you watch him. I know what boys are like."

"Don't worry, I will. Now, tell me why you're calling." It couldn't have been about his transitional support check. She sent those off right on schedule every month, along with a double helping of resentment.

"I want Sabrina to come here for Thanksgiving."

Jenna's left eye began to twitch. "Thanksgiving?" Not happening. Mom and Celeste were coming down for Thanksgiving. They were all going to be together at the beach.

"I haven't seen her since summer," he said.

And whose fault was that? "I don't remember you asking to see her."

"I am now."

"Well, sorry. We have plans."

"Come on, Jenna, don't be bitchy. You have her all the time. The least you can do is let her come here for Thanksgiving. My folks miss her. They want to take her to see *The Nutcracker,* and Mom wants them to go shopping on Black Friday."

"Maybe you should've talked to me before you all started making these plans." Okay, yes, she was being bitchy. After everything he'd put her through, and now, calling as if her plans didn't matter, she was allowed.

"You're always complaining that I'm not involved. Now, when I'm trying to be, you're balking."

"I'm only balking because Sabrina didn't enjoy her last visit very much." There was an understatement.

"If you're trying to make me out to be the villain, let me remind you that she was with me because she ran away from you," he snapped.

That had been a short-lived case of teen rebellion, something that might never have surfaced if Jenna and Damien had stayed together. If he hadn't been self-centered and selfish and unfaithful. If Jenna hadn't been covering for his lack of responsibility.

"Yeah, well, she was disillusioned enough to think you wanted her," Jenna retorted. Once she'd gotten to where her father was, living in his parents' basement with his artist girlfriend, Sabrina's time with Daddy Dearest had been far from idyllic.

"I did want her," he insisted. "That just wasn't good timing. I'm more settled now and I want to see her. I have every right to."

Yes, he knew his rights. When it came to getting what he wanted, Damien Petit was an expert. He so fit his name, and Jenna was glad she'd taken back her own name after the divorce.

But, she reminded herself, their daughter had rights, too. "I'll ask her if she wants to go." If she did, then Jenna would give in and try to do it gracefully.

"I'll ask her," Damien said. "I don't need you poisoning the waters."

He sure didn't. He'd managed to do that all on his own. "Then I don't know why you bothered to call."

"It was a courtesy call, Jenna. I'm trying to keep things civil."

Okay, she could be civil, too. "Fine. If she says yes, you can come down and stay the night at the Driftwood Wednesday so you don't have to spend the whole day

on the road. We've got an extra room I can give you."
Several, actually.

The deal was struck, and the conversation ended, Damien satisfied with how the negotiations had gone and Jenna feeling that, as usual, she'd come out the loser. She didn't bring up the subject at breakfast, half hoping he'd change his mind and not call.

It was a weak hope. His parents loved Sabrina and would want to see her. They'd probably guilted him into asking to have her. But, grandparents or no grandparents, Jenna wasn't going to do anything on her end to further her daughter's leaving on Thanksgiving.

That evening, Damien called her again. "Twice in one day, lucky me," she said.

"What did you say to Sabrina?" he demanded.

"What do you mean, what did I say? I haven't said anything. Neither has she. Did you talk to her?"

"She says she doesn't want to come."

"Well, then, that settles it."

"No, it doesn't. Come on, Jenna, I'm trying here. Help me out."

She didn't want to ever help Damien again. With anything. But he *was* trying. She reminded herself how important daddies were to their little girls and how vital a good relationship was.

Still… "I'm not sure what you expect me to do."

Sabrina hadn't been very happy with how she'd been treated during her last stay, and had felt unwanted. Hardly surprising since the new woman in Damien's life had no desire to welcome her with open arms.

Maybe that was changing, though. Or maybe the Princess Aurora was history. Maybe she'd left him.

Jenna allowed herself an instant of evil glee. That would be poetic justice.

"Talk to her," Damien urged.

"Okay, I'll try. In the end, it's up to her."

"Just don't try to talk her out of coming."

"It sounds like I don't have to," Jenna said.

She ended the call and went in search of her daughter. She'd ask Sabrina if she wanted to go, and if she said no that would be that. Jenna could hardly be blamed if their daughter didn't want to see the rat.

She found Sabrina sprawled on her bed, texting.

"Hey, there. Is your homework done?" she asked, leaning against the doorjamb.

"Almost."

"Okay, then, time to text goodbye."

"Aww, Mom," Sabrina groaned.

"Finish up and then you can text till your fingers fall off."

"Fine," Sabrina grumbled and tossed aside the phone. She was reaching for her math book when Jenna said, "Your dad just called."

Sabrina froze in mid-reach.

"He says you don't want to see him."

"I'm still mad at him."

Jenna came over and perched on the end of the bed. "I get it. You know, I'm still kind of mad at him, too. But he is your dad, and he does want to see you." And Sabrina wasn't the only one who needed to keep that in mind.

"I don't want to be gone all weekend."

This from the girl who, earlier in the year, had complained how bored she was and how desperately she wanted to go see her father. What a difference a friend or two made, especially when one of them was a boy.

"I know," Jenna said. "And I don't want you to go."

"Good. Then I won't."

"You do get to make the final decision. But I think your daddy would like to see you. Did he tell you Grandma and Grandpa Petit want to take you to see *The Nutcracker* ballet?"

Sabrina shrugged.

"I bet there's dinner at the Space Needle involved, too." There would be now.

Sabrina began to gnaw on her lower lip, a sure sign of indecision.

"And then there's the Black Friday shopping." Boy, she had to be nuts to be arguing so hard on the cheating weasel's behalf.

He was trying to be a better father, though, so how could she not? Besides, if she let Sabrina visit him for Thanksgiving, then no way would he be able to claim her for Christmas. She'd sacrifice Thanksgiving for Christmas any day.

"I guess," Sabrina said reluctantly. "But I want to come home on Saturday."

Mom and Celeste would still be here, so they'd all get to be together. They could eat turkey sandwiches and leftover pumpkin pie—if Celeste didn't devour it all beforehand—and watch movies. It was a good compromise.

"I'm sure that'll be okay," Jenna said. "Do you want me to call him?"

Sabrina nodded, and opened her math book, the subject of her disappointing dad closed.

Jenna called Damien and gave him the news. "She wants to come back Saturday."

"Fine. We'll be out of things to do by then anyway."

Out of things to do? Seriously? How sad. Jenna was never out of things to do with her daughter. They helped Aunt Edie in the kitchen, they did craft projects together, watched a movie on a Friday night, talked every afternoon—or rather Sabrina talked and Jenna listened—about Sabrina's day at school, who was seeing whom, and, of course, Tristan. That, ad nauseam. How could you possibly run out of things to do with your kid?

"So, I'll see you that Wednesday."

"Wednesday," she repeated, and ended the call. She could hardly wait. Not.

Meanwhile, though, she had other things to occupy her mind than the upcoming arrival of her ex—and plenty to do. There were posters to distribute, committee meetings to attend and, once in a while, a lone guest at the Driftwood to deal with.

Halloween decorations got taken down and stored away for the next year, replaced by a cornucopia on the dining room table and little Pilgrim candles and figurines sitting everywhere else, from bathroom counters to windowsills. Stores and restaurants in town were also dressed for the coming holiday, and the grocery store was running a sale on frozen turkeys.

"I picked up two," Aunt Edie told Jenna as she prepared to go to the November chamber of commerce meeting. "It's always good to have something extra in the freezer. Anyway, I love turkey, and I have several wonderful recipes for leftovers. Wait till you taste my turkey pot pie."

"Sounds delicious," Jenna said. "Maybe we can have one while Mom and Celeste are here."

"Oh, that's an excellent idea."

Yes, Thanksgiving was shaping up well. In addition to her family plans working out, they actually had some people staying at the motel that weekend. Three reservations, to be precise. And the Driftwood was now fully booked for the festival. Jenna was whistling as she made her way to her car.

Pete and Seth were working on the float, which was taking shape nicely, and she called, "Looking good," and gave them a thumbs-up.

Pete was frowning, but Seth smiled in return.

Seth Waters had the kind of smile women saw in their dreams or imagined on the face of a romance-novel hero. At least Jenna did. If only they'd met before life had left them both burned and bruised.

Her wounds were slowly healing. His were of a different nature, though, so who knew? He'd made it pretty clear he wasn't going to get serious, no matter how attracted he was to her. She'd seen him shooting pool with a woman or two when she went line dancing at The Drunken Sailor on Sundays. A man with a smile like that, with a body like that... Really, how long would he stay out of circulation?

Jenna stopped whistling.

Her mood improved when all the business owners arrived for lunch at their reserved room at Sandy's and she discovered that Susan Frank wasn't among them. "She's home sick," Kiki said.

"Gee, what a shame," Nora said with a smirk.

What a relief, thought Jenna. It would be so much

easier giving her report without their resident doom-sayer present.

After hearing about the progress the Seaside with Santa committee was making, everyone responded with enthusiasm, and when Jenna finally left the meeting she was whistling once more.

The day was crisp and the sky was clear. She had no massage clients lined up for the afternoon. Maybe she'd see if Seth needed some help with the float when she got back to the motel. It was a sure bet Pete would no longer be assisting him.

Yep. He was by himself, straddling the miniature roof, driving nails into the plywood.

She sauntered over for a closer inspection. Of the work, of course. Not the worker. Well, okay, him, too. He'd shed his jacket and his black T-shirt clung to that well-muscled chest.

"I see Pete's vanished. Need help?" she offered.

"You don't do well on roofs," he reminded her, bringing back an embarrassing memory from when she was trying to pull the Driftwood into shape. "And this is higher up than it looks."

"Okay, never mind. But I can do something."

"Yeah, you can. It should be ready to paint by Thanksgiving."

"Good. My sister will be down. She can help." So could Tristan, who, Jenna was sure, would be hanging around the moment Sabrina returned on Saturday. They could have a painting party Sunday before Celeste and Mom left. It would be a fun way to end the weekend celebrations. And speaking of celebrating... "What are you doing for Thanksgiving? Want to join us?"

"Thanks, but I've got plans."

With that cute redhead she'd seen him with the week before? "Oh?" she prompted.

"Going up to see my bro in Tacoma. But don't worry. You'll have Pete around to carve the turkey."

"Yes, we probably will." Jenna would have much preferred to see Seth carving the turkey. Ah, well, he'd be back in time to paint the float. And there were always shared turkey sandwiches to look forward to.

One thing Jenna never looked forward to was going shopping with Aunt Edie because they usually wound up at Beach Babes. Pete was happy to drive her great-aunt to the drugstore and grocery store, since that involved no manual labor, but he drew the line at home décor and women's clothing. And since Jenna wasn't wild about seeing her aunt climb behind the wheel of a car when she could barely see over the dash, it was left to her to chauffeur Aunt Edie to the more girlie places. Including—ugh—Beach Babes.

Aunt Edie caught her on a day when she didn't have any massage clients scheduled and lured her in by saying, "I was hoping to run over to Crafty Just Cuz today."

"I'll be glad to take you," Jenna the sucker said.

Browsing in the arts and crafts shop was fun. Elizabeth was on duty that day and showing off the fabulous oil candles she'd created. "Easy to make," she told Jenna.

And pricey. "I'll have to keep that in mind," Jenna said, determined not to sabotage her budget. Maybe in the new year, or come summer when they had lots of paying guests and a healthy bank account.

Aunt Edie bought some glue and googly eyes and left it at that. And then the real reason for their shopping expedition surfaced.

"I do need to run by Beach Babes and buy some new underwear," she said as they got back in the car. "You don't mind, do you, dear? I know her things aren't your cup of tea."

Susan herself wasn't Jenna's cup of tea. She'd rather have had a root canal than an encounter with the woman, but she couldn't say no to Aunt Edie, so off they went.

"She told me she's having a two for one sale," Aunt Edie said as they pulled up outside the shop. Two for one—twice the ugly at half the price.

Susan had swapped out hideous summer tops for drab and ugly fall wear, but her sale sign in the window had attracted some customers. Two seniors were sorting through a pile of sweatshirts with smiling turkeys on them, and over in the corner by the window, another woman was trying on a windbreaker that had *Moonstruck at Moonlight Harbor* embroidered on it.

Aunt Edie made a beeline for the back corner where Susan kept a limited assortment of lingerie items, Jenna trailing after her.

"Edie, it's good to see you," Susan said, and sneezed. Great. She was still sick and she was at work. Jenna hoped Aunt Edie didn't pick up any nasty bug while Susan was ringing up her purchases. She vowed to douse her great-aunt in hand sanitizer as soon as they got home.

"I had to take advantage of your sale," Aunt Edie said to Susan. "My underwear these days are a disgrace."

So were the ones Susan offered.

"I have some lovely red ones, perfect for the holidays," said Susan. "You'll look very festive in them." Who did Susan think was going to see Aunt Edie in her festive panties?

What Jenna was thinking must have showed on her face because her aunt frowned and said, "A woman is never too old for fancy underthings, my dear. I may be crumbling a little, but inside I still feel fifty and I like pretty things."

It was a gentle scold, but Jenna felt it all the same. "Red underwear's great," she said. Then, chastised, she moved to the display of scarves in a corner of the shop. Her aunt was right. Age was mostly a state of mind, and if Aunt Edie wanted red undies, she should get red undies. And maybe a boyfriend, too.

Aunt Edie and Pete the mooch rockin' around the Christmas tree? Oh, no. Aunt Edie had better taste than that.

Not that it was any of Jenna's business, any more than what kind of panties her great-aunt wore. But she didn't like to see Aunt Edie being taken advantage of, and if ever there was a man with a gift for taking advantage, it was Pete Long.

"Maybe I'll get a cute, knitted cap, too," she heard Aunt Edie say. "I'm planning to ride on our float in the Seaside with Santa parade."

"Don't do it, Edie," Susan warned. "The weather's supposed to be awful, and you'll catch your death of pneumonia." She lowered her voice, but Jenna could still hear her. "Honestly, I don't know what that niece of yours was smoking when she came up with this idea."

"Everyone in town is excited about it," said Aunt Edie.

"They all drank the Kool-Aid," Susan said in disgust.

"Well, *I* think she's brilliant," Aunt Edie said firmly.

"I think she's an idiot."

Jenna the idiot's eyes narrowed, and she felt a sudden desire to throttle Susan with one of her scarves.

"No offense," Susan added.

"Well, I am offended," Aunt Edie said, her voice frosty. "At least Jenna is open to trying new things, and we need that here."

"Not everything you try works," Susan retorted. "She should listen to people who've been around for a while and know something."

"Here, ring these up."

"You don't want to look at hats?"

"I'm done shopping," Aunt Edie snapped. "And if I didn't need panties, I wouldn't be buying these."

"Edie, I'm merely speaking the truth," said Susan.

"Truth or not, you'd be smart to speak less," Aunt Edie informed her.

She was looking far from pleased when she and Jenna walked out the door. "That woman is such a Negative Nellie."

More like the Wicked Witch of the West. If only she'd get on her broomstick and ride out of town.

"I don't think I'm going to shop there anymore," Aunt Edie said. "No matter what she has on sale."

A good decision on so many levels.

The month hurried on and before Jenna knew it, Thanksgiving was almost upon them, and she was checking in their first guests, two twentysomething couples on their way to Grandma's house in Montana, detouring for some fun at the beach. They had scruffy hair, scruffy clothes and a smell of smoke hovering over them. One of the men had meth teeth, rotting in his mouth.

Jenna told herself not to be paranoid. No judging books by their scruffy covers. She smiled and handed over room keys and reminded them that the Driftwood Inn was a nonsmoking facility.

"Well, shit," muttered Mr. Meth Teeth.

"We can smoke outside, Lionel," his lady informed him.

Lionel frowned, shook his head at the world's prejudice against smokers, and lumbered out of the office to unload the trunk of an old car that looked like it wouldn't even make Idaho, let alone Montana.

His buddy spied the plate with Aunt Edie's freshly baked oatmeal cookies. "Are these free?"

"Yes, they are," Jenna said.

"Awesome," he said, and took four. The women each took two, and a moment later Lionel was back in search of free cookies. He cleared the rest of them off the plate. Cookie strip-mining.

Well, Aunt Edie would be pleased that her cookies had been a hit.

Courtney showed up as the new arrivals were hauling coolers and six-packs of beer into their adjoining rooms. "Keep an eye on those guys," Jenna said to her. "They might get a little crazy."

Other than some hooting and shouts around midnight, the foursome was well-behaved. Surprising, considering all the empty beer bottles Jenna found in the rooms when she went to clean after they'd checked out the next day. Someone, probably Lionel, had smoked in the room, and Jenna left it open to air out as she worked.

Stripping beds, vacuuming and cleaning toilets wasn't bad when you only had a couple of rooms to clean, but Jenna wasn't looking forward to the extra workload when they filled up for the festival in December. She'd have loved nothing better than to hire a new maid, but there was no point, not until May, when tourist season kicked off. Meanwhile, she was office manager, bookkeeper and maid at the Driftwood Inn. Livin' the dream.

Actually, she was. She was getting to live at the beach. She had great new friends, and her daughter was thriving. And she loved the old motel and was proud of the job she'd done refurbishing it. People stayed with them, enjoyed the sun and surf and Aunt Edie's cookies, and made memories.

And messes. She wrinkled her nose at the pile of exceptionally dirty towels in the bathroom in Lionel's room. She was glad she was wearing plastic gloves. Ugh.

The rest of Jenna's day was full with massage clients, all wanting the kinks worked out before climbing in the car to drive over to see the relatives, or needing a quick muscle fix before a day of cooking and baking. After that, she had to work the desk. She caught up on some paperwork and checked in an older couple. She wasn't expecting any more people until later when Courtney arrived for her shift, but you never knew.

Surprisingly enough, she did get some more check-ins—a party of millennials, two women and three men on the way to who knew where and full of energy and raucous laughter.

"Are these cookies free?" asked one of the guys.

"Help yourself," Jenna told him, and he did. To two.

"Billie, you are such a pig," said one of the women, a cute brunette. She took a couple, as well. Skinny as she was, she probably needed the calories. And the treats were there for people to enjoy.

Not to be left out, the others swept in like herder ants and cleared the plate.

"I heard there's a cannabis shop in town," said one of the guys.

At the edge of town. Some of the citizens of Moonlight Harbor weren't happy about it, but marijuana was legal in Washington, so, happy or not, Cannabis Central was part of the scene.

"Never mind that," said the brunette. "Where's the liquor store?"

Oh, boy, more party animals. Jenna gave them a list of all the shops in town, informed them that there was no smoking in the rooms, and sent them off with their room keys.

It was dark by the time she got back to the house. She walked into the kitchen for a mug of tea, where Aunt Edie and Sabrina were busy baking pumpkin pies for Thanksgiving and pumpkin cookies for the guests. The kitchen smelled of cloves and cinnamon.

Jenna helped herself to a cookie and pronounced it fabulous. "I'd better get some of these over to the office for Courtney's shift and our next arrivals. We had some unexpected check-ins, and they inhaled the others."

Aunt Edie was pleased to hear that her cookies had

been a success. "We'll have to bake some more, won't we, Sabrina?"

Sabrina, who knew that cookie baking meant cookie dough snatching and cookie sampling, agreed.

Jenna returned to the office with the fresh treats just as Courtney was checking in a couple in their fifties. Both were a little hefty but neither was scruffy, and the car parked outside, while not new, looked like it had been kept in good running condition. No hint of smoke lingering on these two, thankfully. They should be nice and easy. She hoped the partying millennials didn't drive them nuts.

She joined Courtney behind the desk, set out the cookies, and welcomed them to the Driftwood.

"Thanks," the man said briskly. He took the room key and left for the car.

The woman took a cookie, and, with a nod, followed him out.

"Mr. and Mrs. Friendly," said Courtney.

"Oh, well. Heads in beds, and that's what matters. Anyway, they look like they'll be quiet."

"A good change from the partiers," Courtney agreed. "Hey, what kind of cookies are these?"

"Pumpkin," Jenna said, and proffered the plate.

Courtney selected one and took a bite. "These are deadly," she said with a groan. "Your aunt's a sugar pusher. She's turning me into a cookie addict."

"Be glad you're not living with her."

"As if you have to worry," Courtney said, eyeing her. "Do you ever diet?"

"Who needs to diet when I can work off the weight cleaning up after the Lionels of the world?"

At that moment, the older woman who'd checked in earlier with her husband came in. "I was just wondering if you had an ice machine," she said, holding up a small black ice bucket.

The information was printed on a card hanging on the door, but no way was Jenna going to embarrass her by pointing that out, so she directed her to the far end of the motel. "There's also a pop machine."

"Thank you, but we won't need that. My husband brought some juice. We'll be fine." She spotted the cookies and looked longingly at the plate.

"Would you like another one of my aunt's cookies?" Jenna asked, picking up the plate.

"Oh, I would. May I take one for my husband, too?"

"Of course," Jenna said. "They're here for our guests."

"What a lovely touch. By the way, the Sunrise room is simply charming. I love the orange carpet and all the sunrise pictures. It's aptly named."

"Each room has a different theme," Courtney explained.

"Well, we'll have to come back and try a different room next time and see what its theme is," the woman said with a smile. Then she took her cookies and left.

"Another satisfied customer," said Courtney.

"I hope they do come back," Jenna said.

"Speaking of customers." Courtney pointed to a shiny, gunmetal gray new model car of some sort pulling up. "I didn't think we had any reservations."

"Only my ex, but he's got an old truck."

Not anymore, it would appear. The door on the driver's side of the car opened, and a beautifully carved specimen of manhood stepped into the light from the outdoor lamps. He had straight, dark hair, artistically long and slicked back. He wore jeans and trendy sneakers and an equally trendy-looking coat.

"Damien."

"The ex? Uh, that's some truck he's got."

When did he get a new car? And was he paying for it with the money Jenna sent him? When she was driving a beater?

But it wasn't the sight of her former husband's new ride that had her grinding her molars. It was what she saw emerging from the other side of the vehicle—a slender woman with delicate features and long, coppery hair, flowing about her shoulders. She wore leggings and boots and a brown suede coat. Black leather gloves. She looked like a fashion model, but in fact she was a man thief.

Aurora. What was the girlfriend doing here? Jenna had invited him to spend the night at the Driftwood. She hadn't offered a couple's getaway.

She should've known he'd bring her, though. She ground her teeth harder.

"The ex and the bitch," Courtney murmured. "If you want to leave, I can take care of them."

"No, I need to stay and…"

"Be civil?"

Jenna frowned. "Something like that. But hide the cookies." She didn't have to be *that* civil.

Chapter Eight

Jenna put on a smile. It didn't fit well. Leave it to Damien to take advantage of her kindness and bring along the woman he'd left her for. Tacky. Very tacky. But then so was hitting her up for spousal support, dinging her earnings as a massage therapist. Why be surprised by this? Thank God Aunt Edie was keeping the motel in her name until she died. At least he wouldn't be able to get his greedy mitts on that.

He took Aurora's hand as they walked into the office. How touching. They floated in on a cloud of perfume, with her wearing a smile almost as ill-fitting as Jenna's, him looking serious and brooding like the *artiste* he was. Or thought he was.

Normally Jenna would have offered a cheery greeting to a new arrival. This time she stood at the reception desk and waited for him to speak.

"We're here," he said.

No. Really? "I see that. I figured you'd be coming down on your own."

"It's a long way," put in Aurora the princess. "He needed someone to take a turn driving."

"Of course, he did." Because at forty-two he was so old and infirm.

If Aurora caught the sarcasm in Jenna's voice, she refused to acknowledge it. Instead, she smiled at Damien as if they were newlyweds. Ugh.

"I see you got a new car," Jenna said. *With whose money?*

His cheeks suddenly looked sunburned. "Don't worry. I didn't spend any of the money you sent," he said, reading her mind. "My parents helped us out."

"Mommy and Daddy still paying your way, huh?" Jenna said under her breath. Oh, yeah. Let the fight begin.

Courtney stepped into the ring before anyone could get bloodied. "Let's check you in," she said to Damien, and Jenna went to her corner.

If only they still had a nice, leaky room for the rat king and his consort.

No, no, no. Living well was the best revenge, and Jenna was living well. She wished he could see just how well she was living. If only Brody or Seth was around. She'd have loved to parade either of those two in front of him. *See who wants me now?*

But Brody was in Seattle with his family, and Seth had left for his brother's in Tacoma.

"Put them in a Beach room," she told Courtney.

"Has it got a view of the beach?" Aurora asked eagerly.

"No, but it has a beach-themed décor," Jenna replied. "Sabrina took the pictures on the wall," she told Damien. There. See? She could be civil.

"Sounds like she inherited some of your talent," Aurora said to him.

Jenna was a pretty good photographer, too. What was that noise? Oh, yeah. Her teeth, still grinding.

"Can you walk to the beach from here?" asked Aurora.

"Yes, just follow the path." *Feel free to keep on walking once you hit the beach. Right into the water. Up to your neck.*

Stop already, Jenna scolded herself. Did she really need to be jealous of this woman? Damien was no prize. He was a leech and a loser, and she was well rid of him. She probably owed Aurora chocolate for life.

"Where's Sabrina?" asked the leech.

"She's in the house, finishing up her homework."

"I thought we'd take her out to dinner," Damien said. "Can you send her to the room when she's done?"

"Sure."

"Where's the best place to go?" Aurora asked.

"Does she have a favorite place?" Damien wanted to know.

Okay, good for him. He was actually thinking of their daughter. Iceberg Jenna thawed a little. "She loves the Seafood Shack."

Aurora wrinkled her nose. "Is there someplace in town that doesn't serve seafood?"

"This is a beach town," said Jenna. "Everyone serves seafood."

"You're not gonna find much else here," Damien sneered, and the thawing stopped.

"But all the restaurants have other options, as well," Jenna said. Sadly, none of them served rat poison.

Courtney handed over the room key, and Damien took it without another word and left with Aurora and her perfume trailing behind.

"I can see why you fell for him when you were young and stupid," Courtney said after the door shut behind them. "He *is* gorgeous."

"Yes, he is. Just ask him."

Courtney gave a snort. "You're well rid of him. Almost," she added.

Two and a half more years of spousal support left. Then she'd be free of him. But only financially. Down the road Sabrina would fall in love, and there'd be a wedding, followed by grandchildren and family events to which both Jenna and Damien would be invited. She pulled the plate of cookies back out and grabbed one. Self-medicating with sugar.

She left Courtney in charge and went to the house to tell Sabrina her father had arrived. "He's going to take you out to dinner."

"All right! Where?"

"I told him the Seafood Shack."

"Awesome." Sabrina snapped her textbook shut.

Jenna considered telling her that the girlfriend would be joining them, then changed her mind. As far as Sabrina was concerned, Aurora was the Antichrist. Better that she not know the woman had come along. She'd refuse to go out, maybe even refuse to go back with her father. And they needed the time together.

"At least he wants to be with his daughter," Aunt Edie said in Damien's defense after Sabrina had left. "A father-daughter dinner together will be nice."

"A father-daughter-girlfriend dinner."

Aunt Edie frowned. "Oh, no. He brought the other woman?"

"Yep."

"Call the cops," suggested Roger, pacing inside his cage. "Call the cops!"

Aunt Edie shook her head. "I hope they manage to enjoy themselves."

"I hope they manage not to kill each other," Jenna said. Although there were still times when she thought death was too good for both Aurora and Damien. Ah, well. Moving on.

And it was easy to move on when her sister and mom arrived. Celeste was her usual gorgeous, bubbly self, wearing a winter jacket accented with a scarf that she bragged about having knitted herself.

"When did you take up knitting?" Jenna demanded.

"Last month." Celeste held out the furry-looking pink scarf. "You like it?"

"I do."

"Good. Try to act surprised when you get one this for Christmas."

Melody Jones was her usual serene and beautiful self, and a simple hug from her was enough to chase away the fumes of irritation left from Jenna's encounter with her ex and the princess. How great it would be if her mom would retire early and come live with her and Aunt Edie at the beach. Mom would love living in Moonlight Harbor, and everyone would love her.

How old was Ellis West? He looked to be about her mom's age. Maybe they'd hit it off.

Except her mom had been widowed too many years. She'd lost the love of her life, and probably no man would ever measure up. So here they were, a family of single women, all together for the holidays, the only hint of testosterone in the house a grizzled, old mooch. Speaking of testosterone…

"I can't believe you're not having Thanksgiving with Mr. Amazing," she said to her sister as Celeste stowed her overnight case in Jenna's room. "You could've brought him, you know."

Celeste shrugged. "He's off seeing his family."

"He didn't want you to meet them?"

"We're not rushing into anything," Celeste said. "Except bed. Don't tell Mom," she added.

Yes. Their mother wouldn't approve. Jenna wasn't so wild about her sister's impetuousness, either. She knew Celeste was smitten, but she wondered about the new man in her life. Something was off.

"Don't you think, if you're getting that close, it's kind of weird that he doesn't want you to meet his family?" she asked.

"No. He hasn't met mine yet, either."

"Yeah, and what's with that?"

"I don't want to scare him away," Celeste said with a grin.

"Oh, ha ha."

"Seriously, things keep coming up. But I'm sure we'll get to the family meet and greet soon."

"You'd better. Mom's going to want to inspect him, you know."

"I know. Meanwhile…"

Jenna held up a hand. "If you're going to start bragging about your sex life I don't want to hear it."

Mel, who was going to be in Sabrina's room for the weekend, walked in as Celeste was giggling. "Now, what are you two talking about?"

Celeste gave Jenna a warning look. "Nothing," Jenna said. "I hope you guys are hungry. Aunt Edie's made a huge pot of potato soup and some of her amazing cheese bread."

"I remember that cheese bread," Mel said. "You could get fat just looking at it."

"You don't worry about that at Thanksgiving, Mom," Celeste told her. "Not when there's mashed potatoes and gravy and biscuits and dressing. And pumpkin pie. With whipped cream. Oh, my gosh, I'm drooling."

"Wipe the drool off your chin and come on downstairs," Jenna said. "Aunt Edie's probably taking the bread out of the oven now."

"Where's our girl?" Mel asked as they made their way to the kitchen. "I thought I'd find her in her room."

"Out to dinner with her father," Jenna said.

Mel nodded approvingly. "That's sweet."

"It would be sweeter if he hadn't brought Aurora."

"Oh, he didn't," Mel said in disgust.

"He did."

"Talk about a trashy move," Celeste said, sounding equally disgusted.

"But look on the bright side," Mel pointed out. "He cared enough to come and get her."

"Yeah, that cost him a lot since it's probably Jenna's money that paid for the gas," said Celeste. "And he's gotten a free room for the night."

That wouldn't be happening again.

"Oh, well. Who cares?" continued Celeste, who wasn't forking out any money and who didn't have to share a child with a rat. "We're going to have fun this weekend. And she'll be back Saturday, right?"

"That's the plan. The grandparents are taking her shopping on Friday and then to see *The Nutcracker* ballet." How did a single mom on a budget compete with that?

"Well, we'll have DVDs and popcorn," Celeste said. "And, I assume, the boyfriend will be around on Saturday, once she's back home."

Ah, yes, the boyfriend. No fancy ballet performance could compete with *that*, Jenna decided as they entered the kitchen.

Pete, as usual, poked his head in the door just as Aunt Edie was dishing up the soup. He looked like a cross between Captain Ahab and the Ancient Mariner in his favorite old peacoat, a pair of worn jeans and a battered captain's hat. His chin was crusted with gray five-o'clock shadow.

"Thought I'd see if you needed anything done," he said.

At six in the evening? Who did he think would believe that? Certainly not Jenna, who was all too familiar with Pete's subpar work ethic.

"Pete, you remember Jenna's mother and sister," said Aunt Edie. "They're here for Thanksgiving."

Pete took off his cap, sending wisps of gray hair in all directions. "Nice to see you."

"You're probably on your way to The Drunken Sailor," Jenna suggested.

"Oh, I don't have any plans," he said, refusing to take the hint. He sniffed the air. "Something smells good, Edie, my girl."

"We're only having soup tonight since our big meal

is tomorrow," Aunt Edie informed him. Of course, he'd be around for Thanksgiving dinner. Lucky them.

"Pull up that stool and join us," Aunt Edie said. "Pete's my handyman," she explained, just in case someone might have forgotten since the grand opening they'd attended.

"I saw the float you've been working on as we came in," Mel said as they settled around the table. "It looks like a lot of work."

"It is," Pete said, tucking a napkin around his neck. At least he'd been helping with that.

He was about to reach for the French bread when Mel asked, "Who'd like to pray?"

Pete pulled his hand back as if he'd been about to commit blasphemy.

"How about you, Mom?" Jenna suggested.

Her mother nodded, and they all bowed their heads. "Dear Lord, thank you for getting us here safely."

The way Celeste drove, that was a miracle.

"And thank you for watching over us and meeting our needs. Thank you that we can all be together this weekend. Keep us grateful."

Her mother's words reminded Jenna that she did, indeed, have much for which to be grateful. In spite of the fact that her marriage hadn't lived up to her expectations, in spite of the fact that she'd had some challenges with getting the motel up and running and that she was on a budget tighter than new braces, her life was good.

"Amen," she said when her mom had finished.

"Amen," echoed Celeste and Aunt Edie.

"Amen," Pete said, sounding rusty, then reached for the French bread again.

After his free meal, he vanished, and the four women entertained themselves playing cards and drinking hot cocoa.

Sabrina returned from her dinner, and when asked how it was merely shrugged and said, "Okay." Aunt Edie gave her hot chocolate, too, and they switched from cards to Farkle, and soon she was giggling and happy. She wore a smile when she disappeared after the dice game to text with Tristan, who had been commanded to stay home with his family.

"It's a shame he had to bring her," Mel said after Sabrina left, and they all knew to which *her* she was referring.

"Yes, I'm sorry I'm not the only one who has to deal with the other woman," Jenna said. "I wish, for Sabrina's sake, that Aurora would go find some other struggling artist to bond with."

"Maybe she'll get famous first," said Celeste. "That'll end things in a hurry."

It certainly would. Damien's ego could never tolerate it if he got outshone.

"If it wasn't Aurora, it would be someone else," said Mel. "He doesn't appear to be wired for fidelity."

"A lot of men aren't," said Aunt Edie.

"But there are still plenty of fine men out there," said Mel. "I doubt either of my girls will end up alone," she added, smiling first at Jenna, then Celeste.

"I'm already not alone," Jenna said. "I have all of you and my friends back home and here in town."

"And two of them are very handsome," Aunt Edie added with a sly smile.

"Life's good at the beach," teased Celeste.

"It always has been," Mel said. "You're giving Sabrina a good life down here," she said to Jenna.

"You're giving us all a good life." Aunt Edie smiled at Jenna. "Now, let's start a new game. I'm feeling lucky."

They played one more game, then Aunt Edie went to bed. "I've got to get up early and get the bird in the oven," she told them.

Mel made it through a game of cards and one last cup of hot chocolate, then she, too, vanished, tired from having worked a shift before she and Celeste came down, and that left the sisters to snuggle at opposite ends of the living room sofa with glasses of wine.

"Just like when we were kids," Celeste said as she poured herself a second glass. "Well, except for the booze. You're so lucky to be down here."

"We have a school in Moonlight Harbor," Jenna said. "I bet they need teachers."

"Do they need cops?"

Ah, yes. Mr. Perfect. If he was willing to relocate for her sister, that would go a long way toward proving his love. "I can find out," Jenna said. "It would be great if you lived here."

"You've got it pretty great already," Celeste told her. "Now, if you could just get something going with your love life."

Ah, yes. The love life. Her sister never tired of trying to run it.

Her cell phone interrupted just as Celeste was getting warmed up. It was Courtney, calling from the office. At midnight. Not a good sign.

"I think maybe you should come over," she said. "Mr. Petit is here."

"Damien? What's his problem?"

"Noisy neighbors."

Jenna could hear Damien shouting in the background. "Noisy? It's beyond noisy. It's a war in there."

The millenials. "I'll be right there," Jenna said.

"What's going on?" Celeste asked.

"We've got some people who need to settle down for the night. I'll be back," Jenna told her. She slipped on her coat and hurried over to the motel.

She could hear yelling before she even hit the parking lot. Whoo, boy. But as she got closer, she realized it wasn't the rooms the twentysomethings were in. In fact, Billie was hovering in the doorway of his room, as if trying decide what to do.

He looked relieved at the sight of her. "These guys won't shut up," he said, jerking a thumb in the direction of the offenders' room.

Jenna nodded. "Don't worry. I'll take care of it. Sorry you were disturbed."

Out of the corner of her eye, she caught sight of Damien marching toward her like a fire-breathing dragon. "What kind of hot sheets dump are you running here, Jenna? These people have been going at it like rabbits since ten, and now they sound like they're about to kill each other."

"I'll take care of it," she said again. He didn't move. Was he going to shadow her to the door? "You can go back to your room," she added. "I'm on it."

He scowled at her and shook his head. "Great place to raise a kid. Good influence."

"Oh, don't start," she said, her voice rising. "As if it was a good influence on our daughter for you to take up with another woman while we were married? As if it's a good influence for you two to be living together in your parents' basement?"

"Hey, this is not about me." His voice, too, began increasing in volume.

Billie stuck his head back out his door. "We're trying to sleep in here!" he shouted.

Jenna waved a calming hand at him and called, "It's all right." Between gritted teeth, she said to her ex, "Will you please go back to your room?"

Now the screaming and yelling in Room Ten had stopped, and that door, too, opened. The middle-aged man who had checked in earlier, a sight to behold with a hairy chest and pot belly hanging over flannel pajama bottoms, leaned out and demanded to know what was going on. *He* was what was going on.

Jenna hurried over. He smelled like the inside of a whiskey bottle. "Actually, I was just coming to see if everything was all right with you, sir. We had some complaints about noise."

He reared back and looked at her with shocked, bleary eyes. "It wasn't us."

And here was Damien, by her side. "The hell it wasn't."

Jenna turned him toward his own room and gave him a shove. "Good night, Damien."

He pointed at the offender. "You better shut up or I'm calling the cops."

"I'm sure there's no need to do that now, is there?" Jenna said to the offender.

"Of course not," he slurred. "My wife's not feeling well." The unmistakable sound of said wife parting with her dinner could be heard in the background.

Jenna had a sudden vision of a very unpleasant cleanup. *Oh, please, let that noise be coming from the bathroom.* "I hope she feels better soon and that you can both get a quiet night's rest. We hate having to bring in the police when there's a problem."

"There's no problem here." He grabbed the Do Not Disturb sign and after a couple of attempts finally managed to hang it on the doorknob. "Good night," he said and, with as much dignity as a man who was drunk could manage, shut the door.

Jenna heaved a sigh and trudged to the office, where Courtney was waiting.

"Sorry I bugged you," Courtney said, "but I figured since it was your ex, you'd want to handle it."

Yeah, there was nothing Jenna liked better than dealing with her ex. "It's all good now. The rest of the night should be quiet."

"I hope so," Courtney said. She checked her cell phone. "Looks like my shift's over anyway."

"Go home and get some sleep," Jenna told her. "You've got a long drive to your mom's tomorrow."

"I hope nobody gives you any more trouble," Courtney said as she grabbed her coat.

"I'm sure they won't."

"That was some scene out there."

And not one Jenna wanted to reenact.

Courtney shook her head. "Why are there so many shits in the world?"

"It's a mystery," Jenna said. And why people married shits was an even bigger mystery.

"Is everything okay?" Celeste asked when she returned to the house.

"I think so. A couple of our guests had a little too much to drink is all."

"I wouldn't want your job. You're always on call, and you're not even a doctor."

"It's not that bad," Jenna said. "You meet all kinds of people."

"Yeah, so I see."

"Most of them are nice. You're bound to get a dud once in a while."

"I guess this is your once in a while." Celeste yawned. "All your excitement has worn me out. I'm going to bed."

"Me, too," Jenna said. "I have to check people out in the morning." And clean rooms.

And the next morning, while Aunt Edie was happily humming around her clean kitchen, and her mom and Celeste were setting the table and peeling potatoes, Jenna had the joy of checking out guests. The twentysomethings were good sports and happily went on their way. The drunken middle-aged pair, on the other hand, were silent and sullen and the husband complained about the bill.

"Someone was fighting right outside our room last night," he complained as Damien entered the office, a nippy wind blowing in along with him. "We hardly slept at all."

"Yes, someone was being noisy," Jenna agreed, and looked pointedly at his wife, who got busy studying the metal fish sculptures arranged on the wall.

"I think we should get a refund," said Mr. Hairy Belly.

The hospitality business depended on sending away happy campers, so most hoteliers, including Jenna, had coupons handy for a free one-night stay. She was about to reach for one when Damien said, "You should be paying double. It sounded like you were slaughtering pigs in your room last night. You're lucky I didn't call the cops."

The man was bigger than Damien, but he was out of shape, and Damien was young and fit. The guy probably decided the odds would not be in his favor if he picked a fight.

He scowled at Damien and at Jenna. Then, for good measure, scowled at his wife. "Come on, Mariah, let's get out of this dump."

"It is not a dump," Jenna muttered as the door shut behind them. Another gust of wind blew in, and she shivered.

"Well, it's not the Hilton," said Damien. Jenna was about to take up where they'd left off the night before when he added, "But it's kind of cool in a retro sort of way."

That was as close to an olive branch as he'd ever offer, and she surprised both him and herself by smiling at him. "Thanks."

"You're welcome. Is Sabrina ready to go? I want to get on the road. I checked the weather, and it looks like there's a storm coming in."

"I'll see."

He nodded and they started for the door. "Back by Saturday evening, right?" Jenna confirmed. "Mom and Celeste want to spend time with her, too."

"Back by Saturday evening."

"Okay," she said. Then felt, somehow, as though she needed to say more. "Thanks for coming and getting her."

"No problem," he said, and they walked the rest of the way to the house in a silence as companionable as they'd probably ever get.

Sabrina was up but dawdling in the shower. Jenna promised to hurry her along, and Damien returned to his room to pretend to wait patiently.

An hour later, she was standing by his car, hugging her daughter goodbye. "Have fun."

"Mom and Dad are taking her to the Space Needle for lunch Saturday before I bring her back," Damien said, his tone of voice telegraphing that he knew exactly how that had come about. "She'll have fun."

"And Tristan can come over on Saturday night, right?" Sabrina asked Jenna.

"Yes, he can. We'll do a movie marathon."

It was beginning to rain, and Aurora had had enough of the family friendliness. "Damien, we should get going if we're going to be back in time for dinner," she said from her side of the car.

He nodded and got in.

Jenna gave her daughter one more hug, then stepped away and watched her drive off with her father. "It's good to share," she reminded herself, and then went to do room cleanup.

As she'd feared, the problem wife had not made it to the bathroom when she got sick. What a way to start Thanksgiving. At least the older couple in Room Four were quiet. And, hopefully, not slobs.

After cleaning the mess, she moved on to Damien's room. She'd given him one with two single beds, but he and Aurora had only used one of them. She scowled and went to work. One fewer bed to make. There. See? The chocolate box was half full.

She finished the rest of her cleaning, then closed the office and went to the house. The wind was picking up and it tore at her coat with cold fingers. A good day to be indoors.

Especially when there was a feast waiting. As she walked into the house, she was greeted by the aroma of roasting turkey. Ah, turkey and dressing, mashed potatoes and gravy, cranberry sauce, ambrosia fruit salad and Celeste's specialty—candied yams with brandy. Green beans and those peas with the baby onions. And then pumpkin pie with a mountain of whipped cream for dessert.

Next to Christmas, Thanksgiving was Jenna's favorite holiday. Her grandparents used to make the day special with games, fires in fireplaces, and extra servings of pumpkin pie for good little girls, which it turned out Jenna and Celeste always were, no matter how they behaved. She and her sister had also enjoyed a Thanksgiving or two at the beach, where Aunt Edie stuffed them with food and then had a craft for them—turkeys made from pinecones, paper-plate pumpkins, gratitude trees, which were branches with cut-out paper leaves that the girls attached after writing something for which they were thankful on.

Aunt Edie had a craft planned for this holiday, as well. Once Pete left, they were going to make turkey pops. She'd assembled popsicle sticks, mini-wafer cookies, candy corn for feathers and sunflower seeds for beaks. A perfect party snack for Sabrina and the boyfriend on Saturday night. After the crafting, they'd settle in with turkey sandwiches to watch movies, and

Jenna had two she knew everyone would love. She could hardly wait.

So let the rain come. Who cared? They'd be cozy and happy inside—as long as Jenna didn't think about the fact that Sabrina wasn't with her. It wasn't the same not having her daughter present. Thanksgiving was family time.

But Sabrina was with family. The other grandparents had a right to see her once in a while. Anyway, Jenna consoled herself, this would be good practice for the day when Sabrina moved out and turned her and Aunt Edie into empty nesters.

The fun officially started at three in the afternoon. They were assembled around the little dining room table, which was festive with its cornucopia and Pilgrim candles and turkey-shaped salt and pepper shakers. Pete, clean shaven for once and wearing jeans and his best flannel shirt, was about to carve the turkey with Aunt Edie's old electric carving knife when the lights began to flicker.

"Uh-oh," said Pete, regarding the dining room light warily.

"Uh-oh," echoed Jolly Roger from his cage. "Uh-oh, uh-oh."

"It's just a flicker," Aunt Edie said.

"Well, it's starting to blow out there," Pete said.

No blowing allowed. Jenna had rented movies.

The lights flickered again. Then there was a loud boom that made Jolly Roger give a startled squawk in his cage, and both the electricity and the carving knife snapped off.

"Call the cops!"

Chapter Nine

Taylor, Greg and Miranda were on their way to Thanksgiving dinner at her parents' house in Issaquah. She should've been looking forward to the day. Once upon a time, when life was good and money was plentiful, she'd enjoyed celebrating with her family, but this year she was dreading it. Everyone would ask Greg how the business was doing. He'd lie and say it was going great and that would make her mad because she knew it was going nowhere. The investor who was supposed to come on board with a cash infusion had backed out only the day before. She'd hoped to be able to announce that she'd closed on her first house sale, but the deal had fallen through.

So far, her real estate career had consisted of getting two listings and walking through a lot of houses with a lot of people who did a lot of talking about wanting to buy and then never did. Or else came out losers in a bidding war. Even though the Seattle market was hot, she had yet to find the hot spot. Shows like *Property Brothers* and *House Hunters* made the real estate business look so easy, but it wasn't. It was unstable with no guaranteed paycheck.

"We are going to have a good time today, right?" Greg asked warily.

"We're going to try," she said, frowning out the window. These days, fun did not factor in when it came to doing things with her husband. Their sex life had evaporated, and conversation about anything other than Miranda had dwindled to "When are you going to be home?" and "Don't forget to put out the garbage."

Taylor knew all the important dos and don'ts for a happy marriage. Communicate. Don't withdraw sex as a punishment, don't go to bed mad. Well, she was mad most of the time, so good luck with that. How was she supposed to feel romantic when she was constantly pissed off? And she'd communicated until she was blue in the face, but her husband stubbornly refused to quit trying to ride a dead horse. Or beat a dead horse. Or lead a horse to water when it didn't want to drink. Whatever.

"We still have stuff to be thankful for," he said.

"I know," she admitted grudgingly. They had their adorable six-year-old, and she alone was worth a ton of gratitude.

"I'm thankful," Miranda said from the back seat. "I get to see Gramma today. And Christopher and James."

Ah, yes, the rambunctious cousins. People who said there was really no difference between boys and girls had never met her nephews, the mini-whirlwinds. Over the course of the last three years they'd managed to break her glass table wrestling and two expensive figurines, thanks to the basketball that got away when their mother wasn't paying attention, and to take out half her azalea bush playing touch football in the front yard with their father and Greg and his two brothers.

And they were just ten and eight. She hated to think how much damage they'd be capable of by the time they were teenagers.

Even though the boys could get out of control in a heartbeat, they were nice kids, and they were good with Miranda, including her in their games and giving her piggyback rides. Miranda would have fun today.

She'd be the only one.

Taylor's father was on door patrol and let them in with a hearty greeting and hugs.

"I have a new dress," Miranda informed him, parting her coat so he could see it.

Velvet featuring a flared skirt with several layers of glittery Tulle. Taylor had gotten her one in red and one in green. On sale. Fifty percent off. Which she'd be quick to tell her sister if Sarah said anything about Taylor's spending habits.

"Well, you look very pretty," said Dad, giving her another hug and a kiss. "As does my daughter," he said to Taylor. "But then you always look pretty," he added, and she smiled at him.

"Yes, she does," Greg agreed, and she didn't smile at him. After the fight they'd had the night before, she was debating whether or not to ever smile at him again.

Her father took their coats and bore them off to the master bedroom to add to the heap on the bed, and she proceeded on toward the kitchen to drop off her fruit salad. To get to the kitchen, though, she had to traverse the living room, where a set of grandparents, one single aunt, two cousins and her sister's family were camped out, watching the football game. Out in the dining room she could see one small cousin raiding the mints on the buffet, while Christopher and James chased each other around the table.

"About time you got here," Sarah greeted her. In addition to losing her credit card debt, Sarah had lost twenty-five pounds, and she was looking good in skinny jeans and a formfitting white blouse.

Taylor didn't envy her older sister her newly found looks. She, herself, was slender—always had been— and she knew she was cute. She'd figured that out back in grade school when boys started teasing her and showing off for her on the playground. In middle school, she'd perfected the art of makeup, and managed to make lovely hazel eyes even lovelier. Blond hair hadn't hurt, either.

"Dinner's not till four," Taylor said. *Sheesh*.

She'd been so busy transferring the frown she'd had for her husband to her sister that she didn't see Christopher and James barreling toward her. Christopher, in the lead, hadn't seen her either, since he was looking over his shoulder at his younger brother, who was in hot pursuit.

He and Taylor collided with an oomph and a squeal, and the bowl of fruit salad she was carrying tipped inward, dumping fruit and whipped cream onto the front of her gray cashmere sweater.

"Urgh," she croaked.

"Sorry, Aunt Taylor," he muttered, backing away as she pulled the bowl and what remained of her salad away from her chest.

"I hope there's some salad left," joked Chris.
Ha ha.

"Christopher, I told you to settle down," Sarah said.

"Now, go sit on the couch with your father and watch the ball game. Sorry," she said to Taylor. "They've had too much of Mom's punch. They're on a sugar high." She took Taylor's arm and began towing her toward the kitchen. "Come on. We can get the stain out with some dish soap."

Their mother and grandmother were seated at the kitchen table, enjoying a chat over cups of coffee before the dinner prep hit high gear. Grandma said a cheerful, "Hi, sweetie," to Taylor.

She set down the salad and bent to kiss her grandmother and caught a whiff of her vanilla-scented perfume. The older woman put a soft hand to her cheek. "You look lovely as always." Grandma Nelson knew how to make people feel good. Even when they didn't.

"What happened to your sweater?" Mom asked, seeing the mess on Taylor's chest.

"Christopher ran into her," Sarah explained. "I told Dad not to give the boys so much punch. They're buzzing."

"Oh, they'll be fine," Mom said. "But we'd better do something about that sweater."

"It's ruined," Taylor said miserably. The sweater was the last thing she'd bought before she discovered their financial boat was sinking. Even on sale it hadn't been cheap.

"No, it's not," Sarah insisted. "Take it off."

Taylor scowled at her. "And what am I supposed to wear?"

"I'll find you a top," Mom said and disappeared.

She'd get to wear something from her mom's floral blouse collection. Three sizes bigger than she normally wore. But it beat running around in her bra.

Or not. Mom returned a few minutes later, bearing a scoop-necked blouse spattered with large purple flowers. "Not quite your style, but the colors are pretty."

Oh, well, it was only family. Nobody cared how she looked. Taylor thanked her mother, took it and slipped it on. She felt like she'd just aged twenty years.

Gram approved. "Very pretty," she said.

"Thanks," Taylor murmured, and moved to the sink to see what damage her sister was doing to her sweater.

"See? It's all come out," Sarah said proudly, squeezing the sweater in a death grip. "We'll just lay it out on the counter on a towel, and it'll be fine."

"I doubt it." Taylor peered over Sarah's shoulder, bracing herself for a ruined mess. But Sarah had gotten the whipped cream cleaned off. Maybe there was hope for the poor abused sweater.

"Clean," Sarah said. "And no pilling." She put an arm around Taylor. "You're not going to sacrifice my firstborn to the fashion gods, are you?"

"It's a thought," Taylor said, trying to keep her sense of humor.

"If it turns out it's not as good as new, I'll buy you another one. Promise," Sarah said.

"You'd better." Okay, that sounded bratty, so she added a joking, "The fashion gods get hungry." Then, determined to forget her sopping sweater and start again, she asked her mom what she could do to help.

"Come sit down and take a deep breath," said Mom, pouring her a mug of coffee.

She spent the next forty minutes hiding in the kitchen, first drinking coffee with her mom, grandma and sister, then helping with all the last-minute bustle of getting a large holiday dinner on the table—mashing potatoes, bringing out the salads, carefully avoiding the mint-stealing cousin, who was now dancing around the table in pursuit of Miranda. How much punch had Dad given her?

Taylor was returning to the kitchen for the candied yams when she heard her grandmother gasp and Sarah say, "Oh, no!"

She hurried into the kitchen, worried that her grandmother, who'd been about to move gravy from a heavy frying pan into a gravy boat, had burned herself. Gram had, indeed, managed to spill the gravy. Happily, not on herself. Not so happily, the new cashmere sweater had, once more, been a food casualty victim. There it sat, sodden and now covered with a mini-pool of greasy, brown liquid. Time to start making funeral arrangements.

"Oh, dear," Gram said. She looked ready to cry.

"No worries," Taylor assured her, putting an arm around her bony shoulders. "It's just a sweater."

And money down the drain.

But her grandma's feelings were more important than any sweater. Besides, the cost of a sweater was a mere drop down the drain compared to what they poured out on their credit card payments. Ugh. Then there were the house payments, car payments, daycare, groceries, clothes for Miranda, her business expenses, his business-going-nowhere expenses. They even had money still owing on Greg's old student loan from when he went back for his master's in business. Much good that was doing them now.

"I'm so sorry, dear," her grandmother said.

"It's not that big a deal, Gram, really." *People are more important than things*, she reminded herself. "I didn't like that sweater very much anyway," she fibbed.

Sarah raised both eyebrows, but Mom gave Taylor an approving smile.

Time for a sweater burial. Taylor scooped the poor thing up and tossed it in the garbage. There had to be some symbolism in that, but she wasn't in the proper frame of mind to look for it.

The afternoon continued to go downhill. With everyone gathered around the table, Uncle Bill asked her how the real estate business was going, and having to confess that her big deal had fallen through stole her appetite. That commission wouldn't have gone a long way toward pulling them out of the deep, dark hole they were in, but they would at least have seen daylight.

"It's a tough business," said Uncle Bill.

"That's why you should always have at least three months' worth of living expenses in savings," said Chris, who was now an expert on money management. "You never know what's going to happen."

You sure didn't. For instance, someone could get fed up with listening to him pontificate about money and dump what was left of her rutabagas on his fat head.

"Pass the rutabagas, will you, Dorothy?" said her dad, saving Chris.

Mom obliged, then pointed to Taylor's plate. "You're not eating, honey."

"I'm not very hungry," Taylor said. She wasn't very happy, either. Or grateful. And if anybody asked Greg how his business was doing, she was going to throw her plate against the wall.

"Well, Greg, how's your business going?" Uncle Bill asked a moment later.

That was it. Taylor could feel her blood pressure rising faster than a rocket.

Fortunately for the Wedgwood, Mom picked up Taylor's plate and her own to start clearing for dessert.

"It's coming together," Greg said.

In what universe? He was lying to everyone at the table, including himself.

"I don't see anything coming together," she said. *There. Let the truth be told.*

"These things take time," Uncle Bill told her.

"You have to support your husband," added Chris.

"Cut back on expenses," put in Sarah.

Taylor clenched her jaw and got up to help clear the table. She was so done with this Thanksgiving dinner, so done with Thanksgiving. So…done. Period.

Kat was exhausted. Darrell could tell. The dark circles under her eyes looked like coal, and her smile was barely hanging on to her face. She'd sighed three times during dinner.

He'd tried to talk her out of hosting this year, reminding her that if anyone had an excuse to beg off it was her, but she'd insisted. "Everyone will help," she'd said. "Anyway, I want to. I don't even know if I'll be here next year."

That had brought the tears to her eyes and his. "Don't talk like that," he'd said. "You'll pull out of this."

"I want to. But I also want to live every moment to the fullest right now."

He got that. Her own mother had died ten years earlier, never lived to go on that world cruise she and Kat's father had planned. But that wasn't going to be them.

They'd just finished the main meal and were visiting over wine before moving on to coffee and dessert when Kat's sister-in-law Maggie said, "I'm thinking it would be good to share something we're thankful for this year. Or several somethings."

"Sappy," said Kat's younger brother, Mitch, and his wife frowned at him. Their two teenage sons looked uncomfortable at the thought of having to get touchy-feely.

"Just whoever wants to," Maggie said.

"I think that's a great idea," said Jewel, Kat and Darrell's daughter.

"Me, too," agreed their new daughter-in-law, Marina.

"Okay, we'll do it to humor you women." Mitch grinned across the table at Kat. "I'm thankful my sis is such a good cook." Then he sobered. "And I'm glad you're still around."

"And you're going to be around for a long time," Jewel said. "You stuck around to see Luke get married. You have to be here for when I get married."

"She doesn't have a hundred years to wait for you to find somebody," Luke teased, and she stuck out her tongue at him.

"So, what we're thankful for," Maggie said, getting them back on track. "I'm thankful for our family."

"Me, too," Jewel chimed in. "Well, most of them," she added, giving her brother a look and making him snicker.

"I'm thankful for my wife," Luke said. "And that I've still got a job. I survived another round of layoffs."

"That's good news," said Kat. She sounded so tired.

"I'm thankful for my husband," said Marina. "I'm also thankful I got such a great mother-in-law."

Kat blushed and waved away the compliment, but Darrell knew she was pleased. She'd worried that she'd be a stinker of a mother-in-law, not good at sharing her son with another woman. But she and Marina, both avid readers, had hit it off from the start. Marina read Kat's blog regularly and they'd even launched a book club together. Marina's parents were divorced, and her own mother was a walking bundle of issues. She practically idolized Kat.

Kat's dad went next. "I'm thankful for my kids," he said, and saluted each with his wineglass. He'd had a difficult time socializing since losing his wife, and his appearance at family events was usually short. Darrell expected him to bolt soon after the pie was served. Actually, Darrell hoped everyone would leave right after dessert, so Kat could go lie down.

He took his turn. "I'm thankful for my wife," he said, smiling at her. "She's the best thing that ever happened to me."

"Oh, stop," she said, her cheeks flushing again.

"It's true."

He'd fallen for her like a boulder off a cliff the first time he saw her. He'd been at a friend's frat house Halloween party. She'd been wearing a bumblebee costume—funny little antennae bobbing on her head and a yellow leotard with black stripes over black tights that showed off a compact little body with a great butt. Then there'd been that gorgeous hair of hers, long and beautiful, begging him to run his fingers through it. But what had really gotten him was her smile. It had not only lit up her whole face, it had lit up the whole room.

"I'm thankful for you, too," she said to him. "He's been my hero in all this," she told the others. "Going to all my appointments with me, cleaning the house, cooking."

"Dad?" Luke mocked.

"Trying to cook," Kat amended.

"Hey, in case you've forgotten, I can heat soup," Darrell said. "And fry eggs."

Jewel grinned. "And make peanut butter sandwiches."

"So, you see? I'm well-fed," said Kat. "I'm also thankful for all of you. But mostly I'm thankful that I'm still here."

Her father nodded and downed half his glass of wine in one gulp.

"Life is precious," she went on. "Let's appreciate every moment."

"Well put, sis," said Mitch, and raised his glass "To life."

"To life," everyone echoed.

"And to pumpkin pie," added Mitch. "When do we get to eat it?"

"Right now," Kat said.

She braced her hands on the table and started to push up, but Jewel laid a hand on her arm. "We've got it, Mom. Stay put."

The fact that Kat didn't argue spoke volumes about how tired she was.

The other women cleared the table and took orders for pie—pumpkin or wild huckleberry? Whipped cream or not? Coffee?

Dessert was subdued compared to the earlier laughter during the meal. That was what happened when you were reminded how precious—and short—life was. Normally the family lingered after the meal, but this time, after everyone had cleaned up for Kat, they all left. She didn't ask anyone to stay.

Then it was just her, collapsed on the couch, covered with a blanket, and Darrell, seated in the chair next to her.

"You're pooped," he scolded.

She sighed and shut her eyes. "I am."

"I knew we should've let Mitch and Maggie host this year."

"No, I wanted to."

"Well, we're not hosting Christmas," he decreed.

"We'll see," she said, and smiled like women did when they were sure they'd get their way.

But it wasn't happening. She needed to rest.

So now he was wondering if it was wise to haul her down to the beach. What if it rained and she caught a cold? Or pneumonia? "Maybe I should cancel that trip to the ocean," he mused.

Her eyes popped open. "Don't you dare! I'm looking forward to it, and I meant what I said. I want to appreciate every moment of my life. I'm looking forward to this, Darrell. Don't you go cheating me out of it."

"Okay," he said. "Whatever you want."

"That's more like it." The smile returned, and she shut her eyes again.

Darrell sighed and shook his head. He had a sneaking suspicion that they'd be hosting Christmas.

Jenna and her family sat at Aunt Edie's dining room table, playing cards by the light of an oil lamp. After dinner, it had become apparent that the power, which had gone out an hour or so earlier, wasn't going to come back on immediately, so they'd put the turkey in the fridge and vowed not to open the door again. They'd left out the pie for snacking later and had peanut butter and bread ready for breakfast in the morning. Celeste was proud to point out that she'd saved the day by bringing chocolate—caramel M&M's, which they were snacking on as they played. Pete had started a fire for them in the woodstove before vanishing to stay warm with a beer at The Drunken Sailor, and it was crackling away and keeping the downstairs toasty.

"This reminds me of when we were kids," said Celeste. Jenna smiled. "M&M's and all."

"You girls used to love to come down here in the winter," Mom reminded them.

"It was Aunt Edie's woodstove," Celeste told her. "We didn't have one. Of course, the main draw was Aunt Edie and Uncle Ralph," she added. "And the beach and the saltwater taffy."

"But there was something so cozy about having a fire going on a cold day," Jenna said, remembering how warm and comforting the room always felt. Aunt Edie would let them roast marshmallows over it for indoor s'mores.

"Which is why I made sure my apartment had a gas fireplace," Celeste said. "I see a fire in a fireplace and I think of two things—our winter holidays here and romantic Christmas movies on Hallmark."

Celeste was now enjoying her own romantic scenes in front of that fireplace with the new man in her life. When were they going to meet him?

"Everyone should have a woodstove," said Aunt Edie. "They come in handy when the power goes out during a storm."

"You don't have woodstoves or gas fireplaces in the rooms in the Driftwood. What do you do when the power goes out?" Celeste asked.

There was something Jenna hadn't considered. What if the power failed when they were at full capacity?

"Oh, we have a generator for the motel," Aunt Edie said.

Good. Jenna vowed to have Seth check it out and make sure it was working before their festival guests arrived. Not that she was expecting to lose power, but then they hadn't expected to lose power on Thanksgiving, either. You never knew. Best to be prepared.

"Hey, sis, it's your turn. Are you gonna play?" Celeste prodded, bringing her back to the moment.

"Are you going to go out?" Jenna demanded. "You'd better not."

But, of course, Celeste did, leaving the rest of them stuck with a ton of points against them. "Did you have to bring her?" Jenna said to Mel, and Celeste chortled.

By ten o'clock they'd played two more games of cards and Aunt Edie was ready for bed.

"Will you be warm enough?" Jenna asked her.

"Oh, yes, I have plenty of blankets and my flannel pajamas. I'll be fine."

Mom, too, decided she'd turn in, and then it was just the sisters, who stayed up late, keeping the woodstove stoked and talking about diets, dreams and plans for the future. Celeste was sure that by the next Thanksgiving she'd have a handsome cop in tow when she came down. She wanted to be happily married and have at least two kids.

Jenna hoped that things worked out the way her sister wanted, but to her, the fact that Celeste's man hadn't taken advantage of the holiday weekend to introduce her to his family spoke volumes.

Or maybe it said nothing at all. Maybe Jenna's own experience had made her cynical. She supposed, when it came down to it, most people viewed others' lives through the lens of their own experiences. She probably needed new lenses.

"What about you, sis?" Celeste asked. "What do you want the rest of your life to look like?"

"I want to make the Driftwood Inn a success while Aunt Edie's still here to see it. I want to be able to get Sabrina through college. I want to see Hawaii before I die."

"You'll make it happen," Celeste told her. "You're my inspiration, you know."

"Right." Marry the wrong man and live on a shoestring.

"No, I mean it. You've done such an incredible job of restarting your life. I don't know if I could do that."

"You could if you had to."

"I hope I never have to."

"Just be careful," Jenna said.

"I am, believe me."

Jenna doubted it, but a sister could only say so much. Every woman had to make her own choices. She thought of the choose-your-own-adventure books she used to read as a kid. One choice you picked for the hero would send him one way. A different choice would pull him into a different adventure.

She hadn't made the best choice when it came to Damien, but she'd made a good choice when she moved to Moonlight Harbor. At least she thought she had. She supposed only time would tell.

Chapter Ten

"You girls." Doug Owens shook his head.

Lisa and Karen and their husbands were in Icicle Falls, eating lunch at the Bavarian Alps. *(Extra cheese on the pizza. Yeah, Doug, good for your cholesterol.)* Their families had all come up to spend Thanksgiving weekend in the little German-style town nestled in the Cascades, and the various offspring and grandchildren were scattered around town, enjoying the snow and doing their Black Friday spending in the many shops.

The older generation was doing its share of spending also, but had taken a break to eat. And the subject of the sisters' getaway had come up when Doug observed that with all the money they were spending, they probably didn't need to go to a Christmas festival. "Especially without us," he'd added.

"We girls need a break from you boys," Lisa retorted.

"Oh, thanks a lot," said her husband, Dean.

"Every time you two go off together, it's like Lucy and Ethel on the loose," Doug said, making Karen frown.

"Be glad it's not Thelma and Louise," Lisa told him.

Doug had a smart answer for that. "If you drove a car off a cliff, it would be because you were lost."

Okay, her brother-in-law was beginning to irritate her. Just because they'd gotten a little lost in Canada… Anyway, he wasn't so perfect. "You want to start comparing each other to old TV shows and movies? Let's talk Tim the Tool Man, the Doug version."

He scowled and Dean guffawed. "She's got you there, bud," Dean told him. Doug's do-it-yourself disasters were legendary.

"Tim the Tool Man's projects always turned out in the end," Doug insisted.

"More than you can say for yours. How about that revolving shelf you put in my kitchen," Lisa taunted. "Backward."

Karen snickered, but Doug didn't even crack a smile. "Your husband was part of that project, if you remember."

"The Doug and Dean Show," Karen joked. "Always good for a laugh."

"Yeah, but I was just the helper," Dean said. "He was the supervisor."

"Oh, enough already," Karen said. "We're going, Doug, so you can stop being an ass."

He threw up his pudgy hands. "Hey, it's a free country. If you two want to go, fine by me. I'm just saying you could have brought us along."

"Yeah," Dean said. "We like going places with you girls."

"And we like going places with you, but sometimes we need sister time," Karen said.

"Lucy and Ethel," Doug muttered, then let out a yelp, a sure sign his wife had just kicked him under the table.

Lisa wished she'd thought to kick him.

"Seriously," put in Dean. "We worry about you two."

"Honestly," Lisa said in disgust, "we're grown women."

"And trouble magnets," Dean said.

"We'll be fine," Karen assured him. "And it's not like we're taking a cross-country drive. Moonlight Harbor is only a couple of hours away. What can happen?"

"Knowing you two? Plenty," said Doug.

Maybe Lisa could reach him from where she was sitting. She slid down in her chair and aimed for his corner of the table. Her foot made contact with his shin, and he let out another yelp. He frowned at her, and the sisters exchanged smiles.

"You two bring out the worst in each other," he grumbled.

"Yes, we do," said Lisa. Then to her sister, "Isn't it going to be fun?"

"That it is," Karen agreed.

Oh, yeah, this had been a great idea.

The power was on again by the time Damien brought Sabrina back late Saturday afternoon. Jenna had been watching for them and met them in the parking lot to help haul in her daughter's shopping finds. She was laden with shopping bags full of new clothes and in a happy mood, a sure sign that the visit had gone well.

What put Jenna in a happy mood was seeing that the Princess Aurora had opted out of making the drive down.

"Looks like you had fun," she said to them as Damien handed over Sabrina's backpack.

"Oh, yeah," said Damien, sounding self-satisfied.

"We had lunch at the Space Needle today," Sabrina said. "It was so awesome."

"And Mom took her shopping yesterday," said Damien. Jenna's ex-mother-in-law may have raised a rat, but at least she was good to their daughter.

"I got the cutest shoes," Sabrina gushed as Jenna took another bag. "And a sweater and jeans. And a sweatshirt from the Space Needle. And Daddy gave me these earrings," she added, moving aside the curtain of strawberry blonde hair so Jenna could see the little crystals in her ears.

"Very nice of Daddy." So good of him to be generous with the money his ex paid him.

"Grandma and Aunt Celeste are still here, right?" Sabrina asked as if perhaps they'd changed their minds and run away before she could see them.

"Yep. Just waiting for you to arrive so we can start the partying."

Sabrina beamed. "I'll tell Tristan."

Her father wasn't exactly happy at the mention of the boy's name, but she didn't notice. She stood on tiptoe, kissed him on the cheek and said a cheerful, "Bye, Daddy," then ran into the house to show off her treasures and summon the boyfriend.

"You watch him," Damien ordered Jenna.

"Don't worry, I will," she said and changed the subject. "So, it looks like you two had a good time."

"We did. I want her to come for Christmas."

In his dreams. "Oh, no. You just had her for Thanksgiving."

His brows dipped. "Hey, Christmas is important."

"Yes, it is. Which is why she's staying with me. In case you forgot, I'm the primary caregiver."

"I have visitation rights," he reminded her.

"Then you can visit." But she wasn't going to offer him another free room.

"My parents want to see her."

"They can visit, too."

"Come on, Jenna, be reasonable."

She was willing to be reasonable, but she wasn't going to be a doormat. "I tell you what. You can take her the weekend after." Wait. When was New Year's? Sabrina would want to party with her friends on New Year's Eve.

"Generous of you," he said snidely. "You seem to forget she has two parents."

"I'm glad to see *you're* finally remembering," Jenna shot back.

He hadn't been the world's best parent even when they were together, and he'd been especially absent after Aurora sneaked onto the scene. He hadn't fought for joint custody, hadn't made a very good impression when his daughter came to him that past summer. Now he wanted to be Father of the Year?

"What's with this sudden desire to be super dad?" she demanded.

"I love her," he said simply, "and I want to be in her life, not shoved off in some corner. Jeez, Jenna, I'd think you'd be glad. You were always on my case about not spending enough time with her. I can't win with you."

"You're going to make this about me? Really?"

"I'm not the one who moved."

"I moved because I could save money living down

here. And you know full well why I needed to save money."

His cheeks flushed at the reference to his spousal support. "I spent fourteen years home with Sabrina. Not working."

"So you could do your art!" He hadn't sacrificed to stay home with their daughter while she worked. Sabrina had provided him with a great excuse to avoid getting a job. And, in fact, Jenna had been the main caregiver until Sabrina got old enough for preschool. He'd conveniently forgotten that. So had the judge.

He scowled. "You're like a grave robber, Jenna, digging up old bones. Can you just let go of the past?"

It would've been easier to leave the past behind if she wasn't having to drag along the two-legged ball and chain that was her ex. She wanted to kick him. Or cry. Or do both.

"Darn it all, Damien. It would be a lot easier to let go of if you hadn't hurt me so much. And if you weren't still pouring salt in the wound. I'm sending you money, and you're getting your parents to buy you a new car and bringing Aurora down here in it. How would you feel if you were in my position?" Her eyes were starting to prickle. She blinked furiously—not her usual nervous tic—this time in an attempt to hold back tears. She was so done crying for this man.

He softened. "Okay, sorry. I shouldn't have said that."

Damien wasn't one to apologize. It shocked her into silence.

"Look, it won't always be this way. Things are starting to take off for me. Down the road I'll be able to help more with Sabrina. I'll make up for..." He stumbled to a stop.

Hardly surprising, considering how much he had to make up for. Where to begin?

Let it go, Jenna told herself. Giving in to bitterness was a soul-shrinking waste of energy. And maybe he *was* trying to change. Do more, be more.

He heaved a sigh. "All right, forget Christmas. I'll take her the weekend before."

"Okay, but we've got our Seaside with Santa festival that weekend and she may want to be here for it."

"I doubt it. My parents are talking about Disneyland."

Disneyland or Seaside with Santa. Yeah, hard decision there. "She has school that Friday," Jenna said.

"That's why I wanted her for Christmas. We'd have the whole week after."

Christmas and the whole week following? After he'd just had her for Thanksgiving? No way. "Why don't you take her to Disneyland this summer?" There. That was a good compromise. Not one that made Jenna happy but her daughter would be thrilled.

"Okay, fine, we will. But I still want to see her. Like I said, I'll take her the weekend before Christmas."

"And like I said, we've got a festival that weekend."

"Well, you've got to let me have her sometime. Anyway, Mom will think of something to do with her and she won't even miss the festival."

"Mom?" So, he was going to pawn Sabrina off on his mother. "I thought *you* wanted her."

"I do, but they want to see her, too. Okay? It's not fair to them to keep her away."

It wasn't. And, of course, his parents would make the visit worth Sabrina's while with more excursions and spending sprees.

"I have no intention of doing that," Jenna said.

She found herself suddenly jealous. She knew she shouldn't be. She wouldn't have been if she and Damien had still been together. They'd have been one team, working to bring up Sabrina, all four of them contributing to her happiness and well-being. This felt more like competing teams, trying to win her loyalty—Team Mom versus Team Dad.

Still, Team Dad deserved a chance to get in the game. And even if they were now two different teams, they all wanted Sabrina to win.

"So the weekend before. Okay?"

"If she wants to, yes." And Disneyland with the grandparents in the summer. Jenna would have loved to be the first one to take her daughter there, but the important thing was that Sabrina would get to go. Meanwhile, she and Damien could work on building a healthy relationship. Well, as healthy a relationship as one could build with a narcissist.

That settled, he nodded. "Okay."

"Thanks for bringing her home" Jenna said, determined to end the conversation on a positive note.

"No problem," he said, and got in his car and drove off.

She walked back to the house with mixed feelings. Yes, she wanted her daughter to have a good relationship with her father, but she also wanted Sabrina to love her best. Not very noble. Not even very mature. But there you had it.

She sighed. Life got complicated when the love of your life turned out to be the biggest mistake you ever made.

She forgot about Mr. Mistake once the partying started. Tristan came over, bringing along a pumpkin roll his mother had baked. The turkey pops came out, along with the root beer and the microwave popcorn. Tristan and Sabrina stretched out on the floor with the bowl of popcorn between them, and the women settled on the couch and in chairs. The movie played in the new DVD player that Jenna and Celeste had gone in on together for Aunt Edie, the fire in the woodstove crackled, and life was good. And maybe, if Jenna was lucky, her daughter would decide she'd rather stay home for the Seaside with Santa festival.

Of course, Jenna wouldn't say anything to persuade her one way or the other. If she wanted to spend that weekend with her father, then she should.

"Daddy already texted me. I want to go," Sabrina said, when Jenna brought the subject up on Sunday evening after her mom and sister had gone home. Aunt Edie was over at the Oyster Inn, showing Patricia Whiteside pictures of the freshly painted float, and it was just the two of them in the kitchen, making turkey soup.

"It is the Seaside with Santa festival," Jenna said casually. Not that she was trying to influence her daughter. Just mentioning it.

Okay, she *was* trying to influence her daughter. She told herself to cut it out. Damien was making an effort to be a more involved father, and she needed to support that effort.

"I know," Sabrina said. "But Grandma Petit wants to take me to see the Gingerbread House display at the Sheraton. We're gonna spend the night there. And she and Grandpa are going to take me to a musical."

Oh, boy, how to compete with that? You didn't. "What about Daddy?"

"We're going to watch horror movies Friday night."

A horror movie marathon, just what Jenna wanted her daughter doing.

"Don't worry," Sabrina hastily added. "Daddy said to tell you no R-rated sex."

"Just plenty of violence."

"It's all fake anyway." Sabrina's brows knit. "You're not going to say I can't go, are you?"

"Of course not. You need time with your dad."

"Anyway, you'll be busy running the festival," Sabrina said.

She was right. Jenna was going to be busy with the festival. So, everything would work out fine for all concerned.

But darn. She would've loved to have her daughter with her for all the fun. Sharing was hard when you were a kid, but it didn't get any easier once you were a grown-up.

Darrell left school feeling old and worn-out, not a good way for a guy still in his fifties to feel. The kids in his classes had found it hard to settle down after the long weekend and his patience had been frayed to a ragged scrap. Lately, he found himself wishing he could afford to retire early and let some other schlub deal with the next generation. Whether or not Tommy Skinner or

Ariel Ingersol passed Algebra just didn't seem that important compared to the question of whether or not his wife lived. If she didn't, he wasn't sure he'd want to.

He let out a tired breath as he pulled into the grocery store parking lot. They had plenty of leftovers from Thanksgiving, but he didn't have the energy to mess with them, and he was sick of turkey. He'd pick up a pizza and a bag of salad greens. Once in the store, he also got some chocolate for her and a six-pack of beer for himself.

He wandered over to the book and magazine section and picked up a book by Brenda Novak, one of her favorite authors, figuring it would make a nice treat. She hadn't done much blogging lately, other than about her adventures fighting off cancer. Maybe it would do her good to concentrate on something else for a while.

God knew, he wished *he* could think about something else. Sometimes he wished he could run away, forget this was all happening to them. He hated seeing her so miserable, hated feeling so helpless. He should have become a doctor instead of a teacher.

Back in the car he turned on his favorite classic rock station and pumped himself up listening to Huey Lewis and the News. "The Power of Love." Oh, yeah. By the time he pulled into the garage he was able to smile. They'd have pizza, find a movie on Netflix and relax.

"Hey, babe, I'm home," he called as he walked into the kitchen. He looked to the right, hoping to see her in the family room, parked on the couch. It was deserted. He knew what that meant.

He set his groceries on the counter and went upstairs to the master bedroom. The drapes were pulled and the room was dark. A small form was visible under the covers. Had she managed to get up at all?

He tiptoed over to the bed to check on her, make sure she was breathing. Probably irrational, but that was always the first thing he did. She was still wearing her pink sleep hat.

Other than the day she'd had her head shaved and the few times he'd helped her shower, he'd rarely seen her bald. "I can't even stand to look at me without my hair," she'd explained. "I'm not going to make you have to do that."

"As if I care," he'd said. And in a way, he didn't. Yet that little bald head was both a reminder of what she was going through and how fragile life was. He would never tell her, but in some ways he was relieved that she kept her head covered. He didn't like dwelling on what she was facing any more than she did.

As if sensing him leaning over her, she opened her eyes, and he breathed an inward sigh of relief. She was still with him.

She smiled up at him and, as always, that sweet smile squeezed his heart. "Hi," she murmured.

"Hey, you," he said, and touched a hand to her cheek. "You gonna sleep the day away?"

"Maybe," she answered with a sigh. "I'm so tired."

He'd known this would happen. Hosting the family gathering had been too much for her.

She spoke before he could say anything. "I wanted to do it, Darrell."

"I know," he said. "But you can't be pushing yourself like this, babe. You need to concentrate on getting well."

"I am," she insisted. "But I also need to concentrate

on living. I'll be fine by tomorrow." She patted the bed. "Sit down. Tell me how your day went."

He eased onto the edge of the bed. "The kids were shits. I'd rather have been home with you."

"Well, you are now." She started to push herself to a sitting position.

"What do you think you're doing?"

"I'm going to heat us some leftovers."

"No, you're going to stay put. I brought home pizza." He grabbed the remote from the bedside table and aimed it at the TV mounted on the wall. This was new. Before she got sick they'd always found plenty to do in the bedroom and had no need for a TV. But installing one had turned out to be a smart idea. It kept her company when he was gone and she was too tired to read. "Find a show you want to watch and we'll have a lazy night."

She subsided back against her pillow. "I like the sound of that. And maybe you're right. Maybe I did take on a little too much."

"Do you think?" She frowned at him and he added, "But you wouldn't be you if you weren't wanting to do things for everybody."

"Thank you," she murmured.

"But now I want you to start doing something for somebody very important."

"You?"

"No, you. I want you to stop pushing yourself. Give yourself permission to take it easy and concentrate on beating this thing, okay?"

"Okay."

"No more entertaining until all your treatments are done." She pouted at that. "I mean it, Kat. You have got to take care of yourself. I don't want to lose you. You mean too much to me."

"Okay," she promised.

"Good," he said, and took her hand in his. Was he imagining it or were even her hands feeling frail these days? He rubbed her palm, considering.

"What are you thinking?"

He was thinking what he was always thinking, that he couldn't lose her. "I'm thinking I'm going to cancel that trip to the ocean."

"No," she begged.

"It won't have been that long after your next chemo."

"I'll rest right up until the minute we leave. Please, Darrell. I've been looking forward to it. I'll pace myself."

He continued to waffle, and she continued to plead. Finally, he agreed to keep their plans in place and went down to the kitchen to heat up the pizza.

He supposed she was right. Even if this all failed, if it turned out... He stopped the thought before it could go any further. Kat wanted to experience as much as she could while she could. He'd probably feel the same way in her shoes. Heck, he'd probably go skydiving like he'd always wanted to. His wife loved life. He loved his wife. They were going to the beach.

Chapter Eleven

Time seemed to speed up once Thanksgiving was over. Between doing things around the motel, running her massage business and wrapping up details for the festival, not to mention getting her Christmas shopping done—shop local!—Jenna was busy. She still carved out time with Sabrina to make their popular chocolate bark, which they always gave away to friends and neighbors during the holidays. Jenna also carefully packed up some to send to both sets of grandparents, along with an invitation to come visit her at the beach.

Aunt Edie and Sabrina took care of the baking, starting the first weekend in December, making Christmas cookie staples—frosted sugar cookies, spritz cookie wreaths, gingerbread boys and Russian tea cakes, which Aunt Edie had dubbed snowball cookies. Tristan hung around during these baking extravaganzas, earning his keep by helping Sabrina with her math homework.

There'd been no more romantic interludes in the bedroom, and Jenna had decided to reward their good behavior by allowing Sabrina to go to the Christmas ball with him. Plus Hudson and Jennifer, and two boys from church. All in Tristan's mom's old Volvo station wagon.

"Eleven o'clock curfew," Jenna had said. "And no stops between the dance and home."

Sabrina had rolled her eyes but agreed to the rules.

In addition to cookie baking, they put up the decorations, which included everything from a vintage ceramic Christmas tree with tiny lights that Aunt Edie had created back in the seventies to a centerpiece made from pinecones spray-painted gold (another Aunt Edie creation), and a small Nativity set on her vintage buffet. Her love of dolls was also evident. A Victorian girl dressed in a red velvet coat sat on a tiny rocking chair next to a miniature tree in the front hallway, waiting for Santa, and a clown doll popped from a giant red felt stocking hung on the living room wall. An artificial tree stood in one corner, and with Aunt Edie supervising, it had taken Jenna and Sabrina an entire evening to decorate—not simply because two households' worth of combined ornaments had them on ornament overload, but also because many of Aunt Edie's came with a story and had to be examined and properly oohed and aahed over. "This was the first ornament Ralph and I ever purchased for our tree.".... "We bought this one the year we opened the Driftwood for business.".... "Jenna, do you remember making me this little walnut ornament?"

Jenna had her share of memories, too. She smiled at the Baby's First Christmas ornament her grandparents had given her when Sabrina was born. There was also one from her mom and one from the other grandma and grandpa. Sabrina had once asked her why there were so many, and she'd replied, "Because you were a big deal." She still was.

While the women got ready for the holidays, Seth

and Pete worked on pulling the float together for the festival, and now it was almost done. Jenna was delighted with how their mini Driftwood Inn had turned out. It was an exact replica, right down to the fishing net and the driftwood on the outside wall of the office.

She came home from running errands one day to find Seth attaching the fringe to the bottom of it—metallic blue vinyl, which dressed the whole thing up beautifully. "Oh, wow," she gushed, "it's the perfect final touch, like putting on jewels to go with an evening gown."

He stood and stretched. "All it needs is a princess."

Jenna sighed. "I wish Sabrina was going to be here to ride on it."

"You should be riding on it."

"Oh, no," Jenna said with a shake of her head. "I'll be too busy troubleshooting. Anyway, my sister's going to be on it. That will be plenty of eye candy." Besides, Celeste was the ham in the family. She loved doing this sort of thing. Jenna, not so much.

"You can never have enough eye candy on a float," he said.

He was right. She eyed him speculatively.

"Women," he clarified.

"Hey, women like eye candy, too."

"Men don't ride on floats," he said scornfully.

"How do you know?"

"I just know."

"You're a chicken."

"Yeah? Well, looks like I'm not the only one," he said and went back to work.

"Where's Pete, by the way?" she asked.

"He went to the house to get us some water two hours ago. Haven't seen him since."

What a surprise. "That's a long time to be thirsty. I'll get you some now."

"Don't bother. I got my own an hour ago."

"Well, come on over when you're done. Aunt Edie's made up a batch of hot buttered rum batter and she's baking more cookies."

"Sounds good."

Yes, it did. Cookies, hot buttered rum and Seth Waters—an excellent combination. Funny how quickly he'd become like one of the family.

Except she didn't think of him as a brother. She knew he didn't think of her as a sister, but ever since they'd shared a hot kiss on a summer night he'd kept his distance. She got it. She wanted to be cautious, too. Well, other than the times she didn't. Being around the man, she was always aware of the live current running between them, and the temptation to grab on to it and let the sparks fly was hard to resist. Not so hard for him, it seemed.

She found Pete in the kitchen, parked at the table, sampling the hot buttered rum and consuming peanut butter blossoms, Aunt Edie keeping him company. "Seth's still working out there," she informed him.

"I'm going back out as soon as I finish my drink," he said. "Had to try one of Edie's cookies," he added, smiling at her aunt. "Nobody makes cookies like you, Edie, old girl."

And nobody consumed as many as Pete, the two-legged locust. Well, he had good taste. Jenna had to give him that.

"Everybody makes peanut butter blossoms," Aunt Edie said, waving away the compliment.

"I've eaten my share of cookies over the years and yours are the best," he insisted.

"Yours are the best," seconded Jolly Roger from his kitchen perch. "Roger's a pretty bird. Give me whiskey."

"Just don't give him any of my cookies," Pete said, making Aunt Edie giggle.

"Or mine," Jenna said and took one.

"Where's Sabrina?" Aunt Edie asked her. "I thought she'd be home from school by now."

"She went over to Jennifer's house. They're dyeing Hudson's hair."

"Purple?" Pete shook his head. He hadn't been an admirer of Sabrina's pink hair when Jenna let her color it during their summer of adjustment.

Jenna ignored him and poured herself a mug of coffee.

"Well, then," Aunt Edie said, "I think I'll try and get some work done on that blanket I'm crocheting her for Christmas."

"Guess I better get back to work while we've still got daylight," Pete said, pushing away from the table.

Jenna doubted he'd done much work to begin with, but she kept her mouth shut and helped herself to a second cookie. Pete was right about one thing. Nobody baked cookies as scrumptious as Aunt Edie's. They had a cookie exchange with their beach friends coming up, and Jenna doubted anyone would be able to top her aunt's creations.

Seth said as much when he popped in for a sample, and Aunt Edie flushed with pleasure.

"I enjoy baking for people who appreciate it," she told him.

"We all appreciate it," Jenna said. "Well, my thighs don't thank you."

"There's nothing wrong with your thighs," Seth told her, and out of the corner of her eye Jenna could see that matchmaker grin sneaking on to her great-aunt's face.

"There's nothing going on between us," she said to Aunt Edie after Seth had left.

"My dear, I may be old, but I'm not so old I can't see when a man and a woman are attracted to each other."

"Attraction and commitment are two different things, and I don't see that happening."

"It will," Aunt Edie predicted. "Of course, when the time comes I don't know how you're going to choose between him and Brody."

Jenna didn't, either. Although Seth seemed determined to make her choice easy.

Actually, so did Brody. He arrived that evening to take her to The Drunken Sailor for line dancing, wearing jeans and a T-shirt under a vintage leather bomber jacket, a Santa hat on his head. He looked like he belonged on the cover of a romance novel. *A Man for Christmas... Santa's Naughty List... Kisses and Cookies.* Except who cared about cookies with a man this hot? Smear his pecs with icing and put him on a plate.

Oh, good grief. Stop already.

"What's with the frown?" he asked.

"Nothing," she said. "I'll just get my coat."

Of course, he had to visit with Aunt Edie and admire her decorations. "But where's the mistletoe?" he asked Jenna as she stepped away from the coat closet.

And there was that same speculative look on her aunt's face again. "We'll have to get some," Aunt Edie said.

Maybe they would.

Why not spend some time under the mistletoe with Brody? He was fun and generous and had turned out to be a good friend to her and her aunt. He was gorgeous and sexy, and thank God they were only going line dancing. That wasn't a contact sport. Not that Brody ever danced anyway. He preferred to sit at the bar, drink a beer and watch.

"I like watching you in action," he said when she, as usual, tried to coax him out on the floor. "I can't do that if I'm trying to learn all those complicated steps."

So Brody drank beer and schmoozed, and Jenna worked up a sweat and made a fool of herself. Something for everyone.

He brought her home and turned her loose with only a playful tug on her hair since she'd declared a moratorium on kissing early on in their relationship. "But all bets are off once I get your aunt to put up that mistletoe," he warned with a smile that showed off his dimples.

That little tug on her hair was enough to get her hormones stirred up. Ah, yes. She could fall for Brody. But Brody was a ladies' man, a player. She'd been played once and that was once too often.

Still, what if he got serious? Could she?

Take it slow, she advised herself. She didn't need to rush into anything.

At the chamber of commerce meeting the next week Brody was all business. "Jenna, where are we with the festival?" he asked after calling the meeting to order.

"We're in great shape," she was happy to report. "Everyone has posters up and all our restaurants are ready with specials."

Sandy's, where they were meeting, was sure to win a prize for best-dressed restaurant. Holiday wreaths with seashells hung about the restaurant itself, and on the miniature beach in front of its entrance, a big mechanical Santa wearing sunglasses greeted customers, while an elf sat in the lifeguard chair. The restaurant was offering drink specials both Friday and Saturday night.

Sandy's wasn't the only place that had gotten into the spirit of the festival. Santas were everywhere, even at cranky Susan Frank's Beach Babes, where one was modeling a scarf and a beach hat. A miniature sleigh filled with dolls and teddy bears sat in the storefront window, all wearing little Santa hats and sunglasses.

When Jenna had expressed surprise that she was decorating and offering special festival coupons, she'd replied, "I said I thought this was a bad idea. I didn't say I wouldn't participate." If she'd decided not to take part, she'd have been the only one.

"The mayor's going to be on *Beach Beat* tomorrow talking about the festival, so everyone be sure to tune in," Jenna informed her fellow chamber members.

Kiki had been irritated that the mayor was talking about the festival as if it had been *her* idea, and going on the radio was one more way she'd take credit for what Jenna had done. Jenna was fine with it, though. She didn't want to be talking on the radio any more than she wanted to ride on a float in the parade.

And it looked like there'd be plenty of participants in the parade.

"Who all will be represented?" Tyrella prompted Jenna when she got to that part of her report.

Tyrella's employees were going to be marching as the shovel core with shovels slung over their shoulders like rifles. The men and their buddies and boys had been practicing several stunts, which they claimed would dazzle parade-goers. Jenna hoped nobody's shovel went flying. That would be all they needed, to have someone along the parade route knocked out by a shovel.

She read from her list, starting with Beach Lumber and Hardware, then continued, "We've got Something Fishy, the Porthole, the Driftwood Inn, the Oyster Inn, Best Western, Quality Inn, Cindy's Candies and our local Elks chapter. The Quinault Chamber of Commerce is sending their float and we have representatives coming from Icicle Falls and Puyallup, as well. Doggy's is going to have a giant hot dog and their employees will be wearing hot dog costumes. Rian has her pet parade set to go."

Rian nodded. "I think every dog in Moonlight Harbor's going to be present."

"Moonlight Harbor Evangelical is going to have a flatbed truck with Dickens carolers singing Christmas carols, and I believe Our Lady of the Sea is planning some kind of float with a living Nativity. Father Brannon tells me they'll have a sheep and a goat in addition to the holy family and angels and shepherds. Good Times Ice Cream Parlor will be going along the parade route giving out coupons, and the funplex staff is going to be driving go-carts, right?" She looked to Nora for confirmation and Nora nodded. "We've got the Moonlight Harbor Horse Club and the fire and police departments. Oh, and the high school marching band. Then we have our own royal court and, of course, Santa bringing up the rear. His elves will be walking alongside the float and throwing wrapped peppermint candies into the crowd. Thank you, Cindy, for donating the candy," she added.

"Is Santa going to be in a sleigh, then?" asked Susan Frank.

"No, but he's going to be in a horse-drawn carriage."

"Since when does Santa ride around in a horse drawn carriage?" Susan sneered.

"Since the mayor got involved," Nora muttered.

"The mayor knew someone," Jenna said, and left it at that.

"Well, no matter what he's in, I hope he doesn't get blown away," Susan said. "You know the weatherman's predicting a big storm for that weekend."

"The weatherman's always wrong," Brody said and gave Jenna an encouraging smile. "Looks like we're in great shape for the festival."

"We are." She'd never planned something this big in her life, and she had to admit she was pretty darned proud of herself. And, like Brody said, when did the weatherman ever get anything right?

It seemed everyone in town was talking about the festival, and Jenna did her part to fan the excitement, visiting the various shops and restaurants, gushing over their holiday decorations and taking pictures to put on Facebook and post on Instagram.

The Drunken Sailor had decked out their life-size lady pirate wood carvings with blinking Christmas light necklaces, which gave a holiday glow to the massive cleavage spilling out of their pirate vests. The kite shop had a Santa posted by the cash register holding a kite, and Rita Rutledge had gone all out to make Books and Beans festive with a glittering ten-foot tree decorated with teacup and coffee mug ornaments. All the coffee bags on her merchandise rack wore little Santa hats and she was wearing one as well when Jenna stopped in for an eggnog latte.

"I'm sure I'm going to win the best-dressed business award," she said to Jenna.

"You're definitely in the running," Jenna told her.

So was Nora. Both Good Times Ice Cream Parlor and the funplex dripped with colored lights. She'd placed wooden facades of Mr. and Mrs. Santa in the ice cream parlor, and customers were enjoying sticking their faces in the empty space provided in the figures' heads. When Jenna visited, she took a picture of a couple of teenagers posing and got their permission to post it on Instagram.

"Everyone's having so much fun with this," Tyrella said when the women gathered at Aunt Edie's for their cookie exchange that Friday evening. "The festival's going to be great. And, speaking of great, I need the recipe for these rock cookies," she said to Patricia Whiteside. "Please tell me it's not top secret."

"I'll share," Patricia assured her. Everyone was supposed to come wearing an ugly sweater, but the ugliest Patricia could do was a soft, pastel blue pullover accented with a silver scarf. It was beautiful and elegant, like the woman wearing it.

Courtney's sweater was a garish thing sporting a Christmas tree decorated with all manner of pompoms and appliques. She'd embedded it with lights that blinked on and off. If she spilled something on herself she'd get electrocuted. The yellow fringe on the bottom took it to new heights of tacky.

"It makes me think of our float," Jenna told her, "but not in a good way."

Courtney held it out and admired her own handiwork. "I call this design Bad Holiday Trip."

"You weren't on a bad trip when you made these cookies," Nora said, and helped herself to another potato chip cookie.

"That was my aunt's recipe. I love 'em," said Courtney. "They're about the only ones I make. I'd rather play with fabric than bake. Anyway, why bother when I can get Annie to bake for me?"

Annie Albright lived and breathed all things culinary. Jenna hoped someday Annie would be able to make her dream of owning a food truck come true. Meanwhile, though, everyone enjoyed the treats she brought to their gatherings.

She'd outdone herself that night, bringing Kiefles, a Hungarian treat, along with a fudge she'd created using white chocolate and rose water. Those treats, along with Cindy Redmond's whipped shortbread, Nora's holiday drop cookies and Aunt Edie's latest creation, which she'd called Fruitcake Bites, gave everyone a nice selection.

"Are we going to see these at the festival?" Nora asked Annie as she put another Kiefle on her plate.

"I was thinking about it." Her brow furrowed. "I really hope the weatherman's wrong. I want to do at least enough business to pay for my booth."

"You will," Jenna predicted. *Dear Santa, please don't let Mother Nature make a liar out of me.*

* * *

"I kinda wish I could stay," Sabrina confessed to Jenna two days before the festival as she helped Jenna fold event brochures for the motel office.

"Me, too," Jenna told her. "But your dad and your grandparents are looking forward to seeing you. This will be your Christmas with them, and they've got a lot of special things planned."

If you asked Jenna there ought to have been a medal created for single moms who shared with men who didn't deserve their generosity. Not for the first time, she reminded herself that Damien's parents had done nothing to deserve being deprived of visits with their granddaughter.

"I know," Sabrina said and frowned. "I wish you and Daddy were still together."

Jenna didn't. He'd caused her enough grief.

She hugged her daughter. "We did make you pretty miserable and I'm sorry about that."

"*You* didn't," Sabrina said. It would appear that she'd finally figured out who the real culprit was.

It was all Jenna could do not to say, "You're right. I didn't." Instead, she said, "Sometimes things happen."

"Aurora happened," Sabrina said with a scowl. "I hate her."

"But she loves your dad." God alone knew why. "So try to find the good in her," Jenna advised, and then reminded herself that she should do the same, for both Aurora and Damien.

Okay, so he'd fallen for someone else. So he'd turned his wife's and daughter's lives upside down. They'd landed right side up. Sabrina was doing well, and Jenna was happier than she'd been in years. He'd actually done her a favor. Maybe she wouldn't wish him a lump of coal for Christmas.

Anyway, 'twas the season to be merry, and between hanging out with her new Moonlight Harbor friends and getting her daughter ready for the Christmas ball, Jenna'd had plenty of opportunity to be merry.

Sabrina had enjoyed plenty of merriment, too. She'd been smiling ever since the dance, and Jenna was glad she'd given her permission to go.

All the parents had organized a progressive dinner for the kids before the dance, and they'd come to Aunt Edie's for dessert—hot fudge sundaes with peppermint ice cream. Jenna had taken a ton of pictures, which she'd sent to her family and Damien, who'd texted a reminder to make sure Sabrina obeyed the curfew.

I still don't like her seeing him, he'd texted.

They're not dating, Jenna had informed him. They're just hanging out.

Like her and Brody. Except he'd come over that same night to watch movies with her and Aunt Edie and spotted the mistletoe Edie had hung in the entryway. "It's about time," he'd said, making a little shiver of anticipation dance down Jenna's spine.

When they'd finished with the movies and Jenna walked him to the front door, he'd taken full advantage of that mistletoe, drawing her to him. "'Tis the season," he'd murmured, his voice low and sexy.

Then, before she could object (not that she was going to), he'd kissed her, slowly and thoroughly. "Now, that's what I want for Christmas," he said when they were done.

"Only a kiss? Right," she'd teased.

He'd sobered. "Yeah, I want more. You know I do. When you're ready, Jenna, just let me know."

She was getting more ready all the time. She hadn't said that, though. Instead, she'd just nodded. She had to be sure.

Sure or not, it felt good to be wanted, good enough that she managed to welcome Damien kindly when he showed up the Friday afternoon of the festival to get Sabrina for their weekend together.

He looked at her suspiciously. "What are you so happy about?"

"Do I need a reason to be happy?"

"Well, no. But you're never smiling when you see me."

"Maybe I've got the Christmas spirit."

"Maybe," he said dubiously.

And maybe I'm close to finally getting over you and everything you did to me. She hugged Sabrina. "Have fun and I'll see you Sunday night."

"Have fun tomorrow at the parade," Sabrina said, and hugged her back. "Next year I'll ride on the float," she promised.

They got into Damien's car, and Jenna waved them off. A gust of wind caught her coat and pulled. A little wind, so what? It was always a little windy at the beach. Everything would be fine.

The Marshes and the Browns entered Moonlight Harbor on Friday afternoon. The town was dressed up for the holidays with lights strung on frames shaped to look like Christmas trees set up at the white rock gateway. Every shop in town sparkled with lights, beckoning shoppers to come on in, but Taylor couldn't afford to accept the invitation.

The kids caught sight of a family of deer munching grass along the road and were thrilled, and Sarah took a picture.

"How fun is this!" she exclaimed.

Loads of fun, Taylor thought irritably.

They pulled into the parking lot of the Driftwood Inn where she was about to spend a miserable weekend. This was the charming beach motel Sarah had reserved for them? No wonder her sister had gotten a deal. A fresh coat of paint and some driftwood couldn't disguise the fact that the place was a relic. They'd passed a couple of attractive ones—with no-vacancy signs—on their way in. Those had looked more expensive, so, naturally, her sister would've passed them up.

"Try to smile," Greg said under his breath as they got out of the car, and she scowled at him.

"This is lame," she said.

Okay, she was sounding bitchy. But she was feeling bitchy. They'd caravanned down, following Sarah and Chris and the boys, keeping in touch over the phone. They'd all stopped at the Dairy Queen in Aberdeen, and she'd barely had enough cash to cover their burgers and shakes. Nice of Greg to insist they could pay for their own meal. They couldn't pay for anything these days.

The boys began racing around the parking lot, Miranda at their heels. "Miranda, come here," Taylor called.

"Boys, settle down," Sarah ordered, and they came bounding over to her like a couple of oversize puppies. "You shouldn't be running around in a parking lot," she scolded.

"Can we go to the beach?" asked Christopher.

"I want to go to the beach," said Miranda.

"Let's get checked in before we do anything," Chris suggested.

The wind was cold, and it was starting to rain. All Taylor wanted to do was go inside and get warm.

She was freezing and steaming simultaneously. She and Greg had fought about money just before they left, thanks to a past due notice on her car payment. He was pulling them further and further down financially, but he didn't care. He continued to turn blind eyes to the problem and deaf ears to her.

"You don't have any faith in me," he'd said sullenly.

"And you aren't listening to me!" she'd cried.

"That's because all you do anymore is bitch."

"Greg, I'm scared."

"I've told you, you don't need to worry. I'm handling it."

She'd thrown up her hands at that. "Handling it? How?"

There'd been no time to finish the argument. Miranda had entered the room, her backpack in tow, and then Chris and Sarah had arrived.

And Taylor had fumed all the way down.

"I want to go eat," whined James as Chris led their little troupe to the motel office.

"We just ate," his mother reminded him. "We'll go out later." To Taylor she said, "That restaurant shaped like a lighthouse looks like fun."

No, that restaurant shaped like a lighthouse looked like money.

The woman handling the reception desk was pretty,

with big blue eyes and blond hair. She wore a black sweater over jeans and had a red scarf looped around her neck.

"Hi. I'm Jenna. Welcome to the Driftwood Inn," she greeted them.

"We have two rooms reserved—Brown and Marsh," said Chris.

"We have a Groupon," Sarah added, presenting her printout.

"Yes, we've got you down," said Jenna the receptionist.

"Does our room have a hot tub?" Christopher asked eagerly.

"I'm afraid not, but you'll be so busy having fun on the beach and at the festival you won't miss it." Jenna gave him a smile and shared it with the other adults.

Taylor couldn't bring herself to return it.

Christopher spotted the plate of cookies on the reception desk. "Cookies!" he shouted and started to reach for one.

His mother grabbed his hand. "You ask first."

"Can I have cookie?" he asked.

"Please," Sarah prompted.

"Please?"

"Of course," said Jenna, who was irritatingly pleasant. "That's what they're here for."

Both boys dug in.

"I want a cookie," Miranda said and Greg gave her one, too.

He offered one to Taylor, but she shook her head. The burger she'd choked down earlier was still churning in her stomach.

Jenna finished with the business of checking them in, then handed over keys. Keys? Who used keys anymore?

"Our rooms all have different themes," she explained. "You're in the Sandy Beach room," she told Chris and Sarah, "and we have you in the Sunrise room," she said to Greg and Taylor. "If you need anything, let me or my staff know."

"Thanks," Sarah said. She got herself a cookie and led the way out of the office. "All the rooms having themes, that's so clever."

"Clever," Taylor echoed sarcastically. Talk about corny.

Their rooms were side by side, and right before they entered, Sarah smiled at her and said, "This is going to be fun." The F word again.

"Yes, it is," Greg agreed before Taylor could say anything.

Oh, yeah, fun. She was all about staying at a dump and sharing a room with a husband she was barely speaking to. They didn't even have the luxury of enough privacy to fight, since their daughter was in there with them.

Greg opened the door to the room, stepped inside and flipped on the light to reveal...oh, good Lord. The carpet was orange. A bilious burnt orange. The bedspread was vintage and yellow, the walls decorated with framed photos of sunrises. A trundle bed had been placed in a corner of the room for Miranda.

"This is pretty," Miranda said happily, flopping on her parents' bed and checking out the kitschy lamp with its metal base shaped to look like a smiling sun.

Taylor eyed the bed with distaste. Their one at home was a king. This one was too cozy.

She walked to the bathroom, which was microscopic.

The vinyl on the floor was a neutral brown and the walls were cream-colored. There was no shower, only a bathtub with a shower nozzle, hidden by a plastic shower curtain dotted with brown seashells. Ugh. Another picture of a sunrise hung over the toilet.

"This is abysmal," she muttered as she stepped out.

"Knock, knock," called a voice from the doorway, and Sarah entered the room. "Wow, this is wild."

"That's one word for it," Taylor said, making her sister frown.

"Does your room have a sunshine lamp, Aunt Sarah?" Miranda asked.

"No, my room has seashell lamps."

"Can I see?" Miranda asked eagerly.

"Sure, come on," Sarah said.

Miranda dashed out of the room. Sarah followed her, and Taylor trailed behind them, curious to see what her sister's room looked like.

Sarah and Chris's room wasn't the Hilton, either, but it was an improvement over Taylor and Greg's, with brown carpet and the walls painted a subdued shade of tan and hung with beach photos.

A lamp with a glass base filled with shells drew Miranda like a magnet. "Look at the shells, Mommy!"

Meanwhile, the boys were bouncing on the bed, making dents in the light blue bedspread patterned with—surprise, surprise—shells.

"We ready to go check out the town?" asked Chris.

Not really. "I'll get Greg," Taylor said and went next door.

"So, what's their room like?" he greeted her when she walked back into their room. "Nicer than ours?"

She shrugged, refusing to take the bait.

"It's free," he reminded her. "Beggars can't be choosers."

Okay, if he wanted to pick up where they'd left off, she could do that. "Yeah, and whose fault is it we're beggars?" she snapped. "Who just came home one day and announced he'd quit his job?"

"You know, some wives would actually support their husbands when they're trying to start a new business," he growled and gave their suitcase a kick.

"And some husbands would care enough about their families not to be irresponsible and bankrupt them," she growled right back. "You never really asked me what I thought about you quitting your job. You just plunged in and did it."

"I did it for us!"

"No, you did it for yourself."

Miranda was back in the room now, which ended the fight. "Are you and Daddy mad at each other?" she asked in a small voice.

Yes. Mommy wants to feed Daddy to a giant squid. "It's okay, baby," Taylor said and held out a hand to her daughter.

Miranda took it and asked, "When are we going to see Santa?"

"Tomorrow." *Maybe I'll ask him to bring me a new husband.*

Chapter Twelve

"We made it," Lisa Whitaker crowed as she pulled into the parking lot of the Driftwood Inn. "And you can tell Doug that we didn't get lost."

"Well, except for missing our entrance onto Highway 101. I told you that was coming up," said Karen.

"You told me too late," Lisa said, and not for the first time. Honestly, what was it with big sisters that they always had to be right?

"No. You just can't drive in the dark. I told you we should've left earlier."

"I can see fine in the dark," Lisa insisted.

"Right," muttered her sister. "Anyway, we're here now so let's get checked in."

"I can hardly wait to see our room," Lisa said as they walked to the office. "They looked adorable online."

"Then we can go get dinner. I'm starving," Karen said.

"We gorged ourselves all the way down," Lisa reminded her. Cheetos, chocolate and lattes. "I don't know how you even have room for dinner."

"I can manage a salad. And a drink. It's five o'clock somewhere."

"Yeah, here."

A pretty woman with blond hair was working the reception desk and gave them a cheery welcome. "We have you in the Seaside room," she said.

"That sounds so cute," Karen gushed, and the woman beamed. Karen was a gusher, and people loved her for it.

"Be sure and take a festival brochure," said the woman. "It tells you when and where the parade is tomorrow, and it lists all the businesses participating in our Best Dressed for the Holidays contest. Make sure you visit as many as you can and cast your vote. They're all running specials."

"That's what we like to hear," Karen said.

"And help yourself to a cookie. My great-aunt bakes them for our guests."

They both took a home-baked cookie from the plate on the reception desk, then got their keys, and went to their room to begin unloading. "I think we might have overpacked," Karen said, grabbing a tote bag stuffed with goodies. Between the two of them, they'd packed enough for a week—chips, bottled Starbucks coffee drinks, the requisite chocolate, wine, beef jerky and cookies they'd picked up at the grocery store on the trip down. And that was only the food. They'd brought shoes, boots, extra coats and sweaters and, between the two of them, enough hair products to stock a salon.

"I think you might be right," Lisa admitted, pulling out her overnight bag and backpack, which had her extra shoes and a windbreaker.

"Are you sure you're just going for the weekend and not running away?" Dean had joked.

"It pays to be prepared. You know Karen will be packing at least as much."

"You two do not get the concept of traveling light."

"Why should we as long as there's room in the trunk?" she'd retorted.

"By the time you're done spending money down there, you'll be lucky if there's room for the two of you in the car on the drive back."

"Don't worry," she'd said and kissed him. "We can always rent a U-Haul."

He hadn't been amused. Dean was a little on the cheap side. But, hey, it was the holidays, and she intended to do plenty of holiday shopping. She'd find space for her purchases.

She probably hadn't needed to bring her yoga mat, though.

"You're gonna use that?" Karen asked, once they were in their room. It was charming, with a mural of an ocean beach painted on one wall and framed beach photos hanging over their beds, lamps shaped like lighthouses on their bedside tables. But it wasn't exactly spacious. "Where were you going to lay it out?"

"Right here." Lisa pointed to the space between the beds and the bathroom.

"Better hope I don't trip over you," warned her sister. "Anyway, do you seriously think you're going to have time?"

"I might have gotten a little carried away with my packing," Lisa admitted.

"Well, I don't have room to talk," said Karen, who had brought some quilting hand work. She grabbed a chocolate from their stash. "Come on, let's go see what this town has in the way of restaurants."

They opened the room door, and a strong gust of wind blew in like a playful ghost.

"I forgot how windy it gets at the beach," Lisa said.

Karen pulled her coat collar tightly around her neck. "Hopefully it will blow itself out by tomorrow."

"I hope so," said Lisa. "I kind of wanted to take a walk on the beach." She'd envisioned them both getting in some exercise, maybe a little bit of beachcombing.

"I think I'll settle for walking through the shops," Karen said as they hustled to the car for the last of their bags. "This damp and wind will wreak havoc with my hair."

Yep, the sister beach walk probably wouldn't happen. Oh, well, they'd have fun anyway.

They were about to leave the parking lot when Karen's cell phone began to play "I Just Called to Say I Love You," her ringtone for Doug. Their song. More like *I just called to pester you*, if you asked Lisa. Honestly, what didn't he get about the idea of a girls' weekend?

Her moment of superiority was cut short when her own cell rang. "Footloose." Dean. "Why are you calling me on my girls' weekend?" she answered, even as her sister was saying, "No, we didn't get lost." *Good girl, Karen.*

"Just wanted to make sure you guys made it down there okay," Dean said.

"We got down here, no problem. We're about to go eat dinner."

"Okay, well, have fun then. Call me when you start back on Sunday."

"Don't worry, we'll be fine," Karen was saying to Doug. They both ended their calls, shaking their heads over their husbands' unfounded lack of confidence. "You'd think we were twelve," Lisa said in disgust as she started the car. "We should never have told them about Canada."

"That whole getting-lost thing is simply an excuse to call. Bottom line is they don't like being left behind," Karen said. "But it's good for them to miss us. It'll make them appreciate us so much more when we get back."

"Wisely said."

"I *am* the wise one."

"No, you're just the old one," Lisa teased.

"Remind me again why I'm subjecting myself to a weekend with you?"

"Because you love me."

"There is that." Karen consulted her brochure. "Let's try the Porthole. If I remember correctly they've got a nice view of the ocean. We can have a drink and watch the waves come in."

And the wind blow.

It was nearly six o'clock when Darrell Wilson pulled up in front of the little office at the Driftwood Inn. The place was a light blue throwback to the fifties and early sixties, when road trips were the thing to do and mom-and-pop motels populated state highways. It was hardly a luxury hotel. Had he blown it?

"This is so cute," Kat said.

Good. Hopefully, he hadn't. "Reserve judgment until you see the room," he told her. "Wait here. I'll get us checked in." He drew his coat tight against the wind and hurried into the office. "Looks like you've got a storm brewing," he said to the pretty blonde woman behind the desk.

"It gets a little windy here sometimes," she admitted.

A little. That was putting it mildly. He gave her his name, and she gave him a room key and a brochure with info on the weekend festival. "Be sure and take a cookie," she said, pointing to the plate. "They're home-baked."

He did, and one for Kat. Chocolate chip were his favorite, and it had been a while since Kat had baked. He took a bite. Oh, man, that was fantastic.

Back at the car he gave Kat hers, and she bit into it, shut her eyes and smiled. "Oh, that's good."

"Not as good as yours," he said gallantly. Actually, it was better than hers, but he wasn't about to tell her that.

The compliment backfired. She lost her smile and stared out the passenger window. "I wish I had the energy to bake."

He hated it when she got despondent. It was so not her. "You will again," he assured her. "When this is all over."

She nodded and bit her lip. The rest of the cookie went untouched. Oh, yeah, they were getting off to a great start.

"Hey, you need to finish that," he said with mock sternness.

"I'm not very hungry." She handed it over. "You finish it."

He'd lost his taste for cookies, too, but he took it anyway. They couldn't both be down at once. "Okay, fine. Your loss." It didn't taste as good as the first one had.

In addition to the wind, the clouds were spitting rain,

and he hustled her into the room, turned on the light, then hurried out and dragged in their suitcase. When he got back she was sitting on the bed, looking around.

"It's really charming," she said.

It was the sort of room a woman would like—a bedspread with seashells, framed black-and-white beach photos on the wall. The nightstands had lamps shaped like blue crabs. A little chair sat in one corner, a small pillow on it printed with the message *Life's Good at the Beach.* He hoped so. He wanted them to have a good weekend, to make some happy memories they could slip in between the hard times and the struggles.

"So, what do you say we grab a bite to eat?" he said.

"Is there room service?" she asked.

Even though she'd napped most of the way down, she was still looking tired. "Probably not, but I'll go see what I can find."

Kat nodded and scooted back against the pillows, and he returned to the office. With every step he questioned the wisdom of this weekend getaway. She'd had chemo only a couple of days before, and by about the third day it always caught up with her, leaving her exhausted, her whole body aching. He hoped she'd be up for seeing the parade the following day. And darn, he wished he'd gotten them some place with a view. She could at least have sat at the window and watched the waves.

"I think we're going to try and find some place that does takeout," he told the receptionist, who, he learned, was also the manager. "What restaurant would you recommend?"

"They're all good," she said.

"Do you have a favorite?" he pressed.

"Well, we don't play favorites here at the Driftwood."

"I do," said a stylish dark-haired woman, coming in behind him. She was shedding her coat. Probably the next shift. "You can't go wrong with anything at Sandy's. They're right down the street."

"How about that place across the parking lot?" he asked.

"The Seafood Shack?" The receptionist smiled and nodded. "They have great fish and chips."

Kat loved fish and chips. He thanked her and ran across the parking lot to the fast-food joint with a giant wooden razor clam perched on its roof. Inside it was festooned with red tinsel and smelled like grease and frying fish. A string of fish-shaped Christmas ornaments hung on one wall, and as he walked past it, a mounted fish on a nearby wall turned its fishy head and began to sing, "Take me to the River." Mr. Fish was accompanied by the sound of visiting and laughter. Several people sat at tables, and there was a line of customers waiting to order. Lots of customers, the best testimonial a food place could have.

Darrell ordered fish and chips, popcorn shrimp and a couple of chocolate shakes, then hustled back to the room. Kat had gone from sitting to lying and her eyes were shut. He set the bag of food on the nightstand and looked down at her. She was so gaunt. It scared him.

As if sensing his gaze, she opened her eyes and smiled. He sat down on the edge of the bed and put a hand to her cheek. "You poor kid."

"I'm not a poor kid. I'm a happy woman with a great husband."

"An idiot husband. You should've told me to forget this. We should've stayed home."

"I didn't want to stay home. I like getting out." She motioned to the bag. "That smells good."

"Fish and chips."

"Yum," she said, and worked to move herself to a sitting position.

He placed pillows at her back, then laid the meal in its take-out box on her lap. "Don't say we never travel in style," he joked.

"This is perfect," she said. "Turn on the TV and see if they've got cable. Maybe we can find a movie."

He got his food and the remote control and settled next to her on the bed. "Ah, this is the life," he cracked.

"It is," she agreed, and he knew she meant it.

Most of their guests were checked in, and Jenna had turned the reception desk over to Courtney for the night when her sister arrived at the house. The wind had gone from a whisper to a shout, and the rain was coming down in buckets.

"It's pouring out there," Celeste informed her as if she couldn't tell from her sister's wet coat and dripping hair. "If you think I'm riding on a float in this you're nuts."

"It'll be fine tomorrow," Jenna insisted.

"Easy for you to say. You're not the one stuck on the float," Celeste grumbled and went upstairs to stow her suitcase in the room they were sharing.

"You're such a baby," Jenna called after her.

Aunt Edie had come out of the living room by then. "Is your sister here?"

"Yes."

"Oh, good. I'll heat water for our hot buttered rum."

"Thanks," Jenna said. "She could use some sweetening up."

Ten minutes later, they were all settled in Aunt Edie's cozy living room with hot buttered rum and a plate of Christmas cookies. Roger, who'd been put to sleep for the night, was quiet beneath his cage cover. Which was just as well, as there would've been much whining for him to parrot.

"I'm going to get pneumonia in that." Celeste groaned, looking at her costume, a glittery turquoise mermaid tail and a body suit with a turquoise bra.

"It's the Driftwood Inn. You have to look beachy," Jenna said. "And you'll be sitting under a beach umbrella. That'll serve as a wind break."

"That's not a wind out there. It's a hurricane."

"All this complaining from the woman who went skydiving on her spring break? Where's your sense of adventure?"

"Gone with the wind."

"Ha-ha. Anyway, the weather will be fine by tomorrow," Jenna said. "These storms always blow themselves out."

She'd said the same thing to Seth earlier when he'd asked if she still wanted him to drive the float. "Fine by me," he'd said with a shrug. "I'm under the thing. I won't be stuck sitting on top in a mermaid costume. I hope your sister's still speaking to you after this." Now, listening to her sister, Jenna hoped so, too.

Her cell phone rang, and she picked it up to hear Kiki Strom on the other end. "I don't want to discourage you or rain on our parade—so to speak," she said. "But I'm wondering if we need to cancel. The weather report doesn't look good. There's supposed to be a big storm blowing in tomorrow."

"I think it already got here," Jenna said. "It'll probably be on its way out of town by the time the parade starts."

"That does happen sometimes, but I'm worried that the weather we have now is just the warm-up act."

"Let's cross that bridge when we come to it," Jenna suggested, and hoped they wouldn't get to the bridge only to find it washed out.

"Okay. It's your call," Kiki said, and left Jenna wondering if she was making the right one.

Of course, she was.

Or was she simply being stubborn? This festival was her baby, and it was always hard to part with one's baby. It was also hard to fail. Was she doing all this to prove she wasn't a failure? Who was she trying to impress, the people of Moonlight Harbor? Her ex?

There was an ugly thought. She sent it packing.

"Who was that?" Aunt Edie asked her.

"Kiki, wanting to make sure the parade is still on."

"Oh, I do hope so," said Aunt Edie. "People have worked so hard on their floats. It would be a shame to let a little wind ruin everything."

There, thought Jenna. She wasn't doing this just for herself. Other people wanted the parade to happen as much as she did.

"A little wind," Celeste repeated. "All we're missing is Dorothy's house and the Wicked Witch of the West."

"It'll be fine by tomorrow," predicted Jenna the weather girl. "Anyway, the show must go on."

"You'd better pray the curtain doesn't fall on us," Celeste said.

"Since when have you become such a Debbie Downer?" Jenna demanded.

"Since you decided to stake me to a float in nothing but a mermaid tail," Celeste retorted.

"With a body suit," Jenna reminded her.

"Anyone like more buttered rum?" asked Aunt Edie.

"Yes, please." Celeste held out her mug. "And make sure you send a big batch with me tomorrow. Maybe if I get drunk enough, I won't realize I'm freezing to death."

"Oh, very funny," Jenna said in disgust.

But after fielding four more calls from worried parade participants, her resolve was starting to falter, and worry edged its way into her mind as she lay sleeping. Her dream put her on the Driftwood Inn float in a wind so strong she found herself gripping the roof of the little motel with both hands while the rest of her body (in a mermaid costume) flew out like a human flag.

She was the only one on that float and the only one on the street, while all along the parade route angry people booed her as she passed, throwing tomatoes and clamshells at her. Her sister stood among them, all bundled up in a warm coat and scarf and laughing uproariously.

Susan Frank came into sight and she was dressed like Glinda, the good witch from the *Wizard of Oz*. But she wasn't smiling. "I told you this would happen," she hollered.

Meanwhile, Jenna was trying desperately to hang on to her miniature motel. Finally, the wind became too much for her and she lost her grip.

"Good riddance," called Susan as the strong wind caught Jenna up, blowing her toward a tall stand of fir trees. Head over heels she tumbled, trying to straighten herself out, until a big tree loomed in front of her. She was going to get hit!

She woke up with a cry, her heart racing. In the bed next to her, Celeste was lightly snoring, oblivious to her sister's nightmare.

That was all it was, Jenna assured herself. A silly dream.

The next morning the wind appeared to have died down. The sky was still gray and threatening, but, so far, the clouds had only been able to squeeze out a light mist. Mist was okay. They could deal with mist.

"See?" she said to her sister as they made the coffee for breakfast. "It's going to be fine."

"It doesn't *look* fine," Celeste retorted.

Pete walked in at that moment. "Is the coffee ready?"

"Not yet," Jenna said. "Sit down and have a bagel." Had she just offered food to Pete the mooch? Good grief, she was turning into her aunt.

He plopped down at the kitchen table. "Weatherman's predicting a big storm for later today."

"Well, it's not going to come until after the parade," Jenna said firmly.

"You better hope it doesn't."

"It'll be fine," she told both him and herself.

"I do wish I could be on the float with Celeste," Aunt Edie said wistfully.

Yes, that was what they needed, her aunt out in the freezing cold, getting pneumonia. "I know," she said. "I'm sorry you have to work the desk." Thank God she'd come up with a reason to keep her aunt inside and warm.

Aunt Edie sighed. "Ah, well. That's the hospitality business."

"Courtney will be in to help later this afternoon," Jenna said. "Maybe you and Celeste and I can check out the booths at the pier if the weather turns nicer." It could improve.

Maybe. In a parallel universe.

A cloudy sky still scowled at them as she and Celeste drove behind the float to the start of the parade route, where everyone was to assemble. The wind had come to the party. But it wasn't too bad yet. Hopefully, the worst of the storm would hold off until after the parade... Or, better yet, wait and come in at night, after everyone had shopped and eaten. Yes, nighttime would be okay. Sort of.

Most of the participants were present, and Brody and Ellis were on hand with their clipboards, directing traffic, when the Driftwood Inn float pulled up. The fire and police departments had brought only one police car and fire truck. Frank waved at her from behind the wheel of his patrol car and called, "Good luck!"

"This is all the patrol cars you could spare?" Jenna asked the chief of police. "And what happened to the motorcycles?"

"Can't spare 'em," he replied tersely. "With the storm

about to break, we need to be ready for emergencies. You should've canceled," he added, giving her a disapproving frown.

Her cell phone rang, and the mayor's name showed on the screen. Had Parker been talking to the chief? Jenna opted not to take the call and shoved the phone in her pocket. People were already gathering along the parade route. They'd paid good money to the various motels and B and Bs, and they'd come expecting to have a good time. And that was what they were going to get.

Celeste had put on her mermaid costume only to discover she couldn't walk, so Seth had carried her to the car back at the motel. Now he helped her out, walked with her to the float and set her on the little bench they'd disguised as a rock. The beach umbrella in back of it was swaying like a palm tree in a typhoon, but Jenna noticed her sister wasn't looking quite so cranky anymore. Even though she was with Mr. Fabulous, the cop back home, she never seemed to tire of male attention.

A lone plastic flower from one of the floats blew off and danced past.

"Are we ready?" Brody asked Jenna.

She checked the time on her cell. "We still have ten minutes." The last thing she wanted was to get to the viewing stand and be stuck with the mayor ten minutes before parade time.

He pointed to the leaden sky. "I don't think I'd wait."

The high school marching band was in place, ready to kick off the parade, but she hated to start early. What if some people were still making their way there?

A burst of wind whipped past her, nearly taking her hat in the process. That decided it. "Okay, let's go," she said, and a fat drop of rain landed on her nose.

Chapter Thirteen

"Are you sure you want to go to the parade?" Darrell asked Kat. She still looked dragged out, and the weather wasn't exactly beckoning. The sky seemed ready to dump at any minute.

"I do," she said. "I feel better today, and I want to take advantage of that."

"It's about to rain," he warned her.

"We've got an umbrella," she reminded him and slipped on her heavy coat. "Come on, let's go. The parade's beginning soon, and I don't want to miss it."

"I doubt you'd be missing much," he said. "How about we hit a couple of shops instead?" At least she'd be warm and dry inside, and he wouldn't have to worry about pneumonia.

"We can do that after. Come on, don't be a sissy," she teased and opened the door before he could argue further.

"Okay." If this was what she wanted to do, then this was what they'd do. But, crap, it was cold out.

They walked the short distance to the parade route, the wind pushing against them all the way. And, sure enough, it was starting to rain. He put up the umbrella and held it over her, hoping the wind didn't turn it inside out.

"Where is everyone?" she asked, looking up and down the main drag. "Are we in the right spot?"

Only a smattering of people lined the parade route, all hunched inside their coats like so many turtles. "The smart ones are inside the shops or at the restaurants, drinking hot coffee," Darrell said. "We're going to freeze our butts off out here."

"We'll be fine," she said, and linked her arm through his. "This was such a good idea. I'm glad we're here."

Yeah, right. He should've found a festival someplace warm.

Taylor stood on Harbor Boulevard, bundled in the warmest clothes she'd brought, which weren't that warm, sort of scowling. It was hard to maintain a proper scowl when your teeth were chattering. She wished she'd stayed in the room and watched TV, but Miranda had been excited about seeing Santa, and Sarah wouldn't permit any slacking, so off they'd all trudged to watch what would probably be the lamest parade on the planet.

The boys were busy trying to punch each other, and Miranda was jumping up and down as if she had springs on her feet. All that energy. Where did it go after you grew up? Responsibility and worry sucked it out of you. Taylor felt tired all the time. If only her sister had found a Groupon for a spa weekend.

"When are we going to see Santa?" Miranda asked.

"Pretty soon," Taylor said. The sooner the better. A couple of raindrops spattered on her cheek, and she pulled her coat collar tight. It had already been cold and windy. Rain had been all that was missing to make this event truly miserable. Now the picture of misery was complete. She sighed.

Greg, who was standing next to her, put an arm around her, and she shrugged him off. He looked hurt but didn't make another attempt at comfort. Or solidarity. Or whatever he'd been going for. Taylor experienced a sense of righteous triumph. That showed him exactly where he stood these days.

The righteous triumph faded into sadness. What was happening to them? To her?

A big gust of wind gave her an angry push. The kids were now running with their hands stretched out in an effort to get airborne. She remembered when she was a kid, trying to fly on a windy day. Back then she'd believed if she spread her coat wide enough she could take off like Peter Pan. She'd also believed in Santa Claus and the Easter Bunny and magic, and she'd believed she would fall in love and live happily ever after. Those days were long gone, and she was beginning to doubt that she and Greg would ever find their way back to happy again.

"Let's go," she said to her sister.

"Oh, come on, stay. Look, the parade's starting," Sarah said.

"So's the rain. We're going to get drenched."

"Look, Mommy!" Miranda cried, jumping up and down again, pointing to the high school marching band. The slightly off-key rendition of "Santa Claus is Coming to Town" drifted toward them. It was accompanied by the whistling of the wind. Ugh.

Greg put up the umbrella, and the wind turned it inside out, which made Miranda laugh. Oh, yeah. Funny.

Behind the marching band lumbered the first float, shaped like a giant shark with its mouth open. "Don't let him eat you," Greg joked with Miranda and gave her a quick tickle, making her squeal in delight.

Anyone watching would've thought he was the perfect father. But what kind of father gambled with his family's financial security?

"At least you've got more clothes on than those poor women," Sarah said to Taylor as the float passed. The women wore mermaid tails and nude body suits, which were obviously producing little warmth. They were waving, then rubbing their arms for warmth. Their smiles looked forced. The wind was pulling the fake seaweed from the float, sending it flying everywhere. And, speaking of going everywhere, people were starting to drift away, even though there were floats still to come.

"This is getting bad," Taylor said to Sarah. "We really should leave. Come on, baby, let's go back to the room," she said to Miranda.

"We can't go yet," Miranda pleaded. "We haven't seen Santa."

"I'll take you to see him at the mall," Taylor promised.

"I want to see him here! You said we could."

She and her big mouth. Santa probably wouldn't show until the end of the parade. She clamped her jaw shut in an effort to keep her teeth from rattling. They were all going to be drenched before this stupid parade was over. Like the poor bedraggled princess coming by in a classic red convertible. She looked like she'd just taken a shower. In her clothes. The red velvet cape she wore over her gown was sopping, and her hair was hanging in strings. She was waving, but her smile was pained. The man driving the car didn't appear much happier than she did.

The woman on the Driftwood Inn float looked as if she was contemplating murder, and Taylor pitied the poor fool who'd convinced her to ride on a float in a mermaid costume in the middle of December.

The wind became fiercer by the minute, and sea-weed from the fish float was now swirling everywhere. Taylor let out a yelp and dodged a flying plastic elf that had escaped another float. "Okay," she said, taking her daughter's hand. "That's it. We're leaving."

"I don't want to go," wailed Miranda. "I want to see Santa."

"You will, but not today," Taylor said. An escaped umbrella cartwheeled by, spooking one of the horses trotting past, making him toss his head and half rear up.

"Yeah, I think it's time to go," Sarah agreed. "We don't need to get hit by flying debris."

"Enough is enough," Darrell said, pulling a piece of pretend seaweed out of his hair. "You're freezing and we're leaving." What had started out as a little wind and rain was quickly turning into the full-fledged storm the weatherman had predicted for the coast. Darrell had never paid much attention to weather predictions. It seemed half the time they were wrong. Not this time, though.

Kat didn't argue with him. "I'm ready to go back to the motel," she admitted.

"Forget the motel," he said. "We're going home."

The sisters had braved both the wind and the rain, but Karen drew the line at flying objects. The plastic elf that tried to take off her kneecap was the final straw.

"I think I've seen enough of the parade," she said to Lisa.

"Me, too," Lisa agreed.

"In fact, I think I've had enough of the beach," Karen continued as they started back to the motel. "This is shaping up to be a major storm. Let's go to my house. We can watch movies and drink wine. And if you're dying to shop we can go to the mall."

"Oh, come on. We've got the room for two nights. Let's get our money's worth and stay."

"Are you kidding? This is get-the-ark weather. Let's scram while we can."

"Don't be such a wimp. It's only a rainstorm. It'll blow over," Lisa said. "Anyway, do you really want to go home in defeat? The guys are bound to give us a hard time."

"It's not as if we can control the weather."

"No, but we can control our paranoia. By tomorrow it'll be beautiful. We can have a nice breakfast and kick around town before we head back."

"I guess." Karen held on to her knitted cap and leaned against the wind. "Good grief. I feel like I'm in a hurricane."

"It's not *that* bad," Lisa scoffed. Then they arrived at the motel in time to see the wind blowing a dumpster across the parking lot. "On second thought, wine and spending the night at your place sound perfect to me."

Jenna was on the viewing stand with Mayor Parker Thorne and Aaron Baumgarten from the newspaper. The stand was shaking in the wind and a deluge of rain was pelting them, but the mayor was smiling gamely and reminding the few brave souls remaining on the parade route that Moonlight Harbor residents never let a little wind and rain spoil their good time.

Good time? Who among the parade participants was having a good time? The high school marching band was drenched, the plumes on their hats drooping over their dripping faces. The goat and sheep had bleated pitifully when the live Nativity rolled past, and Mary had looked anything but beatific. Brody's real estate agents, inside their appliance-box houses, had to be cursing his name. One had blown over, struggling on the wet street to right himself. He'd probably never have made it to his feet if one of Tyrella's shovel-wielding marchers hadn't left their formation to help him. (Brody had realized he couldn't be in the parade and keep it moving, so he'd escaped public humiliation, but he was probably going to get a very public punch in the face as soon as that agent found him.) The wind was tearing decorations off floats right and left. "Joy to the World," the Dickens carolers sang even as their faces said, "End of the world."

How would the paper report this disaster? Jenna could almost see the headlines. *Seaside with Santa Parade Big Failure.*

Susan Frank had been right. This had been a stupid idea. Why, oh, why hadn't they all listened to Susan?

"Our Moonlight Royal Court is a little wet," the mayor observed as the cars bearing the princesses rolled past. "But they're smiling. We coastal residents are tough, aren't we, Aaron?"

"Oh, yeah," Aaron said, and the mayor ignored the sarcasm in his voice.

Yes, they were tough, and as the various floats and people marching in the parade trudged past, Jenna waved encouragingly at each one. The Driftwood Inn float lumbered by, and she noticed that some of its shiny blue fringe was missing. She smiled at her sister, and Celeste glared back at her and hollered something. The wind whisked the words away, but the expression on her sister's face gave her a pretty good idea of what Celeste was trying to tell her. The only thing that kept her from jumping off the float and coming to strangle her big sister was the fact that she couldn't walk in her mermaid tail.

"And here's the float from the Driftwood Inn," announced the mayor. "Jenna Jones, who manages the inn, was the inspiration behind our festival." She may as well have added, "So talk to her if you have any complaints." A herd of raindrops came at them, and Parker covered the mike and leaned over. "Is this going to electrocute me?" she demanded.

"No, you'll be fine," Jenna assured her and hoped that was true.

The wind was now blowing so hard that both she and the mayor were having trouble staying upright. "Oh, my, that was quite a gust," the mayor said and tried for a lighthearted laugh.

But she wasn't laughing when a melting papier-mâché clam came loose from a float and whacked her in the leg. She glared at Jenna as if it were all Jenna's fault.

Maybe, in a way, it was. Jenna gave her a helpless shrug.

The last of the parade-goers were now leaving, pushed along by the wind, but the mayor, the reporter, and Jenna, the organizer of the ill-fated event, were stuck on the viewing stand.

Finally, Santa and his carriage came into view. The driver wore a rain slicker, and rain was pouring from his hat like a waterfall. Poor Brewster Thorne was drenched. He'd lost both his Santa hat and his smile. The elves walking beside the carriage looked equally miserable.

A couple of old men in the departing non-crowd happily taunted him. "Having fun up there, Brewster?" he called, and Santa gave him the finger. Fortunately, there were no children left to witness Santa's naughty behavior.

"And that's it for this year's parade, everyone," said Mayor Thorne, even though there was no one there to listen.

Without a word to Jenna, she climbed down from the viewing stand and joined her husband in his carriage, and Santa and the Mrs. disappeared down the street.

"I'll try to put a positive spin on it," Aaron said to Jenna as the sound man hurried to rescue his equipment. They'd been under cover, but it hadn't spared them from the rain.

She nodded and thanked Aaron, although she knew there was no positive spin. A moment later Brody showed up with one of his helpers. "We'd better take this stand down before the storm gets any worse," he said. She nodded miserably, and he gave her a one-armed hug. "Hey, it's okay. It was a good parade."

"It was a disaster," she said miserably.

"It's not your fault Mother Nature's being a bitch."

"Storm's gonna get worse," said his helper.

Brody frowned at him. "We don't know that," he said to Jenna.

"Yes, we do," she said, resigned. She'd seen a few ocean storms when she was a kid, and she knew what was coming. "Where's Ellis?"

"Wiping down his car."

"He's probably mad at me."

"He'll get over it."

Jenna's cell phone summoned her. It was Nora. "We're shutting down the rides," she reported. "It's too dangerous on the pier. I've got the vendors taking down their booths, too."

"Okay," Jenna said. "Do what you have to do."

Just as well. No one would want to be out in such nasty weather. She didn't even want to be out in it. In fact, she wanted to be far, far away. Seaside with Santa was an abysmal failure. Could this day get any worse?

Chapter Fourteen

"**I**'m done," Taylor announced as the families walked back to the motel.

"Done?" repeated her sister.

"Done. As soon as we get back to our room, we're packing up."

Sarah was silent, and Taylor could tell by the set of her jaw that she was angry. Well, let her be.

"Don't you think you're overreacting? The storm will probably pass in another couple of hours," Greg said.

"I'm not going to sit around in that dinky room all afternoon, hoping it stops," she informed him.

"Fine," Sarah said. "We'll all have more fun if you're not here complaining."

Her sister's words stung. She hadn't complained before this, and she wouldn't be complaining now if they weren't in the middle of a typhoon. Or if they were staying at a halfway decent motel with fireplaces in the rooms and an ocean view. She clamped her lips shut, determined not to get into an argument. She'd reimburse Sarah for what she'd spent on the rooms and then…never talk to her again.

Okay, that was a momentary fantasy born out of irritation, rather like when she was a child and would stamp off to her room in a snit when she was feeling misunderstood, sure that the offender would be sorry and come to apologize. Of course, that never happened, and estranging herself from her sister wouldn't happen, either. Sarah was bossy and self-righteous, but she also cared. They had their fights and yet in the end they always made up because that was what sisters did.

But that didn't mean sisters couldn't get mad at each other. And that was where Taylor was. She'd had enough family togetherness to last her until Christmas...of next year.

It was a sad procession back to the Driftwood Inn. The float was missing fringe, shells and its resident mermaid, who sat shivering in the car next to Jenna.

Celeste cranked the car heater up even higher. "I don't want to hear ever again about the dumb things I've tried to rope you into," she growled.

"I'm sorry," Jenna said for the fifth time.

"You owe me chocolate for life."

"Yes, I do." If only everyone else in town could be so easily placated. Businesses had invested time and money in this festival. Nobody was going to see a profit.

They pulled into the parking lot behind the storm-buffeted float, and Seth and Pete, his wingman, emerged from underneath it, dry and warm.

"Next year put Seth on top of the float, and *I'll* drive it," Celeste muttered.

There would be no next year. The tears Jenna had been holding back demanded to be set free, and she laid her head on the steering wheel and turned them loose.

"Oh, hey, I'm sorry," Celeste said, instantly penitent.

"This whole festival is a disaster," Jenna sobbed.

"It'll be okay, sissy. Don't cry," Celeste said, and scooted closer, putting an arm around Jenna.

Seth chose that moment to open the passenger door. "Hey, what's this?"

"This is my sister blaming herself for the weather," Celeste told him.

"I've let everyone down," Jenna said miserably.

"Cheer up. No good deed goes unpunished," Seth said. "Come on, Celeste, we should get you into the house."

Jenna let them go and stayed in the car and cried.

A few minutes later, Seth was climbing in and settling into the passenger seat. "You gonna get on yourself for doing something good for the town?"

"Yes," she said, and sniffed. "It was a stupid plan. People tried to tell me that." Well, one in particular. "But I wouldn't listen. Like my mom says, pride goeth before a fall." Her mom also told her to look for the rainbow in the storm, but any rainbow in this storm had been blown away.

"Hubris, huh?"

"Leave him out of this," Jenna said, indulging in a moment of black humor. Except she was in no mood to laugh. A fat tear leaked out of her eye and rolled down her cheek.

Seth reached over and wiped it away. "It's gonna be okay," he said gently. "Nobody's going to prison."

Their private code for "things could be worse." It always put her circumstances into a proper perspective. She sighed and wiped her eyes.

"What's the worst that can happen?" he continued.

"I lose customers."

"More will come when the weather gets nice."

"Everyone in town will hate me."

"For doing something good? Yeah, right. Want to try again?"

"No. That's all I can think of so far," she said and managed a smile.

He smiled back, giving a lock of her wet hair a playful tug. "I'll see you later, then. I'm off to get some gas for the generator, just in case."

She'd been so worried about the festival she'd forgotten about the ultimate thing that could go wrong. Losing power would be the final nail in the tourist coffin. "Thanks," she said. "For everything."

"You'll get my bill," he joked, and left.

Seth Waters should have become a shrink. Jenna still felt miserable, but not half as miserable as she had before she talked to him. And not half as miserable as she'd feel if they lost power. There was no sense going down that worry road, though.

She trudged to the office to relieve Aunt Edie.

Her aunt had missed the parade, but she'd gotten into the spirit of the festival and was wearing a green sweatshirt over her favorite elastic-waist jeans. She'd dolled up her outfit with a Santa hat, a necklace of blinking Christmas lights and dangly earrings to match.

"How was the parade?" she asked.

"Awful," Jenna said.

"Oh, dear. I'm so sorry."

"The storm's getting worse. I don't think people will want to go out in it."

Of course, Aunt Edie knew what that meant. No business. "Well, dear, you can't control the weather."

That was what everyone kept telling her, but she *could* control when to hold a festival. This really had been a dumb idea.

"It might blow over by tonight," Aunt Edie said.

Pete stopped in at the office to snag a couple of cookies from the plate. "The parade didn't go so well."

Thank you, Pete, for pointing out the obvious. Jenna scowled at him.

"I knew it wouldn't, not with the storm," he continued.

"That will be enough, Peter," Aunt Edie said sharply, shocking Jenna. Aunt Edie favored and fussed over Pete like a fourteen-year-old girl with a crush. It wasn't like her to speak harshly to him.

He looked a little shocked himself. "Hey, I'm just saying."

"Well, don't. Jenna's already upset over how things went."

"Sorry," he said. "Guess you don't want to hear that there's another parade—lots of cars leaving town."

No, she didn't. But she wasn't surprised. It was only a matter of time before their guests joined the crowd of people fleeing Moonlight Harbor.

"I'll go tie down the dumpster," he said and started for the door.

He avoided work like a germophobe avoided a handshake. This was an olive branch, and Jenna accepted it. "Thanks, Pete."

"Honestly, I don't know what got into him," Aunt Edie said irritably as he slouched across the parking lot.

As if he'd suddenly been taken over by rude aliens? He'd been a rude, old crumb ever since Jenna met him. Hard to believe her aunt had never noticed. Hard to believe she thought this was a momentary aberration. Maybe Seth was right. Maybe her aunt did have the hots for the old guy, even though he had to be at least ten years younger than her.

Eew. There was a place Jenna didn't want to go.

"Anyway, don't you pay him any attention," Aunt Edie said and patted Jenna's arm.

"Don't worry, I won't," Jenna promised. "Why don't you go back to the house before the wind gets any stronger? I can take care of things here until Courtney comes in."

"I'll go make us some corn chowder and cheese biscuits. Something hot we can reheat on the stove later if the power goes out."

Don't even say that, Jenna thought. The festival flopping was bad enough. She didn't think she could cope with a power outage on top of it. Surely they would at least be spared that.

Obviously some of their guests weren't going to wait and see. Jenna watched out the window as one of the two families who'd checked in on Friday stowed a suitcase and a couple of bags in their car trunk.

She remembered them. The husband and wife and little girl. The woman had been pretty and stylish and had looked like she had a bad case of PMS. From the frown on her face, it appeared nothing had changed. There would be no good reviews on Yelp from her. Jenna sighed.

Aunt Edie had seen them, too. "People come and people go. Don't you worry."

Oh, yeah. No worrying here. Jenna could feel her nervous tic returning with a vengeance as her left eye began to twitch.

"I'll bake some Christmas brownies, too," Aunt Edie said as she headed for the door. "Our cookie supply is running low, and I think, after this day, we'll all need something sweet."

They needed more than that. Pete had been right about the parade out of town, and it appeared to be leaving from the Driftwood Inn.

Darrell Wilson, the nice, middle-aged man who'd asked Jenna to recommend a restaurant, was the next to scram. He came in just as Aunt Edie was on her way back to the house. "My wife's not well. I think I need to get her home where she can rest more comfortably."

Jenna understood perfectly. She wasn't feeling so well, either. "Of course," she said.

Two more of their guests came in. Lisa Whitaker and Karen Owens, the sisters who'd come down for a weekend getaway. "We're sorry to have to check out early," said Karen, "but we're thinking maybe we should head home."

Jenna wanted to say, "Stick around. It's bound to get better." But that would've been wishful thinking. The lights in the office flickered, and her eye twitched again. "Of course. I understand."

"Your place is really cute," said Lisa. "We'll have to come back in the summer."

"I hope you will," Jenna said earnestly.

"We will," Lisa assured her. "We've been here before, years ago, and we know how pretty it is when the weather's cooperating."

They paid their bill and left. Jenna could see more people hurrying in her direction across the parking lot. Oh, boy.

She put in a quick call to Courtney. "If you're not afraid to get blown off the face of the earth, could you come and help me? I've got a stampede of people leaving."

"That sucks," Courtney said.

That was putting it mildly.

Courtney promised to be over in five minutes, and Jenna braced herself to greet the next evacuees. "We're going to be checking out," said an older man.

She didn't blame him. If she could have, she would've checked out, too.

By the time Courtney arrived there were several people in the office, tapping their toes, watching the wind blow branches around outside the window, checking watches and cell phones and calling relatives and pet sitters to let them know they were coming home.

"Bunch of lightweights," Courtney whispered.

That at least made Jenna smile.

Finally, the crowd left, and it was only the two of them in the office. "Wow," said Courtney. "You'd think we had a tsunami coming."

"It probably feels like it to them," Jenna said.

"Is that everyone?"

"Almost. Half of the Brown party left, but the other family is still here. So are the two guys and the newlyweds. I don't think they were planning on leaving their room much anyway."

"The sun will probably be out tomorrow, and then people will wish they'd stayed," Courtney said.

"You believe that?"

"Not really, but I thought it would make you feel better."

Jenna's mom called. "How's it going down there? I heard you've got a big storm."

"Who told you? Celeste?"

"Yes, but it was also on the news. I'm sorry, sweetie. I wish I was down there with you."

"Trust me," Jenna said. "You don't. Good thing you had to work."

"You know I'd always rather be with you girls."

"You wouldn't want to be here to witness this disaster."

"I'm sorry your parade got rained on."

"Rained on and blown away," Jenna said. "Just like all the people who'd been staying here. Almost all our guests have run off."

"Hey," Courtney said, pointing to the parking lot. "Look."

Jenna looked to see a car pulling into the lot. The couple with the little girl had come back. They got out of the car, and the stylish crabby woman began banging on the door of the room next to theirs.

"I guess they forgot something," Jenna said.

But they were followed by another car pulling in. It stopped in front of the office, and Jenna saw the Wilsons, the middle-aged couple who'd left a little earlier.

He'd had a commiserating smile for her when he'd checked out, but he wasn't smiling now. And here came that stylish crabby woman, marching across the parking lot, looking ready to strangle someone with a string of Christmas lights.

Right along with her came the tic. Blink. Blink. Blink, blink, blink. *Stay calm*, Jenna told herself. Blink, blink, *blink*.

"Hello," she greeted Mr. Wilson. "Did you forget something?"

He shook his head. "No. I'm hoping I can get my room back."

"Of course, you can. But why?" Like she should look a gift horse in the mouth?

"We can't get out of town. A couple of big trees have come down over the roadway, as well as some power lines. Nobody can get past, and there's a traffic jam on the highway with people trying to turn around. It's a mess."

Power lines. *Don't panic. We still have power.*

But for how long? Jenna felt twitchy as she retrieved the Wilsons' room key. Had Seth made it to the gas station? Most of their guests hadn't been happy when they left. *Now* how were they going to feel? The lights in the office flickered.

"Uh-oh," said Courtney.

Okay, panic.

"I imagine we won't be the only ones coming back," Mr. Wilson said.

"Well, don't worry. We'll take care of you," Jenna said with a confidence she was far from feeling.

The crabby woman entered the office. "We left the key in our room."

"No problem," Jenna told her. "We keep spares."

"You've got trees down on the highway," she informed Jenna. "People are stuck here."

"I'm sorry," Jenna said. "But we'll take good care of you." She felt like Jolly Roger, parroting the same phrase over and over.

The woman frowned as though she didn't believe it, took her key and stomped out of the office.

"Another satisfied customer," Courtney murmured.

Jenna grabbed her cell phone and called the house. "Tell Aunt Edie to make as many cookies as she can," she told Celeste when she answered. "I have a feeling we're gonna need them."

"What's going on?" asked Celeste.

"The highway's blocked. A lot of the people who checked out are returning."

"That's good news, right? People will have to come back."

With the frame of mind everyone was in, Jenna wasn't so sure it was good.

"Here come some more," Courtney said.

"Okay, gotta go," Jenna said to her sister. "You guys keep baking like crazy. Whatever you can make that's fast and easy."

"Got it," Celeste said.

Jenna ended the call as two more families walked back in the door. Well, the good news was that the Driftwood would be back at full capacity. She only hoped they were ready for whatever came next.

Brody's sporty 'Stang pulled into the parking lot. "Here comes the stud," Courtney said. "I'll watch the desk and feel jealous if you want to go out with him."

As if Jenna dared leave the sinking ship. "You know there's nothing between us."

"Just keep telling yourself that," Courtney teased. "I hope you brought booze for her," she said to Brody as he walked in.

"Actually, I was thinking maybe you'd like to go out and grab a drink," he told Jenna. "After the day you've had, I figure you need one."

"After the day I've had, I need to run away," Jenna said.

"So, run away with me. Where do you want to go, Tahiti?"

She shook her head at him. "What would you do if I took you up on that offer?"

"Get online and order tickets and buy you a bikini. But due to your overactive sense of responsibility, I doubt you're going to take me up on the offer. So how about the Porthole? The bartender makes a great eggnog martini. We can find a warm corner and storm watch."

"Go on," Courtney urged. "I can handle things here."

With his easygoing attitude, Brody would be the perfect man with whom to unwind. Except Jenna didn't want to do her unwinding in public where fellow business owners would look at her like she was the Grinch in drag, the author of their holiday festival misery. Anyway, she didn't want to leave her sister. After what she'd roped Celeste into, she owed it to her to stick around.

"I can't," she told Brody. "I need to spend some time with Celeste."

"She can come with."

She'd like to have said yes, but she resisted. "I need to help her and Aunt Edie bake cookies. You might not have heard yet, but the road out of town is blocked. I don't think any of our guests are happy to be stuck here, and we're going to have to try and placate them with carbs."

"Okay," he said. "How about dinner and line dancing at The Drunken Sailor on Sunday then?"

Everyone would've checked out by then, her sister would be on her way home and Jenna would need to decompress. "Deal," she said.

"Meanwhile, no feeling guilty about how the day went," he said. "You've done a great job of spearheading this festival, and don't let anybody tell you any different."

She didn't need anybody to tell her different. She had herself for that.

"He's such a sweetie," Courtney said as he drove off. "You should take him up on the Tahiti offer. Or are you holding out for someone else?" she asked slyly.

A certain dark-haired man with swarthy skin and brown eyes came to mind. No point in pretending she didn't know who Courtney was talking about. "He's not interested."

"Right. I've seen the way Seth looks at you."

"Looking and following through are two different things," Jenna said. "Anyway, I don't want to be in a hurry to jump into anything."

"Jump? You haven't so much as stuck a toe in the water," Courtney said. "But hey, I get it," she added. "I felt the same way after losing my loser. Still, I gotta say, after a while going to bed alone sucks."

"We need to find someone for you…"

"I actually started looking. I'm trying the online dating thing. Going to meet someone for coffee the night before Christmas Eve. I'll be in Seattle to see my mom anyway, so what the heck."

"Good on you," Jenna said.

"A woman can't wait forever. And I'm sure done waiting for Santa to come through."

"I think he only specializes in toys."

"He should branch out. And you should get back to the house and get in some sister time."

"You sure you don't mind being here on your own with everything that's going on?" Jenna asked.

"Absolutely not. If I get bored, there's always the TV in the office. I can stretch out and nap on the couch in between reruns of *Project Runway*."

"Okay," Jenna said, and left for the house. She did, indeed, need some downtime, and helping her great-aunt and her sister bake cookies would be the perfect way to recharge her batteries.

It was now five o'clock, and daylight had been eaten up. The darkness, coupled with the howling wind, felt more like Halloween than Christmas, and she was happy to get inside where it was warm and dry. The house smelled like sugar and chocolate. Oh, yeah. She felt better already.

She found her family busy in the kitchen with Roger on his kitchen perch, supervising. "Chocolate is good for you," he greeted Jenna.

"I see you've been teaching him some new words," she said to Celeste.

"It was time to expand his vocabulary." She held out a bag of mint chocolate M&M's to Jenna.

"I hope you didn't try and feed those to him," Jenna

said, taking one. "He's plump enough, and God knows what those would do to his birdy constitution."

Roger almost looked ashamed. "Roger's a pretty bird. Give me whiskey."

"He never quits," Aunt Edie said with a chuckle. She opened the oven and the aroma of brownies danced out of it like a genie from a bottle.

"Those look delicious," Jenna said, and inhaled deeply.

"They'll taste delicious, too," Aunt Edie said, and set the pan on the stove top. "We've also got some snow-balls done."

"Great. That should make our guests feel better," Jenna said.

"It'll make *me* feel better." Celeste helped herself to more M&M's. "Aunt Edie's got corn chowder heating on the stove and the water's ready for hot buttered rum. See, life's not so bad."

"Maybe not," Jenna decided. "After all, things could always be worse."

And then there was a big boom. Followed by darkness. Goodbye, power.

Chapter Fifteen

"I'll go get us something to eat," Darrell said to Kat. "What would you like?"

She already had her shoes off and was climbing into bed, clothes and all. "I don't care. Get whatever you want."

He knew she just wanted to sleep. But she needed to eat. "How does clam chowder sound?"

"Good," she murmured, and rolled over onto her side.

"Okay. I'll run across the parking lot to that fish place. Be right back."

"Take your time," she said. Her voice was faint, smothered in exhaustion.

He left the room, cursing the damned cancer that had done this to her, cursing the weather for ruining their anniversary getaway, cursing whoever should've been clearing the road and wasn't, and cursing himself for not getting them out of town at the first hint of a storm. As he crossed the parking lot he pulled out his cell, called the fancy restaurant where he'd wanted to take Kat and canceled the reservation.

The Seafood Shack was packed with people, some of whom he'd seen around the motel. Two couples had three little kids bouncing around like characters in a video game. One of the women was trying to settle them down. The other one looked ready to murder somebody. Oh, yeah, fun times at the beach.

He was finally able to place his order and came away with two containers of clam chowder and some crackers. Not exactly the elegant meal he'd planned. But then nothing had gone according to plan.

He got back to the room to find Kat asleep. Should he let her continue sleeping or wake her up and make her eat? He set the bag with their meals on the nightstand and eased onto the bed next to her and thought of anniversaries past, when they'd wasted very little time in bed sleeping. After they made love, she'd cuddle up to him with that soft little body of hers and tell him he was the best lover ever. As if she had anything to compare him to. He'd been her first and only, and she'd been his.

Was it selfish of him to urge her to go through all this so he could keep her with him longer? He was a selfish man; he'd be the first to admit it. He hogged the remote and drove her crazy with his constant request for spaghetti dinners every week. He'd balked at taking ballroom dance lessons when she'd begged him to, all because he hadn't wanted to look stupid. He should have taken those lessons. He would once she was better. He'd do anything. *Please, God, let her come through this.*

He must have said that prayer a thousand times since her diagnosis. Was it doing any good? Was God listening?

He slid under the covers and spooned against her, pulling her close. "We'll get through this, babe," he whispered just as the lights went out.

* * *

"Uh-oh," said Celeste.

"Uh-oh," Jolly Roger repeated, then subsided into silence as darkness took over the kitchen.

More like *oh, no.* "Okay, don't anybody panic," Jenna said as panic flooded her entire body. "We need candles." And flashlights. And she had to get outside and start the generator. She made a dash for the drawer where Aunt Edie kept her matches and emergency candles and collided with her sister, who was obviously on the same hunt.

"Whoa," squeaked Celeste as she ricocheted against the kitchen counter. This was followed by the plink of cookies tumbling to the ground. "Oh, no! The snowballs."

"Don't move," Jenna said as she slid along the floor, feeling for the drawer. She got to it and fumbled around inside until her fingers closed around a thin candle and then a box of matches. She managed to light the candle without setting her fingers on fire and held it up.

There, in the thin circle of light, stood Celeste, staring at the floor, horrified. Jenna bent to inspect the damage. Cookies lay scattered across the vinyl like pebbles, most of them broken.

"Some of them are okay," Celeste said and began to scoop them up.

"You can't give people cookies that have fallen on the floor," Jenna protested. All they needed was for someone to get sick and sue them.

"Sure, you can. Two-second rule," Celeste said. "Anyway, Aunt Edie's floor is so clean you can eat off it. Right, Aunt Edie?"

"Yeah, with Pete trooping through here all the time in his muddy boots? Toss 'em," Jenna ordered and dug a candle holder from the drawer. "At least we still have the brownies."

"And a few of the snowballs didn't fall," Aunt Edie said. "With them and the brownies, we should have enough to put on some small plates. And we can make some non-bake chocolate cookies to add."

Jenna set the candle on the counter, then pulled out a flashlight. "Round up some of the scented candles," she told her sister. "And get a fire going in the wood-stove. I'll bring in the lantern and the oil lamp from the garage when I come back."

"Where are you going?" Celeste asked.

"To start the motel generator." And to have a quiet nervous breakdown.

She heard the generator buzzing as she stepped out onto the back porch. Thank God. Seth was already on it. The motel would at least have power for heat and light. She hurried down the steps and to the side of the motel to find him walking in her direction.

"I was just coming to tell you the generator's up and running," he said.

"Thank you," she said, and gave herself permission to breathe again. "At least that's going right."

"For the moment."

"We'll probably have power back sometime tomorrow." Wouldn't they? Of course, they would.

Was she lying to herself? Of course, she was. But they had a generator. Granted, it was an older model, but it was working fine.

"I don't want to freak you out," he said, "but don't

hold your breath waiting for the power to come back on. We're at the end of the world down here, and it might take a while."

Even when you weren't at the end of the world it took a while. All those beautiful green trees that made the Pacific Northwest so lovely also created problems when they came down in a storm, taking out power lines right and left.

"We'd better get more gas for the generator," she said.

"Uh, Jenna, the pumps aren't going to be working with no power."

Oh, yeah, that.

"I got some extra, but you'd better be thinking about a Plan B."

Plan B? The generator *was* Plan B.

"And you should probably invest in something bigger for the next time. Meanwhile, don't worry," he added. "We'll get through this."

Easy for him to say. He wasn't the one running the place.

"Let me know if you need anything else. I'll be in my room."

Probably reading a book by candlelight. Seth Waters might have had a job that used more brawn than brain, but he never let his brain stay idle. If he hadn't done jail time, he could have been a teacher, a college professor perhaps. It saddened her to think that one hasty decision could have had such huge lifelong consequences. But then, wasn't that how it worked? Every choice, big or small, had consequences.

She shrugged off her philosophical moment, thanked

him, then got the oil lamp and lantern from the garage and beat it back to the house to help put together goody plates for their guests. Celeste and Aunt Edie had lit several candles, and now the fragrances of cinnamon and pine swirled through the house.

Celeste set a match to the paper and kindling in the woodstove and shut the door. "Okay, we're ready to go."

"Good," said Jenna. "Let's get those cookie plates made up." *And think of a Plan B.* Blink, blink, blink.

Electricity was on in the motel to keep the guests from stumbling around in the dark, but Aunt Edie didn't have a generator for the house, and the kitchen felt eerie with only scented candles for light and the fridge silent.

"Oh, wonderful, more light to work by," she said as Jenna set the oil lamp on the kitchen counter. Not that the dim glow of candlelight had stopped her aunt from working. She had the kitchen table covered with little red paper plates and plastic wrap and ribbons.

Jenna put oil in the lamp and lit it, and the room's glow became less eerie. Celeste returned, and the three women got busy loading cookies onto the plates and wrapping them festively. Aunt Edie put the corn chowder on the woodstove to stay hot while they worked. Jenna couldn't help wondering what the people staying at the motel would be doing for dinner. If the power was out all over town, how long would the restaurants be operational? She hoped some of them would be able to stay open.

Of course, Pete put in an appearance. "Power's out everywhere," he reported.

"Are any of the restaurants serving?" Jenna asked.

He shrugged. "Don't know. The Drunken Sailor's got an emergency menu—sandwiches and chips and pop."

"Is the grocery store open?" Aunt Edie asked.

"It looked kind of dim in there," Pete said, "but I think so. They'll probably only take cash."

"I have some cash in my purse," said Aunt Edie.

"Then you and Pete had better run to the store and see if you can stock up on bread and peanut butter and bottled juice," Jenna said. "If the power doesn't come back soon, we have to be ready to feed people."

"Okay," Pete said. "But how you gonna keep 'em warm if the generator's not working?"

There went the nervous tic. Blink, blink, blink. "We'll have to…" Jenna stalled. What *would* they do?

"We'll have to put people up here at the house," said Aunt Edie.

Twenty rooms' worth? "Where would we put them all?"

"I can bunk in with Edie," Pete offered, making Celeste snicker and Aunt Edie blush and Jenna remember the red panties her aunt had bought.

"We may need to house some of the women in my room," Aunt Edie said.

Pete frowned. "It's gonna get cold in my room in the motel."

"You can sleep on a cot in here," Jenna told him. She might not have been Pete's number one fan, but she didn't want him freezing to death, either.

Hmm. Pete unsupervised in the kitchen. Maybe that wasn't such a smart idea. She'd bunk Seth in there as well, to keep an eye on him. "Seth can sleep here, too."

"You still got a lot of people to find beds for," Pete said.

There was a long moment of silence in the kitchen before Aunt Edie said, "Well, in hard times we all pull together. I'm thinking we might have to ask some of our friends to make room."

Okay, there it was, Plan B. Jenna hated to drag other people into her drama, but when it came to keeping her guests warm, she had no pride. And no choice.

Brody was her first call. "You having fun over there?" he asked as she waved goodbye to Aunt Edie and Pete, on their way to the store for supplies.

"Oh, yeah. Loads. We've got the motel generator running, but if this power outage lasts for more than a day, we could be in trouble."

"You're right. The pumps at the gas station aren't working."

So she'd heard. "I'm trying to get a backup plan in place. If worse comes to worst, could you take a few people at your house? You've got a fireplace, so they won't freeze. I'll pay you," she added. There went her profits. But oh, well. Profits were overrated.

"Sure. And no need to pay me. This is what we do down here."

"Thank you," she breathed.

"Oh, wait. What was I thinking? Yeah, you should pay me. With a kiss."

"You never miss a beat, do you?" she teased. Actually, she could have kissed him right then and there, she was so relieved. At least she had one place lined up.

"Nope," he said. "In the meantime, you need anything?"

"Xanax would be nice."

"I'll come over later with some wine," he promised. "And chocolate."

That sounded good to her. She thanked him and called Tyrella, who assured her she could fit several people in her house. "I've got a woodstove and a store of extra gas for the generator, and my fridge and freezer are full. Bring 'em on," she said.

Courtney was also fine with taking in some boarders. "May as well. I think my plans for Christmas just went up in smoke now that the road's closed."

"The guy you met online?" Jenna remembered Courtney had planned to see him before Christmas Eve.

"Looks like he'll have to wait to meet me in the new year. Meanwhile, if any hot single guys checked in on your shift, I'll be happy to take them off your hands."

"Two did, but I think they're gay."

Courtney heaved a dramatic sigh. "All the best ones are. Oh, well, maybe they're into fashion."

"If they are. I'll send them to you."

"I'll take whoever. I've got candles, a woodstove and enough canned tuna to last for a couple of days. And plenty of instant coffee and tea bags."

Jenna thanked her and told her to go home. At this point there was no need to keep the office open. Each room had Jenna's cell phone listed as an emergency number, and they were now officially in emergency mode.

"Fine with me. I'm going to crawl under my blankets and work on some new designs."

Okay, among all of them, they should be able to take care of everyone. If it came to that. Maybe it wouldn't.

Maybe the power outage would be an easy fix. One could always hope.

Jenna and Celeste finished with the plates, laying them carefully in Aunt Edie's covered wicker picnic basket. "You want me to help you distribute them?" Celeste asked.

"No. You spent enough time out in the storm today." Had the parade only been a few hours ago? It felt like ages.

Jenna pulled on her coat and went out into the cold to make her deliveries and reassure everyone that all would be well.

Some of the people weren't in their rooms, probably out looking for food. She made a note of the ones who were missing so she could go back later. The newlyweds were happy with the cookies and not remotely bothered by the fact that the lights in their room were dimmer than normal and that the restaurants would most likely be offering only emergency menus. Living on love.

Darrell Wilson, the man who'd planned the getaway for his wife, opened the door looking like a weary soldier peeking out from the trenches. She caught a glimpse of his wife, lying in bed, tucked under blankets, and wondered if the woman still wasn't feeling well.

"I brought you some cookies, courtesy of the inn," Jenna said. "I'm sorry the power's gone out."

"It's okay," he said with a fatalistic shrug. "How long does it normally stay out down here?"

"Hard to say." There. How was that for a nice, evasive answer? "But don't worry. If it's out for longer than we expect and our generator runs out of gas, we'll have someplace for you to stay. I'll keep you posted." Then, concerned about his wife, she asked, "Is Mrs. Wilson feeling all right?"

"As well as can be expected," he said.

"If you need some medicine…" Aunt Edie had enough cold remedies in her medicine cabinet to treat half the residents of Moonlight Harbor.

He shook his head. "She had chemo earlier this week."

Cancer. Everyone's bogeyman. "I'm so sorry," Jenna said. As if this poor couple didn't already have enough to deal with, now they were stuck in a motel running on half power. She hadn't caused the storm or the power outage, but she couldn't help feeling somehow responsible for their misery.

"It's okay," he said. "Thanks for the cookies. Kat will love them."

What a nice man. If only everyone else would be as nice. Jenna suspected they wouldn't, though.

The two families who'd come down together were returning to their rooms just as she walked up with her basket of goodies. She noticed they had a couple of grocery bags and breathed a sigh of relief. At least they had food. And heat and light.

"I wanted to check on you folks and make sure you're okay," she said.

"We're fine," said the pleasant woman.

"Sort of," added the frowning one.

Jenna reached into her basket and pulled out two plates of cookies. "I brought you all some cookies."

"Yay!" crowed one of the boys.

"Cookies!" cried the little girl, jumping up and down.

"Never mind the cookies," said the crabby woman. "How long is the power going to be out?"

The burning question. Jenna gave her vague answer, knowing it wouldn't make this woman happy.

Sure enough. It didn't. "When will the road get cleared so we can get out of here?" she asked through gritted teeth.

"I wish I knew," Jenna said. "Of course, I'll be in touch as soon as I learn something."

"Oh, well, you've got a generator so we're good to go," the pleasant woman said.

"Only until the gas runs out," her husband put in.

"If that happens, we'll have homes for everyone," Jenna assured them. "Our house has a woodstove and emergency supplies." Or they would have, once Aunt Edie got home.

"Hey, a real adventure," said the other man, and the frowner frowned at him.

"It probably won't come to that," Jenna said. *Please let it be true.*

"It's cold out here," said the grump. "Open the door, Greg."

The younger man obliged, and his wife went into their room, the little girl skipping behind her. He followed, looking sheepish.

The other woman turned to Jenna. "Thanks for the cookies. You're really going the extra mile, and we appreciate it."

Some of them did. Jenna thanked her and went on to the next room, where the two sisters were staying. "Wow!" said Karen, taking Jenna's plate of cookies.

"Look at this, Lisa," she said as her sister came to stand next to her. "Sustenance. We're saved."

Jenna caught sight of a take-out bag from Sandy's sitting on the bed. "It looks like you already saved yourselves."

"That's just sandwiches. We didn't get dessert," Karen said. "This is going to be a real treat." Then she moved on to the question of the day. "Any idea when the power might come back?"

"I wish I did," Jenna said. "But don't worry. We'll take good care of you." Oh, yeah. Jolly Roger with his repetitious phrases had nothing on her. Next she'd be saying, "Give me whiskey."

"You are taking good care of us," the woman said. "Thanks."

Those words were balm to her frazzled spirit. The wind was bitterly cold and the rain was trying to slash Jenna's cheeks, but she left the sisters feeling warmed and encouraged.

"That was sweet of them," Lisa said as the sisters returned to their card game. They added the cookies to the feast they'd spread out on Karen's bed, and she took one.

"Yes, it was," Karen agreed. "So, who cares if the power's out?" she said and helped herself to a brownie. She did love her creature comforts, but she could manage when she had to. "We've got food, we've got cards." And, in spite of the storm, she was having fun.

"Sunshine on a rainy day," crooned Lisa, and played a card. Her cell phone rang. "Oh, boy. It's the husband patrol," she said, and put the phone on speaker. "Hi, babe. Miss me?"

"I heard you've got a major storm down there. Are you girls okay?"

"Of course, we are. And in case you want to talk dirty to me, don't. We're in the middle of a high-stakes card game, and you're on speaker."

"So, power's on? You've got heat?"

"We've got heat."

"And power?"

"They have a generator."

"So, no power. You need to come home."

"Oh, yes, we want to be out driving around in this," Karen muttered.

"We can't," Lisa told him. "The only road out of town has trees across it, and there are power lines down."

Dean swore. "Why isn't someone getting them off the road?"

"I'm sure someone will as soon as the storm blows over. Anyway, you wouldn't want us out in this. We'd probably have a tree come down on us."

There was silence on the other end, and Karen could picture Dean with the proverbial steam coming out of his ears. His wife in a mess, without him there to save the day. The man pictured himself as a senior version of a Marvel action hero.

"Deano, it'll be okay," Lisa said, as reassuringly as she could.

"I don't like this. I wish I was down there with you."

"Don't worry. We're totally fine."

"Until their generator runs out of gas."

"The woman who runs the hotel has that covered. She just stopped by with cookies."

"Cookies. Great. You may wind up freezing to death down there with no power, but at least you'll have cookies."

"We're not freezing to death. Like I told you, we're fine."

"I worry about you," he said.

"I know, and I'm glad you do, but there's no need."

"Well, you'd better charge your phone while you've got power."

"I will," Lisa assured him, then quickly changed the subject. "How was your dinner?"

"Good, but lonely. I miss you."

"Oh, brother."

"I do."

"You'll survive."

"Yeah, well, I hope you do, too."

"Bye, Deano. Love you," Lisa said and ended the call. "I wonder how long it'll be until we hear from Doug."

"I give him ten minutes."

It was five. Karen didn't put him on speaker.

"Dean says you guys are stranded down there with no power."

"There's a generator here," Karen told him, "and we have light and heat and we're eating cookies."

"And playing cards," Lisa threw in. "Hi, Doug."

"Lisa says hi," Karen relayed.

"Never mind that. You need to come home as soon as the road is clear," said Doug.

"We will," she told him. "Don't worry."

"*Don't worry?* You two are down there pulling a Lucy and Ethel, and you tell me not to worry?"

"We didn't cause the storm, Doug," Karen said irritably, and Lisa shook her head. "And quit calling us Lucy and Ethel. It's not cute anymore."

"I knew something would happen," he muttered. "Your sister comes up with these harebrained schemes and you go along with them."

"Taking a trip to the beach is hardly harebrained. We'll be fine. I'll see you tomorrow," she said and pressed the off button.

Lisa raised an eyebrow. "Harebrained?"

"You know how he gets," Karen said in her husband's defense.

"Yeah, controlling. I don't understand why you let him get away with it. He can be such a jerk."

Doug had his faults, but nobody got to diss him except her, not even her little sister. "Look who's talking! Whose husband called first? And you can thank Dean for getting Doug all stirred up."

"As if Dean's to blame for Doug being insulting? Dean was worried."

"Well, so's Doug."

"No, he's just spoiled. The only thing he's worried about is that you won't be home in time to make his dinner tomorrow."

"You know, your husband's not so perfect, either," Karen said.

"At least he doesn't call people names."

"Oh, shut up and eat your sandwich," Karen said. She grabbed another brownie and stuffed it in her mouth. A sister getaway had seemed like a good idea at the time. Right now a getaway from her sister sounded even better.

They had light and they had heat and the TV was working. Taylor told herself she needed to stop feeling so pissed. But she was having trouble listening to herself. She sat on the bed and took the potato chips out of the grocery bag.

Their evening feast consisted of chips, apple juice and apples and some crackers—they'd been lucky to get those. It had been like the end of the world in the town's little grocery store with its dim lighting and emptied freezer and refrigerator shelves.

"Can't sell 'em," one of the workers had said when someone asked him about the frozen items. "Store policy. Possible food contamination." Which, of course, made what was left even more valuable. People were scooping things off the shelves and elbowing in front of each other to get bread and peanut butter. One old lady had almost gotten trampled by a man determined to grab the last loaf of bread. But she'd gotten there first.

"Hey, lady," he'd protested. "You already have three loaves in your shopping cart."

"I have a lot of people to feed," she'd informed him, and the crusty old man with her had told the guy to back off or he'd sock him in the nose.

Taylor had been sure Greg was going to get punched when he'd snatched that apple juice. The woman he beat to it looked mean enough. Obviously, emergencies didn't bring out the best in people. This one certainly wasn't bringing out the best in her. But then, lately, nothing had.

Someone knocked on their door, and she opened it to find her nephew standing there. "Mom wants to know if you want to come over and play Crazy Eights with us."

Miranda was already off the bed. "I do!"

"You can go over after you've had something to eat,"

Taylor said. "Tell your mom Miranda will be there in a few minutes."

"Tell your mom we'll all be there in a few minutes," Greg corrected her.

"I don't want to play cards," she said as she shut the door.

"Why?"

"I'm not in the mood."

"Fine," Greg said, his voice sharp. He took an apple out of the bag and some crackers. "Come on, Miranda. We'll eat over at Aunt Sarah's."

Miranda looked from one parent to the other, her little brows knit.

Greg got her coat and handed it to her. "Put your coat on and let's go have some fun." She did as she was told, and he gave her the apple. "You go on over, and I'll be right behind you as soon as I talk to Mommy. Okay?"

"Okay," Miranda said. The earlier excitement had disappeared from her voice, and she sounded subdued. She slipped out of the room and closed the door behind her.

Greg shoved into his coat and took another apple. "I don't know how to break this to you, Taylor, but the world doesn't revolve around you."

The disgust written on his face fanned her anger to a blaze. "Yeah? Well, it doesn't revolve around you, either," she retorted. "This is all your fault."

"Don't blame me for the weather!"

"That's not what I'm talking about, and you know it."

"I thought maybe this weekend we could actually have some fun, like we used to. Forget our troubles for a while."

"Oh, yes, you'd like that, since all our troubles are your fault. Well, guess what, Greg. I don't want to forget our troubles. I want to be done with them."

He pressed his lips together so tightly, they turned white around the edges.

"It wasn't my idea to come here," she reminded him.

"Yeah, well, too bad we didn't leave you at home. We'd all have had a better time without you," he said, and left, slamming the door behind him.

How dare he! "You bastard!" She marched over and locked the door, then returned to the bed and her chips and struggled to open the package. Finally, with a vicious yank, she succeeded, sending potato chips flying in all directions. She scooped a handful off the bedspread, then dropped them. Who knew what had been on that bedspread? She threw the bag down in frustration and indulged herself in a good cry.

Whatever circle of hell she was in, she needed to find a way out of it soon.

Chapter Sixteen

Aunt Edie and Pete returned with two bags filled with staples. "We have bread and peanut butter and juice and carrots and celery and cocoa mix, and some canned soups," Aunt Edie announced. "That, with what I have in the pantry, should get us through."

"We're lucky we got that," Pete added. "It's a war zone in there. I had to get rough with a couple of people."

Pete brawling in Beachside Grocery. Hopefully, he hadn't mentioned the Driftwood Inn.

"I'm glad I had you with me," Aunt Edie said to him, and in the dim glow of the lamplight, Jenna could see his crinkly, bristled cheeks turning rosy.

"Aw, you'd have been fine on your own," he told her. "Your aunt's quick," he told Jenna.

"Survival of the fittest," Aunt Edie said as she stowed the peanut butter. "I'm sure our chowder's hot. Let's have something to eat."

And so they did. Roger was tucked into his cage for the night, and they made themselves comfortable in the living room with bowls of chowder. The room was cozy, and the fire dancing behind the woodstove's glass door gave out both heat and comfort. Jenna would happily have settled in for the night, enjoying the experience to the max, if it had been only them and she didn't have other people to worry about.

But it wasn't. And in between Pete and Aunt Edie's reminiscences of storms past, she could hear the wind tearing around outside, slapping the windowpanes. And howling. (Wind really did howl.) There'd be more than wind howling if the generator went on strike. Jenna found it impossible to enjoy her chowder and finally set the bowl aside.

Celeste, on the other hand, was tucked in for the night, happy with her corn chowder and the cocoa they'd made. She sat under a blanket on the couch next to Aunt Edie, as enthralled as a little kid during story hour at the library.

"One time when the power was out, we were marooned down here for five days," Aunt Edie said.

"How did you manage to keep the motel running?" Jenna asked.

"I didn't. It was the winter after Ralph died. We didn't have anyone staying here."

Jenna wished that was the case now. She also wished she'd thought to look into getting a bigger commercial generator that could power not only the lights and heaters, but the hot water tanks, too. Cold showers lurked in her guests' future. Honestly, when it came to running this place, was she going to have to learn every lesson the hard way?

"It was just Jolly Roger and me, here in the house, keeping each other company," Aunt Edie continued. "Of course, people checked in on us. Brody came by every day and brought wood for the stove. Year before last, we had a storm but not such a bad one. People went beachcombing afterward. A lot of treasures wash up after a storm—glass floats, buoys, sometimes things that have fallen off boats. Patricia Whiteside found a case of whiskey once."

"I wouldn't mind finding that," Pete said.

"Oh, yes. It's always an adventure when there's a storm," Aunt Edie said with a chuckle.

Jenna couldn't concentrate on the stories. She was too busy fretting over what the following day might bring.

She hated to think what their guests were going to say about the Driftwood after this. Ugh. Time to go back out and deliver the rest of her cookies.

She found the last of the missing guests back in their rooms, and they seemed to be taking the storm in stride. "Cookies, what a kind gesture!" exclaimed one woman.

Jenna could only hope the woman mentioned her kind gesture somewhere online.

The storm was showing no sign of blowing itself out, and she scooted back to the house, her coat clutched tightly around her. She'd barely gotten in the door when Brody arrived with two bottles of wine.

"We're saved," cracked Celeste.

"I can't believe you braved the storm," Aunt Edie said to him.

"It's not that bad," he replied cheerfully.

Jenna gave a snort. "Compared to what?"

"Florida. Puerto Rico."

That put things in perspective.

"We'll have a few shingles flying and some driftwood on the road down by the pier and a certain amount of inconvenience, but we'll be okay," he said with an easy grin. "Now, can somebody get me a corkscrew and some glasses?"

"Gladly," Celeste said, and hurried off to the kitchen.

"Of course, it could always be worse," Aunt Edie said, "but I am sorry the storm had to pick this weekend to hit us and ruin your festival."

"There'll be other festivals," Brody said. "Meanwhile, we're warm inside." He lowered his voice and added, "And somebody might owe me a kiss, so I'm hoping the storm keeps it up."

Was it suddenly hot in here? Jenna could feel her cheeks sizzling.

Celeste returned with the glasses and corkscrew, and Brody got busy pouring wine.

"This is how you weather a storm," Pete said, raising his glass in salute, and after a glass Jenna felt they might, indeed, weather it. After a second glass she went to bed with a smile on her face. Maybe she owed Brody a kiss, whether or not he wound up housing Driftwood Inn evacuees.

Sunday morning there was still no power and it was still raining, but at least the generator was humming happily along. And the wind had stopped. It looked like the day after the end of the world, with tree branches scattered everywhere and only a faint glow of candlelight or weak power from a generator shining eerily in windows.

Phone calls and texts had gone out. No church service that morning. Unlike the Driftwood, the church didn't have a generator, and Pastor Paul Welch and his leadership team had decided their members could be just as spiritual at home, huddled by the fire, as they could sitting in a freezing sanctuary. Good call, Pastor.

Jenna probably wouldn't have gone anyway. She had too many things to do, like checking on everyone at the Driftwood and putting together a plan for who would go where. Maybe it wouldn't come to that, but she wanted to be ready in case it did. She'd finished with her housing assignments and was in the kitchen with Aunt Edie, listing their supplies, when Damien called.

"It's all over the news. You guys really took it bad down there."

"The whole town's out of power, but that's nothing new. We had power outages in Lynnwood," she said. She remembered one when she and Damien were first married. It had lasted two days, but they hadn't cared. They'd played cards by candlelight and had wild monkey sex. He'd sketched a picture of her naked.

Someone new was posing naked for Damien now, but who cared? Jenna had an offer on the table of Tahiti and a bikini. She half wished she'd taken it.

"So, should I bring Sabrina back?"

Yes. But of course, there was no point when the road into town was impassable. Jenna explained the situation to him, and they agreed it would be best to wait. "I'll call you when the power's on again," she said. If her cell phone was still charged. And what if the road didn't get cleared before Christmas?

But surely it would. The idea of not having her daughter with her at Christmas was too depressing to contemplate. And the idea of still having their guests stuck at the Driftwood was nearly as depressing. *Don't go there*, she told herself. The power company would get busy, the road would get cleared, and she would get rid of the headache she'd awakened with.

She dropped in on her guests, who all greeted her hopefully, sure she was bringing good news. Instead, she was merely instructing them to come to the office if the generator ran out of gas.

"How likely is that to happen?" asked the woman who never smiled. To her daughter, who was by her side, she said, "Miranda, don't stand in the cold doorway," and the little girl, who'd been smiling and happy to greet their visitor, dropped the smile and slumped her way back to the trundle bed Jenna had brought in for her.

The husband was nowhere to be seen. Maybe he'd run away. If so, Jenna didn't blame him.

"I mean, aren't you supposed to be prepared for this sort of thing?" the woman demanded.

"We were. We are. We're trying," Jenna ended lamely. Yes, list-maker that she was, replacing the generator with something more powerful should've been at the top of her list. She should at least have been pricing them. But she'd been too busy organizing a festival. Ah, priorities.

But no generator could run indefinitely if the pumps at the gas station weren't working.

"Well, thanks," the woman said, sounding far from grateful, and shut the door, leaving Jenna on the doorstep feeling both inadequate and irritated.

"I hate my job," she told Seth when she stopped by his room with corn chowder from Aunt Edie.

The room looked manly and welcoming. It wasn't cutesied up as much as the others. No sand dollar bedspread, just a plain brown one. The lamps on the night-stands were mismatched but cool. One was an antique oil lamp that had been converted to electric, and the other had a simple brass base. A framed picture of two women who were probably his mom and sister sat next to it, along with a thermos, and a book lay open on the bed. No clothes on the floor, or take-out bags. Seth Waters had made a good and simple life for himself by the sea.

"You're still riding a steep learning curve," he said to Jenna. "You'll get this all sorted out eventually."

"How much longer do you think we have until the generator dies?"

He shrugged. "I'd have to see the manual that came with it. Probably a few more hours. You got a Plan B yet?"

"Yes, but I sure hope I don't have to use it."

"Well, like my grandma always said, expect the best but prepare for the worst."

"I wish your grandma was here to help us," Jenna grumbled. She hesitated at the door. "Am I whining?" She hated whining, especially when she was the one doing it.

He grinned. "Maybe a little, but you're allowed. It's called letting off steam."

"I like that better than whining." But really, she *was* whining. *No more of that*, she told herself. She didn't have time for it.

Come afternoon, she was in the office, bundled in a hat and coat and gloves, working by the light of a pro-pane lantern and debating whether or not to distribute candles to the rooms. What if someone put their candle near the curtains and set the room on fire? On the other hand, what if someone tripped in the dark and broke a wrist? She should invest in some little flashlights for the rooms in case this happened again. But maybe it wouldn't if she got a decent generator.

Too late, she thought grimly as the lights winked out in the rooms. There would now be a stampede to the office. Thankful she'd charged her cell, she pulled it out and called in her reinforcements. All three promised to come immediately and drive people to their homes. Each of those homes would be overflowing, and Jenna couldn't help feeling grateful that a few of her guests had escaped before the road became impassable. Who knew where she'd have put them?

She'd just finished her May Day calls when the first guests showed up, a couple with a toddler. "Our power's gone," said the mother.

"Don't worry. We have a great place for you to stay until it comes back on," Jenna assured her. "And this woman loves babies." Tyrella kept hoping for grand-kids, but so far her son in South Carolina was not co-operating. She'd be thrilled to have a little one in the house to fuss over.

Next came Darrell Wilson. "I guess you're aware that the power's off."

"I'm afraid our generator's run out of gas, and we can't get any more because the pumps at the gas station are down." Now was when he'd erupt, threaten to sue her, come across the counter and throttle her.

Instead, he said, "These things happen."

This man was a treasure.

"Is there any place in town that has fireplaces in the rooms?" he asked. "Maybe we can move."

"We are moving you. To my house. It's right next door," she said, pointing across the parking lot, "and we've got a fire going in the woodstove. Go on over. My great-aunt loves company, and she'll give you something hot to drink as soon as you get there."

His face was the picture of relief. "Thanks," he said, and hurried out of the office.

Jenna called over to the house. "Our first guests are on their way," she said to Celeste, when she answered. "Tell Aunt Edie to have tea or hot chocolate ready. Mrs. Wilson's just gone through chemo and she feels like crap."

"We've already got the mugs out and bowls full of pretzels and peanuts on the coffee table."

"Good. Because it's going to be a regular invasion."

"We're ready. I've got the list of who's sleeping where. I'll get everyone settled."

Celeste actually sounded excited. No surprise. She loved to party, and in her mind this was going to be one big party. Jenna decided not to burst her bubble. Keeping eleven strangers happy under less than ideal conditions wasn't going to be an easy feat.

More people showed up, and Jenna had accommodations ready for all of them. "I can guarantee your hosts will make you feel welcome," she said to the growing crowd.

Brody piloted guests to his place in his hot red Mustang, thrilling both a fourteen-year-old boy who opted to ride with him and a sixty-seven-year-old man who'd talked fondly of the 'Stang he'd had when he was young.

Thank God Brody had such a big house. He'd be taking most of the Driftwood Inn evacuees. Tyrella had a van and stuffed it full of people and luggage. Just as Jenna had thought, she was delighted to take the couple with the toddler.

Courtney took the newlyweds and the two hot guys who were stylishly dressed and who Jenna figured might enjoy hanging out with a clothing designer.

The sisters, Karen and Lisa, had arrived, along with the other pair, Sarah and Taylor, the frowner, and their families. "You'll all be staying in our house, which is the one right across the parking lot," she said, pointing.

"A giant slumber party," joked Sarah.

The frowner kept her frown in place. Oh, boy. She was going to be good for morale. That one Jenna would've loved to farm out to someone else, but it would have been a rotten way to repay her friends for their kindness.

"Come on, grumpy," said her sister, "let's go get our stuff." Yep, only sisters got away with name-calling.

And that was it. Everyone had a place to stay. Something to be grateful for. Jenna took her lantern and left the office, falling in step behind the two families and their three little kids.

Aunt Edie was at the door to welcome everyone. She was wearing red slacks and a black sweatshirt and a Santa hat, which didn't go well with her hair or her coral lipstick. She'd completed her ensemble with her blinking Christmas-light necklace. It wasn't an outfit Courtney would approve of, but it did look festive.

"We're so glad to have you here with us," she said to the newcomers. "Gentlemen, you'll be sleeping in my niece's office here. Ladies, you're all upstairs and Celeste will show you to your rooms. After you've put away your things, everyone come on into the living room where we've got a good fire going in the wood-stove. I have water on for hot chocolate and hot but-tered rum."

One of the men rubbed his hands together. "All right. I haven't had hot buttered rum in years."

"Just give me the rum," the pill said under her breath as the women followed Celeste upstairs, leaving Jenna with a strong desire to bitch-slap her.

Darrell Wilson and his wife, whom he'd introduced as Kat, were already in the living room. She was en-sconced on the couch with a blanket over her and a steaming mug of something. She had dark circles under her eyes, but she was smiling. Jenna walked over and introduced herself.

"Your motel is charming," the woman told her.

"I'm sorry you haven't seen it at its best."

"Oh, I think I have," Kat said. "You've been noth-ing but kind, and you're certainly going the extra mile for us."

"Well, we can't have you all freezing to death in your rooms," Jenna said. Death! Why had she said that? Her cheeks burst into flames.

"It would make for bad reviews on Yelp," Kat re-marked, and the corners of her lips turned up.

Yelp. Let's not think about that, either.

The families were back now, the children bound-ing into the room with enough energy to power up all of Moonlight Harbor. If only they could find a way to harness that.

The parents followed at a more sedate pace and squeezed onto the couch and into the chairs, while the kids hit the floor. One of the boys spotted the pretzels and dived into the bowl.

"Christopher," his mother scolded. "Wait until you're offered."

He looked guilty and dropped his handful back into the bowl.

"Don't do that once you've taken them," she groaned and leaned over to fish out the contaminated ones.

"It's all right," said Aunt Edie. "Little boys love to eat."

The other boy positioned himself in front of Jolly Roger's cage. "Does your bird talk?"

"Yes, he does," said Aunt Edie, and the little girl came to the cage to check out Roger, too.

"Ask him if he's a pretty bird," Celeste suggested.

"Are you a pretty bird?" asked the boy.

"Roger's a pretty bird," Roger said, bobbing his head. "Give me whiskey."

That made the boy laugh. "What else can he say?"

"Ralph, Ralph," cried the bird. "Call the cops."

That had all three children giggling.

The giggles were overridden by the sound of thumping and a surprised screech. Jenna turned to see that one of the other sisters—Karen—had tripped on her way down the stairs and was bouncing down them like an oversize, misshapen beach ball. She landed with an *oomph*, her sister hurrying down the stairs after her.

The noble, kindhearted side of Jenna thought, *Oh, no!* The terrified motel manager side of her thought,

Don't sue! Both sides rushed to help the woman and ask, "Are you all right?"

"I'm fine," Karen assured her. "Just didn't watch where I was going." She tried to take a step and winced.

"Are you okay?" asked her sister.

"It's nothing, probably just a mild sprain. And we're not telling Doug about this," Karen added.

"For sure," her sister agreed.

Between Jenna and Lisa, they managed to get the injured party to the couch, where she joined Kat Wilson. Celeste brought a footstool, then vanished upstairs to the bathroom to find some Advil while Jenna hurried to the kitchen to get ice from the freezer while there was still ice to be had.

"I'm so sorry," Jenna said as she put the ice pack she'd made on the woman's ankle.

It was hard to tell if the ankle was swelling or not since Karen wasn't exactly small. What if it was broken? They had insurance. They'd be fine. *Please don't let it be broken.*

"It's nothing, really. I'm a klutz."

Such a good sport. Jenna could have kissed her.

Meanwhile, Aunt Edie was taking drink orders.

"The hot buttered rum is wonderful," said Kat Wilson.

"Now, that sounds like the perfect cure for what ails me," the accident victim said with a nod.

The other adults decided they'd try it, too, and Jenna was pleased to see that they were all smiling. Even the frowner managed a faint one, which gave Jenna hope that maybe they'd all survive being stranded in such close proximity.

As Aunt Edie distributed drinks, she told her captive audience the history of the motel. "My husband and I were one of the first ones to build a motel down here," she said. "He's gone now, God rest his soul, but I have my lovely niece to help me. We've only recently renovated it. I hope you all like your rooms."

The rooms they weren't in. They needed a change of subject fast.

Celeste the party-planner came to the rescue. "What's not to like about being at the beach? When the weather's nice," she added and was rewarded with a few chuckles. "I can tell you all, I've been coming here since I was a little girl, and Moonlight Harbor is the best place in the world. Well, next to Disneyland," she said, and winked at the kids. "But obviously, Mother Nature didn't get the memo that we were having a festival this weekend, and managed to mess things up. Still, my aunt's got plenty of wood in the stove and we've got plenty of hot buttered rum. So we may as well party while we're here."

"Good idea," Karen approved.

Celeste smiled, happy to find a kindred spirit. "I'm thinking it would be good to get to know each other a little bit. Let's go around the room and exchange names and where we're from. And what we like to do for fun."

She smiled at everyone around the room, and they all smiled back. Even the grump managed to force a smile. Jenna couldn't help admiring her younger sister for her ability to insert enjoyment into any situation.

"I'll go first," Celeste said, reminding Jenna of when they were kids.

No matter what game they played, her sister had always wanted to go first. This time Celeste was making

a concerted effort to break the ice, and Jenna appreci-
ated it. Ice-breaking wasn't her specialty.

"I'm Celeste," she said. "Aunt Edie is my great-aunt,
and Jenna here is my sister. My older sister," she added
with a teasing smile. That brought out some chuckles
and she continued, "I came down for the festival. You
may have seen me riding on the Driftwood Inn float.
I was the frozen mermaid," she finished, shaking her
head and bringing out more chuckles. She leaned over
to Jenna and gave her a goofy stare. "And who are you?"

"You've all met me," Jenna said. Oh, how she wished
it had been under different circumstances. "I recently
started managing the Driftwood Inn." *So pleeease be
patient with me.*

"She's also a massage therapist," Celeste said. "If
any of you are feeling stressed, she can help you relax."

"I'm sure I must be feeling stressed," joked Lisa.

"Just for that, you have to go next," Celeste said,
pointing at her.

"I'm Lisa Whitaker, and I came down with my older
sister, Karen, for a girls' weekend," she said, following in Celeste's teasing footsteps by emphasizing *older*
and making her sister frown. "The klutz," she added.

"Are you sure you didn't push me?" joked her sister.

"I'm still in the will, right? Inheriting everything?"
Lisa joked in response.

"Including Doug."

"Never mind. Take me out of the will."

"And what do you like to do for fun?" Celeste
prompted. "When you're not trying to bump off your sis."

"I love to play tennis and dance," Lisa said. "And
read. We both do." She smiled at her sibling.

"My wife's a big reader," put in Darrell Wilson. "She has a blog."

"Yeah? What's your blog?" Lisa asked.

"Under the Covers with Kat."

"Oh, my gosh! Really? I follow that blog," said Karen. "I'm Karen Owens. I've actually won a couple of your book giveaways."

"Karen Crazy Quilter?" asked Kat.

Karen nodded eagerly. Then her smile grew pinched. "I've been reading about your battle with cancer. I just want you to know how much I admire you."

Kat blushed at that. "There's nothing admirable about having cancer."

"There is when you're fighting it with such a good attitude," said Karen.

Kat's fingers slipped up to touch the black knit cap on her head as she murmured a thank-you, and Jenna, seeing her discomfort, moved them on.

Introductions continued. Sarah and Taylor and their husbands, Chris and Greg, were from the Seattle area.

"When you're not coming to the beach for adventure, what do you do for fun?" Celeste asked Sarah.

"I like to read, go out to lunch with my girlfriends whenever I can," Sarah said. "I'm a stay-at-home mom, and I need a break every once in a while."

Celeste turned to the sister. "What about you, Taylor?"

"I'm a real estate agent," the woman said.

"Oh, very cool. I'd have done that," Karen told her, "except drawing up those contracts looked way too complicated."

"So she settled for being a math teacher," Lisa said.

"Which is so much easier than writing contracts, right?" she teased.

"You'd have had no problem with real estate," Taylor said to her.

"My husband, Darrell, is a math teacher," Kat said.

"Come to the dark side. We have pi," Darrell quipped.

"Oh, yes," Karen said. "But I'm retired now. I'm done with the dark side."

"Sometimes I'd like to be," Darrell said. "But we need the insurance." The minute the words were out of his mouth, he looked like he wished he could swallow his tongue.

His wife reached out a hand to him and he took it. "He's my hero," she said.

"That's what guys like to hear," said the man named Greg.

"Just for that, you'll have to go next," Celeste told him. "But first." She turned her attention to the kids. "Okay, guys, tell us who your favorite comic book hero is."

The kids, who had gone through the snacks and were starting to look bored, came to life and joined the conversation. The adults listened indulgently and soon were sharing more about themselves.

The Marshes and the Browns had never been to Moonlight Harbor. They'd taken advantage of Jenna's Groupon offer and come down for the festival. The older sister, Sarah, and her husband, Chris, seemed amiable and happily married. Her younger sister, Taylor, and her husband, Greg, were along for the ride but not enjoying it. While the other couples sat close with arms around each other, Greg sat on one side of the room and Taylor was on the floor with their daughter. There was no smile for him, no softening of her features when he talked. They were the powder keg couple, ready to blow up at any minute. They were trying to hide the tension between them, but ever since her divorce Jenna had developed a sixth sense for that sort of thing. She could feel it, almost hear it thrumming. She only hoped their toxicity didn't ruin this forced togetherness for everyone else.

"What do you do for a living?" Darrell asked Greg.

"Actually, I've just started a company."

"Trying to," his wife corrected, looking far from happy about it.

Ah. There it was, the match to the powder keg. "Well," Jenna said heartily. "I'm sure you're all hungry. We do have food on hand for anyone who doesn't want to go out in search of it—tuna or peanut-butter-and-jelly sandwiches, some fruit and chips. We'll have a spread set up for you on the dining table in a few minutes."

"Sounds great to me," said Karen Owens. "I'm in for the night. And we have beef jerky we can share."

"Plus cookies," added her sister, Lisa. "Not that they're as good as what we've had here."

"We're in for the night, too," Darrell Wilson said.

"And us," said Chris Brown.

The moment of tension passed, and Jenna let out in inward sigh of relief. Maybe, if the subject of Greg Marsh's business was avoided, everyone would have a nice evening.

She checked in with Brody as she and Aunt Edie prepared the evening feast. "What are you feeding the multitude over there?"

"Got the grill up and running, and we're barbecuing salmon," he said.

Brody's guests had landed at the five-star house. Lucky them. She called Tyrella and learned she was serving homemade potato soup and French bread. Courtney had fruit, brie cheese and crackers, as well as wine for her gang. The two men had also contributed wine, and the newlyweds had brought leftover wedding cake.

And Jenna was serving tuna sandwiches. She hoped none of the guests had an opportunity to compare their culinary experiences. *We have hot buttered rum*, she reminded herself, and took comfort in that.

"Tuna sandwiches are great," Seth told her when he came in. "Everybody loves tuna sandwiches."

It would appear that way. No one complained about the food they were offered, not even Taylor, as they gathered around the spread on the dining table. Maybe listening to Pete, who was always around for the food, had inhibited her.

"This storm is nothing," he said, as he grabbed a sandwich. "You know, back in the forties in Eastern Washington, nobody had power. Ever. My gram cooked on a woodstove all her life."

"Well, I'm glad I don't normally have to," Aunt Edie said. "I like my modern conveniences."

"Women today are spoiled," Pete said, earning nasty looks from all the women present. It was time for Pete to go to his kitchen bunk.

After dinner, Karen and Lisa shared their cookies and some of their chocolate, which made the kids happy, and Celeste, who taught first grade and loved kids, played games with them, which made them even happier.

Around nine, Kat excused herself. "I hate to leave, but I'm kind of tired."

Kind of? The poor woman looked like a zombie.

"Of course," Jenna said, ready to escort her upstairs.

"I'll see you to your room, babe," said Darrell, and since Celeste had already given Kat towels and showed her where she was going to sleep, Jenna stayed put and let them have some privacy.

Not that there'd be much privacy for anyone. Kat was in Sabrina's room with Sarah and Taylor, sleeping in Sabrina's bed while the sisters shared an inflatable mattress. Karen and Lisa were stuck in the doll room with Jenna and Celeste. The kids were going to be put in the office to sleep until the grown-ups went to bed, then the dads would cart them into the living room, where they could stay warm by the woodstove. Chris and Greg would take the office and Pete was bunking on a cot in the kitchen with Seth. In short, there'd be bodies everywhere. It made Jenna think of youth group lock-ins at church when she was a teenager, giant non-slumber parties where the kids would spend the night in the church and stay up until dawn playing games. She'd loved those parties.

But she'd known everyone there. This she wasn't so sure about.

The grown-ups got the kids settled, then hung out a little longer to visit, enjoying another drink and, in Karen's case, more Advil. By ten thirty, everyone was pretty much done for the day, and people scattered to their respective sleeping corners.

"This is an interesting room," Karen said diplomatically as she and her sister and Celeste and Jenna settled in for the night. They'd given the guests the bed and they were on the floor with another air mattress, right next to the three-foot-high doll.

"My aunt's a doll collector," Jenna explained.

"They don't come alive at night, do they?" Lisa asked, eyeing the clown doll on the dresser. "That little guy makes me think of a Stephen King book I read."

"Don't worry," Celeste said. "They're very quiet."

Lisa slid down in the bed and pulled the covers over her face. "Don't let him get me, Celeste," she said, and Celeste giggled.

"Oh, brother," Karen said in disgust. "Shutting off the light now, which means it's time for you to shut your mouth."

Yep, it wasn't hard to tell who the younger sisters were in this room. Jenna dug deeper under her covers and smiled. These two made good roommates. She hoped everyone in the other room was adjusting, as well.

Chapter Seventeen

"Did Santa come?" Miranda murmured as Greg transplanted her, sleeping bag and all, from the office to the couch in the living room.

"Not yet, baby," Taylor said, kneeling beside her. "Santa's still getting ready to leave the North Pole." What if they got stranded in this town and didn't make it home in time for Christmas? The gifts from Santa were at the house, hidden in the garage. "Go back to sleep."

Miranda sighed and settled against her pillow. "Okay. I love you, Mommy. I love you, Daddy."

"We love you, too," Taylor said, and kissed her cheek. Their finances were a mess and their marriage was sick, but Miranda was the one thing they'd gotten right.

"'Night, baby girl," Greg said. He, too, kissed her, then followed Taylor from the room, stepping over the cousins, whom Chris and Sarah had just settled on the floor.

The woodstove cast a soft glow over the room. The Christmas tree sat in a corner in all its finery. It was a charming family picture, but Taylor was in no mood to appreciate it.

"'Night, sweets," Chris said to Sarah at the bottom of the stairs and kissed her.

Taylor slipped past them, up the stairs, without a word to her husband.

"You could at least have said good-night to him," Sarah scolded as they reached the landing.

"And pretend that everything's great? What's the point of faking it in front of you?"

"How long are you going to make him pay for trying to start a business?"

It wasn't hard to see whose side Sarah was on. "A business he plunged into without even talking to me. Maybe you should ask him how long he's going to make *us* pay?"

"He told Chris things are about to turn around. Can't you hang in there a little longer?"

"He's been saying that for months, and trust me, they're not. We can't keep living on dreams. You know, I thought you'd be on my side."

"I am on your side," Sarah insisted. "I want you guys to get through this."

Taylor said nothing to that. She wasn't sure what to say. Wasn't sure what she wanted. She'd reached the point where she wondered if she even loved her husband anymore. Could you be so mad at someone that the heat of your anger fried all those tender feelings? She'd never thought so until recently.

"He's got us in quicksand. You know that."

"If you'd just let Chris help you with a budget," Sarah began.

Taylor whirled around. "We don't need a budget. We

need money. Is Mr. Knows Everything going to manufacture some for us?"

"He could help you. Taylor, you've been spending money like you've got it. You guys need to get it together. You can't keep racking up the credit card debt."

It was so easy for her sister to be judgmental. Taylor would like to see how well Sarah would do in *her* shoes.

"How am I supposed to pay the bills?" she hissed. "If you want to lecture someone, why don't you lecture Greg? He's the one who needs it."

"So do you," Sarah hissed back.

Taylor could feel the sting of tears in her eyes. Again. It seemed that lately she was either fuming or crying. Her life had gone from perfect to an out-of-control roller-coaster ride, and she couldn't shake the feeling that any moment the car wouldn't make the turn and she'd go flying off into space.

She marched into the bedroom, wishing she could slam the door. She couldn't. Kat Wilson was in bed asleep.

Now, there's a woman with something to complain about, but she's not complaining, is she? whispered her conscience.

Well, good for her. Taylor was no Kat Wilson. And Greg was no Darrell Wilson. Darrell was willing to do anything for his wife. Greg wasn't. If he was, he'd have pulled his dead business off life support by now.

He kept saying he was doing this for all of them, but that was a lie. He was doing it for himself, wanting to become a big-shot businessman, a millionaire before he hit forty. When he'd first jumped off the financial cliff he'd claimed he wanted to give Taylor the lifestyle she deserved. But she'd been happy with the lifestyle they had.

What made her unhappy was insecurity, and they now had that to the max. Where was it all going to end? There was the question that kept her awake nights.

A waning crescent moon provided no light, and she had to fumble blindly to find her cami and pajama bottoms. The room was arctic. This was like being at camp. In Alaska. In January. She changed quickly and settled onto the air mattress on the floor, pulling the pile of quilts over her.

She could hear Sarah rustling around, getting ready for bed, felt the mattress bounce when her sister got on it. She didn't whisper good-night. Neither did Sarah.

There was still no power the following morning. Jenna got up and restarted a fire in the woodstove. The kids slept through it. She filled the kettle with water and put it on the stove to heat. Thank God they weren't on a well and could flush toilets and wash up, even if the water was cold. Although with this many people in the house, that might be interesting.

The food they had would, hopefully, get them through the next twenty-four hours. She'd love to have used the milk left in the fridge but decided against it. The milk was probably fine, but there was no sense in taking chances.

She was setting out plastic silverware and napkins when Aunt Edie came in. "My, I slept late," said her aunt.

Unlike Jenna, who was exhausted and felt like Atlas in drag, holding the entire world on her shoulders, Aunt

Edie looked chipper and refreshed. She'd put on a red sweatshirt over her elastic-waist jeans and was wearing her Santa hat. Aunt Edie was in her element with houseguests to fuss over and feed.

"Did you sleep all right?" Jenna asked.

"Oh, yes. But I felt bad having a room to myself when all you girls are doubling up."

"We're fine," Jenna said, speaking for everyone else and hoping it was true.

"Well, now," Aunt Edie said. "I've got some canned milk and a lot of oatmeal. What if we have cinnamon oatmeal for breakfast? Do you think everyone will like that?"

It sounded good to Jenna. "I'm sure everyone will love it." She thought of the sour-faced Taylor Marsh. Almost everyone anyway.

Slowly the house came awake, with the kids up first and getting fed. Jenna couldn't tell whether it was Aunt Edie's hot chocolate or the brown sugar in the oatmeal or simply the need to burn energy, but by eight thirty they were bouncing off the walls. Poor Jolly Roger was happy to stay safe inside his cage and keep begging for whiskey.

Jenna was glad when Celeste came down and jumped in to entertain them, settling them on the living room floor and teaching them how to play Spoons, a dangerous game involving cards and diving for a limited number of spoons. When they'd played it as kids with Mom and Aunt Edie and Uncle Ralph, they'd all come away with scratches. But they'd loved it, and so did these kids. And when they tired of Spoons, Celeste found a penny to hide and sent them all over the house looking for it.

Meanwhile, the other adults were up, and the men got busy bringing in more wood for the stove while the women congregated in the kitchen and speculated as to when the power might come back on.

"It would be great if it came on today," said Lisa, who was seated at the table with her sister and Kat Wilson. "Then we could at least get in some shopping."

Karen, who had taken another painkiller earlier—"One for the road"—stuck out her foot and rotated it. "I'm ready for that."

"I'll go check to see if the stores are open," Jenna told them. "I'm sure some of them have generators."

"Yeah, but isn't everything computerized now?" wondered Karen. "I doubt they'll be able to take our credit cards if their machines aren't working."

"Some of our merchants still have the tools to do that the old-fashioned way," Jenna said. Didn't they? They had to.

"They can always take cash and write you a receipt," said Aunt Edie. "Sometimes I think with all our new-fangled technology things haven't really changed for the better. People are lost when they have to make do without it."

"I know how to make do," said Karen. "We eat chocolate. In fact, I have some left."

"You can never go wrong with chocolate," Sarah said with an approving nod, and even her sister smiled.

"I'll go get it," Karen said.

"Let me," offered Lisa.

"No, you stay put. I need to move," Karen insisted and left the room, barely limping.

Kat sighed. "I'd love to buy some fancy shells."

"You can get some for free on our beach," Jenna told her, then wished she could cut out her tongue. Kat was thin enough to blow away in a breeze, let alone a strong wind. She probably didn't have the energy for beachcombing.

Her husband walked through at that moment, his arms laden with wood. "I'll make sure you get some shells, babe."

"You have such a nice husband," Taylor said to her.

She said it so wistfully, Jenna couldn't help feeling sorry for her. Taylor's husband had to be a major cause of her grumpiness. He seemed like a nice guy, too, but Jenna knew from experience that a man could present one face to the world and quite another to his wife.

"I've been blessed," Kat admitted. "We've been having some tough times lately. I don't know how I'd be getting through them if I didn't have Darrell."

Karen returned to the kitchen carrying an empty candy bag. "Okay, Miss Piggy," she said to her sister, "you could've told me you ate the last few pieces."

"I didn't eat your chocolate," Lisa said. "You probably finished it off last night and forgot. Dementia's settling in early," she joked.

Her sister wasn't amused. "There were almost a dozen chocolate kisses left. Now there's nothing but air, you sneaky little chocoholic."

"Well, I didn't eat them," Lisa insisted.

Celeste came into the kitchen just then, giving clues to the little boy named James. "You're getting warmer," she coached as he moved in the direction of the canisters, her latest hiding spot.

"There's your culprit," teased Jenna. "Celeste, have you been in Karen Owen's chocolates?"

"Chocolate? There was chocolate in our room and my radar missed it?"

James stilled a moment, then frenetically renewed his search. His mother studied him, her brows dipping. "James, come here a minute."

He came, not looking her in the eye. Jenna knew what that meant. Probably every woman in the room knew what that meant.

Sarah turned him to face her and studied his mouth. Sure enough, there was a dab of chocolate at one corner. "Did you find some chocolate when you were playing your hunt-the-penny game?"

He bit his lip and studied his feet.

"Did you?" his mother prompted.

He nodded and his lower lip began to wobble.

"James," she chided, "that wasn't yours to take. That's stealing."

The little boy burst into tears. "It was on the bed."

"In someone's room. You just took it and you didn't ask permission."

"Better his tummy than my thighs," Karen hurried to say.

"You need to tell Mrs. Owens you're sorry," Sarah instructed her son.

"I'm sorry," he said in a small voice.

"It's okay," Karen said, looking uncomfortable.

"It's never okay to take what doesn't belong to you," Sarah said, her expression stern. Now James was really crying. "But we still love you," she said, and pulled him to her for a hug.

The hug didn't help, and as soon as he was free the little boy ran from the room.

"Guess we're not the only ones who need to get it together," Taylor murmured.

Her sister's eyes narrowed. "And what's that supposed to mean?"

Taylor shrugged. "Maybe that you're not so perfect, either."

"Oh, that's mature!"

"I never claimed to be mature. Or to know it all," Taylor shot back.

They had a whopper of a storm brewing right there in the kitchen. "I think I'll go on a scouting mission," Jenna said, and slipped from the room. As she passed through the living room, she saw her sister on the couch with the unhappy little boy, while his brother and cousin sat on the floor, watching.

"Santa won't come now 'cause I was bad," he sobbed.

Ah, the Santa business.

"Santa understands that we all do wrong things sometimes," Celeste told him. "You said you were sorry, and I'm sure Santa heard that." She looked over the boy's head at Jenna and a silent message passed between them. *How am I doing?... Great.*

Which was more than they could say for the boys' mom as voices were beginning to rise in the kitchen.

The kids had bigger concerns. "What if we don't get home by Christmas?" James worried. "How will he find us?"

Jenna was about to step in and assure the children that Santa would find them no matter what, when her sister said, "You know, that's a good point. How about you write him some letters to tell him you might still be at the beach? You write them and I'll mail them."

Brilliant, Celeste. It not only reassured their three worried little guests, it was also yet another activity to keep them busy.

"But how will he get them?" asked Miranda.

"I've got that covered. I'll make sure he gets them. Okay?"

The children all nodded eagerly, and Celeste went to get writing paper.

That took care of the kids. Now, if they could find something to keep the adults happy… Jenna put on her coat and left in search of stores that might be open.

One by one, the other women in the kitchen had all slipped away as the sisters escalated their argument. "You can stop the snotty attitude anytime now," Sarah finally snapped. "It's really wearing thin."

"Well, so is your superior attitude," Taylor snapped back. "You know, you don't have to be in charge of my life. We're not kids anymore."

Sarah cocked an eyebrow. "Then maybe you should stop acting like one."

Taylor could think of no reply to that, so she shot up from the table and marched out of the kitchen. Almost everyone had gathered in the living room now, and she could feel their gazes on her as she hurried through. Every man and woman there was judging her, she knew it.

And maybe they should. Maybe she was behaving like a child. But darn, she was so sick of her sister acting like…a big sister. Sarah had always been bossy. She needed to outgrow that.

And Taylor had always been…hmm. Okay, the baby of the family. Spoiled. Bratty. And now she was going upstairs to…what? Pout? Give herself a time-out?

Her nephew wasn't the only one who needed to say he was sorry. She did need to apologize to her sister. Maybe to all the women for making an uncomfortable scene in the kitchen.

She plopped down on the window seat and looked out at the sky. It was still gray, but at least the wind had settled down. The storm had passed. Outside anyway.

She was still stewing over her bad behavior when, a few minutes later, Kat Wilson slipped into the room. "I thought I'd rest for a bit. I hope you don't mind."

"No," Taylor lied. "I love my sister," she blurted.

"Of course, you do," Kat said, settling on the bed. "But sisters fight sometimes. I have one myself. I know. Funny how, when you get a life-threatening disease, some of those little things you squabble over just don't seem to matter."

It was said kindly, with a smile, yet it produced more guilt than any of Sarah's lectures. "I've been under a lot of pressure lately," Taylor said. "Of course, it's nothing compared to what you must be going through," she hurried to add.

"We all go through hard things."

Taylor sighed. "I don't know how you can smile."

"What's the alternative? Waste time feeling sorry for myself and being angry?"

Taylor had been doing plenty of that. It hadn't felt

like a waste of time. "You have such a great husband," she said, and realized she was jealous.

"He's a wonderful guy. We've been married thirty years. We came down here for our anniversary. Have I mentioned that? Chemo brain." She shook her head.

"Some anniversary," said Taylor.

"I'm having fun. It's kind of an adventure, really. Better than some of what we've been through."

"Like what? If you don't mind me asking."

"A lot of stuff many people go through. We lost a baby. Our first. That was hard. We had our share of financial struggles, too, but then everyone does at some time or other."

"How did you survive all that?" Taylor wanted to know.

"By putting everything in perspective. What was having to do without a few things compared to losing a child?" Kat sighed and shut her eyes. "Even though it was awful, in the end it brought us closer. The best asset you ever have is each other."

Taylor sighed, too. Then she went to find her sister and apologize.

But Greg. She still wasn't sure if he was an asset or a liability.

Chapter Eighteen

Jenna left the house, hoping she'd find stores open. That would go a long way toward making her guests happy. Most of them, at any rate.

She ran into Seth in the parking lot. "How's it going?" he asked.

"So far nobody's murdered anyone, although I thought we might come close this morning. I'm off to see if any of the shops are open. That way people can get out."

"Good idea. Pete and I are going to do some clam digging later when low tide hits, so anyone who's interested can join us. If Tyrella's open, she'll probably have rubber boots for sale."

Jenna couldn't envision the stylish and cranky Taylor in a pair of rubber boots out in the cold, digging in the mud for clams, or any of the other women for that matter, but she suspected the men and the kids would enjoy the experience.

"I'll pass that on," she said. "And thanks for everything you're doing."

"Going hunting for anything, especially clams, is no hardship for a guy," he said.

"And here I thought you were being so heroic."

"That, too."

"Seriously, I don't know what I would've done without you in all this."

"I'm there for you, Jenna."

When his voice softened and she caught the hint of tenderness in his eyes, she couldn't help wondering if something could work out between them. Someday... "I owe you," she said, her own voice getting a little mushy. Maybe, like Brody, he'd take that as an invitation to ask for a kiss. Or more.

He didn't. "You don't owe me anything and you know it. How about we build a beach fire tonight?"

That brought back memories and made Jenna's heart skip. The last time she and Seth had sat on the beach together, their driftwood fire had been nothing compared to the combustion they were creating between the two of them. Was he remembering that?

She waited a beat in the hope that he'd allude to it. He didn't. "A fire sounds good," she said. "I'll see if any of our other guests want to join in, as well."

Although a fire with just Seth and her *really* sounded good. She told herself to stop indulging in stupid daydreams as she made her way to town. Her Romance Road was pitted with holes and lined with brambles, and she didn't need to be dragging a reluctant Prince Charming down it. Anyway, he wasn't the only prince out there. She had time to find her way to her fairy-tale castle and her happy ending.

Meanwhile, she turned her attention to the task of checking out the shopping. The air hummed with the sound of generators as she drove around town, and she saw a faint glow in the windows of the little cabana shops. Cindy's Candies was open, and she stopped in to pick up some chocolate to replace Karen's depleted stash.

"I'm glad to see you're open," she said to Cindy, who was bundled up in a jacket and fingerless gloves. She was wearing a headband with felt reindeer antlers and a smile.

"It's freezing in here and we're back to the Stone Age," she told Jenna, "but we're doing business."

To prove it, a trio of women walked in. "Wow, look at all this," said one.

"Better stock up in case we're stuck here for Christmas," said another.

Jenna decided to follow their example and filled a basket with saltwater taffy. At another shop she found some cheap Christmas stockings and bought those, too, just in case. Although she hoped it wouldn't come to just in case. If only she'd set an earlier date for the festival. They wouldn't be in this mess now.

"You couldn't know," Kiki consoled her when she stopped in at Something Fishy for some trinkets to stuff in those stockings. "Anyway, this is all working out. Thank God I still have my manual credit card imprint machine. It pays to hang on to things."

It was certainly going to pay off for Kiki. The shop was crowded with people milling around, checking out the baseball caps, shot glasses, T-shirts imprinted with pictures of sharks, and abalone jewelry.

Her next stop was the hardware store where Tyrella was also selling merchandise the old-fashioned way. She, too, had plenty of customers.

"How are my people doing?" Jenna asked her.

"I left them eating the cinnamon rolls I took out of the freezer and drinking hot cider. I suspect by now they're all out shopping or beachcombing for post-storm treasure. And that toddler, what a doll. Of course, we're finding it a challenge to keep him away from the wood-stove."

"I don't know what I'd have done without you," Jenna said. How did you ever repay friends who went such a long extra mile?

Tyrella waved away her gratitude. "You'd have managed."

"I think some of my people will be in later for rubber boots. Pete and Seth plan on leading a clam-digging expedition. And we're going to build a bonfire on the beach, so if anyone at your end wants to come, they're welcome."

"Sounds like fun," Tyrella said. "Can I come, too?"

"You have to ask? Of course!"

Jenna extended the same offer to Brody when she ran into him outside the hardware store. "Sounds great," he said. "But even by the fire it'll probably be cold. You might need someone to warm you up."

"And you're just the man for the job?" she joked.

"Glad to see you realize that."

Maybe she was beginning to. Getting warm next to Brody was tempting, but with so many people around, the only sparks flying would be from the wood.

Jenna's last stop was the food bank, run by Bob and Sandra Harley and staffed by volunteers from the various churches in town. It had been turned into an emergency supply depot, offering oil lamps, candles, socks, scarves and coats, as well as food. Most of the food was gone, but Jenna did manage to score a couple of cans of chili and another bottle of juice.

"How's everyone doing over at the Driftwood?" asked Pastor Paul, one of the volunteers on duty.

"We're surviving," Jenna said. "But I'm praying hard that the road will be cleared by Christmas."

"I think we all are," he said. "But if that prayer doesn't get answered, there's probably a reason."

Not what Jenna wanted to hear. She wanted her daughter back home.

And she wanted her mother. Funny how, even when you were a mother yourself, you never outgrew that.

She put in a call, in the hope that her mom was on break and could answer her cell.

"I was just going to call you," said Mel. "Are you doing okay? You've made the local news up here, and it looks awful."

"We're making do," Jenna said, and filled her in.

"How nice that everyone's pulling together," Mel said. "What an experience for your guests. They'll be talking about their storm adventure for weeks."

"Not all of them in a good way," Jenna said, then went on to tell her mother about the unhappy Taylor.

"It sounds like something's amiss there," Mel said. "People aren't unhappy for no reason."

"You're right. I think they've got some money problems. I just wish she'd keep her misery to herself. She and her sister got into it this morning, and it was really uncomfortable to be around."

"That is awkward," Mel agreed.

"I don't remember Celeste and me fighting like that," Jenna said.

"That's because you didn't. Well, rarely," Mel amended. "You two were always there for each other. Maybe that was because of losing your father so young. We were all we had and we had to stick together. Family's important."

"Maybe somebody needs to tell that to Taylor Marsh," Jenna said.

"Let's hope at some point she'll figure it out for herself, which is the best way to learn those life lessons."

"As in *don't butt in*? Don't worry. I wasn't planning to. I've got my hands full keeping everyone fed and entertained."

"I'm sure you're doing an excellent job."

"Between Celeste and Aunt Edie and me, I think we've got it covered." And Brody, Tyrella, Courtney and Seth. Even Pete, who was pitching in, not to mention all the volunteers in town doling out emergency supplies, and the businesses doing their best to stay open for the trapped festival attendees. Talk about a group effort.

"I'm afraid my break's over," Mel said. "I need to get back to work."

Jenna was reluctant to let her go. "I wish you were here. Well, except we don't exactly have the best living conditions at the moment." So, it was just as well she wasn't.

"I'll be there for Christmas," her mom promised. "Or as soon as the road's clear."

Oh, please let that be by Christmas.

Jenna said goodbye to her mom and made her way back home. She arrived to find Celeste had the kids bundled up and ready to go beachcombing. "We're going to see if we can find some good crafting material so we can make some special presents for the parents," she told Jenna.

"Fabulous!" When it came to keeping kids busy, Celeste was a regular idea factory. Of course, it helped that she was a teacher.

"We wrote letters to Santa," Miranda told Jenna, "and Miss Celeste mailed them Reindeer Express."

"That'll get them there," Jenna said. Reindeer Express, the same mail service their mother had used when they were little and writing to Santa. Mom would love it.

The thought of her mom possibly not making it down for Christmas saddened her. The idea of her daughter not being home at Christmas was downright depressing. *Santa, please come through for us all and get that road open.*

"Reggie Hinkle says there's no such thing as Santa," announced Christopher, the oldest boy.

Was it Jenna's imagination or did kids stop believing in Santa at increasingly younger ages? "Those presents must come from somewhere," she said. Kids should believe in magic and happy endings as long as possible.

"And he who doesn't believe doesn't receive," added Celeste.

He smiled and shrugged. "That's why I wrote the letter."

Hedging his bets. Good plan.

"Okay, guys," Celeste said, "let's go see if we can find some rocks and shells to paint."

She took the kids out for their field trip, and Jenna shared the news that the shops were open, and her guests scattered like leaves in a strong wind. Except for Kat, who decided she was perfectly happy parked on the couch by the fire with a book.

"You won't miss me, then," Darrell told her. "I have to run a secret errand for Santa," he said with a wink.

"Don't go spending a lot," she cautioned.

He made no promises, just kissed her goodbye and scooted out the door.

Jenna found herself feeling a little jealous. As far as men were concerned, there were still plenty of winners out there. What had she done to deserve a loser?

You picked him, she reminded herself. And at least they'd had a lovely daughter. Feeling the need to connect with her baby, she put in a call.

Sabrina sure wasn't suffering stuck up north with Daddy and the grandparents. "We're going to *Disney on Ice* this afternoon," she informed Jenna. "Then Grandma and Grandpa are taking me to Red Robin."

Obviously, her daughter's life wasn't being ruined by the fact that she couldn't get home. "I'm glad you're having fun," Jenna said. And it was probably just as well Sabrina wasn't stranded without her hair dryer or a way to charge her iPod. She certainly wouldn't have been thrilled at having to share her room. Jenna wisely chose not to mention the fact that it was currently overrun with strangers.

Still, even though it was all for the best... "I sure miss you, sweetie."

"But tomorrow's Christmas Eve. Daddy will be bringing me back then, right?"

"If the road's finally clear."

"It *has* to be," Sabrina said. "I don't want to spend

Christmas up here with Aurora. I want to be with you and Grandma and Aunt Celeste and Aunt Edie. All my presents are down there," she added. "And Tristan was going to come over."

This was news to Jenna.

"It'll be clear by tomorrow," Sabrina insisted as if saying would make it so.

"I hope it will," Jenna said. "But if not, we'll do Christmas as soon as you get down here."

"With eggnog cake?"

"With eggnog cake."

"Don't open my present to you until I'm there."

"I won't," Jenna assured her.

"I wish I'd stayed home," Sabrina grumbled.

"Come on, now," Jenna coaxed. "You've had fun with Daddy and the grandparents, right?"

"Yeah, but Aurora doesn't like me, and she hogs him. And I miss Tristan. And Jennifer and Hudson and I were going to do presents tomorrow, and I was going to ask Seth to build us a beach fire. And the youth choir is supposed to sing for the Christmas Eve candlelight service."

Ah, yes, her daughter was definitely plugging in here at the beach. "Well, let's hope they get the road cleared," was all Jenna could say. She decided not to share that there'd be clam digging and a beach fire later that night. Then her daughter, who was being taken to an ice show and a popular restaurant chain, would feel deprived. "But if they don't, we'll make up for it when you're back."

"Okay," Sabrina said, resigned to her fate.

"I love you, baby. I'm sorry you're not here."

"I love you, too, Mom."

Jenna ended the call with a sigh. She'd envisioned a very different holiday than the one she was getting.

Taylor picked up a pair of silver earrings shaped like sand dollars from a display in Beachcomber, a shop with all manner of chick-centric treats. Two years earlier she would've bought them. Now she could only wish to buy them. Aware of her sister hovering at her elbow, she put them back.

"Would you like those?" Sarah asked.

"No. I don't need them." It almost felt good to be noble. (Did passing up cute earrings qualify as noble? She hoped so.) She'd apologized to Sarah but still felt guilty over her behavior, and it was making their shopping outing more uncomfortable for her than pleasant.

"I didn't ask if you needed them."

Sarah picked up the earrings, and Taylor laid a hand on her arm. "No, don't. Really."

"I want to. For Christmas."

"This trip was our Christmas present," Taylor said.

"And some present it turned out to be. Let me buy the earrings, Tay. I can afford it."

There it was again, the reminder that at least one of them had her act together. "No, don't, please," Taylor said, and then distracted her sister by directing her attention to a display of candles embedded with shells that Taylor would've loved to be able to afford. Sarah snapped one up, as well as a dish towel with a quarter moon on it that said *I Heart Moonlight Harbor*. Taylor drifted over to another section of the store and checked out a collection of party dip mixes, all the while wishing she'd stayed at the house.

She hated going from store to store, each visit a reminder that she had no money to spend and no way to pay the bills they already had.

At the kite shop Sarah purchased kites for the boys and a little mermaid doll for Miranda and a puzzle. "In case we don't make it home in time for Christmas."

"Please don't say that," Taylor said.

"It could happen. Best to be prepared."

At Books and Beans, Sarah bought them both lattes. All purchases made with cash, because of course credit was for losers who had to live from paycheck to paycheck. That, according to Chris, Mr. Knows Everything.

Maybe Chris had the right idea, though. After all, who could afford earrings and who couldn't? Still, if Greg hadn't quit his job…their finances still would've been a mess. They'd been living beyond their means long before that final nail hit the coffin.

And had that all been Greg's fault? How many unnecessary purchases had she charged while rationalizing why she needed them?

Okay, so she'd played her part, but he was still the archvillain. Thanks to him and his stubborn refusal to sign the death certificate for his dead company, she was trailing her sister from half-lit shop to half-lit shop, watching her spend money on kites and candles while Taylor wondered how they were going to make their next house payment. No matter whether she was marooned here at Moonlight Harbor or at home surrounded by presents she couldn't afford and shouldn't have bought—either way, her life was a mess.

They were walking to the car when Chris called Sarah to tell her a clamming expedition was planned for later and asking her to pick up rubber boots for him and the boys at the hardware store. "I guess we're having a beach fire tonight, too," she said to Taylor once she'd told her about Chris's request.

That should have sounded like fun. Taylor frowned.

"I have to get rubber boots for the clam diggers. Want to come in?" Sarah asked as they pulled up in front of the hardware store.

Taylor had seen enough things she couldn't afford. She shook her head. "No. I'll wait here."

"Okay. I won't be long."

Taylor watched as her sister ran into the store. She seemed positively lighthearted, which was funny considering the fact that Sarah had always been the more serious one.

She'd gotten married long before Taylor had met Greg, putting her in a different world. Then she'd had the boys and moved to a different universe, where life was about back-to-school shopping, staying current on immunizations, trying to find an SUV they could afford. Back then, it seemed that her sister's life had consisted of penny-pinching and drudgery. Taylor had found it hard to identify. She and Greg had student loans, but Greg had made good money. She'd worked part-time and had plenty to spend. Even after Miranda came along, they'd been okay. Some hospital bills to pay that insurance hadn't covered, but so what? They had money. Funny, now they didn't, and she was the one whose life consisted of penny-pinching and drudgery, and her sister was carefree, happily running into stores to drop a wad of bills.

Actually, it wasn't funny. Not at all.

Sarah was back out in ten minutes, carrying a big, plastic bag filled with rubber boots. "I got some for Miranda, too," she said as she tossed them into the back seat.

"You didn't need to do that," said Taylor, torn between resentment and gratitude.

"Her tennis shoes will probably be wet from beachcombing, and she's going to want to go clamming," Sarah said. "You don't want her to miss out."

"You're right, I don't." Taylor didn't want her daughter to miss out on anything. What was she going to miss out on if their finances kept spiraling downward? Only the other day she'd been asking if she could have ballet lessons.

"I hate this," Taylor said, jaw clenched. "I hate that we don't have any money and that you're paying for everything. I hate being where we are." Sarah opened her mouth to speak, but Taylor cut her off. "And don't say Chris will help us with a budget."

"Tay, everyone needs help once in a while."

"Then how about a loan?" That was what they needed.

"Would that turn you into a better money manager?"

"It would turn me into a happier person," Taylor muttered. Except did she really want a loan from her sister and brother-in-law? She didn't even want rubber boots. "You're right," she said with a sigh. "A loan wouldn't change the real problem."

"Which is?" As if Sarah didn't know.

"Greg. He's thrown us all in quicksand. His business is a disaster but he won't give up on it. We're going to wind up bankrupt. Even if I sell my car like you keep telling me to do and we eat nothing but rice and beans, how's that going to help if he keeps hanging on to a business that's going nowhere?"

"I don't know, Tay," Sarah admitted. "I'm really sorry."

"We're going to lose our house," Taylor fretted. "We're going to wind up losing everything." Tears erupted, and she scrambled in her coat pocket for a tissue.

"Hey," her sister said, laying a hand on her arm. "No one's going to let you end up on the street. You know that."

More kindness from her big sister after she'd been such a brat—it made her cry all the harder.

"I think we'd better go see if that candy store is open," Sarah said and started the car.

"You going to replace the candy James took?"

"James is going to replace the candy James took… out of his allowance. But that's not the main reason. I think you need chocolate."

No, she needed money. But she wouldn't turn down chocolate.

They found the candy shop open and decked out for the holidays, a tree standing in the corner with multi-colored lights, tinsel garlands and ornaments shaped like lollipops and peppermint twists. A wreath of peppermint discs hung on one wall and a sign claiming *Santa Shops Here* on another.

"This is darling," Sarah said as they walked in. "I'm casting my vote for them as the business best-dressed for the holidays."

The woman behind the counter greeted them warmly.

"I'm glad you're open," Sarah told her.

"Oh, yes. We can't let a little thing like a storm shut us down. In tough times people need candy."

"We sure do," Sarah said. She bought some licorice and saltwater taffy for the kids, some truffles for Karen and chocolate-dipped Oreo cookies for her and Taylor.

"You're going to turn us into blimps," Taylor protested, but she took the treat anyway. And ate every bite on the way back to the house.

Before they went in, she laid a hand on her sister's arm. "I really am sorry. For everything."

"I know," Sarah said, and hugged her. "You'll get through this."

Taylor wasn't so sure, but she nodded agreement.

Once inside, Sarah went upstairs to hide the kids' candy. Taylor dawdled over hanging up her coat, embarrassed to face people after her earlier snotty behavior.

"Did you girls have fun?" called Mrs. Patterson. She and Kat Wilson were cozy on the couch. It was an invitation to join them. Both women smiled at Taylor as she walked into the living room.

"It was good to get out," she said. *And make up.* "I guess I needed it," she added. "I'm sorry I made things uncomfortable for everyone earlier."

"We all have our moments," Kat said.

Taylor couldn't picture Kat Wilson ever having a moment, but she thanked her. "Are the kids back?"

"They're out in the kitchen getting ready to start a special project," said Mrs. Patterson.

Taylor nodded and went to the kitchen.

The kids had been busy, and Miranda was excited to

show Mommy the clamshells they'd found when they'd gone beachcombing. "We're going to do something special with them," she said, pointing to the collection drying on a towel on the counter. "It's a secret." She held up a lovely, delicate-looking one. "This is mine."

"It's beautiful." Oh, to be a little girl again with no worries, taking pleasure in simple things like pretty shells found on the beach.

Celeste was at the sink, rinsing off some rocks. She smiled over her shoulder at Taylor. "Her shoes got a little damp. They're drying out by the woodstove. I hope you don't mind. Your husband said it would be okay," she added.

Was she trying to shift the blame or appease the monster? Probably some of both. Taylor hadn't exactly shown herself in a good light since they'd arrived.

"It's okay," she said. "Thanks for doing that."

Chris and Greg came in the back door. "We're about ready to dig clams," Chris announced. "Did Sarah get the boots?" he asked Taylor.

She nodded.

"Tell her to send the boys on out then," he said and disappeared.

"Can I dig clams?" Miranda asked Greg, and he looked questioningly at Taylor.

Her daughter would probably never get ballet lessons, but here at least was one small treat she wouldn't have to miss. *Thank you, Sarah.*

"Yes, you can," Taylor told her. "Go find Aunt Sarah. She bought you some boots. Good thing," she added, "because Mommy couldn't afford to." She looked pointedly at Greg, and he gave up on the uneasy smile he'd been wearing and went out, slamming the door behind him.

Taylor sighed. That had been a waste of breath. Everything she'd been saying was wasted breath. Her complaints and jabs only made Greg dig in deeper.

As she went back to the living room, she was almost trampled by the boys, anxious to get outside. Miranda was hurrying into her boots, crying, "Wait for me."

"Don't worry, you won't get left behind," said Sarah, and handed Miranda her coat.

Then Miranda, too, joined the clam stampede.

Karen and Lisa returned from their shopping expedition, happy to settle in the living room. "Out in the cold, digging in the mud. Doesn't sound like fun to me," Karen said.

"I swear, you've lost your sense of adventure," Lisa said to her.

"My sister thinks I'm turning into a pet rock," Karen told the other women in the room.

Lisa's cheeks turned rosy. "Well." She stopped at that.

Karen shrugged. "So I'm not as active as I used to be? I'm happy."

"You'd be happier if you'd get out more," Lisa said. "And healthier."

"I just had a checkup. I'm fine," Karen replied in a tone of voice that ended the discussion.

What was it about sisters that they tried so hard to run each other's lives?

"Anyway," Karen continued, "being without electricity is enough real-life adventure for me. Anything more dangerous I prefer to watch on TV or read in a book."

"You can't go wrong with a book," Kat said, and held up the one she'd been reading. "I'm loving this story."

"Is that the new Brenda Novak book?" Karen asked. "I've ordered it."

"It's good," said Kat.

"I'll bet it's even better with chocolate," Sarah put in, and produced her offering.

"You shouldn't have," Karen said, but she was smiling as she took the little box of truffles.

"Oh, I didn't. My son will be paying me back for these out of his allowance."

"Very wise," Kat approved.

Yes, that was Sarah, the picture of wisdom. Bossy wisdom. Interfering wisdom.

No one's going to let you end up on the street. You know that. Her sister's words returned to wrap around her troubled spirit like a warm blanket. Maybe interfering wasn't always so bad. Maybe, as with those football players running interference, having someone who cared jumping into your life to save you from getting pummeled to death wasn't such a bad thing.

Karen was just sharing her goodies when Darrell Wilson returned with a surprise for Kat. He bent to kiss her on the cheek and then put a gift bag in her lap. "I know you wanted some seashells. Happy anniversary, babe."

"Oh, Darrell. I wish you hadn't," she moaned. "I didn't do anything for you."

He sank to the floor by her feet. "You've been a little busy getting well," he said. "Anyway, you've given me all I could ever want. You've loved me, believed in me, and have always been there for me."

Every woman in the room heaved a sigh. "That was like a line right out of a movie," Lisa said.

"I don't remember the last time my husband said something like that to me," Karen said wistfully.

Neither did Taylor. If only she could find a bottle on the beach with a genie in it who could fix her marriage.

"Open your gift," Darrell urged.

Kat removed the tissue paper and took out a little net bag filled with exotic shells. "Oh, they're so pretty!"

"I don't think they're all from here," he said.

"I don't care. I love them." She reached back inside the bag and withdrew a candy box with a clear top that showed off the chocolate clamshells inside.

"Since you don't feel up to going clamming," he said.

She bent down and threw her arms around him. "You're the best husband ever."

Yes, he is, thought Taylor. Lucky Kat. If only Greg cared as much about her as Darrell cared about his wife. What was it going to take? Would she have to get some life-threatening disease?

"And now," Darrell said, "I think I'm going to go supervise the clam digging."

"You've got a great guy there," Karen said as he left.

"Yes, I do," Kat said with a smile.

Too bad we can't clone him, Taylor thought.

Darrell had heard Karen Owens's comment. Boy, did he have them fooled. They hadn't had to live with him dumping his dirty socks and underwear on the floor or failing to step in and discipline the kids, leaving it to Kat to always be the bad guy. Those women hadn't been there when he bought that car they couldn't afford. It had been a miserable three years paying the damned thing off. But Kat had hung in there with him, and now he was hanging in there with her. That was how it worked when you were married.

The rest of the Driftwood Inn gang wasn't far down the beach. Out on the tideflats, Seth Waters and Pete Long, the motel's two handymen, were showing the boys how to use a clam gun, while Greg Marsh and his brother-in-law were attacking the mollusks with shovels.

"How's it going?" he called.

"We'll be having clam chowder tomorrow," Pete called back.

Darrell strolled up to the bucket and saw they already had a couple in there. "Cool."

Pete pointed to his sneakers. "You need boots."

"Should've thought to pack some," Darrell said with a shrug. "But then I hadn't planned on having to scrounge for food. Thought I'd be taking my wife to a fancy restaurant or two."

"There's no such thing down here," Pete scoffed.

"Looks like she's having fun anyway," observed Chris.

"Yeah, I think she is."

"Sorry she's sick," Chris added.

Darrell shrugged again. "We'll get through it."

"She doesn't look like a complainer," said Pete. "Most women can be a real pain in the butt."

"So can a lot of guys," Darrell pointed out. "I guess we all have our moments. But you hang in there and get past 'em." Okay, was he getting a little preachy? Probably, but somehow, he felt he needed to say that. Particularly because of Greg Marsh and his wife, who didn't strike Darrell as being in a good place.

The philosophizing ended, and the men turned their attention back to the all-important manly-man task of clamming. Darkness dropped like a curtain, and Seth lit the lanterns they'd brought, and the search continued. Other people were on the beach now, too, and dots of light were scattered about the shore or danced along as people walked the beach, looking for the small holes in the sand that indicated good digging. Laughter and conversation floated on the air as people visited.

"Seems to be a popular sport," Darrell remarked.

"A lot of people out here, just like us, figuring they could be running out of food," said Pete. "Who knows when they'll get the road cleared and get the power back on? Better not start singin' 'I'll be Home for Christmas.'"

Kat had been looking forward to having Christmas with the kids. Darrell didn't know how he was going to break this news to her.

Seth Waters had been saying something. Darrell jerked himself back into the moment. "What?"

"Want to give it a try?" Seth repeated.

"Sure," Darrell said, and took the clam gun. Okay, this was serious fun. He brought up a clam and was hooked.

"There's another one for the bucket" Chris said as his oldest son proudly held one up. "We're gonna have some good eating. Right, gang?"

"Right!" exclaimed both his sons.

"I like clams!" cried little Miranda, jumping up and down.

"You've never had a clam," her older cousin informed her.

"But I like them," she said.

"You've got a cute daughter," Darrell said to Greg after they'd finished and were walking back.

"Yeah, I do," Greg agreed, watching fondly as his little girl chased after the two boys.

"And a lovely wife. You're a lucky man."

The smile disappeared faster than a fleeing razor clam. Darrell could feel a wall going up. Hardly surprising. Guys didn't like to talk about their problems, especially with people they barely knew.

"Yep, nothing better than a nice family," Darrell said, then veered away from the subject. "So, I never did hear. What do you do for a living?"

This didn't appear to be a welcome topic, either. Greg frowned. "I'm starting my own business. Some real innovative stuff that's going to make the internet search engines we're using now look like dinosaurs."

"Yeah?"

"We're currently in the development stage. I just need a few more investors."

Uh-oh. Was that a pitch? When it came to investing, Darrell wasn't a risk tasker, and he said as much. "Sounds pretty cool, though."

"My wife doesn't think so."

Ah, there it was, the bone of contention. That would explain the discontent surrounding those two. "Well, that can be hard," Darrell said.

"I'm gonna make it work."

Darrell caught the stubborn set of the jaw. "I hope you can." He wondered how high a price the guy would have to pay to do that.

Back at the house he had his own situation to deal with. Under cover of a myriad of excited conversations about the great clam expedition, he joined Kat on the couch and broke the news that they probably wouldn't be back home for Christmas, then braced for her disappointment.

Instead, he got a comforting hand on his arm. "I figured as much. I already called the kids."

"Were they disappointed?" He thought of the presents they had waiting under the tree—a digital camera for Jewel and a Keurig coffee maker for the newlyweds.

"A little," Kat said, "but they're going to get together and party no matter what. Luke and Marina want to have us all over on New Year's Day, and we'll open presents then."

So, everything was working out. "That's a relief."

She kissed him. "I'm having a really good anniversary. In fact, I know it's going to sound silly, but this is one of the best anniversaries ever." His perplexity must have shown because she said, "We've survived a giant storm and are making new friends. I got shells and chocolate and have been waited on hand and foot. And I've had so much hot buttered rum I feel like a pirate. Fancy dinners are nice, but you tend to forget them. This is one getaway we'll never forget. It's a bit of an adventure, and I think I needed some fun, a little adventure."

"Fun, huh?"

"You're having fun, aren't you?" she asked.

It wasn't exactly sex on the beach, and now they weren't even in the same bed. But he'd gotten a kick out of digging clams, and he'd loved seeing Kat's delight over the shells.

So, yeah. "I am," he said.

"Well, then, happy anniversary," she murmured and kissed him again, her fingers threading through his hair.

Funny. Sometimes things didn't go at all the way you planned. Sometimes they went even better.

The clam digging had been a success, and there was a promise of clam chowder for Christmas Eve. Meanwhile, the men had a bonfire going, and several of the other displaced guests and their temporary hosts had arrived to roast marshmallows and party.

Seth Waters, one of the men who appeared to work around the place, had brought a guitar and played it for everyone, and Jenna Jones and her sister taught the kids some silly campfire songs. The grizzled, old guy named Pete told a ghost story Taylor was sure would give Miranda nightmares, and Mrs. Patterson, the actual owner of the Driftwood Inn, reminisced about Christmases past.

"It's such a special time of year," she finished. "And so important to celebrate together. And you know, one of the things I used to love to do when I was a girl was to go caroling with my family and friends. Seth, do you know any Christmas carols?"

"I think I could manage a few. What would you like to sing?" he asked.

"'Joy to the World,'" said Aunt Edie.

"Oh, yeah. Jeremiah was a bullfrog," Pete began.

"Not that one, Pete," Mrs. Patterson said. "The other one. Do you know it?" she asked Seth.

"I do," he said, and began to play.

Taylor found it hard to sing about joy when she was so worried and angry. Greg scooted next to her on the log where they were sitting. "Could you at least try to enjoy this?" he whispered.

"How can I?" she muttered. "I'm worried about the future, Greg. Can't you understand that?"

This was all too much. All this jolly, jolly, happy, happy. She left the fire and started off down the beach.

Greg fell in step with her. "Tay, I know you're worried. But if you could hang in there a little longer—"

She cut him off. "How much longer, Greg? Until our cars get repossessed? Until we lose our house? I just lost a sale. We have no money coming in, and you've burned through our savings. Where are we going to end up if you can't make something happen soon? What about Miranda?" He didn't have an immediate answer for that. She went on. "Did you know that Sarah had to buy her mud boots because I didn't have any money?"

"You already said that. But listen, I'm going to make this happen, I promise. Can't you believe in me?"

"And can't you care about me?" It was dark, but even without seeing, she knew his lips were pressed tightly together and his jaw was clenched. Why, every time they had this discussion, did it have to come down to her being disloyal if she pointed out that they were in trouble?

"Greg, not every idea is a good one. Not every business gets off the ground. That has nothing to do with me believing in you."

"Yes, it does," he insisted. "You think I can't do this."

"I think you're a very smart man. I think you're worth your weight in gold. I don't think you're an entrepreneur. Does that have to mean I don't believe in you?" He said nothing and she continued. "We set a deadline. Remember? You were going to give this two years, and if it didn't look like anything was happening you'd get a job. Well, guess what. We passed the deadline and we're in trouble. And not just financial trouble. I can't go on like this."

She hoped he'd finally get it, would see what his stubbornness was costing him. Instead, he said, "You've never believed in me."

That again. "I've had it, Greg. When we get back home, I'm leaving."

"Leaving?" he repeated as if she was speaking in a foreign language.

"If you want to go down the tubes you can, but you're not taking Miranda and me with you."

"You can't afford to leave," he protested.

Not, "I can't live without you." Not, "How could you even think I'd hurt you and Miranda?" It was all about money now. And the company, his mistress.

"That was not the right thing to say," she snapped, and turned back toward the house.

"I didn't mean it that way," he said, keeping in step with her. "I meant how would you…? Why…? What are you thinking?"

"I'm thinking there's something you love more than me. I hope you and your company will be very happy together."

"This is crazy talk," he said.

"Maybe it is. But you've made me crazy."

They were almost back at the fire now. "Daddy, come help me roast a marshmallow," Miranda called.

"Go hang out with your daughter," Taylor said to him. "She still loves you, which is more than I can say."

He left without another word, fists clenched, shoulders hunched. A man torn between crying and hitting something.

Okay, what she'd said had been cruel. And now that she'd said it, now that she'd claimed she didn't love him, she knew it wasn't true. *So* not true. What had she done?

Chapter Nineteen

Jenna had observed Greg and Taylor Marsh out there, two figures beyond the light of the flames. Even in the dark their body language was easy to read. This was no reconciling couple enjoying a stroll on the beach. This was a marriage in big trouble. She knew the symptoms.

"Hey, there," said Brody at her elbow, "cheer up. Everyone's having fun. Your disaster party is a success."

Yes, everyone except Taylor and Greg was having fun. Brody and Courtney had both brought wine, and people were visiting and drinking from plastic cups as they roasted marshmallows. Even the newlyweds had joined them. She was glad the others were enjoying themselves, but she felt such empathy for Taylor and her husband. A marriage foundering on the rocks was worse than any storm Mother Nature could bring.

She watched as Greg returned to the fire and put a marshmallow on a stick for his little girl. Darrell Wilson said something to him, and he smiled and nodded, but the smile didn't reach his eyes.

"Have some wine," Brody said, and handed her a cup.

Yes, party on. Wasn't that how life often went? You

bled internally while all around you, clueless people went on with their happy lives, no one noticing.

Of course, sometimes you denied there was a problem. Or you tried to hide it. Jenna had done both. She hadn't wanted to give up on her own marriage for the sake of her daughter, and she hadn't wanted to tell anyone that there was a snake in paradise for her pride's sake. But eventually you couldn't hide from the snake or hide it from others.

The people with children left around nine to get them settled. Darrell and Kat Wilson also went in. She looked tired but happy, and he had his arm around her as they walked back down the path through the dune grass to the house. If only every woman could have a Darrell Wilson.

The party finally broke up around ten thirty, with Brody, Courtney and Tyrella and the last of their houseguests heading home. By eleven it was just Jenna and Seth putting out the fire.

"Okay, what's wrong?" he asked.

She didn't bother to pretend. "I feel bad for the Marshes."

"I thought so. You lost your smile the minute they took off down the beach."

"It makes me sad to see people having marriage problems. She's so mad."

"You can't know what's really going on. And you shouldn't. It's none of your business."

She frowned at him.

"Take it from me, Jenna. You shouldn't interfere in other people's lives. It gets messy."

"You did," she pointed out. He'd taken interfering

to the max when he took the rap for something his sister did.

"And look what it cost me."

"But wouldn't you do the same thing if you had it to do over again?"

"Of course, I would," he said, sounding shocked that she'd even ask.

"So maybe sometimes it's a good thing to interfere," she said.

"Most of the time it's not."

And maybe this was one of those times. Close proximity gave the illusion of closeness, but she barely knew these people. Still, as they made their way back through the dunes, Jenna resolved to say something encouraging if the opportunity presented itself.

The next morning, the marooned guests were in the kitchen helping themselves to the last of the muffins Aunt Edie had pulled from the freezer when Pete returned from a scouting expedition.

"Road's still out," he reported before grabbing a muffin and vanishing.

"Why is it taking so long?" Taylor Marsh demanded.

If only Jenna knew. "I have no idea," she said. "I wish it was open, too." Maybe the mess would be cleared up by afternoon. If that turned out to be the case, there'd still be time for Damien to get Sabrina back to her for Christmas.

"Don't worry, dear," Aunt Edie said. "I'm sure the road will be open in time for Sabrina to come home."

Jenna was beginning to have her doubts. "I think I'll

call and check on her," she said, and excused herself from the kitchen.

Her daughter answered the phone after just two rings. "Can I come home now?"

"The roads aren't clear yet," Jenna said. How long did it take to cut up some trees and move them off the road anyway? Forever, when you were living at the ends of the earth.

"This sucks," Sabrina said. "I want to come home."

"Believe me, I want you home, too. Meanwhile, though, you get to be with Daddy and Grandma and Grandpa, and Grandma will come up with all kinds of fun things to do."

That put a good spin on things for Sabrina. Now, if Jenna could find a way to positively spin the situation for herself… She'd never done Christmas without her daughter. Where was the upside to this? Practice for those looming empty-nest years? No, no. Surely even once her baby bird had flown off to college she'd return to the nest for the holidays.

"I want to be with you and Grandma and Aunt Celeste and Aunt Edie," Sabrina said. "I'm tired of being here. There's nothing to do."

"I'm sure that's not true," Jenna said. There was always texting. "Have you seen Marigold?" Maybe Damien could arrange a quick visit to the BFF from the old neighborhood.

"Her family went to Disney World for Christmas," Sabrina said irritably. "Daddy's out looking for stuff for a new sculpture and Aurora went with him, and they didn't even ask me if I wanted to go. Grandma's getting her hair done and Grandpa's watching TV. It's so boring."

"But at least you have power," Jenna pointed out. She was still making do with candles and oil lamps and charging her phone in her car.

"I don't care. I'd rather be there. Have you guys had a beach fire?"

"Just a little one."

"This sucks," Sabrina said once more.

Yes, it did.

"Poor Jenna," Celeste said after her sister had left the kitchen.

"What's wrong?" asked Lisa.

"Her daughter's stuck up in Lynnwood with the ex. If they don't get the road cleared, she won't be down for Christmas," Celeste explained. "Neither will my mom," she added with a frown.

Jenna Jones seemed so together, so nice. It was hard to picture her with an ex. And not to have her daughter with her at Christmas—Taylor couldn't imagine how that would feel.

Yet she'd laid the groundwork for a similar situation only the night before. Her appetite died, and she set aside her muffin.

"At least we're not marooned on an island with no hope of rescue," said Mrs. Patterson.

"Like in that old TV show," Karen said. "You know, *Gilligan's Island*."

"A three-hour tour," sang her sister. "What would you think about that, Roger?" she asked the parrot, who was on his perch in the kitchen. "Can you say three-hour tour? Three-hour tour."

"Three-hour tour," Jolly Roger repeated. "Give me whiskey."

"He's got his priorities straight," joked Darrell. "Speaking of, we'd better bring in some more wood."

"Good idea," Chris said. "Come on, boys."

He and his sons and the men left to don their coats, Miranda trailing after them.

"How many men does it take to bring in wood?" cracked Sarah.

"I think the guys are actually enjoying this," said Karen.

"How can anybody be enjoying this?" Taylor demanded. "It's Christmas Eve, and we're stuck here and all our presents are back home."

"But we're together," said her sister. "And isn't that what's most important?"

Taylor wanted to scream, "No! We all need to get home and back to our lives." But what kind of life would she be returning to? Especially after what she'd said to Greg. He hadn't so much as looked at her all morning. They were in trouble, on their way over the cliff.

"Things can always be worse," put in Kat Wilson. She held up her mug of instant coffee. "We could be out of coffee."

That made the other women chuckle.

Taylor didn't want to chuckle. She didn't even want to smile. She picked up her discarded muffin and started shredding it. "I guess I'm not going to be happy this year no matter where I am," she muttered. And why had she said *that*? Now she'd get a lecture from her sister.

But it wasn't her sister who said something. Jenna Jones had come back into the kitchen in time to hear her. "You know, I think I've been where you are. Not that it's any of my business," she hurried to add.

It wasn't, and Taylor wasn't sure she wanted to hear Jenna's story. It was bound to depress her even more than she already was.

"I was pretty unhappy myself not so long ago," Jenna continued. "My husband and I had split."

"No loss since he was a cheater," put in her sister.

"It wasn't. But it was still hard to accept. If we'd had any other kind of problem short of abuse, I'd have stuck it out. In fact, I could have forgiven him for cheating and stayed with him if he hadn't wanted the other woman more than me."

Yikes. Jenna had been through a lot, and yet here she was, smiling and gracious, trying to keep them all happy. How was she managing? Did she give lessons?

"That's awful," said Kat. "I'm sorry."

"It is what it is," Jenna said. "I wish it could be different, though. I feel sorry for my daughter. Girls need their daddies." With this she looked straight at Taylor, igniting a flame on Taylor's face.

"My husband is bankrupting us," Taylor said. "His business is going nowhere, but he won't let go."

It wasn't up there with cheating or beating, but as far as she was concerned such lack of care for her feelings ran a close second. How was she supposed to deal with that? How were they supposed to live when his greedy company was sucking the lifeblood out of them? Just like Audrey, the bloodthirsty plant in *Little Shop of Horrors*.

"Ah, money problems," Lisa said with a sage nod. "Been there, done that. My husband and I went through some bad years. I had some health issues." She looked over at Kat. "Ovarian cancer."

"Mine's uterine," Kat said, and the two women nodded at each other in understanding.

"Dean had gotten laid off and our COBRA had run out," Lisa continued. "We had medical bills coming out our ears. Not good when you don't have insurance. We finally had to declare bankruptcy."

"And I thought we'd had money problems. That's awful," Sarah said.

"It was, but I'm still here and I never take a single day for granted. You never know what tomorrow might bring, and let me tell you, it's a lot easier to go through the hard stuff with someone rather than alone. Right, sis?"

Karen nodded.

"What happened to you?" Taylor asked her.

"We lost a child. Spinal meningitis."

"Been down that road, too," Kat said to her. "It's so hard to lose a child."

There was the understatement of the century. Taylor felt she was shrinking with every story that was told. She was with giants. Warriors.

"Like I said, it's none of my business. But your husband seems like a nice guy," Jenna observed.

"He is," Taylor admitted. Then had to add in her own defense, "But he's being stubborn. And selfish."

"When it comes right down to it, aren't they all?" Karen joked.

Kat shook her head. "Not Darrell."

"He must have some flaws," Lisa teased.

"Okay, he refuses to take dancing lessons. He's worried about looking stupid in front of strangers."

"A guy thing," Sarah said. "They hate looking like losers."

"That might be why your husband's hanging on to his business so tightly," Kat said to Taylor. "He doesn't want to look like a loser to you."

"He already does. I don't know what else to do to get him to listen. I'm ready to leave him," Taylor confessed. "I told him as much last night."

There was silence as all the women digested this news.

Sarah was the first to speak. "Oh, Tay," she said, her voice heavy with sorrow.

"I can't take any more," Taylor said. "I really can't." And look who she was saying this to, women who'd been through harder things than what she was going through.

"My first husband beat me," said Mrs. Patterson. "I didn't stay. You do whatever you have to, dear."

Finally, someone who was on her side.

Taylor was about to thank her when she added, "But you weigh your choices carefully."

Taylor nodded and then excused herself. She'd had all the counseling she could stand for a while.

The day moved on. After a lunch of canned soup Sarah and Aunt Edie started working on the clam chowder while the other adults scattered around the house. Celeste and Jenna kept the kids busy at the kitchen table painting shells, which made them happy. Until the shell that Miranda was painting for her mother broke. Since the other two she'd found had already met the same fate, this was artistic tragedy.

"It's okay," Celeste told her. "You have that pretty rock you painted. Your mommy will love that."

"But I want a shell," Miranda said, sniffling. "Can we get another?"

It was getting late in the day and would be dark soon. The temperature had fallen. "I'll tell you what," Jenna said. "Tomorrow we'll go look for some more."

"But tomorrow's Christmas. I want to give Mommy a shell for Christmas," Miranda insisted.

"You can give her mine," offered James, sliding his across the table. It was a splattered mess of a shell painted in the Seahawks' colors of blue and green and had a sloppy number twelve on it. Thanks to clever marketing, James, like every Seahawks fan, was a twelfth man.

Miranda, who'd been meticulous with hers and painting it pink, looked at it scornfully. "I want to paint one myself."

"We will tomorrow," Celeste promised. "Meanwhile, we'll let our rocks dry, and while they're drying we can make Christmas cards." She glanced up at Jenna. "You think Sabrina will mind if we use her colored pencils?"

"Of course not," Jenna said. "I'll get them and some paper."

She went to the office, where she walked in on Greg, Chris Brown and Darrell Wilson, deep in conversation. "How badly do you want to keep her?" Darrell was asking.

At the sight of Jenna, Greg's cheeks turned russet.

"Sorry," she said quickly. "I just need to grab some paper from my printer." She got the paper, then hurried off. Hopefully, the men were having better luck getting through to Greg than the women had with his wife.

She returned and helped Celeste put the kids to work drawing. Taylor had vanished, and Kat went upstairs to rest. Lisa and Karen settled in to play cards in the living room, and Sarah and Aunt Edie continued to work side by side on Christmas Eve dinner. Everyone seemed happy and convivial.

"It's almost like one big family," Jenna said to her mother when Mel called to check in.

"Sounds like you're all doing okay."

"Pretty much. People have had a chance to do some shopping, and the men got clams for us. We're having clam chowder for dinner. Celeste's had the kids painting shells and rocks to give their parents for Christmas. I just wish you and Sabrina were here."

"I can bring her down as soon as the road's passable. I'm off until the day after New Year's. The road's bound to be open by then."

"I hope that happens soon," Jenna said fervently.

"I'm sure it will. Meanwhile, think of the adventure you're having."

"I've had enough adventure," Jenna said. She wanted a long, hot shower, wanted to be able to run the washer and dryer. "I don't know how those pioneer women managed."

"They had vision," Mel said.

"Well, I can tell you now, I'd never have been on one of those wagon trains heading west. I'd have been the one waving goodbye, saying, 'Write when you find work.'"

"I don't know. I think you're tougher than you realize," her mother said.

Toughness was overrated.

After the group shrink session in the kitchen, Taylor had decided she needed some alone time—not easy to get in a house full of women—so she'd bundled into her coat and gone for a walk, going down the main road toward town.

Stores were still open, and she'd popped into a couple, but not being able to buy anything reminded her of the mess they were in and made her cranky. She passed a restaurant where a large mechanical Santa greeted her, one of his elves on duty in the lifeguard chair on the miniature sandy beach landscaped outside the entrance. That ratcheted her level of crankiness even higher because it made her think of Miranda's gifts from Santa waiting at home. Gifts she couldn't afford and had charged. Those charges had been the final straw for her Visa card, and she'd reached her limit. She thought about what she'd said to Greg the night before. There was a limit to how much bitterness you could spill into a relationship, too, and she suspected she'd gone over that. What a crappy Christmas.

But the new year wasn't looking any better.

The light was fading, so she turned around and walked back to the house. By the time she arrived, the sky was as black as her mood and the air was arctic. The faint glow of candles showed in the window, making the house seem cozy and inviting. She hurried inside, thinking how good it would feel to stand in front of the woodstove.

But everyone would be looking at her, judging her. Never mind the stove. She'd go to her room.

Or not. "You're back just in time," Mrs. Patterson called to her from where she stood by the stove. She was wearing oven mitts and lifting a big pot from the stove top. "We're about to dish up the chowder."

Well, she *was* hungry. No one seemed to be staring at her. They were all too busy following their hostess out to the dining room.

Miranda ran up and took her hand. "Come on, Mommy."

Greg fell in behind them, saying nothing to her. She could hardly blame him. She kept silent, too. What was left to say?

Everyone sat around the little dining room table and in the living room, eating chowder and soda crackers. The men and kids accepted compliments on their clam-digging prowess and Mrs. Patterson happily accepted compliments on her cooking.

After they'd finished the chowder along with some no-bake chocolate cookies, Celeste took charge, teaching them silly parlor games. "Picture-taking spoon" was a favorite; she'd pretend to use a spoon to take a picture of someone, while her sister, acting as able assistant, would leave the room. Whenever Jenna returned she always managed to know whose picture Celeste had snapped.

"How did you do that?" Christopher asked.

"Magic," Celeste replied, and they played until most of the adults and Christopher had figured out the secret.

After that, Karen recited *The Night Before Christmas* and her sister performed an off-key rendition of "Santa, Baby," which had most everyone laughing. Taylor managed to smile politely.

Finally, it was time to put the children to bed. Taylor tucked her daughter into her sleeping bag, told her she loved her and kissed her good-night. "Go right to sleep," she said.

"So Santa can come," Miranda added.

Oh, boy. Why, oh, why were they stranded here?

"Santa's going to find us, isn't he, Aunt Taylor?" James asked.

"If not, he'll leave something for you back at your house," Taylor reassured him.

"No, he's going to find us here," Miranda said. "Miss Celeste sent our letters by Reindeer Express so they'd get to him in time."

"Well, then, as long as the reindeer don't get lost you'll be fine," Taylor said, giving Santa an out.

Miranda giggled. "The reindeer live with Santa, Mommy. They can't get lost."

No, it was only grown-ups who lost their way. Taylor gave her daughter one more kiss and left the room.

Greg had come to say good-night to Miranda. Neither of them spoke as Taylor brushed past him.

The living room was turning into Santa Central. Jenna Jones brought out some goodies she'd picked up for the kids, along with three stockings to hold the treats.

"That was really kind of you," Sarah said to her.

"Yes, thank you," Taylor added. These people were doing everything they could to make the situation tolerable for their stranded customers. Even though she wasn't happy about where she was, she could at least be grateful for their kindness.

"I know it's not going to be the same as if you were home and with the rest of your families," Jenna said, "but it'll be something."

"And the kids will have letters from Santa waiting for them," said Celeste, holding up three envelopes.

Mrs. Patterson had wrapping paper squirreled away, and they wrapped what Sarah had gotten for the kids and arranged them under the tree.

"I hope it'll be enough," Taylor said, looking at the small collection.

"It will be more than many children ever get," Mrs. Patterson said, and, once again, Taylor felt small.

She decided it was time for bed and ducked out, leaving the others to enjoy themselves. Which, of course, they would, because after this they'd go back to their happy, steady lives while she and Greg returned to their financial mess.

Except not everyone's life was perfect. Kat Wilson would still be fighting off cancer, and Jenna Jones would be dealing with her ex.

At the rate she was going, Taylor, too, would soon be dealing with an ex.

That thought didn't make for pleasant dreams. In one she found herself trying to get to the bank, but she was in quicksand and the harder she tried to run, the deeper she sank.

She woke to gray predawn light with a whimper. Christmas morning. Yeah, Merry Christmas.

It wasn't long before the kids were up and then the

adults with them. Even Kat dragged herself down to the living room, although she looked exhausted with dark circles under her eyes. Mrs. Patterson made oatmeal while the kids opened their presents. The letter from Santa, explaining that these presents were special beach ones and he had more goodies waiting for them at home, was enough to pacify all three.

The boys proudly presented their rocks and shells to their parents, who showed the proper enthusiasm. Miranda's lower lip was sticking out when she held out the rock she'd painted. "My shell broke."

"That's okay, baby," Taylor said. "Your rock is very pretty."

"But you like shells," Miranda reminded her.

"Yes, I do, but I like rocks, too."

Miranda frowned but didn't say any more.

Jenna and Celeste and their aunt opted not to open their presents until the rest of their family could come down, but it turned out Chris had bought candles for them. "Oh, you shouldn't have," Mrs. Patterson said. It was evident she was pleased nonetheless.

"We've gone through enough of yours," he said, shrugging off her thanks.

He and Greg had obviously gone to the same store to shop for their wives, as they'd both purchased fancy soaps for them. Taylor was surprised Greg had even bothered to give her anything.

"Love it!" Sarah exclaimed and kissed her husband.

Taylor couldn't get beyond murmuring an embarrassed thank-you to Greg. Where had he found the money? Chris had most likely lent it to him. Ugh.

She'd grudgingly bought him something, which was

back home under the tree, and she was embarrassed to be the only person not handing over a present. She was even more embarrassed when her sister presented her with the earrings she'd seen when they were out shopping, as well as the candle with the shells embedded in it.

"I didn't get you anything," she protested, her face sizzling. She hadn't given anyone anything—except a hard time.

"We're not keeping score," Sarah said. She hugged Taylor and whispered, "Anyway, I thought you could use some cheering up."

As if a candle and earrings could manufacture enough cheer to lift the dark cloud hanging over her. Still, it was a sweet thought.

"Merry Christmas, babe," Darrell said to Kat, handing over a small wrapped box.

"Oh, Darrell, my gift for you is at home."

"You're the only gift I need. Open it."

She did and found a necklace with a sterling silver disk-shaped pendant with an ocean wave etched on it. "It's beautiful."

"So are you," he said.

Taylor watched with jealous eyes. It was as if there were only the two of them in the room. How long was it since she and Greg had been like that?

Mrs. Patterson heated apple juice on the woodstove for the kids, and the adults drank instant coffee. The children spent the morning playing with their toys, then after a lunch of raisins and peanut butter sandwiches, they were ready for a change. Miranda, still mourning her ruined shell, wanted to beachcomb, but it was raining, so Taylor nixed that.

"It's pretty nasty out there," Sarah agreed.

To keep restlessness at bay, Celeste organized another coin hunt and as the children scampered around the house, the adults visited. Everyone was having a good time. Except Taylor.

And Greg. She could feel his gaze on her but avoided looking in his direction. If she looked at him, she'd cry. This year all she was getting for Christmas was a crumbling marriage and a headache. And what about Miranda? What were they giving her if they split?

She should stick it out. The three of them could live with her parents. Mom would love that. Then, once Taylor's real estate career took off, they could start over. And drag the ball and chain that was Greg's business everywhere they went, came the bitter thought.

She escaped to the bedroom and hoped he wouldn't follow her. And she really hoped the ever-cheerful Kat would stay downstairs on the couch.

Even with the heat rising and bedroom doors left open, the room was freezing. Taylor shut the door, knowing that would make it even colder. She didn't care. All she wanted was a little privacy. She burrowed under the blankets on her blow-up mattress and, exhausted from her poor night's sleep, actually dozed.

The room was dark when she woke. Good. That meant most of this miserable Christmas Day was over. Maybe the next day the road would be clear, and they could leave. She was sick of wearing the same clothes over and over and having to wash her underwear in the sink.

As if that was any big deal compared to what was really going on? Being at home would give her a chance to put on clean clothes, but it wouldn't help her clean up her life.

She brushed her hair, then went downstairs to check on Miranda. Once upon a happier time, Christmas Day meant presents and playing with her daughter and watching a Christmas movie on TV… Going over to her parents' for Christmas dinner.

She found the men all squeezed around a card table, playing poker. Karen had a quilt square she was embroidering, and she and Lisa and Kat were visiting with Mrs. Patterson. Roger, her parrot, was muttering in his cage. Jenna and Celeste were in the kitchen, foraging for munchies, the boys hovering. But where was Miranda?

Taylor walked back into the living room. Maybe she'd been sitting by the tree or in a corner. But no, she wasn't there.

"Greg, where's Miranda?" she asked her husband.

He looked up, puzzled. "I thought she was with you."

"No."

"She's not in the kitchen?"

"No." There was no need to panic. She had to be somewhere.

"She's probably upstairs," said Chris.

Yes, that was it. She was upstairs. Maybe in the bathroom.

Taylor hurried up the stairs. The bathroom door was wide-open, a trio of flicker candles on the counter. There was nothing in the room but the shadows they cast. She hurried down the hall, checking the bedrooms, calling her daughter's name. No response.

Greg was upstairs now. "Did you find her?" He sounded as panicked as she felt.

"She's got to be here somewhere," he said, and made the exact same rounds she'd just made. "Okay, she has to be downstairs."

"She's not," Taylor said. She could feel her heart fluttering in her chest. *Oh, God.*

"Did you find her?" Chris asked when they came back.

Taylor shook her head. She could feel tears stinging her eyes.

"She's got to be here," Sarah said. She left the couch and went to the kitchen. She returned a moment later with Jenna and her sister and aunt behind her. The expression on her face must have mirrored Taylor's.

Taylor rushed to the closet where Miranda's coat was hanging.

The hanger was on the floor and the coat was gone. *Oh, dear God. No.*

Chapter Twenty

"Her coat's gone!" Taylor cried. "Didn't anybody see her leave?" How could a little girl manage to get her coat and leave a house filled with people—and nobody saw?

"Stay calm," said Chris.

Was he insane? "It's pitch-dark out!"

The men were already grabbing coats. "We'll find her," Greg said. "She's probably right out in back."

Yes, that was it. Maybe she was on the porch. Taylor pulled on her coat and rushed through the kitchen and out the back door. No Miranda. She called her daughter's name, but only a cold night wind answered her.

More people had come out now, all wearing coats and ready to search for Miranda. Seth Waters took charge, holding up his lantern so everyone could see him. "Let's split into groups. We can cover more ground that way."

"I'll go with you," Chris said. "Sarah, call 911 and wait here."

Sarah nodded and pulled out her cell.

"I'll come with you, Seth," said Darrell.

"Me, too," said Celeste.

"We'll go toward the pier," Seth told them, starting down the stairs. "Pete, you take the road."

"Karen and I will go with him," Lisa offered as Pete took the second lantern.

Jenna Jones had two flashlights. She handed one to Greg, saying, "We'll take the other direction down the beach."

Taylor fell in behind her and Greg, stumbling her way down the stairs. He caught her arm and shone the flashlight so she could see. Her tears made the steps look blurry, as though she was underwater. All she could think of was the posters she'd seen on grocery store bulletin boards. *Have you seen this child?* A cute little girl with blond curls and brown eyes would be a molester's dream. Her throat caught on a sob.

"It's going to be okay," Greg said.

"I should've been watching her. I should never have gone upstairs," Taylor said. Her throat was so tight with tears she could barely speak. Like Kat had said, there was nothing worse than losing a child. What if Miranda was gone for good? What if they never found her, never learned what happened to her?

"No, I should have kept an eye on her," Greg said miserably.

"It's nobody's fault," Jenna told them. "The house was full of people. We all assumed somebody was watching her."

"She's always with the boys," Greg said. "It's not like her to go off by herself."

Greg was right. Whatever had possessed her?

Jenna swept her flashlight beam along the beach as they walked. There was nothing but sand. She pointed the light to where the driftwood lay in misshapen heaps, reaching wooden claws toward a blackened sky.

Taylor shivered, and it had nothing to do with the cold and the light rain that was falling. "What if we don't find her?"

"We'll find her, Tay," Greg said, and pulled her close.

Taylor clamped an arm around him and hung on. "She's probably so scared."

"She can't be far," Jenna said, making another sweep with her flashlight.

"Miranda!" Taylor called. "Miranda!" The wind blew the words right back in her face.

From down the beach she could hear her brother-in-law calling her daughter, too. Surely, Miranda would hear one of them.

Unless she was in a strange car being taken who knew where. The tears began pouring down Taylor's face.

"Miranda!" Greg called, and Taylor could hear the panic in his voice.

They walked farther, illuminating nothing but sand, seaweed and driftwood, until finally, after Greg had called their daughter's name again, they heard something faint.

"I think it came from over there," Greg said and began to race toward a huge piece of driftwood. "Miranda! Miranda!"

Taylor and Jenna stumbled along behind, both echoing him.

Suddenly the light caught a little head matted with wet hair. Miranda stood up from behind the wood and held out her arms. "Daddy!"

Taylor allowed herself to indulge in some serious crying as Greg rushed to their little girl and scooped her up. Thank God, her baby was safe.

She and Jenna arrived in time to hear Greg asking, "Why did you leave the house all by yourself?"

"I wanted to get a shell to paint for Mommy," Miranda said in between sobs.

"Baby, I don't need a shell, not when I have you," Taylor said, brushing a wet curl from her cheek.

"I didn't want you to be sad."

It had been evident all weekend that Taylor wasn't happy. Guilt washed over her like a tidal wave.

"Oh, sweetie," she said, and kissed her daughter's cheek. "You don't have to worry about making me happy."

"Are you happy now?" Miranda wanted to know.

"Now that we've found you? Yes, I'm very happy."

"I'm glad. I was scared, Daddy. I got lost."

Miranda wasn't the only one who'd been lost.

Jenna got out her cell phone and alerted the other searchers that Miranda had been found, and Taylor called Sarah and told her to cancel the 911 call.

"At least she didn't run away," Jenna said as they made their way back to the house. "Been there, done that."

Taylor couldn't even imagine having to cope with such a thing. "How old was she?"

"Barely fourteen. It was only last summer. She wanted to go back where we used to live and visit with her father. I didn't get her there quickly enough, and she decided to take matters into her own hands." Jenna shook her head. "Just some of the lovely fallout from divorce."

It seemed that whether you stuck together or separated, there was fallout. Still, that moment of shared panic, of clinging to each other, had confirmed for Taylor that, no matter what she had to go through in life, she didn't want to go through it without Greg. Maybe money problems really weren't the worst kind of problems to have, not if you had each other.

But after what she'd said, did they?

They were almost at the house when the lights came on. *Welcome back to civilization.*

"Thank God you found her!" Sarah greeted them as they trooped in the back door. "We sure are glad to see you, peanut," she said to Miranda and rumpled her hair.

"It was dark out there," Miranda informed her and shivered.

"I'm going to get her a blanket," Greg said. He handed her to Taylor and disappeared into the living room.

Miranda rummaged in her coat pocket and pulled out a small clamshell. "I found your shell, Mommy."

Tears flooded Taylor's eyes as she took it. "Thank you, baby." *I think I might have found something, too.*

"You're a drowned rat," said Sarah. "I'll grab a towel."

"We have some apple juice left. I'll make some hot cider to warm your tummy," said Mrs. Patterson. She already had a bowl out and flour and sugar. "And now that we've got power and a working oven again, I'm going to bake some cookies. We need to celebrate."

"I like cookies," Miranda said through chattering teeth. Greg was back with a blanket, and he peeled off her wet coat and pants and wrapped her in it. "Now, I'm snug as a bug in a rug," she said happily.

Taylor realized her knees had turned to mush, and she collapsed onto a chair. Mrs. Patterson opened a cupboard and removed a bottle of schnapps and poured some into a small glass. "You'd better drink this."

Taylor took it, murmuring her thanks.

Their hostess gave Greg some as well, which he downed in one gulp.

Sarah was back with a towel, and she dried Miranda's hair, then Greg carried Miranda into the living room and set her down in front of the woodstove. Taylor followed and sat next to her, pulling her close.

"We need to get the heat on in your rooms again," Jenna said.

"I think we left ours on," Greg told her, "but I'll go check."

"I'll go with you," Taylor said. Then, to her daughter, "You stay right here with Aunt Sarah, okay? No going outside by yourself."

"I don't want to go out there," Miranda said. "It's scary in the dark."

It sure had been. Taylor gave her daughter a fierce hug and a kiss, and then went out with Greg. They started down the front stairs and encountered Seth's search party coming up.

"Where was she?" Chris asked.

"Crouched behind some driftwood," said Greg. "She went to look for a shell and got lost."

"Thank God you found her," Chris said. "Are you putting her in warm clothes so she doesn't get hypothermia?"

Good old Mr. Knows Everything. Who'd gone out in the dark and cold to look for her child.

"She's wrapped in a blanket, and Mrs. Patterson's

making her hot cider," Greg said. "We're off to make sure the heat's on in our room."

"We left ours on," Chris said. "But I'm not going back until it's warm in there. I about froze my ass off out here."

"Thank you," Taylor said to him, and hoped he understood how fervently she meant it.

"Mrs. Patterson's pouring something to keep you warm," Greg told him, and he and Taylor kept walking.

Neither of them spoke as they crossed the parking lot to their room. The outside lights were on again, and Taylor could see the sober expression on her husband's face. Now was when he'd tell her he'd had it with her complaining and angry outbursts, that it was fine if she wanted nothing more to do with him because he felt the same way. How she wished she'd never said what she'd said.

Their frantic search in the dark had shown her husband to her in a whole new light. He was a poor businessman, and deluded, but a good man.

They could fix their situation. Their marriage. She'd get a job with a regular paycheck to keep them going. Sell houses on the side. They could make it. If he could forget all the awful things she'd said to him.

"Greg, what I said the other night..."

His jaw clenched tighter than a clamshell and he shook his head.

"I was wrong. So wrong."

They were at their room now. A car drove up, washing them in its headlights. Driftwood Inn guests coming back from their temporary lodgings.

Greg unlocked the door and opened it. The room was dark and cold.

He flipped on the light, grabbed her arm and pulled her up against him. "Tay," he said even as she said his name. Then he kissed her, giving her the best Christmas present she could ask for—hope. "Aw, Tay, I'm sorry."

"Sorry?"

"I've been wrong to keep hanging on to this business. I couldn't let go, and I took us all down."

Exactly what she'd been thinking, but suddenly she felt so bad for him that amnesia set in. "Don't say that."

"It's true." He dragged his fingers through his hair. "Out there on the beach..." He shook his head again. "It was a wake-up call. There's nothing more important to me than you and Miranda. If I lose you, I don't know what I'll do. I know I've messed us up, but give me a chance to fix it."

She'd done her share of messing up, too. "Oh, Greg." She threw her arms around his neck and began to cry. "I'm sorry for all the angry things I've said. And I'm really sorry for what I said last night. I didn't mean it."

"Just say you love me. I need to hear it."

"I do love you."

"That's all that matters," he said, and kissed her again. "I'm going to make things right," he promised. "I'm going to pull the plug on the business."

"Oh, no." Perversely, now that he was going to do what she'd been after him to do for months, she didn't want him to. Taylor the dream-crusher. She'd finally gotten what she wanted, but she'd also killed Greg's dream.

"Oh, yes."

"You wanted that business."

"I want you more." He reached over to the thermostat and turned up the heat. Then he kissed her again, turning up her thermostat, as well.

Fumbling, hands, fumbling apologies—they kept at it until she didn't notice that the room still wasn't warm. It was warm enough for them to be together in a way they hadn't in months, with enough heat to set the whole motel on fire.

Half an hour later, they walked back across the parking lot to fetch their daughter. And to thank everyone for helping them find her. Once again, they weren't speaking. But they were holding hands.

None of the guests seemed in a hurry to return to their rooms. Edie Patterson was in the kitchen, happily baking, Kat was comfy on the couch, sipping tea and visiting with the sisters and Sarah, watching the boys play with little Miranda, who seemed to have come through her ordeal unscathed. The men had all enjoyed finishing off the schnapps and were talking about another poker game.

Except Darrell. He passed on joining in. Much as he'd enjoyed getting to know these people, he was ready to go back to the room and have his wife to himself. But he wanted to make sure it was warm enough, so he slipped out of the house to go over and crank up the heat.

On his way, he walked by the Marshes coming back. They were both smiling and holding hands. He liked to think the advice he and Chris had dished out had sunk in, but suspected this new closeness had more to do with the trauma they'd just experienced. Hard times had a way of throwing a couple into the furnace and burning away the dross. If there was something there, something still between you, then you came out better and stronger in the end.

He felt that was what had happened with Kat and him. They'd always had a solid marriage, but this latest trial had welded them together more closely than ever. They were a team, and they would beat the cancer. Inside the room, he turned up the heat. It was a funky room, decorated in beach overload, but Kat had been pleased with it. For the short time they'd been in it.

Boy, had his plans for a fun, romantic getaway blown up in his face. Storms, power outages, peanut butter sandwiches instead of fancy meals in restaurants. And yet she'd loved it.

Back at the house he came in to hear her laughing at something Lisa had said while the parrot called, "Merry Christmas," from his cage. She looked at Darrell and smiled. The woman was a trouper.

"Come try these oatmeal cookies Edie made," she said to him. "You're going to love them." He sure loved the way they smelled. Between the cookies and the cinnamon candle Edie had burning on her hall table, the place smelled like a bakery.

He joined Kat on the couch and helped himself to a cookie. It tasted even better than it smelled.

Looking around the room, you'd never know everyone had survived a storm and gone days without power. The scene made him think of some old Norman Rockwell painting. Greg and Taylor Marsh had joined Celeste, Jenna, and Sarah, and were sitting on the floor, playing a game with the kids. The other men had set up the card table and were into their poker game. Karen and Lisa were comfy in chairs, holding steaming mugs and Edie was passing around more cookies. The Christmas tree cast a colorful glow over everyone.

"We need another victim over here, Wilson," Chris said. "Waters is fleecing us big-time."

He liked these men, even crusty old Pete, but he didn't want to sit around playing poker with them all night. He had every intention of enjoying a game that was best played by only two.

But then Kat said, "Go ahead, Darrell. I'm in no hurry to leave."

So it looked like he wasn't, either. He moved over to the card table and sat in for a couple of hands.

At last little Miranda was yawning. "I think it's time we got you into bed," said her mother.

"You boys, too," Sarah said. "You've all been up since the crack of dawn."

"I'm not tired," protested Christopher.

"Oh, yes, you are," said his mother.

"I think I've had enough," Chris said. "Any more poker with these guys and I'll have to sell a kid."

"Don't sell me!" cried James.

"How about I sell you to Santa?"

"Okay," James agreed, making several of the grownups chuckle.

"You've all been so great," Kat said to Edie as she and Darrell started out the door. "You've really been so generous to us."

"We were happy to do it," said Edie.

"Yes, we were," Jenna added.

"This has been so much fun," Kat gushed.

Darrell wasn't sure he'd go that far, but he also thanked the women and then hustled his wife out the door.

She linked her arm through his as they walked back to their room. "This has been a wonderful anniversary," she said. "Of course, I hated missing Christmas with the kids, but if it wasn't for that, I'd have to say it's been one of the best anniversaries we've ever had. You did everything in your power to make it wonderful for me. Darrell Wilson, you're the best husband ever."

The best husband ever. He smiled. If she thought he was the best now, just wait till they got back to the room.

Back in their room, Karen and Lisa charged their cell phones and called their husbands to let them know they had power again.

"Good," said Doug when Karen told him. "If the trucks got in to fix the power, that means the roads should be clear and you can come back home."

"You're probably right."

"About time, too," he said. "The kids stopped by and were bummed that you weren't home yet. They've got an announcement to make, and they want us both there."

Karen knew what that meant. "I'll bet Jillian's finally pregnant."

"Yeah. They looked pretty happy. Which was more than I could say for myself. I had to go over to Gwen and Randy's for dinner. They might be good friends, but that woman is the worst cook in the world. Man, I missed your red velvet cake. But I missed you even more. It's not the same without you here."

Aw, sweet.

And then he ruined the sweet moment by adding, "No more of these sister trips. You get in too much trouble."

What was that in her husband's voice? Condescension? "Douglas Owens, you make it sound like I can't survive on my own. Well, guess what. I did. I even helped rescue a lost child." Okay, so she hadn't been one of the ones to find Miranda. She'd been out there searching, though. "And there'll be more sister trips in the future because I want a life."

"What are you talking about? We have a life."

"Sitting around like a pet rock isn't a life. I'm going to get out and start doing. Maybe, once in a while, I'll let you join me. If you're nice."

"Your sister is a bad influence," he informed her.

"Finish off the Christmas cookies and I'll see you when I get back," she said and ended the call. "And I hope he enjoys them because those are the last cookies we'll see until we've both managed some serious weight loss."

"Whoa, who are you?" Lisa teased.

"The same woman I've always been."

"I'm proud of you, sis."

Karen smiled. "I hate to admit it, but you were right. I do need to get out more. This weekend showed me how much life I've been missing. I want to live it while I still can."

"Amen to that," Lisa said. "Maybe come spring, we can go to Harrison Hot Springs. And take our tennis racket."

"I don't know about that," Karen said. "I haven't picked up a racket in years."

"Good. Then maybe I can finally beat you."

"Don't count on it," Karen said.

Lisa's cell rang. "It's Dean. How much you want to make a bet that Doug's called him? Hi, Deano," she answered.

"Doug says you guys have power again. Does that mean you're coming home?"

"If the roads are clear."

"Good. I've missed you. It was really weird not having you with me today."

She'd missed out on spending Christmas with his obnoxious family. Gee, what a shame. But it did seem strange not to have her husband with her on such an important holiday. She'd make it up to him when she got back.

Or better yet... "Hey, Deano. What do you think of kidnapping Doug and you boys coming down here to spend New Year's with us at the beach?" she asked.

She looked at her sister, and Karen nodded and said, "I'm game. Maybe some of the kids would like to come down, too."

"You know, that sounds kind of fun," Dean said. "I'll call him."

"Great. I'll talk to the manager tomorrow and find out how many rooms they have available," Lisa said.

"Ask if we can use their washer and dryer," put in Karen.

"You guys bring us down some fancy New Year's Eve clothes. Oh, and I hope you don't get lost on your way," Lisa goaded him, and winked at her sister.

* * *

Jenna's scattered guests began to return, chauffeured back by Tyrella, Courtney and Brody. "It was quite the adventure," one woman told Jenna as she greeted them. "But we actually enjoyed it."

"I'll stay with Brody Green anytime," a woman in her fifties told Jenna while eyeing him as if he were a giant candy cane.

"Looks like you've got a new member of the Brody Green fan club," Jenna said to him after the woman had given him a finger wave and sashayed off to her room, along with her friend.

He frowned. "That one should've come with a cougar alert. I slept with my bedroom door locked."

"Poor baby."

"Anyway, I only want one member in that club," he said. "Don't forget, you owe me a kiss."

"How could I forget I have such a treat coming?" she teased, then sobered. "Seriously, Brody, you saved us. I can't thank you enough."

"Yeah, you can. And you have. I was happy to help." He turned back to his car. "I'd better go home and pick up the rest of the gang. I've got to get the place put back together. My kids want to come down for New Year's Eve. Speaking of, what are you doing?"

"Aunt Edie's already talking about a party on the beach."

"I hope I'm invited," he said. "You'll need somebody to help build the fire."

"Of course." Brody was pretty darned good at building fires. But then, so was Seth.

At least he had been. Before he decided to keep her

at arm's length. Well, his loss, she told herself as she went back into the house to help the last of their guests relocate.

While the Marshes and the Browns were gathering up their things, Jenna put some cookies on paper plates for them. She had the treats ready when they came to check out.

"This has really been great," Sarah told her as she took the plate. "*You've* been great."

"I'm glad you had a good time," Jenna told her.

"The boys had a blast," Sarah said, watching her rambunctious sons tear down the front steps.

"Thank you. For everything," Taylor said, and surprised Jenna by hugging her. "This was life-changing."

"I'm glad," Jenna said. Coming to Moonlight Harbor had sure been a life-changer for her, and she wasn't surprised it had been for someone else, as well. Life was good at the beach…regardless of the weather.

"We want to be debt-free like you guys," Taylor said to her sister. "We're going to sell the house and the second car and get out from under all our debt."

"Good for you," Sarah said.

"Greg's going to close his business and look for a job," Taylor continued. "Who knows? Maybe he'll even find one down here. Uh, do you think Brody Green would let me sell real estate out of his office?" she asked Jenna.

"I'm sure he would," Jenna replied.

"I'm ready for a new start," Taylor said.

Jenna hoped they'd be able to make one. "This is a good place to do that."

"I think maybe it is," Taylor agreed.

Jenna watched them go back to their rooms, a feeling of immense satisfaction settling over her. They'd all coped with inconvenience and even a scare, and maybe they'd all come out of the experience a little better for it.

With all the guests either checked out or back in their rooms, the house fell quiet. "It feels rather strange," Aunt Edie said. "But it is nice to have the power back on."

"Finally, a hot shower," Celeste said.

"If we've got power, the road into town has to be clear," Jenna said. Which meant she'd finally get her daughter back.

"I'll go see," Pete offered. He grabbed another cookie and left.

"If you don't need anything, I guess I'll go back to my room now," Seth said and put on his coat.

Jenna walked him to the door. "Thanks for everything you did for us."

"No, thank *you*. You and Edie were the ones keeping everyone fed and happy. Including me."

"You were an easy bunch to please."

Suddenly he was looking at her in a way that made her insides melt. "You're an amazing woman, Jenna Jones. You know that?"

Amazing? Her? The compliment made her blush. Before she could correct him, he leaned over and kissed her on the cheek. Oh, yeah. The power was back on again.

She watched him go down the front porch steps and walk across the parking lot.

"That man is one sexy beast," her sister said from behind her, making Jenna jump.

"Were you spying on me?" Jenna demanded.

"Of course," Celeste said with a grin. "It's what little sisters do."

Little sisters also pitched in and helped when their big sisters were in need. "You know, I don't think I could have pulled this off without your help."

"You're changing the subject," Celeste observed.

"Yes, I am. I love you."

"Good to know, because I'm taking first dibs on the shower," Celeste said, and ran up the stairs.

Jenna went into the living room and settled in her favorite chair, the little one upholstered with seashell dotted fabric, and called her mother.

"The last of our house guests just left," she announced.

"So your power's back on?"

"Yes, it is," Jenna said. *Merry Christmas.*

"Does that mean the road's open again?" Mel asked.

"I'm pretty sure it does. Pete's gone out to check."

"If so, then Sabrina and I will be down tomorrow."

"I can hardly wait. It wasn't the same without you two here."

"But you managed."

Jenna thought back on how her guests had pulled together to find a lost child. She remembered how happy Taylor and Greg Marsh had looked when they came back from turning on the heat in their room. Kat Wilson had been inspiring, and Karen and Lisa fun to have around. She and her unexpected houseguests had shared more than living space. They'd shared lives.

"We did better than that," she said.

She thought of the famous phrase from *A Christmas Carol*. God bless us everyone. The day had, indeed, been blessed.

Chapter Twenty-One

By the next day, life in Moonlight Harbor was returning to normal. Trucks were coming in, and the grocery store and restaurants were restocking and readying for New Year's.

Jenna's mother and Sabrina made it down, and that night the women celebrated a belated Christmas with pizza from Pizza Palace, as well as dried fruit from the gift basket Jenna's cousin Winston had sent for Aunt Edie.

"Trying to butter me up," she'd said in disgust as she helped herself to a dried apricot. Considering the fact that he'd alternately used her and ignored her, it was going to take a lot of butter.

Jenna's gift, on the other hand, had been a success. Aunt Edie loved the wineglass, which sported a woman's face complete with false eyelashes and earrings dangling from her glass ears. Mel was delighted with the gift pack of scented soaps and candles, and Celeste had hugged the holiday coffee box with three different blends as if it was gold. Sabrina was happy with her gift cards for the funplex, Good Times Ice Cream Parlor and Books and Beans, and after an enthusiastic hug for

Aunt Edie, spent the rest of the morning wrapped in the blanket Edie had crocheted for her. Aunt Edie and Mel had loaded Jenna up with Mastercard gift cards, which she planned to spend at Beach Lumber and Hardware stocking up on more emergency supplies like flashlights and candles and lanterns. And rubber boots for clamming. In addition to that, she'd be saving up for a bigger and better generator. Aunt Edie had also given her a gift card for Crafty Just Cuz, and she was looking forward to finding a craft to work on when she finally got some downtime.

She was especially pleased with her sister's thoughtful gift—a cloth journal and expensive pen. "So you can keep a record of all the cool things that happen down here at the Driftwood," she explained. "I bet you won't have any trouble filling it."

"That's a lovely idea," said Aunt Edie. "It'll be a wonderful treasure to pass on to Sabrina…when she takes over someday," she added.

Sabrina grinned. "Start with writing about the storm," she said. "And the little girl who got lost."

"And how you tried to turn your sister into a Popsicle." Celeste said as she handed Jenna one final present from under the tree.

That one was from Sabrina and turned out to be her favorite present of all. In a wooden frame trimmed with tiny shells, it was a selfie of the two of them that Sabrina had taken at the Driftwood's grand opening, their faces close together. Their smiles said, "We love each other. Always. No matter what."

Tristan showed up later that day and gave Sabrina a necklace with a silver clamshell hanging from it. "I love it!" She threw her arms around him and kissed him. Damien's head would have blown off if he'd seen that. But hey, it was Christmas.

Come New Year's Eve, the Driftwood Inn was at full capacity. Darrell and Kat had decided to stay on, and their kids had joined them. Lisa, Karen and their husbands and children were there, too, and all were invited to the bonfire Aunt Edie had planned. So were Sabrina's friends, plus Courtney and a group of local businesspeople, including Tyrella, Cindy Redmond and her husband and Nora and hers. Pete, Brody and his two teenage kids, and Seth were present, as well. Everyone brought something to share. Cindy, of course, brought candy. Quiet Annie Albright came with her daughter, bearing mini quiches and snickerdoodles. Tyrella and Brody both brought champagne. "We've got our priorities straight," she joked. Nora brought a giant thermos of hot chocolate and a pan of piping hot twice-baked potatoes to add to the hot dogs Seth had bought and Aunt Edie's famous baked beans. Sabrina's friends came with soda pop and chips. Even Pete had contributed something, a six-pack of beer.

In addition, Jenna's friend Vanita had come down from Seattle with a bottle of champagne. Her other friend Brittany was on hand, too, with her family, and they'd provided the makings for s'mores, which all the kids were enjoying.

"A regular feast," Brody said. "Thanks to our hosts." He raised his glass of champagne.

"And what we're all doing out here when we finally have power will forever remain a mystery," Tyrella said, laughing as she poured more champagne into her plastic cup.

"We're celebrating that we survived the storm," said Karen.

"And my sister's snoring," Lisa added.

Karen sniffed. "I don't snore."

"Yes, you do," said her husband, "but I love you anyway."

"This has been so much fun," Kat said to Jenna.

Jenna had found Kat's blog and read her latest entry titled *Beach Adventure*. She'd made the Driftwood look like the Marriott and had painted Jenna, Celeste and Aunt Edie in such glowing tones they sounded like Cinderella's three good fairies. Holiday magic-makers.

"I'm glad we stayed on," Kat said. "It's the perfect way to start the new year."

Which Jenna knew was going to include a final chemo treatment and the beginning of radiation. But they were planning to come down for Valentine's Day, and Aunt Edie had already promised to bake them something special to commemorate their love.

Seth had been ordered to bring his guitar, and he produced it and accompanied everyone in their favorite camp songs. He also accompanied the sisters and Celeste and Vanita, who gave a slightly tipsy rendition of "Girls Just Want to Have Fun."

"Speaking of fun, I think I've had enough for one night," Aunt Edie announced. "I'll leave it to you young ones to clean up."

"Are you sure you want to go inside before midnight?" asked Lisa.

"No, but my old bones get tired sitting on these hard

logs," Aunt Edie replied. "Anyway, it's midnight in New York."

"I'll go with you, Edie old girl," Pete offered, and she smiled up at him and let him lead her away.

Heaven only knew what those two were going to get up to alone in the house. Whatever it was, they were certainly old enough. But Aunt Edie and Pete the mooch? Jenna supposed she'd have to get used to the idea. Pete was there to stay.

"Told you something's going on between them," murmured Seth, who had slipped in to sit beside her when Brody got up to roast her a marshmallow.

"You have a dirty mind," Jenna said.

"Nothing dirty about what those two are planning to do," he replied easily. "A good way to ring in the new year."

Yes, it was. She half wished she had someone to ring it in with. Like Seth Waters? Was he hinting? He stretched his legs toward the fire, and his thighs brushed hers, setting off fireworks in her chest.

Speaking of fireworks, people were already setting theirs off along the beach. Brody's kids and their friends had brought some down and lit them, adding to the show. And thanks to a clear night, the show was great.

"This time last year, I felt like my life was over," Jenna mused. "Now I feel like it's just beginning."

"It's never too late for a new beginning," he said. How right he was. She smiled up at Brody as he returned with her treat and sat down on her other side.

Seth frowned and moved to the other side of the fire to talk with Darrell.

Once midnight approached, the singing turned serious with "Auld Lang Syne." The song always made Jenna sloppy-sentimental, and on this night she was particularly so as she looked at the people gathered around the fire—family, and friends who had come to feel like family. People who were there for you when you needed them. Whatever challenges the new year held, she knew she wouldn't be facing them alone.

"It's midnight!" cried Sabrina, and Tristan used that as an excuse to kiss her. Oh, boy, Jenna didn't want those two making a habit of that. But, as with Christmas, it was a special moment. A kiss could be allowed.

Jenna didn't have long to think about her daughter. "I'll take that kiss you owe me now," Brody said with a smile. And he did. Oh, yes, Happy New Year. A kiss was allowed for her, too.

She finally opened her eyes to see everyone hugging and toasting each other with champagne. She searched the shadowy figures around the fire for Seth but couldn't find him. Just as well, she told herself.

"Happy New Year, darling," her mom said and hugged her. "I'm so proud of you. You dealt with some hard things this year, but you still managed to discover the rainbow in the storm."

It would appear she had.

Toasts, hugs and well-wishes done, the revelers packed up their things, doused the fire and made their way back across the beach. "See you at the chamber meeting if not before," Cindy said to Jenna.

Oh, yeah. That. She could only imagine how eager her fellow chamber of commerce members would be to see her after her fiasco of a festival. She decided not to ruin her night thinking about it.

In spite of her decision, the vision of that upcoming encounter followed her back to the house like a hungry puppy. She was lost in thought, trailing her mom and sister up the back stairs, when a hand reached out from the dark and grabbed her arm, making her yelp.

Celeste turned. "You okay?"

"She's fine," Seth Waters said and pulled her around the corner of the house.

"What are you doing?" she demanded. "You scared the snot out of me."

"Sorry. I just wanted to wish you a happy New Year."

"Which you could've done back at the fire."

"You were busy with the house-peddler."

A little jealousy? Hmm. She rather liked that.

"You into him, Jenna?"

Yes. But she could easily be into Seth, too. She still didn't know exactly what—or who—she wanted. Each man was special in his own way.

There was only one thing she knew for sure. "I said I was through with men after Damien dumped me, but I don't want to be scarred for life."

"Looks like those scars are healing. You're better off with the other guy."

"Am I?" She wished she could be certain of that. Seth seemed to have a gift for stirring up doubts.

"He's got his life together."

"He has baggage, just like everyone, but at least he isn't going to let it hold him back."

"So, what are you saying, Jenna?"

"I'm saying... I don't know what I'm saying. I don't know what I'm doing. All I know is that I'm not going to close myself off to love. I'm going to give it a second chance. This is going to be a new year for me."

He slipped his arms around her, and it felt like someone had set off a sparkler inside her. "Well, then, Happy New Year."

His lips on hers set off more sparklers. No, not sparklers. A firecracker. A bottle rocket. He smelled smoky from the fire, and he tasted like beer and new beginnings.

She pulled away and bit her buzzing lower lip. "That was some kind of happy. Did it mean anything?"

"Yeah, that I'm a fool. Sorry. But it was a nice way to start the new year," he said with a smile.

She had to agree as she watched him walk away. But it looked like things were ending for them before they'd even begun. Was Seth going to get brave and take a chance on love or was he going to make her decision easy? The coming months would surely give her the answer.

Her mom had gone to bed, but Celeste was waiting for her, seated at the kitchen table with a mug of chamomile tea for each of them. "You're such a pig," she greeted Jenna. "Two men when some women don't even have one."

Was she talking about herself? Jenna slid onto a chair and picked up her mug. "What happened to the cop? Is there something you're not telling me?"

"No, no. We're fine." Celeste frowned at her mug. "I invited him to come down here for New Year's, and he turned me down."

"Maybe he had to work."

Celeste shrugged. "I'd kind of thought we'd reached

the meet-the-family stage, but I guess not. Things'll come together when they're supposed to. But never mind me. We're talking about you." She pointed at Jenna with her mug. "You've got two great guys interested in you. You need to make up your mind."

Jenna *had* made up her mind. To be through with men. But that was before Brody and Seth came into her life. It was a new year, time for new resolutions. Resolution Number One: be open to love.

"I'm going to make some changes this year," she vowed. Her sister had a good point. She did have two great men in her life. One of them had to be right for her.

"I hope so," Celeste said. "You need to have sex again before you die."

"I'll keep that in mind," Jenna said. "And now I'm going to bed."

"Me, too," said Celeste. "It's been fun, but I need my beauty sleep."

They turned off the lights and went upstairs, Celeste humming "Girls Just Want to Have Fun." "It's stuck in my brain," she said when Jenna told her to stop already.

And then it was stuck in Jenna's. And once she fell asleep there it was, playing again. She was on a yacht anchored off the pier in Moonlight Harbor, holding a fancy drink with an umbrella in it and dancing to the music and singing at the top of her lungs. It was a balmy summer night with a full moon and she was wearing a bikini. She'd lost fifteen pounds. Yeah, she was dreaming. And she was wearing a Santa hat.

And look who was joining her. Here came Brody in a red Speedo. He was wearing a Santa hat, too, as he shuffled up to her. "Happy New Year, Jenna. This year's gonna be a good one," he said and put an arm around her.

Seth Waters approached from the other side. He, too, was in a Speedo. His was green. And he had on a pirate hat. "Yes, it is," he said. He held up a sprig of mistletoe. "Come on over here and give your favorite pirate a kiss."

Jenna started toward him, but Brody pulled her back. "She doesn't want a pirate. She's through gambling on losers. She wants a Santa baby with some money. Don't you?"

"I don't know what I want," Jenna wailed.

Now here came her sister, jumping up from the sea in a mermaid tail. "It's okay," she called. "You don't have to know yet. Just be open to finding out. And give me your drink," she added, scooping it out of Jenna's hand as she flew past.

"My drink! Where's my drink?"

Jenna woke to find her sister staring at her. "You didn't have enough to drink tonight? Is that the problem?"

"Sorry," Jenna muttered and rolled over.

"What were you dreaming?" Celeste asked.

"I guess I was dreaming about the new year," Jenna said with a smile. Then she shut her eyes and went in search of that yacht.

She never found it again, but she did get the message loud and clear. She was done with closing herself off. Whatever the new year offered, she was ready for it.

That took care of Resolution Number One. Resolution Number Two was to never again suggest a holiday festival.

Annie Albright was finishing her morning shift at Sandy's when Jenna walked into the restaurant, headed for the meeting room. "Are you okay?" Annie asked. "You look kind of scared."

"I am kind of scared," Jenna admitted. "It's the first time I've seen a lot of these guys since the festival."

"Nobody blames you for the weather," Annie assured her.

"All the same I'll bet you were glad you didn't end up doing a food booth, after all."

"Well, yeah," Annie admitted. "But don't worry. Some of the members have already come in, and nobody seemed too mad." She'd hardly finished speaking when Susan Frank walked through the lobby looking like a thundercloud about to burst. "Well, almost nobody," Annie amended. "Good luck," she added, and then went to clear a table, leaving Jenna with no excuse to postpone going in to face the festival firing squad.

Many of her fellow chamber members were in the meeting room already, standing in groups, visiting. She swallowed and walked in, bracing herself. "There you are," Kiki Strom called, beckoning her over. "We were just talking about you."

Since Kiki was talking with Nora and Tyrella, Jenna figured it couldn't have been all bad. These women were her friends. "We survived the big storm," Kiki said to Jenna with a smile.

"Barely," muttered Susan Frank, inserting herself into the group.

Once again, Jenna braced herself.

But she was spared as Brody, who'd been on the opposite side of the room talking with Ellis West and Patricia Whiteside, summoned everyone to the table. Jenna scooted over to Brody and sat next to him, figuring that if anyone could save her from tarring and feathering it would be the president of the organization.

Ellis West sat down on her other side. "Looks like you guys survived the storm okay," he said. "Sorry we had to close down and couldn't help your people out. Thought for a while there I was going to save some of my food, but in the end, I tossed it all."

"Oh, Ellis, I'm sorry," she said.

"Hey, that's the food business. Sometimes you take a hit. You gotta roll with it."

Kiki had settled on the other side of him. "Well, I must say, we did okay. Sold out on those mini-flashlights shaped like sharks, and we moved a lot of sweatshirts."

"We all survived. That's the main thing," said Ellis. "Even the upholstery in my convertible." He pointed a finger at Jenna. "But I'm not letting you have it again next year."

Who was he kidding? There wouldn't be a next year.

Lunch was served, and Jenna picked at hers, feeling like a prisoner trying to enjoy her last meal.

Finally, Brody called the meeting to order. Jenna endured the secretary's reading of the minutes and the treasurer's report. Then it was time for old business. She took a deep breath and waited for the lethal injection.

"So," Brody said, giving her an encouraging smile, "the festival."

"I told you we shouldn't do it," said Susan Frank.

"And you were wrong." Kiki's sharp response made Susan blink.

She recovered. "Weren't you at the parade?" she challenged.

"Of course, I was," Kiki snapped. "We had a float in it."

"Well, if that wasn't the biggest disaster," Susan began.

No, probably the biggest disaster had been the mess down on the pier, with booths closing before the people who'd rented them had even been able to cover their costs.

"We had some challenges," Nora admitted.

"But we rose to them," Tryella said.

That they had.

"My guests actually found it all rather an adventure," said Patricia.

"I did a ton of business," Cindy announced.

"So did I," said Wilma Spike, who owned Sunken Treasures Consignments.

"A lot of my people decided to stay on through the new year." This was from Wendy Burton, one of their newer members, who'd recently opened a B and B.

"So did a lot of mine," said Jenna, emboldened.

"I managed to keep the coffee coming," Rita Rutledge told them.

"I sold out of stock," Courtney said.

That goaded Susan into saying, "I made sales."

"Then why are you squawking?" Nora demanded.

"I'm not squawking. I'm just saying that having a festival down here in the winter is a bad idea."

"Well, I disagree," Kiki said firmly. "I think we

should do it again next year. Maybe a little earlier in the month, though."

"The first weekend in December," suggested Rian LaShell. "That way, even if we have another storm, people will still have a chance to get home by Christmas."

"Good idea. All in favor?" asked Kiki, taking over.

"That comes under new business," Susan scolded.

"Well, let's get down to new business, then," Kiki said and cocked an eyebrow at Brody.

"I guess we could move on to new business," he said. "We have a motion on the floor to put on the Seaside with Santa festival again next year. Do I have a second?"

"I'll second that," said Nora.

"Okay," Brody said. "All in favor."

They almost all raised their hands.

"Opposed?"

"Me," said Susan, raising hers. "You're all nuts."

"Or maybe we're all visionaries," Kiki said.

"It's a sick vision." Susan consoled herself by grabbing another dinner roll from the basket in front of her.

"We need to go back to old business," Kiki said. "The committee didn't get to give their report on how the festival went."

"Oh, brother," Susan groaned. "We *know* how the festival went."

"We need to announce who was voted the best-dressed business for the holidays. Don't you all want to know who won?"

"Yes," said Cindy eagerly and Susan let out a disgusted snort.

"Well, the winner of this year's contest is…Beach Babes," she finished with a smirk.

Susan blinked in surprise.

"Unless, of course, you don't want to accept the prize on general principles," Kiki suggested.

"The people voted," Susan said haughtily. "I'll accept."

"I guess everyone liked those colored lights on the clothes racks and all the mannequins wearing Santa and elf hats," Kiki said. "It was cute," she said later to Jenna after the meeting broke up. "And she had that darling miniature sleigh filled with dolls and teddy bears in the window, all wearing little Santa hats and sunglasses. If she could dress people as well as she did her shop, she'd be rich."

"Maybe she won't whine so much next year," said Nora, who'd joined them.

"Don't hold your breath," Kiki told her. "You do realize what all this means," she said to Jenna.

"I get to live another day?"

"You get to be in charge again next year," Kiki said with a smile.

Heaven help her.

"You definitely should be in charge next year," Brody said when he took her out to dinner that night to celebrate. "You did a really impressive job of pulling the festival together in a very short amount of time."

"I almost had a nervous breakdown," she said.

"Nah, you didn't even come close. You were great. But then, you were great even before you came up with the festival idea," he added, making her face heat with embarrassment. He raised his wineglass to her. "So, here's to a new year and new adventures."

"I'll drink to that," she said and they clinked glasses. She had no idea what the new year would bring. But one thing she was certain of. No matter what, life was good at the beach.

* * * * *

Holiday Recipes from your Friends at Moonlight Harbor

Since you couldn't be at the cookie exchange at Aunt Edie's, some of the women thought it would be nice to share their recipes. Happy holidays from your friends in Moonlight Harbor.

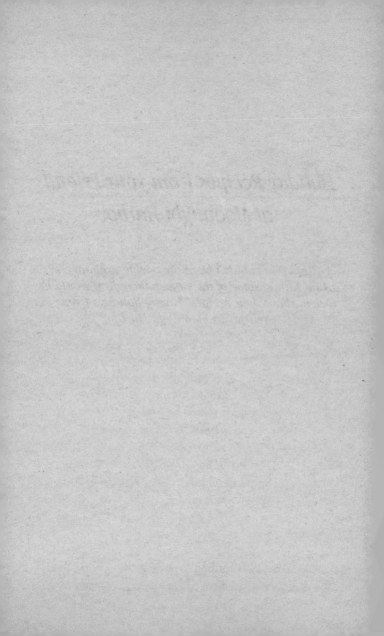

Aunt Edie's Fruitcake Bites

Courtesy of Kathie Follett

These can be baked in muffin pans or in mini-muffin pans.

Ingredients:
1 box pound cake mix and the ingredients that are
listed on the box to bake the cake
(usually butter, eggs and water or milk)
½ cup mini chocolate chips (or more to taste)
Maraschino cherries (from a 10 oz jar or larger),
chopped and drained on paper towels
½ cup dried cranberries or currants
And if you prefer:
½ cup of chopped dried apricots
½ cup of chopped pecans

Directions:

Make the cake mix according to package directions. Fold in each additional ingredient one at a time and gently mix.

If desired you may add ½ teaspoon vanilla or almond extract and a tablespoon of orange zest.

If baking in muffin tins fill each ¾ full. Bake according to package directions. (Baking time may vary depending on what size muffin pan you use.)

Store in airtight container and enjoy!

Patricia's Rock Cookies

Courtesy of Shirley Rembold

Ingredients:
½ cup brown sugar
½ cup butter
3 eggs
1 tsp baking soda dissolved in 1/4 cup warm water
2 ½ cups flour
pinch of salt
1 tsp cinnamon
1 tsp ground cloves
1 lb pitted dates
1 lb chopped walnuts

Directions:

Mix all ingredients and drop by teaspoonful onto a cookie sheet. Bake at 350° for 10 to 12 minutes.

Annie's Hungarian Kiefles

Courtesy of Cathy Marrone

Ingredients:
2 cups sifted flour
½ lb cream cheese (room temp)
½ lb butter (room temp)
Fillings: prune, apricot, raspberry jam

Directions:

Mix ingredients for dough and refrigerate 1 hour. Roll dough out thin.

Cut into squares approximately 2 ½ inches. Place ½ teaspoon filling on each square. Pull opposite corners up so they meet in the middle and press with a fork to seal so they don't pop open in the oven (but even if they do, it doesn't matter). Bake at 350° for 5 to 8 minutes.

Courtney's Potato Chip Cookies

Courtesy of Deanna Willis Simmers

Ingredients:
1 cup shortening
1 cup brown sugar
1 cup granulated sugar
2 cups flour
1 tsp baking soda
1 tsp vanilla
2 cups crushed potato chips
1 cup pecans, chopped
2 eggs

Directions:

Cream shortening and sugars. Add eggs and vanilla and beat well. Add flour and baking soda and mix well. Add chips and nuts. Drop onto ungreased cookie sheet and bake 11 to 13 minutes at 350°.

Cindy's Whipped Shortbread Cookies

Courtesy of Linda Thorpe Moore

Ingredients:
1 lb butter
1 cup powdered sugar
½ cup corn starch
3 cups flour
1 tsp vanilla

Directions:

Using a mixer, cream butter and sugar together, then add corn starch. Add flour gradually to blend and then add vanilla. Mix till it looks like whipped cream. Drop by teaspoon on cookie sheet and bake at 350° for 10 to 15 minutes. Add some holiday sprinkles on the top before baking!

Nora's Holiday Drop Cookies

Courtesy of Renee Brancato Durdan

Ingredients:
1 cup granulated sugar
3 cups flour
3 tsp baking powder
dash of salt
4 heaping tsp shortening
3 eggs
½ cup milk
1 tsp vanilla

Directions:

Combine flour, sugar, baking powder and salt. Mix in shortening. Make a well and add eggs, milk and vanilla. Batter is a little tacky. Drop by tablespoonful onto cookie sheet lined with parchment paper. Bake about 8 to 10 minutes at 350° until slightly brown and transfer to wire rack to cool.

To frost cookies, make a thick icing from confectioner's

sugar and milk to get desired consistency; ice cookies and decorate immediately with red and green sprinkles, nonpareils or other Christmassy decorations. These cookies do not stack well at all, so serve them on a platter. Makes about 3 dozen depending on size.

Happy Eating!

Acknowledgments

I want to thank my wonderful editors Paula Eykelhof and Michelle Meade for helping me with this project and all the special people at Harlequin who continue to give me gorgeous book covers and support my endeavors so wholeheartedly. Thank you to my fabulous agent Paige Wheeler. You're the best! A special thanks to Cheron and Harold Wittman and Jane and Bob Hughes, float-making experts who tried to explain to me how the process works. I probably still didn't get it all right but I appreciate your efforts guys! And finally, a big thank you to all my friends on my Facebook like page who so kindly shared their cookie recipes for this book. I can hardly wait to try them!

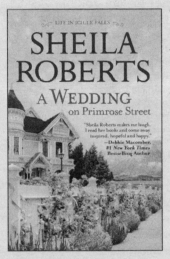

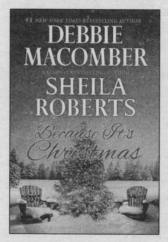

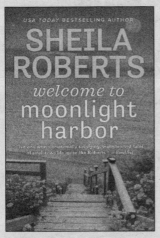

Turn your love of reading into rewards you'll love with
Harlequin My Rewards

SHEILA ROBERTS

36805	WELCOME TO MOONLIGHT HARBOR	___$7.99 U.S.	___$9.99 CAN.
33003	STARTING OVER ON BLACKBERRY LANE	___$7.99 U.S.	___$9.99 CAN.
31879	HOME ON APPLE BLOSSOM ROAD	___$7.99 U.S.	___$9.99 CAN.
31815	A WEDDING ON PRIMROSE STREET	___$7.99 U.S.	___$8.99 CAN.
31661	THE LODGE ON HOLLY ROAD	___$7.99 U.S.	___$8.99 CAN.
30790	CHRISTMAS IN ICICLE FALLS	___$7.99 U.S.	___$9.99 CAN.

(limited quantities available)

TOTAL AMOUNT	$ _____
POSTAGE & HANDLING	$ _____
($1.00 for 1 book, 50¢ for each additional)	
APPLICABLE TAXES*	$ _____
TOTAL PAYABLE	$ _____

(check or money order—please do not send cash)

To order, complete this form and send it, along with a check or money order for the total amount, payable to MIRA Books, to: **In the U.S.:** 3010 Walden Avenue, P.O. Box 9077, Buffalo, NY 14269-9077; **In Canada:** P.O. Box 636, Fort Erie, Ontario, L2A 5X3.

Name: _____

Address: _____ City: _____

State/Prov.: _____ Zip/Postal Code: _____

Account Number (if applicable): _____

075 CSAS

mira

*New York residents remit applicable sales taxes.
*Canadian residents remit applicable GST and provincial taxes.

Harlequin.com

MSR1118BL

Get 4 FREE REWARDS!

We'll send you 2 FREE Books plus 2 FREE Mystery Gifts.

ROBYN CARR
Any Day Now

CARLA NEGGERS
the RIVER HOUSE

BJ DANIELS
HERO'S RETURN

KAREN HARPER
SHALLOW GRAVE

FREE
Value Over
$20

Both the **Romance** and **Suspense** collections feature compelling novels written by many of today's best-selling authors.

YES! Please send me 2 FREE novels from the Essential Romance or Essential Suspense Collection and my 2 FREE gifts (gifts are worth about $10 retail). After receiving them, if I don't wish to receive any more books, I can return the shipping statement marked "cancel." If I don't cancel, I will receive 4 brand-new novels every month and be billed just $6.74 each in the U.S. or $7.24 each in Canada. That's a savings of at least 16% off the cover price. It's quite a bargain! Shipping and handling is just 50¢ per book in the U.S. and 75¢ per book in Canada*. I understand that accepting the 2 free books and gifts places me under no obligation to buy anything. I can always return a shipment and cancel at any time. The free books and gifts are mine to keep no matter what I decide.

Choose one: ☐ **Essential Romance**
(194/394 MDN GMY7)

☐ **Essential Suspense**
(191/391 MDN GMY7)

Name (please print)

Address   Apt. #

City   State/Province   Zip/Postal Code

Mail to the **Reader Service:**
IN U.S.A.: P.O. Box 1341, Buffalo, NY 14240-8531
IN CANADA: P.O. Box 603, Fort Erie, Ontario L2A 5X3

Want to try two free books from another series? Call 1-800-873-8635 or visit www.ReaderService.com.

---

*Terms and prices subject to change without notice. Prices do not include applicable taxes. Sales tax applicable in NY. Canadian residents will be charged applicable taxes. Offer not valid in Quebec. This offer is limited to one order per household. Books received may not be as shown. Not valid for current subscribers to the Essential Romance or Essential Suspense Collection. All orders subject to approval. Credit or debit balances in a customer's account(s) may be offset by any other outstanding balance owed by or to the customer. Please allow 4 to 6 weeks for delivery. Offer available while quantities last.

Your Privacy—The Reader Service is committed to protecting your privacy. Our Privacy Policy is available online at www.ReaderService.com or upon request from the Reader Service. We make a portion of our mailing list available to reputable third parties that offer products we believe may interest you. If you prefer that we not exchange your name with third parties, or if you wish to clarify or modify your communication preferences, please visit us at www.ReaderService.com/consumerschoice or write to us at Reader Service Preference Service, P.O. Box 9062, Buffalo, NY 14240-9062. Include your complete name and address.

STRS18